"Patricia Rice's historicals are deliciously fresh, sexy, and fun."
—**Mary Jo Putney**

The Rebellious Sons Series

The Wicked Wyckerly

"A heartwarming tale that kept me smiling all the way through. Every character entertains and satisfies, from the engaging scapegrace hero, whom I loved more and more through the book; his wild insecure love child; and the loving, down-to-earth heroine, right down to the devious old butler and the dyslexic assassin. It's a sweet, sexy, fun romp with so much heart. I can't wait to read the next book in the series." —Anne Gracie, author of *The Accidental Wedding*

"Charming, witty, and completely wonderful. A delightful book from start to end."
—*New York Times* bestselling author Jillian Hunter

"Filled with engaging characters and astute dialogue, Rice's new Rebellious Sons series gets off to a rollicking start. With her voice she combines a bit of whimsy, mayhem, and a lot of love and laughter in this delicious and highly entertaining read." —*Romantic Times* (4½ Stars)

"Rice is a master storyteller as she takes her endearing if roguish hero and spunky, stubborn heroine through all the trials evildoers and Regency society can concoct. A wonderful blend of humor, pathos, adventure, and charm, this page-turner is book one in Rice's promising Rebellious Sons series." —*Booklist*

The Mystic Isle Series

Mystic Warrior

"With its complex characters, Rice's last book in the Mystic Isle series pits a stubborn, seasoned warrior against an equally determined young woman. Rice combines an overview of the French Revolution, depths of emotion, mysticism, and great love into one passionate and fiery story."
—*Romantic Times* (Top Pick, 4½ Stars)

continued . . .

JUL 2011

W9-BXV-440

"Definitely a good addition to any library."
—Once Upon a Romance Reviews

Mystic Rider

"With whimsical and subtle touches of humor and memorable characters, [Rice] cleverly blends the paranormal with the historical events of the French Revolution in this passionate, very sensual romance. Her powerful voice and talent as a great storyteller make this one another keeper."
—*Romantic Times* (Top Pick, 4½ Stars)

"Filled with history, romance, and passion, a story that pulled me in and held me captive.... Ms. Rice makes the Revolution come alive. I can't wait for the next installment in the amazing Mystic Isle series! I am hooked!"
—Romance Reader at Heart

"An enthralling tale that should not be missed."
—Romance Reviews Today

Mystic Guardian

"Extraordinary characters ... subtle touches of humor and clever dialogue." — *Romantic Times* (Top Pick, 4½ Stars)

"Will enchant readers."
—The Romance Readers Connection

"A fine, fresh series kickoff, Rice's latest is passionate, rich in historical detail, and peopled with enough captivating secondary characters to pique readers' curiosity for many volumes to come." —*Publishers Weekly*

"Charming, magical." —*Midwest Book Review*

The Magic Series

Magic Man

"Never slows down until the final thread is magically resolved. Patricia Rice is clearly the Magic Woman with this superb tale and magnificent series."
—*Midwest Book Review*

Much Ado About Magic

"The magical Rice takes Trev and Lucinda, along with her readers, on a passionate, sensual, and romantic adventure in this fast-paced, witty, poignant, and magical tale of love."
—*Romantic Times* (Top Pick, 4½ Stars)

This Magic Moment

"Charming and immensely entertaining."
—*Library Journal*

"Rice has a magical touch for creating fascinating plots, delicious romance, and delightful characters both flesh-and-blood and ectoplasmic." —*Booklist*

"Another delightful magical story brought to us by this talented author. It's a fun read, romantic, and sexy with enchanting characters." —*Rendezvous*

The Trouble with Magic

"Rice's third enchanting book about the Malcolm sisters is truly spellbinding." —*Booklist*

Must Be Magic

"Very sensual." —*The Romance Reader*

"Rice has created a mystical masterpiece full of enchanting characters, a spellbinding plot, and the sweetest of romances." —*Booklist* (Starred Review)

"An engaging historical romance that uses a pinch of witchcraft to spice up a tale.... The story line mesmerizes.... Fans will believe that Patricia Rice must be magical as she spellbinds her audience with a one-sitting fun novel."
—*Midwest Book Review*

"I love an impeccably researched, well-written tale, and *Must Be Magic*, which continues the saga of the Iveses and Malcolms, is about as good as it gets. I'm very pleased to give it a Perfect Ten, and I encourage everyone to pick up this terrific book." —Romance Reviews Today

Merely Magic

"Simply enchanting! Patricia Rice, a master storyteller, weaves a spellbinding tale that's passionate and powerful." —Teresa Medeiros

"Like Julie Garwood, Patricia Rice employs wicked wit and sizzling sensuality to turn the battles of the sexes into a magical romp." —Mary Jo Putney

"One of those tales that you pick up and can't put down.... She is a gifted master storyteller. With *Merely Magic* she doesn't disappoint. Brava!" —*Midwest Book Review*

PATRICIA RICE

The Devilish Montague

THE REBELLIOUS SONS

A SIGNET ECLIPSE BOOK

SIGNET ECLIPSE
Published by New American Library, a division of
Penguin Group (USA) Inc., 375 Hudson Street,
New York, New York 10014, USA
Penguin Group (Canada), 90 Eglinton Avenue East, Suite 700, Toronto,
Ontario M4P 2Y3, Canada (a division of Pearson Penguin Canada Inc.)
Penguin Books Ltd., 80 Strand, London WC2R 0RL, England
Penguin Ireland, 25 St. Stephen's Green, Dublin 2,
Ireland (a division of Penguin Books Ltd.)
Penguin Group (Australia), 250 Camberwell Road, Camberwell, Victoria 3124,
Australia (a division of Pearson Australia Group Pty. Ltd.)
Penguin Books India Pvt. Ltd., 11 Community Centre, Panchsheel Park,
New Delhi - 110 017, India
Penguin Group (NZ), 67 Apollo Drive, Rosedale, Auckland 0632,
New Zealand (a division of Pearson New Zealand Ltd.)
Penguin Books (South Africa) (Pty.) Ltd., 24 Sturdee Avenue,
Rosebank, Johannesburg 2196, South Africa

Penguin Books Ltd., Registered Offices:
80 Strand, London WC2R 0RL, England

First published by Signet Eclipse, an imprint of New American Library,
a division of Penguin Group (USA) Inc.

First Printing, July 2011
10 9 8 7 6 5 4 3 2 1

Copyright © Rice Enterprises, Inc., 2011
Excerpt from *The Wicked Wyckerly* copyright © Rice Enterprises, Inc., 2010
All rights reserved

SIGNET ECLIPSE and logo are trademarks of Penguin Group (USA) Inc.

Printed in the United States of America

Without limiting the rights under copyright reserved above, no part of this pub-
lication may be reproduced, stored in or introduced into a retrieval system, or
transmitted, in any form, or by any means (electronic, mechanical, photocopying,
recording, or otherwise), without the prior written permission of both the copyright owner and the above publisher of this book.

PUBLISHER'S NOTE
This is a work of fiction. Names, characters, places, and incidents either are the
product of the author's imagination or are used fictitiously, and any resemblance
to actual persons, living or dead, business establishments, events, or locales is
entirely coincidental.
    The publisher does not have any control over and does not assume any re-
sponsibility for author or third-party Web sites or their content.

If you purchased this book without a cover you should be aware that this book is
stolen property. It was reported as "unsold and destroyed" to the publisher and
neither the author nor the publisher has received any payment for this "stripped
book."

The scanning, uploading, and distribution of this book via the Internet or via any
other means without the permission of the publisher is illegal and punishable by
law. Please purchase only authorized electronic editions, and do not participate
in or encourage electronic piracy of copyrighted materials. Your support of the
author's rights is appreciated.

Acknowledgments

To the St. Louis brainstormers, who kept me from bashing my head against the wall while deciphering Percy's antics and Jocelyn's motivations, and particularly to Chi and Pam, who reminded me that romance is about romantic tension and not parrots.

And, as always, to the Cauldron, who let me simmer in my own juices while stirring the pot and flinging mangel-wurzels into the brew.

1

"I should marry to save England?" Blake Montague asked, not hiding his sarcasm.

His thick dark hair had been marred with a silver streak since birth, lending an air of authority to his demeanor. He had the stern features and military bearing of an experienced officer, standing with legs apart, hands clasped at his back—except he wore the tailored clothes of a civilian with a casualness bordering on the disrespectful.

The youngest of Baron Montague's three sons, Blake had sought out Lord Castlereagh, Secretary of State for War, in the Duke of Fortham's library while the rest of the house party played at spillikins and cards in the salon. The interview had not gone well. Blake continued with hostility, "Without a position in the War Office, I have no other means to pursue decrypting this code except to buy officer's colors and rejoin the army to obtain more examples. For that, I must marry money."

"It's just that kind of insolence and intolerance for

the way things are done that holds you back," the secretary retorted acidly. In his middle years now, Viscount Castlereagh had breathed the heady power of government for most of his adult life, and his impatience with this interview was plain. "For all your intellect, you could not even finish Oxford without waving the flag of your noble code of honor and getting yourself kicked out."

"Without honor, we are not men," Blake argued. "The dean gave the grade and the prize I deserved to his lover. If a dean cheats in choosing award winners, is he any more right than a student caught cheating on an exam? Are men of power allowed more leeway than others?"

In response to Blake's righteous anger, the molting parrot perched in a cage in the corner woke with a start and cried, *"Égalité!"*

Blake fisted his fingers to prevent flinging an inkpot at the bird. His frustration oftentimes got the better of him. With his future riding on this audience, he couldn't afford to vent his annoyance here.

"Sometimes, yes," Castlereagh said. "Men of power are in a position to know more than the common man. Had you obeyed your commanding officer in Portugal and not galloped down a hillside to save a damned enlisted soldier, you might not have taken a bullet to your leg, and you could have earned your colors and been working on your wretched code by now. Your behavior will not suit our office, Montague."

"It cost me the price of a uniform, a horse, and transportation to volunteer as an officer, my lord. With all due respect, I cannot afford to volunteer again. I will have to enlist as cannon fodder in the front lines, with little chance of obtaining what I need."

"If you do not want to be cannon fodder," Castlereagh retorted impatiently, "then yes, I suggest you purchase an officer's colors, join Wellesley, and learn to take orders, even if doing so means marrying for wealth. Or is that beneath your dignity also?"

"The future of England is at stake!" Blake retorted, ignoring the insult. "All I need is more examples of this code, and I'm certain I can break it. Wellesly can stop Napoleon in his tracks if he has the ability to read French messages. I'll work at home if I'm such an irritation to your office."

"And if we do not provide sufficient copies of the code, will you shoot us as you shot Carrington? Don't think we don't know about your duels. It was only because you provided discreet witnesses and were not caught that you were not prosecuted."

"Lord Carrington is a cheat and a fraud and a plague upon society. He is fortunate I chose not to kill him," Blake said maliciously, aware he'd lost the argument and would get no sympathy in this quarter. Carrington was a viscount, a lord of the realm. Blake was nothing but a thorn beneath his aristocratic instep.

Castlereagh's scorn was apparent. Blake did not flinch as the great man gestured dismissal. Throwing back his shoulders, he offered a mocking salute, turned on his heel, and marched out. Or rather, limped out. The bullet from his brief stint in Portugal had torn ligaments in his left leg that had not yet healed. The bullet may have ended his volunteer status and sent him home with the wounded, but he did not regret having saved a man's life.

Physical frustration was as much a part of his fury as his indignation at the obstacles thrown in his way by those in power. Until the wound knit properly, he'd been ordered to stay off horses and forgo fencing. Without physical release, he had no means of venting the ire boiling inside him.

Avoiding the laughing company in the parlor, Blake aimed for the study, where the brandy was kept. Entering, he encountered a languid, elegantly tailored figure already occupying a wingback chair, his boots propped upon the desk. Nicholas Atherton held out the decanter to his old friend.

"Irish boy turned you down, did he?" Nick asked, without much sympathy. "Probably for the best. You would have punched his snout the first day at a desk."

"I am not a barbarian," Blake said crossly, finding a glass and adding a goodly portion of the duke's finest. "I'm quite capable of carrying out a civilized argument when all else is equal. Castlereagh made it plain that I am not his equal and, therefore, my opinion is of no importance."

"Men in power have been known to be wrong," Nick said idly, swinging his glass and admiring the portrait of the voluptuous late duchess hanging on the far wall.

"If I thought even for a moment that he would take the information I've given him about Jefferson's wheel to someone in a position to work on this damned code, I'd let it go. But he won't. Yet the fate of Wellesley's army could depend on reading these ciphers." Blake pulled a folded paper from his pocket and shook it open. It had come into his hands when he'd served briefly in Portugal. Deciphering puzzles was his expertise.

"You wouldn't let it go," Nick said with a laugh. "You never let anything go. You chew a problem to death until you decide whether to spit it out or swallow."

"That's a disgusting image." The brandy didn't mellow Blake's humor. "I enjoy a good conundrum. Generally, however, they don't affect the fate of armies and possibly the future of England. If the French are using a code wheel for communication, we'll never decrypt it by our standard old-fashioned methods."

"Chewing it to death," Nick reiterated through a yawn. "You haven't the blunt to volunteer again, and the War Office won't have you. You know your only choice if you want to see more of that code is to marry wealth and buy colors. So either give up the problem or marry. A simple enough choice."

Blake ran a hand through the silver hair at his temple and spoke through clenched molars. "What, precisely, have I to offer a wealthy wife?"

"Certainly not charm," Nick said, amused by his own wit.

Blake knew he couldn't throw a punch at his best friend, not in a duke's study leastways. Besides, despite all his indolent manners, Nick had a punishing bunch of fives of his own. And he was right, confound it. Content with the freedom of his bachelor life, Blake had never cultivated charm.

"This party is a waste of time," he said. "I'll head back to London in the morning. Maybe I'll have a better idea after I've cleared my head." To hell with doctor's orders. He'd ridden sedately earlier, but at the moment, he needed a bruising fight or a punishing ride.

"You'll leave without telling your family farewell?" Nick lifted his golden-brown eyebrows skeptically.

Damn and blast. If he bade them farewell, they'd flutter and protest and ultimately wouldn't let him leave at all. But sneaking away wasn't an option. Setting down his glass, he stalked out. Agreeing to this house party had been a huge mistake. Only the presence of Castlereagh had tempted him out of his usual lairs.

To compound his annoyance, his father was waiting for him at the bottom of the stairs. As much as Blake's overprotective family nettled him, he could not return their benevolence with disrespect. It irritated him that they did not recognize he was a grown man of nearly thirty, but he could not change his parents. Nor, he privately conceded, would he wish to.

"Your mother and I would like to speak with you," the baron said affably, catching his son's elbow and steering him toward the ladies' parlor.

"I will not become a vicar," Blake warned, anticipating a much-argued subject.

Portly, balding, and half a head shorter than his youngest son, the baron did not respond to this opening volley. "I've had a bit of good luck at the tables. Your mother and I have discussed this for some months, and we thought perhaps we could put the prize to good use."

Blake had long since given up hope that his superstitious mother would allow money to pass into his hand. She was violently opposed to his joining the army, which is what she knew he would do if he could afford an officer's colors. She had wished for her youngest son to stay in Shropshire as a rural vicar and marry a local girl to provide her with more grandchildren to dandle on her knee. Blake's bachelor freedom in London was a severe disappointment to her. His penchant for sport horrified her.

"Mother." Entering the parlor, he greeted Lady Montague with a nod, noting that even his unmarried sister, Frances, had been excluded from this tête-à-tête. Seeing his spinster sister matched with some respectable bachelor was the presumed reason they had attended the house party.

With resignation, Blake prepared himself for the onslaught of pleas to cease his careless existence and knuckle down to family duty.

"Oh, you're limping!" Lady Montague cried. "Your

leg must still be hurting. Sit, sit, why aren't you in bed by now?" His mother gestured at the cushion beside her on the love seat.

Blake waited for his father to take the big chair beside the fireplace, then leaned a hip against a writing desk and crossed his arms. His chances of escape were better if he did not make himself comfortable.

"It is not even midnight, and my leg will heal better if I stand," he said in answer to his mother's admonishments. "I'll be leaving in the morning, so I trust you'll enjoy the rest of the house party."

"Oh, no, no, you cannot leave yet!" Lady Montague cried. "You must hear us out, then stay. There might be dancing! Are you set on breaking my heart?"

Having heard this plaintive cry since childhood, Blake managed to withstand it. "I hardly believe dancing appropriate on one good leg," he said dryly.

"Oh, dear, of course not, but we have had the most interesting conversation with Lady Belden. You must meet—"

"Perhaps we should explain our intent first," the baron suggested with good humor. He clasped his hands across the waistcoat straining over his belly and regarded his son with the fondness that always made Blake feel like a guilty child. "I cannot enjoy watching your mother fret over your well-being. Since being tossed from Oxford over the contretemps with the dean, you've been involved in three duels that I know of, nearly broken your neck racing horses across country, fought against some of the toughest pugilists in the ring, and now nearly got yourself killed by shipping out to Portugal without a word to us."

Blake might have explained that he did these things for money and because he was damned bored, but his father's solution was for him to become a vicar, have no money, and be damned bored. There was no winning that circular thinking. So he waited to see where his parents' latest whim might lead.

"Your mother and I have talked about it," the baron continued, "and we've decided you simply need a little incentive to look around and find a nice girl and settle down."

Blake refrained from sighing with impatience. His lack of enthusiasm did not deter his parents.

"Your father has won the most darling house in Chelsea!" Lady Montague said with enthusiasm, waving her plump hands as she spoke. "We thought perhaps we should use it for Frances's dowry, but she dislikes London, so it did not seem right."

"Chelsea is not London," Blake reminded her. "It is at the very least half an hour or more outside the city. Frances should be fine there."

"But Frances has a dowry, and you do not," his mother continued. "With a lovely house to offer, you might have a choice of young ladies. Why, we have met the most charming—"

With the practice of experience, the baron diverted this overflow of information. "It's Carrington House. A fairly large, respectable estate, I'm told. I've not been out to inspect it, but the late viscount often entertained there. He was well known in political circles, so I'm assured it is a substantial asset."

Carrington House. The devil in Blake smirked in satisfaction. Harold, Viscount Carrington, had finally lost his family home at a gaming table. At last, the bastard had suffered the penance he deserved. Outwardly, Blake merely tilted his head to show he was listening.

"I thought to offer the use of the house as a marriage settlement if you decide on a gal before the end of the year," his father said. "But if you do not, then I'll have to sell it. A place like that cannot be left empty for long, and I haven't the interest in maintaining it." The baron settled back in satisfaction, having said his piece.

"That is extremely generous of you, sir," Blake said politely. "I'll certainly take it into consideration should I chance upon a marriageable female. But I will remind you that marriage is not likely to change my habits, so if that is your intent, you may as well sell now."

His mother patted her chest and blinked away tears. "You will be the death of me yet. You know I lost two brothers to war and another to accident who all bore the same silver streak in their hair that you have. It is not just superstition that those who wear it die before they're thirty. Do not make me bury my son, I beg you! Going off to war and fighting are just asking for trouble."

Blake did not need to be reminded of mortality. He had been a lad of six when he'd watched as his uncle was swept away in a flood. But neither did he believe in foolish wives' tales. "If it is my fate to die before I'm thirty"—which gave him a mere six months to live—"I'd rather go courageously, and with honor, than sleeping in my bed. What is the purpose of living if we do not improve the world we inhabit? I thank you for your generosity, and I give you good day, madam, sir."

He bowed himself out, leaving his mother weeping and his father to console her. It had ever been thus. He saw no means to change it.

Nevertheless, the possibility of owning Viscount Carrington's home filled him with wicked satisfaction. The bastard had cheated a good friend of his, forcing Acton Penrose to enlist in the army just to have food in his belly, and he was certain Penrose wasn't the only one Carrington had cheated over the years. In retaliation for Penrose's fate, Blake had pierced the viscount's shoulder with a bullet in a duel. It seemed perfect justice that the fat lordling should lose his home after causing others to lose theirs.

Perhaps he ought to consider his father's offer for the pure gratification of seeing "Carrion's" expression when he learned who now owned his family estate.

2

"That is my bird," Jocelyn Byrd-Carrington said, seething, as the Duke of Fortham's stout nephew, Bernard Ogilvie, crossed the lawn some distance away with a piteous African Grey parrot on his shoulder.

"Surely not, dear," Lady Isabell Belden replied, languidly flourishing her fan as they strolled toward the latest entertainment. "A duke's nephew has no reason to steal a molting fowl. He is merely attempting to impress you with his knowledge of birds."

"I vow, that is Percy. My brother Harold must have sold him to one of his wretched friends. And I told you before, duke's nephew or not, Mr. Ogilvie will not suit me as a bridegroom. He's as old as Harold, and twice as mean-spirited, and I want my bird back." In frustration, Jocelyn twirled her parasol and stalked after their host.

It was August. The Season was well over, and Jocelyn could not decide on a suitor, although she'd certainly had offers. She did not particularly wish to marry, but living alone would limit her ability to go about in society, and she dearly adored the parties and salons her lovely inheritance had opened to her these past months.

This house party was one last chance to consider a suitor. The Duke of Fortham had offered the use of his estate outside the city—purportedly in hopes of marrying off Ogilvie, his heir. That Jocelyn had been included suggested that His Grace must be desperate to find a bride for his nephew. She was merely the half sister of a viscount, and the fact that her father had been the duke's good friend hardly signified.

The party had seemed an opportune time to examine her marital choices in a charming rural setting. So far, Jocelyn was even less impressed with London's gentlemen in the country than in the city.

"It's the duke's bird, dear," said Lady Belden. "Surely you are not thinking of starting another aviary?" A youthful widow, the dark-haired dowager marchioness glanced at Jocelyn in concern. "I doubt there is a house in London that could hold one."

"No house that I can afford," Jocelyn admitted. "I have enjoyed my recent return to society very much, and you cannot know how much I appreciate the opportunity you have offered by opening your home to me. But as much as I have dreamed of London, I see now that it was foolish to believe I could return to town as the carefree child I once was."

"You were not a child when your father died. You were seventeen! I truly cannot understand why your father's heir would throw you from his home when he could have given you a Season and arranged a suitable marriage."

Jocelyn shrugged. "Our house was too small to hold the disparate personalities of my family. My mother insisted on ruling the study as she had always done when my father was alive. My younger brother, Richard, threw tantrums if anyone disturbed his birds in the conservatory. My sister-in-law didn't wish to spend coin on a Season for me, and Harold, who thought inheriting the title meant he should be stuffy, was embarrassed by poor Richard's admittedly erratic behavior. The arguments were quite fearful. Harold solved his difficulties by foisting us off on my half sisters. They got a nanny and nursemaid in me, although at the cost of poor Richard's birds and my mother's eccentricities. It is all quite simple."

The sensible marchioness did not protest. She knew of Jocelyn's family liabilities and patted her arm. "It is a sad pity that your father had no unentailed wealth with which to support you, but now that you have my late husband's bequest, you have choices. I will not hurry you into making a decision that will affect the rest of your life. If your family comes first, so be it. But your social flair would be an asset for so many men, and even if you do not marry, I'm sure you could find other means of employing your talents. Why, your eye for choosing just the right fabrics and ribbons could make you an arbiter of fashion!"

Jocelyn laughed as they joined the other ladies at tea tables set up on the lawn. Very few of the women sipped their tea, however. They were all too busy watching the masculine prowess of the men fencing by the garden wall.

"Blake will be maimed for life!" the Baroness Montague mourned, flapping her fan in agitation. "He can barely walk on that leg!"

"Which is why he chose a position against the wall," Lady Bell murmured, looking about to find a table that would give her the best view of the show. "No one can come up behind him, so he need not swing on his bad leg."

"Mr. Montague is fencing?" Jocelyn settled at the table her benefactress had chosen and turned to watch as two powerful young men stabbed at each other with deadly skill.

Stripped to their shirtsleeves and sweating from their efforts, both men were extraordinarily fine physical specimens. Unfortunately, Jocelyn's needs in a man included understanding and sympathy. Corinthians did not qualify, so she merely admired their athletic prowess.

"What has the disrespectful Mr. Montague said this time that has him dueling . . ." She strained to identify his opponent. "Mr. Atherton? Surely Mr. Atherton is accustomed to his friend's rudeness."

Lady Bell gestured toward a servant for a teapot and continued to observe the spectacle. "Mr. Montague possesses an inner devil that must be unleashed occasionally. I daresay Nick draws him out simply to avert an explosion of incivility."

Jocelyn snickered, but now that she recognized both men working themselves into a lather, she returned her attention to her host's parrot. England did not abound with African Greys. There was only one other to her knowledge, and that was Percy's mate, Africa. She could tell them apart by the pattern of white on their faces.

Richard would weep for joy if she could return at least one of the birds he'd been forced to leave behind after Harold had cast them from their home. He'd been devastated by the loss of his aviary and had never truly recovered. Her troubled little brother didn't have much joy in his life. The physicians had never been able to determine why Richard had irrational tantrums when anyone interfered with his obsessive interests. He did not adapt well to social situations, and the birds were his only friends. Returning Percy would be a goal worthy of her time and effort.

Adopting the vapid smile she had learned to wield at an early age to please an audience of adults, Jocelyn excused herself from the table and, lifting the frill of her muslin skirt from the grass, tripped daintily in the direction of the gentlemen watching the match.

As she neared Mr. Ogilvie and the bird, she pretended to stumble, emitted a peep of distress, and caught herself on her host's sleeve as he and his companions turned in response to her cry.

Percy squawked a bored, "Acck, swive the fart-catcher!"

"Ogilvie, damn you!" Mr. Montague cried abruptly, halting the fencing duel. "I told you to keep that obscene creature caged away from the ladies! That is my mother and sister sitting over there."

Although she was appalled that the bird had been taught such phrases, Jocelyn merely righted herself, covered her mouth, and tittered. "Law, I didn't mean to stop the match. I just wanted to pet the pretty bird."

"'Pologize, Miss Carrington," Ogilvie said gruffly. "Bird don't know what he's saying."

If Mr. Ogilvie seriously meant to court her, he was making a poor show of it, Jocelyn thought. She doubted the older man would have even offered his arm if she hadn't caught it on her own. He was simply another selfish twit more interested in the beef on his plate than in the people around him.

"Someone return the lady to the tables where she belongs," Montague called in disgust, sweat-soaked linen clinging to his wide chest. Clearly, even in his impatience, he made the more gentlemanly suggestion that hadn't occurred to Ogilvie.

Jocelyn pouted prettily and held out her hand to Percy. "Pretty bird. Come to Mama, baby."

"Ack, bugger off, looby," Percy cried, hopping from

Ogilvie's shoulder to hers and affectionately nuzzling her ear.

"Naughty bird," Jocelyn cooed, flapping her long lashes at all the gentlemen, who now openly stared at her. "I'll just take him off your hands, shall I?"

Lifting her hem, revealing a flash of ankle, she set off across the lawn with Percy nibbling one of her carefully curled blond ringlets.

"Flibbertiwidget," she heard Montague mutter. "Ogilvie, you'd better escort the lady back before she trips in those foolish shoes and your creature flies away."

"Obnoxious bully, that Montague, with all the social graces of a turkey," Jocelyn muttered under her breath as Ogilvie hastened to catch up with her. *Flibbertiwidget,* indeed!

"Can't lose that bird," her host announced, alarmed, taking the bird from her shoulder. "Duke would have my head."

Ogilvie left her with Lady Bell and strode back to the house, carrying the shrieking parrot in his paws. Jocelyn wanted to weep, but she would not. It seemed poor Percy had been horribly mistreated since she'd last seen him. Greys did not like drastic changes in their circumstances.

"Oh, Miss Carrington, it was so thoughtful of you to try to stop their foolishness!" Lady Montague came to their table, her eyes wet with tears. "You tried, but that son of mine is as stubborn as the day is long."

Still stinging from his insult, Jocelyn merely patted the lady's plump hand. At least she knew enough not to say rude words, even when she thought them—unlike Blake Montague, who apparently said whatever came into his head. *Flibbertiwidget!* He scarcely knew her.

Rather than think impolite thoughts, it was far better to plot how she would retrieve Percy now that she had come close enough to identify Richard's pet. She had wondered what Harold had done with Richard's aviary, but she'd been helpless in the wilds of Norfolk for so long that she had given up all hope of ever seeing the birds again.

Now that she knew one still lived, she had a mission.

3

"Percy wanta chippie. Africa knows," the parrot squawked sleepily later that evening.

His cage should be covered by now. Flirting with an amused Mr. Atherton, Jocelyn hid her frown behind her fan. It was either that or conk the whiskey decanter over Mr. Ogilvie's oblivious head and walk out with the bird.

As the next youngest in a family of much older half siblings, she had always lacked any sort of authority. She'd learned long ago that subterfuge was the best method of accomplishing what she wanted. Better than conking people over the head, at least.

Apparently not so reticent, Mr. Montague growled from near the library fireplace, "I told you to stubble that bird, Bernie. There are ladies present."

"It's my uncle's bird," Mr. Ogilvie protested. "His Grace would have *me* stubbled."

Mr. Montague had avoided the ladies all evening, as he was avoiding her now by standing at the opposite end of the room and pretending Jocelyn was a piece of furniture. Being ignored rankled when she'd dressed to impress tonight, but her interest wasn't in surly Montague, even if his father had hinted that he might include a house in a marriage settlement. A house was scarcely compensation for a man who was prone to violence and who would never possess the patience her eccentric family required. They would not suit.

Over the past few days, she had easily dismissed every man here as a potential suitor. Despite all his elegant sophistication, Mr. Atherton was a notorious rake. From Lady Bell's investigations, Jocelyn knew Mr. Ogilvie had no income beyond an allowance from the duke, and he seemed to have no ambition toward improving his lot. Couple that with his friendship with her repulsive brother Harold, and he was the last man she'd consider. Lord Quentin was older and even more intimidating than Mr. Montague. He hadn't noticed her existence. Why should he? He was already rich.

In frustration, she gave up the dream of reentering the society that she'd been denied upon her father's death. Instead, she would find a home where Richard could own as many birds as he pleased. Since society frowned upon an unmarried lady living on her own—and her younger brother would scarcely be considered a competent guardian—she would start looking for a house outside London. Just escaping the life of drudgery in her half sisters' households would be a satisfying use of her inheritance.

For the moment, she kept her goals simple—retrieving Richard's abused pet.

To distract the argument brewing on the far side of the room, Jocelyn tapped her fan on Mr. Atherton's shoulder. Another younger son, he was on everyone's guest list simply because he looked pretty and his affability smoothed over many awkward social situations.

She flapped her lashes at him, and nodded at the blank spines of the books on the wall they stood beside.

Being of an accommodating nature, he readily agreed to divert the quarrel over the bird by calling out, "I say, these books have no titles, Bernie."

"That's the servants' door, silly," admonished Frances Montague, Blake's sister, leaning past them to examine the false facade. "Those are *faux* books."

"They still need titles." Mr. Montague joined them, his mood apparently more suited to playing word games than discussing parrots. Or perhaps that was the result of the quantity of brandy he'd consumed these past hours. "*Johnson's Contradictionary*," he suggested.

Mr. Montague was of a similar height to Atherton, but somehow he vibrated with a restrained energy that all the other gentlemen lacked. Jocelyn disliked the way she was drawn to his formidable presence—and admittedly clever wit—so she inched away.

"*Boyle on Steam*," Lord Quentin added, sipping brandy and looking bored now that Lady Bell had retired for the evening. It was well past midnight, and he generally did not attend social occasions except as the marchioness's escort.

With the argument redirected, Jocelyn removed herself from the game, picking up a genuine book and settling into a wing chair in a dark corner. Her original plan had been to hope they'd forget she was here until she could abscond with the parrot. But she feared that Mr. Montague forgot nothing.

"Percy Vere in forty volumes," Atherton added languidly. "That should name the rest of them."

"Acck! Stick it up her bum! Roger her, boyo!" the parrot declared.

"That's quite enough of that!" Mr. Montague said in

frustration, swirling to glare at Ogilvie. "Remove that rude creature or I will!"

"Perhaps it will be best if the ladies withdraw, Blake," Frances suggested shyly. "We're keeping the poor thing awake."

Hurray for Frances! The woman showed a little sense after all. The men gallantly protested but the ladies demurred, and eventually, the scents and sounds of perfumes and silks wafted from the room, accompanied by a few more of the gentlemen, including Lord Quentin.

"Now see what you've done, old boy," Mr. Atherton protested. "Who wants to look at your ugly mugs without the ladies about?"

"I won't have a bloody parrot insulting my sister," Blake protested. "Ogilvie, you need to tie the bird's beak shut or remove it to a barn, where it belongs."

"Can't," Bernie argued morosely. "I'm to guard it with my life."

"Fair enough. Then I'll shoot you before I shoot the bird."

Jocelyn's eyebrows soared upward. Mr. Montague sounded bored, hostile, and frustrated, always a volatile mixture when combined with alcohol. Should she intervene?

"Codswallop!" the bird screeched.

"Did anyone bring their weapons?" Montague asked ominously.

Jocelyn shuddered at the image of the soldier using Percy as a target.

"I've my weapons with me. Prime Mantons, they are," one of the more drunken chaps cried happily. "Surely you won't shoot the creature in here?"

Jocelyn buried her head in her hands and wondered if there was any beast on earth more stupid than a man full of brandy. She waited for Mr. Montague to tell them all to jump off a cliff. She had a feeling they would do anything he suggested.

Instead, Mr. Montague drawled a bored, "Why not? Whatever it takes to stop the bird from insulting ladies."

"Montague, you idiot, you cannot shoot a bird," Ogilvie shouted in protest.

"Did you just insult me?" Mr. Montague asked in a dark tone.

"A card game," Atherton interjected. "He who wins the set decides the bird's fate."

Mr. Ogilvie protested, but he'd lost control of his guests. Various gentlemen rushed off to find their cards and their pistols. Disappointed that Mr. Montague did not assert his leadership skills, Jocelyn decided she did not care if a bunch of drunken sots killed one another, but she could not allow them to kill Richard's bird.

Just as she thought they'd all gone away, and she was free to take Percy and run, Mr. Montague's shadow fell over her chair. "Are you lost, Miss Carrington? Shall I send your maid to find you?"

Now he deigned to notice her, when he was foxed and she was preoccupied with birdnapping. She threw her book aside. "I am not lost. Nor am I the *idiot* fighting over a bird." She emphasized the insult Mr. Ogilvie had used. That was unlike her, but the knowledge that Mr. Montague couldn't call her out for the offense gave her childish pleasure.

Without looking back, she stalked from the room, cursing interfering men. She would have to hide elsewhere until she had a chance to retrieve poor Percy. Her bags were packed. Lady Belden meant to leave at the break of day so they'd be home in time for an evening engagement. She could sleep while they traveled. She need only wait until they left the bird—

At a cry from Percy, she swung around to see Ogilvie carrying the parrot with him as the men strolled from the room in search of cards, weapons, and presumably more sensible heads.

Well, drat. That complicated matters.

Refusing to give up on Richard's parrot, she settled into a window seat and drifted off to sleep while waiting for the men to return with the bird. At some point, she heard the drunken louts arguing over the card contest and some significance of the code of duello, but they still had Percy.

She woke up again when Mr. Ogilvie roared someone was a bloody cheater, and he'd shoot the cheat before he'd let the bird be shot. Glancing outside, she couldn't see dawn, but she did see raindrops on the glass.

Percy screeched a protest as someone carried him out the front door into the cold drizzle. They would kill the bird in this weather, of a certainty! Finding her bonnet and cloak in the closet beneath the stairs, Jocelyn slipped out after them, determined to put an end to their bird depredations.

Standing in a field outside a duke's mansion, in a drenching predawn downpour, surrounded by a crowd of equally drunken young men, Blake Montague decided that getting shot by an overbearing imbecile over a rude parrot and a card game possessed potent symbolism, if only he could fathom what it might be.

He had attempted to divert the sots with cards, but Bernie Ogilvie's second insult had only added fuel to the flames, and Blake's honor came into question. Over a bird. That had to be the effect of too much brandy on both their parts. He could not think why else a duke's nephew would intentionally insult someone so far below him on the social scale.

Damn Jocelyn Carrington and her flirtatious eyes and bold insults. He should not have partaken of that last glass of brandy while attempting to ignore the arousing effect that vivacious Venus had on his frustration. He was a hopeless mutton-head when it came to champagne-colored curls and blue eyes.

More likely, he should not have attempted his friend Fitz's trick with counting cards. Bernie didn't like to lose.

Blake examined the assortment of bloodthirsty weaponry placed at his disposal. Shooting anything might relieve some of his many irritations. He'd far prefer to find a woman than a weapon for physical release, but he'd take what he could get.

Hair tied unfashionably at the nape, whiskers in need of scraping, and torso stripped to shirtsleeves, embroidered vest, and loosened neckcloth, Blake was aware that he looked the part of disreputable highwayman. Perhaps if he accidentally killed Bernie, he'd take up thievery for a living. But he had no intention of hitting a target as wide as Bernie. The dolt merely needed a layer or two of privilege removed from his hide.

"'He's a most notable coward,'" Blake pronounced, the words tripping effortlessly off his well-oiled tongue while he held up a pistol and checked the length of the barrel, "'an infinite and endless liar, an hourly promise breaker, the owner of not one good quality.'"

Oblivious of his opponent huddled with friends farther down the hedgerow, Blake pointed an ornate Manton at the moon. "'I desire that we be better strangers.'"

"Damnation, he's quoting Shakespeare." Staying dry beneath the spreading branches of an oak, Atherton did not seem overly anxious about Blake's impending confrontation with death. "We could all drown out here before he's done."

Blake would miss his callous friends if he took up

thievery. He wouldn't, however, miss Miss Carrington's infectious laugh. Or that riveting cleavage she'd flaunted all evening. Ladies be damned.

Bernie's second sounded more concerned than Nick. "We're supposed to resolve this, not let them further insult each other."

"We tried," Nick noted. "Ogilvie's the poor sport here."

"Montague cheated!" Ogilvie protested, as he had done ever since the drunken party had whooped its way from the duke's mansion to this distant field. He ignored the proffered box of weapons while he affixed the duke's molting parrot on a perch he'd planted in the ground. "It's a matter of honor."

The wet creature flapped its wings and squawked a bored protest. "Acck! Friggin' cock snatcher. Roger her, boyo!"

The very words that had set Blake off this evening.

"'Methink'st thou art a general offense, and every man should beat thee,'" Blake quoted, filling his weapon with powder.

Shoulders propped against the oak, Nick sighed in exasperation. "You're not on the battlefield anymore, old friend. Let the poor boy toddle to bed and sleep it off. You may not mind fleeing the law for a stint on the Continent, but it's a damned poor way to treat your host."

"That's Bernie's choice, not mine," Blake corrected, testing the sight on the barrel. "It is my duty to defend the delicate sensibilities of the ladies. How can I find a rich one so I might return to war if I allow them to be insulted?" Blake asked. "Although it is hard to come by a wife who wants me dead," he added with drunken wisdom.

Bernie's second lifted a questioning eyebrow.

"Not a quote," Nick explained. "Blake needs a dowry

to buy colors. He thinks he can run the war better than the current crop of hen-hearted rattle-pates."

"You're serious?" the other man asked in disbelief, water dripping from the brim of his hat.

Nick shrugged. "He possesses the intellect to run the country but hasn't a ha'pence to his name. What do you think?"

"War heroes get titles." Bernie's second nodded in understanding.

"Acck, tup her good, me lad!"

Maintaining the deadly focus that had kept him alive on the battlefield, Blake ignored Nick's idea of repartee. In boredom, he aimed the loaded pistol at the half-featherless creature, which was barely discernible against the backdrop of yew. "'Scurvy, old, filthy, scurry lord.'" He fired a test shot in the general direction of the bird and hedge. A flurry and scuttle shook the evergreen branches, as if some animal's sleep had been disturbed, and the parrot squawked incomprehensible curses.

"Not the bird, Montague!" Ogilvie shouted, seeming in more fear of the parrot's life than his own. "His Grace will disown me! Someone move Percy behind the hedge."

One of Bernie's companions obligingly pulled up the perch and moved the scurvy lord out of sight, if not out of hearing. Obscenities and squawks screeched against the silent dawn, raising songbirds into protest.

"The ladies are leaving this morning," Nick called from his position beneath the oak, making no effort to verify the safety or accuracy of the next pistol Blake hefted. "Shooting Ogilvie won't do you any good now. Apologize and have done."

"'I must be cruel only to be kind.'" Blake again sighted along the length of a barrel, in the direction of the hedge where the bird now resided.

The shrubbery rustled as if retreating from his aim.

"Shakespeare?" Bernie's second asked.

"One never can be quite certain," Nick concluded. "Montague's brainpan is stuffed with an encyclopedia."

Eager to escape the chilly September rain, one of the onlookers finally herded the duelists into position, back to back, and gave the signal for them to begin pacing off their distance. As Blake took long strides across the wet grass, a demonical shriek from the hedge—*Ackkkk, kidnapper, murderer, help, hellllppppp!*—dispersed the tension of the final count.

Undeterred by the parrot's warning, Blake swiveled steadily at the count of ten and aimed his pistol. But Bernie was no longer in position.

Instead, coattails flapping, the duke's stout nephew was racing for the shrubbery. "She's stealing Percy!" he roared.

Sure enough, a dark, cloaked shadow—with a silly plume bouncing on its head—could be seen darting up the hill, into a grove of trees, the bird perch with it.

In disgust, Blake fired at Bernie's hat, sending the inappropriate chapeau bouncing across the saturated grass with a hole through its middle. The rain had stopped as suddenly as it had begun, and a glimmer of predawn light appeared on the horizon. His opponent's balding pate glistened as he fought yew branches in hopes of reaching his pet.

The bird screamed again from the field beyond the hedge.

Pointing, looking for all the world like a shorter version of the Prince of Wales, Bernie shouted, "A thousand pounds to anyone who catches her. Devil take the damned witch!"

"I say, did he promise a thousand pounds for that paltry poultry?" Blake asked, reloading the smoking pistol.

"He did, old boy, he did." Nick unfurled himself from the oak's trunk. "But everyone knows Ladybyrd took him. He'll never see the creature again."

Blake snorted. "For a thousand pounds, I'll follow her to the Outer Hebrides." Chasing Jocelyn Byrd-Carrington anywhere was just exactly what he needed. At this point, he would do so for nothing. He could still smell the damn woman's exotic scent. Shooting her might be good for the soul and relieve the world of a foolish, bird-stealing widget.

"For all your education, you have ale for brains, Professor," said Nick. "With that game leg, you can barely walk. You're supposed to be recuperating. Haring after a crackbrain will only get you killed all the sooner."

"She's carrying a squawking damned parrot. How far can she get?" Donning his coat, Blake tucked the loaded pistol into his trouser band and trudged toward the hedge.

He had despised his enforced idleness. The last fumes of liquor evaporated with the exhilaration of action priming his blood. He didn't know a woman alive who would travel without bags and boxes. If she was fleeing with the parrot, she wouldn't part easily with them. *Voilà*, she and the parrot would be found with the baggage.

Even if idle Bernie didn't actually possess the full reward he'd offered, the duke might. Just five hundred pounds would buy Blake's colors and free him from the need to marry for money. For the first time in recent memory, his spirits soared, and the thrill of the chase was on.

4

"Methinks he thinks too much," Jocelyn crooned to the parrot, stroking it beneath the dark cloth covering the warm dry box she'd appropriated for the mistreated creature. The parrot batted its head against her soothing finger, then settled into sleep.

Shivering in her wet cloak, her mangled bonnet plume sticking to her cheek, Jocelyn tried not to think too hard about Blake Montague aiming a pistol in her direction, looking the part of a dangerous rogue.

Tucking the bird's box among the rest of the baggage in the wagon, she heard the uneven crunching of gravel up the carriage drive and glanced toward the towering ducal mansion nearly a quarter mile from the stable where she stood. She had hoped the combatants were all too drunk or involved in the duel to follow her, but she didn't underestimate the provoking soldier's determination. The angry stride with a halting limp was probably his.

Montague was a lethal weapon. And for all his education, he didn't seem to like anyone very much.

With no hope of reaching the house before he caught up with her, she abandoned the wagon and slipped into the shadows of the stable, out of the lingering drizzle. Nickers and whoofs and the pungent odor of manure permeated the morning air as the animals stirred in anticipation of their breakfast.

She'd learned the value of stealth and a good diversion while avoiding Harold's rages. Spreading her thick cloak, Jocelyn pulled the hood over her bonnet and settled in a rear stall where a barn cat was nursing newborns.

"I know you're in here," a husky baritone called from the entrance. "I had hoped to have to hunt you down. You have disappointed me."

Jocelyn wanted to ask what he intended to do, shoot her? But she saw no reason to disturb the kittens.

She suffered a nervous chill at the thought of being alone with an enraged man, but for all his brooding gloom, Mr. Montague was widely reported to be an honorable gentleman. He might scald her with the acid of his scorn, but a gentleman would never lay a hand on a lady. Behind him, dawn was lightening the wet day, silhouetting his square shoulders as he brushed raindrops from his hair. She wished she didn't admire his physical strength so much. He had looked like a dangerous pirate in that duel, and his fencing this afternoon . . . Not to be considered. She had her goals, and Montague didn't fit in with them.

She scratched mama cat's head to reassure her as her pursuer stomped from stall to stall, waking the mares. Fortunately, the stallions were stabled elsewhere, or they'd be breaking down their doors at this intrusion.

She'd stationed herself so she could see the length of the barn and knew when he drew near. Her dove gray cloak blended nicely into the shadows this far from the door. When his tall outline loomed close, she pulled back her hood so he could see her white face against the stall. Good soldier that he was, he spotted her instantly.

She surreptitiously studied Mr. Montague's stern, steely-eyed expression as he approached. She knew the value of most of the young men of society, and Blake Montague's worth lay in his intellect, not in his pockets.

Except—the sight of the distinguished silver in his thick hair produced in her an oddly delicious shiver of excitement. She must admit that he was a handsome, if formidable, figure of a man—not one easily manipulated by the deceptive smiles and beguiling ways she'd learned to employ.

She was entirely too aware of Blake Montague's powerful body as he came to a halt and regarded her as if she were a strange insect. His square jaw and angular cheekbones were made harsher by the bronze of a Portugal sun. Sinfully dark-lashed eyes accompanied his thick, overlong locks, creating an almost poetic image, if only the streak near his temple didn't look like a dangerous lightning bolt.

It was that intense, hawk-eyed expression he bestowed upon her that set her nerves trembling, nearly preventing her from teasing him as she might tease another man.

She could almost swear he growled as he limped forward. She held a finger to her lips to indicate quiet. He quirked a menacing dark eyebrow at her.

"Quit posturing and admit the bird is better off free," she whispered.

"Free?"

If he'd worn a hat, she thought he might have stomped on it. Picking up a kitten, she returned his glare. "What else could be done but let free such a rude creature?"

"You did not let a tropical bird loose in chilly England. You may be nicked in the nob, but no one ever said you were stupid."

She slanted her eyes thoughtfully. "Actually, Harold said it quite often. And my brothers-in-law had occasion to mention it once or twice. Mr. Ogilvie certainly said it over these past days. I think I prefer *nicked in the nob.* What, precisely, does that mean?"

He ignored her effort to distract him. "The bird belongs to the duke. You cannot keep it. It's theft. Just tell me where you've hidden it, and I'll see it's returned without question." He crossed his arms over his soaked coat and glowered.

Jocelyn beamed at him in return. "Nature cannot be owned, sir."

He blinked as if he'd just realized she truly was dimwitted—the reaction she was most accustomed to receiving. In keeping hapless Richard and his fowl from being murdered by angry family and strangers alike, she'd learned to act helpless. They usually quit shouting when she presented guileless smiles and pretty pleas.

Mr. Montague recovered more quickly than most, unfortunately. He reached down, grabbed her arm, and hauled her to her feet, much to mama cat's consternation. "That's the most preposterous idiocy I've heard all week, and I've heard a lot. *Where is the bird?*"

"Really, sir, you'll ruin the drape of my gown." She probably ought to be afraid. Blake Montague was more raw male than she normally encountered. He didn't stink of perfume or hair pomade but male musk, perspiration, and damp wool. His hands on her weren't the polite escort of a gentleman. She sensed he was passionately determined for reasons she could not perceive, but she couldn't believe he would harm her because of a bird.

"Would you like me to summon an audience?" he

asked maliciously. "What would Lady Bell have to say if we were discovered here alone at dawn?"

Jocelyn cocked her head thoughtfully. "Oh, something pithy and intelligent like *birds of a feather flock together.* Or *dross sinks to the lowest depths.*"

She thought she almost caught a quirk of humor in the curl of his lip, and a thrill of totally unjustified pride swept through her. She really ought to be concerned about her reputation, but he was a rural baron's youngest son, and until recently, she had been no more than the impoverished daughter of a deceased viscount. Their families were of Quality, but not of vast import to society.

But Lady Belden had been more than kind to her, and Jocelyn always tried not to disappoint her hostess. She set the kitten down and left the stall so the mama cat might rest easy. "Wouldn't you rather explain your interest in a half-dead old bird than cause a scandal?"

"Personally, I'd wring the foulmouthed featherbrain's miserable neck, but Ogilvie has placed a thousand-pound reward on its return, and I have good use for the blunt."

"Your mother said you had given up on buying colors!" Jocelyn declared in dismay. "You've already been grievously injured. It would be suicide to return to the battlefield."

Blake Montague bared his strong white teeth and hauled her past the stalls. "I have an entire family smothering me with such witticisms, thank you. What I choose to do is no concern of yours. Now tell me which of these stalls contains the damned bird, or I shall open them all."

"Then I hope you enjoy chasing the duke's cattle," she replied merrily.

Montague shot her a disgruntled look, studied her

amused expression, and withdrew a pistol from beneath his coat. He aimed it at the luggage cart that was clearly visible through the barn doors. "What if I proceed to shoot those boxes?"

Jocelyn shrieked, jerked his arm downward, and the delicate firing mechanism of the expensive pistol exploded.

In dismayed horror, Jocelyn covered her mouth to prevent crying out as Montague lifted his boot to reveal a smoking hole through the toe.

"Oh, my, you are bleeding! We must remove that boot." Near tears, the lethal blonde dropped to her knees on the barn floor beside Blake and struggled to grasp his ruined boot.

Blake could scarcely believe the birdbrained Venus had had the audacity and immense stupidity to attend a duel with the intention of stealing a damned bird, much less *shoot* him. And if he did not mistake, Miss Carrington was now about to faint over his wound.

He was none too happy with the sight of his own blood pouring from the smoking hole, either.

"You should never carry a loaded pistol!" she sobbed while kneeling over his legs and tugging at his boot. He wished her concealing cloak to damnation so he might have a better view of her luscious bottom. "Violence only leads to violence," she continued, although he wasn't listening.

She pulled so hard on his boot, she practically toppled into his lap when he jerked his foot away at the sharp pain. Recovering quickly, she scrambled to her knees beside him and peered at him through long-lashed violet eyes nearly hidden beneath a preposterously frivolous bonnet. Her eyes alone could bring a strong man to his knees.

The ridiculous plume of her bonnet framed a heart-shaped face, an upturned excuse for a nose, limp blond ringlets, and a wide mouth designed specifically to destroy him.

"Leave the boot alone," Blake ordered, biting back a groan of pain for both the inanity of his reaction to a flibbertiwidget and the throb of his wounded appendage.

She was kneeling entirely too close for his peace of mind. He pushed her hands aside and attempted to ease off the leather. "Did no one ever tell you to keep your hands away from men with guns?" he grumbled, just to refrain from emitting every curse in his capacious vocabulary.

"Gentlemen generally do not wave weapons in my presence," she countered, recovering from what little remorse she'd suffered, although she wiped suspiciously at the corner of her eye. "Give me your neckcloth for a bandage."

"It's a flesh wound. I don't need a bandage." In truth, it felt as if he'd shot off his toe, but he couldn't wiggle his foot free to tell. He directed his gaze away from his smoking boot, which left him looking into eyes that tilted deliciously at the corners when she glared at him, but she finally showed some sense by not arguing.

"Will you bleed to death if I run to the house for help?" she asked.

"It would be preferable to enduring your prattle." Blake hated the sight of blood, especially his own, but he supposed it was better than studying this addlepated Venus.

He finally tugged off the boot and waited for her to depart before peeling off his stocking. Even with the sock on, it looked as if the bullet had merely nicked a toe, but blood soaked through the knit, spreading everywhere. He'd rather not offend her with the sight.

"Far be it from me to wound your pride as well as your toe." Proving herself to be an unexpectedly dangerous judge of character, she retained her dignity, stood up, and began to brush off her hay-littered skirt—until the chatter of voices in the yard halted her.

"I heard a shot!" an excited female called from outside. "We are already too late to stop them from fighting! I should not have taken time to dress! Could you tell the direction?"

Blake groaned in recognition of his mother's voice. "Run. *Now*."

To his amazement, the scatterwit obeyed. She raced to the open doorway, which revealed that the rain clouds had finally dissipated. Her bonnet fell off and flopped down her back, allowing the first rays of dawn to strike a rosy tint on her creamy complexion and highlight the golden strands of a heavy chignon deteriorating with moisture. In her haste, she failed to lift the sagging hem of her loose cloak, causing straw and dirt to fly up in a cloud that clung to the wet cloth.

She looked like a woman who had just been tumbled.

"Over here, come quickly!" she cried to the women in the stable yard. "Someone fetch a physician."

Blake went from admiring the vision of a dawn goddess to covering his eyes in defeat. "I meant run and hide, Miss Carrington, not greet our doom and direct it toward us."

He could easier shoot a bee from a bonnet than finesse his way out of the scandal sure to be raised by their presence together at this hour and in this condition. His companion had wits to let.

A feminine babble joined that of the geese honking overhead. From somewhere outside, the parrot woke grumpily and squawked, "Pretty bird wants a canary."

Blake wished he'd shot the obscene creature when he'd had the chance.

A gaggle of females darkened the doorway, whispering, gasping, and otherwise dithering rather than enter the dim stable.

"Jocelyn, whatever is going on here?"

Blake recognized Lady Belden's modulated tones and wondered if there was any place in all the kingdom where he could hide without the delicate dowager hunting him down and shooting him. *Of course* she was up and about. That was her wagon loaded outside. She was no doubt looking for Jocelyn and prepared to depart for London at this ungodly hour. The widow did not let time or distance stand in the way of her entertainment. She certainly hadn't come to save his hide from a duel. But it would be just like his mother to do so. One of the maids must have awakened her.

"Lady Belden, Mr. Montague has been injured," Miss Carrington cried. "I need bandages to stop the bleeding, and—"

"Blake!" his mother exclaimed frantically. "Frances, call for a physician. Find a groom. We need to carry him to the house at once."

Blake groaned in exasperation. "It's just a scratch, Mother," he asserted, reluctantly revealing his presence. "I am fine. Send the ladies away so the damage does not offend them."

His mother ignored his admonitions, of course, shoving past his sister and Lady Belden to enter the barn. "Miss Carrington, I need bandages and alcohol," she called at the sight of his bloody toe.

Without asking his permission, his not-so-delicate mother jerked off the stocking that had become matted to his wound. Blake nearly came up off the floor at the explosion of pain.

In the doorway, Miss Carrington folded her hands in her skirt, raised expressively blond eyebrows, and refrained from smirking. He had the choice of displaying his *wounded pride* by telling her to get the hell out again, or pretending she didn't exist. He grabbed the stocking and used it to mop blood from the nick while his shy sister stood in the doorway, covering her eyes.

"It was an accident," he muttered from between clenched teeth. "I am no longer in the nursery, Mother, so if you would cease and desist, it would preserve my dignity for another few hours."

After rummaging through the luggage, Lady Bell returned with a clean white cloth and a brandy flask. She held them out for someone else to bring to him, not deigning to enter a stable containing a man with a naked foot. "I cannot conceive of any rational reason for this incident, Jocelyn," the dowager said. "You have blood on your skirt."

"And straw," his mother added absently, kneeling on the floor at an excellent advantage for observing Miss Carrington's attire. "I do hope she accepted your proposal if the two of you were out here all night."

Damnation! His mother was a woman dedicated to seeing him wedded. She would stick tighter than a leech if he did not divert her.

"We were not out here all night." Blake gritted his teeth and whisked the cloth and flask out of Miss Carrington's fingers so she might flee—which, of course, she didn't do. He took a healthy swallow of the brandy before dumping the contents over his wound, then whipped the linen around his toe to hide it. "Our soaked conditions should be proof enough of that," he added. "And Frances was with me until just a few hours ago." Five or six, to be exact. Small matter.

Miss Carrington stooped down again, this time to offer aid in helping him up. Her damp attire revealed far more of her curves than he had any right to notice, and his blood thrummed in inappropriate reaction.

He blamed his response on the blond strand that had once been a ringlet dangling damply beside her ear. When he brushed aside her interfering aid, she nibbled a delectably pink bottom lip and cast him a look that he preferred not to interpret. The woman would no doubt blow off another toe if he allowed her closer.

"I was merely checking on my horse, and Miss Carrington was helping a mother cat." Wobbling, Blake pushed off the floor without anyone's assistance, hoping to escape this ambush of delicate femininity until he recovered from his light-headedness, which had probably been brought on by loss of blood. Certainly not from Miss Carrington's presence.

He'd shot his good foot, leaving him to hobble unsteadily with one boot on and one boot off. It would be simpler to volunteer for the army again rather than suffer another house party like this one.

The least he could do was collect the reward for his troubles. He'd heard the filthy-mouthed bird in the cart as the hordes descended, but it was impossible to listen for it while his mother, Frances, Lady Belden, and Miss Carrington chattered all at once.

"That's sweet of you to protect her reputation after she saved you from a duel," his mother simpered, following close and prepared to catch him should he topple, although he towered a foot taller, several stone heavier, and would likely flatten her. "She's a darling girl, and we thoroughly approve."

"I am not protecting anyone, and I was not aware that I needed your approval, Mother," he replied stiffly. Saved him from a duel! As if he needed saving. Ogilvie was such a bad shot, he could only have hoped to hit Blake by accident.

Any attempt at argument with his parents felt as if he'd been reduced to a snot-nosed boy in short breeches, but he couldn't let his mother entertain ridiculous hopes about an addlepate who would no doubt get him killed. "Miss Carrington was not with me, as Ogilvie and Atherton can attest."

Not that Ogilvie would be inclined to help him or that anyone would believe a rake like Nick. Blake ignored the imagined noose tightening around his neck and limped toward the wagon, eyeing the stacks of trunks, satchels, and other assorted luggage piled high. They were less than a day's journey from London, but it looked as if Miss Carrington and Lady Belden had packed enough for a year on the Continent.

Miss Carrington hastened to come between him and her boxes.

Rather than suffer the continued humiliation of being dithered over, Blake risked her tempting perfume to lean over and whisper in the bird lady's ear, "If you will not tell me where you have hidden Ogilvie's fowl, I have nothing further to say in your defense, Miss Carrington. Your reputation may go hang."

"Oh, I believe you are wrong there." She caught his arm and steered him toward the house, away from the cart, steadying his limping stride while pretending he supported her. "But men are often so caught up in seeing the world at large that they fail to comprehend the social niceties. That's where women are eminently useful, is that not right, Lady Montague?"

Blake politely refrained from rolling his eyes at her apparent reference to the straw on her skirt and the noose dropping over his head. Instinct warned that she had turned the table and was holding the situation over *his* head as a threat. He had the urge to fling off her hand and stalk into the house, except with a bad knee and an injured toe, he feared he'd fall flat on his face.

"Precisely, Miss Carrington," his mother happily replied. "Blake is a brilliant visionary who could lead men out of darkness if he applied his talent appropriately, but he cannot see the food beneath his nose sometimes."

"Perhaps it has not been the proper food," Ladybyrd suggested, patting Blake's coat sleeve and offering him a dimpled smile as he limped up the stairs to the portico.

As if she understood he'd like nothing better than to heave her down the stairs they'd just ascended, Miss Carrington slipped blithely into the house after Lady Belden, who had her pert nose so out of joint that it was a wonder it didn't brush the door lintel as she passed under it. Women! He'd never understand them. Nor did he want to.

"I forgot to leave instructions with the stable lad about my horse," Blake said abruptly. "I shall see you at breakfast."

"Your foot!" his mother protested as he hobbled away. "It will become infected!"

His head was likely to become infected if he lingered longer among musical voices and feminine scents while any chance of claiming Ogilvie's—or a duke's—reward rolled away with the luggage wagon. Why on earth would a duke want an obscene parrot?

Leaving the ladies to dither inside, he reversed course and limped back to the stable.

5

Having discarded her damp cloak and bonnet, but still wearing her wilted evening gown, Jocelyn kept an eye on the stable yard out the window while Lady Belden paced up and down the parlor. The lady harangued the fates that had put Jocelyn and Blake Montague in the same location at the unfortunate hour of dawn, with more than one witness. She ended up bewailing the need to return Jocelyn to her family.

"You must marry! I cannot let you return to Norfolk in the state I found you in," the lady finally cried. "Your half sister behaved appallingly!"

With a weary grimace, Jocelyn recalled the day Lady Bell had arrived, a particularly disastrous occasion if she did say so herself. One of Richard's ducks had nested on her brother-in-law Charles's head the previous night. Her half sister Elizabeth had rolled into an egg the duck had laid on her pillow. And when Charles had wrung the duck's neck and roared down the stairs to swat at Richard with the carcass, Jocelyn's kitten had crossed his path, tripping him until he'd fallen face-first into the maid's slop bucket. She could almost smile at the memory now.

She hadn't been smiling when Charles had gone after the kitten with an ax and sworn that Richard would be sent to Bedlam and the rest of the damned family could go with him. She'd heard that threat from her other relations over the years. It inevitably meant more upheaval, and at the time, she had run out of options. Lady Bell had saved her.

"Baron Montague has said he will provide his Chelsea home as a settlement on his son if Blake marries a wife of whom he approves," Lady Belden was saying, disrupting Jocelyn's reverie. "But I fear Blake Montague is a confirmed bachelor with violent tendencies and little income of his own who will not appreciate your social skills."

To be perfectly honest, after being relegated to rural desolation for so many years, Jocelyn had been having such a good time whirling about society these past months that she truly hadn't given much thought to what kind of husband might suit her. She'd given a great deal of thought to ones who would *not* suit her, however.

If it weren't for her little brother and the desperate need to find a stable home for him, she would not worry about marrying at all. But she feared Lady Bell was making it clear that her own home wouldn't be indefinitely available, and even with the caretaker Jocelyn had hired to keep Richard out of trouble, the time had come to make a decision. She truly didn't want to be thrown out of still another home.

"I can see that you might not be happy living in the country, although you could certainly afford to hire a companion and do so," Lady Belden continued, her voice softening as it usually did once she vented her an-

ger or dismay. Slender and elegant, she looked like a disapproving angel. "But if you wish to live in town and go
about in society, you must marry. Blake Montague may
be a decent man, but he does not meet your require-
ments by any means."

Standing in the bay window, Jocelyn watched the
wretched man in question. He was systematically dis-
mantling the baggage wagon's load under the bemused
gaze of the driver.

Hardheaded, determined, with a strong streak of
cynicism and snobbery, Blake Montague would not be
easily manipulated. His clever wits would spin circles
around her. But she had tricks he'd not encountered,
ones developed out of necessity and over the course
of many escapades while dodging Harold and her half
sisters, who disliked bird poop in their soup. Getting
caught in a stable was just one in a long string of misfor-
tunes that would have flattened her by now if she wasn't
resourceful.

Besides, Blake Montague apparently had something
she might use—a house in Chelsea. She and Richard
had grown up on their father's estate in Chelsea, and
her younger brother would be ecstatic to be back by the
river again. The village was less than an hour's ride from
London, so it wasn't entirely rural oblivion. Lady Bell
was correct, though. Blake Montague did not suit her
in any way—except that he wished to go off to war. A
house in exchange for his colors. That was something to
consider.

There were any number of reasons why the incred-
ible notion forming in her addled brain was probably
terribly, horribly wrong—starting with the fact that she
just might need to kill the man if he didn't leave her
brother's parrot alone.

She preferred confronting problems to dithering

over them. Now that she'd found Percy, the bird would require Richard's care. Richard needed a home with an aviary. She could afford no suitable house in London.

Her brother-in-law would not tolerate Richard's childishly inappropriate tantrums and her mother's disconnection with reality for very much longer. Charles would insist that Richard be institutionalized. Or worse yet, that he be returned to his proper guardian, Harold. Richard had no defense against Harold's rages. That would be an abomination. Mama was not quite so intrusive and might escape his fury, but Lady Carrington deserved a home of her own, too.

Jocelyn needed a husband so she could have a home. Blake Montague needed a wealthy wife so he could go to war. He'd recklessly stained her reputation. The conclusion seemed obvious.

Montague might conclude otherwise, but she wasn't above a little blackmail. He was a gentleman, after all. His reputation had as much to suffer as hers.

If she hadn't killed Harold in all these years, then she should be able to hum along just fine with an overeducated snob who would spend the better part of a year a thousand miles away.

Jocelyn swung about, dropped an elegant curtsy, and hurried across the parlor, forcing Lady Belden to halt in midsentence. "Perhaps Blake Montague belongs on a battlefield," Jocelyn acknowledged. "But he does not belong in my baggage. If you will excuse me, my lady—"

She left without waiting for permission. She knew better. She was extremely well versed in etiquette. She could converse eloquently with a queen or a housekeeper. She might be as simpleminded as others called her, but she had learned all the rules so she knew how best to work around them.

She also knew how to play the rules to get what she

wanted, and right now, despite all her misgivings, she had Blake Montague in her crosshairs.

She took the side steps to the cobblestone stable yard and hastened across, wishing she had a riding crop. "Stop that this instant!" she shouted in a most unlady-like fashion.

Not that a mere shout would stop a tenacious rogue like Montague. The man could scarcely walk! Yet he was unloading her baggage while hobbling about on a bloody bandage and a gimpy leg. Even so, without a pistol of her own, she couldn't physically force him to cease his depredations. He was far larger than she. With his short-waisted coat unbuttoned, his neckcloth unfastened, and the damp linen plastered to his formidable chest, he revealed far more of his muscular physique than she wished to encounter.

Fortunately, physical strength failed before her arsenal of weapons.

"If you do not stop that this instant, I shall tell your mama that you lied and that we spent the night together in the stable!" she called.

The annoying man narrowed his eyes and immediately removed his hands from the crate next to the bird box. She could hear Percy stirring. In another moment, the poor creature would be screaming for his breakfast, in words that would make a seaman blush.

Ignoring Mr. Montague's escalating temper—as indicated by his ominous silence—Jocelyn stalked toward the side of the stable where Lady Belden couldn't see them from the parlor window. And where the miserable rogue couldn't disturb Richard's parrot.

She tried not to glance down at his bandaged toes. She hated that she'd shot him, but she couldn't stifle her curiosity. She'd never seen a man's bare foot. His was arched high, with long, elegant—manly—toes.

"That is the stupidest threat I've ever heard," he finally said, limping along beside her. With his overlong hair coming loose from its unfashionable queue, he looked more disreputable than ever.

When she lifted her skirts to step over a puddle near the horse trough, he cupped her elbow and assisted her over, even though he was the one who could barely stand. She glanced at him in incredulity when he continued to rant as if his fingers weren't still gripping her arm.

"You would ensnare yourself as well as me in my family's coils," he protested. "And for what? A feather-brained fowl?"

He was protecting *her* from her own actions? What kind of man was this? Not one her experience would allow her to believe.

"Percy is from a rare and ancient lineage and should be treated with the respect of kings," she informed him. "He should not be fed ale and carried about at dawn. Really, if there were a bird police, the duke would be shot for leaving Percy with his nephew. Mr. Ogilvie is a spiteful sort who probably pulls out Percy's feathers when no one is looking."

She tried to ignore the strength of Mr. Montague's hand clasping her elbow, but now that the treacherous notion of marriage had taken root, she couldn't help thinking of his strong, capable hands elsewhere on her person. That made her a trifle uneasy, but not enough to give up.

She would do anything to provide her small family with the home they deserved. What good was a fortune if it could not create happiness for the ones she loved best?

Mr. Montague emitted the long-suffering sigh she'd heard from countless men over her twenty-three years. She had innumerable arguments to counter those sighs, but she was tired of spouting them. She had her own wealth now. She didn't have to care what men thought.

She really, really loved that freedom. She owed Lady Belden her life. She shouldn't flout the lady's wise advice so hastily. But she had already set this wheel in motion, and she couldn't seem to stop.

Perhaps a man who argued with her as if she had thoughts of her own, instead of ordering her about as if she were a beagle, excited her hopes. Then again, she suspected Mr. Montague simply liked to argue.

"You don't care about Percy." She halted on the far side of the stable and climbed up on a mounting block so she could meet Blake Montague eye to eye. He did not look his best after a night of carousing, with his icy gray eyes shadowed, his black hair tangled, and his jaw covered in heavy whiskers. Despite his general dissipation, he'd just assisted her over a mud puddle while she was threatening him. She knew his type—all blazing arrogance, but with the social graces so ingrained he couldn't cut them out with a knife.

"I think the bird ought to be shot," he agreed, not in the least intimidated by her stance. He crossed his arms over his powerful chest, his broad shoulders pulling his shirt linen taut beneath his unfastened waistcoat. The lack of neckcloth revealed more of his bronzed throat than was respectable. "But I promise not to shoot it. I just want the thousand pounds Ogilvie offered for its return."

Jocelyn straightened her shoulders and clenched her fists at her side. It was a good thing she seldom took time to ponder her decisions or she'd run screaming into the woods, never to be seen again. "Ogilvie lies. He does not have a ha'pence to his name. Lady Bell's man of business has already advised us that he lacks funds. He lives off his uncle's goodwill, which is why he wants the bird back, even though he despises Percy."

Montague scowled so blackly that Jocelyn feared

he'd frighten the sun into falling. He had understandably been counting on such a large purse. To his credit, he refrained from uttering the curse that was so blatantly on the tip of his tongue.

"You cannot be faulted for believing him," she offered generously. "Men are inclined to believe in the honesty of their fellows. Unfortunately, women cannot be so sanguine, or we fall victim to scoundrels. Lady Bell says investigating potential suitors is good business."

"I'll keep the blasted fowl until the duke pays up," he growled.

He was about to turn on his heel and hobble off, which was what she really ought to let him do. He'd be willing to give Percy away soon enough. But that choice did not solve her long-range difficulties. Nor his, come to that. Annoyed that she should even remotely consider his problem, Jocelyn daringly grabbed his lapel and tugged him back. "You do not have the bird!"

He captured her hand to pry it loose but hesitated when he caught sight of her expression. Perhaps she was demonstrating her desperation a little too forcefully. "Lady Bell's man of business also confirmed that your father would provide his Chelsea home for your use if you marry a wife of whom he approves," she said, before releasing him.

"My parents want me to marry a woman they've chosen," he corrected. "And my father will surround the settlement with all sorts of disagreeable stipulations."

"I have already met the approval of your parents," she countered. "Unfortunately, Lady Bell has rejected you due to your propensity for violence."

Outrage hardened his already harsh features. "I don't wish to hear more. If you will excuse me—"

Jocelyn sighed as she watched him stride—or hobble—away. Blake Montague was a fine figure of a man, admittedly, but probably too hardheaded—and much too smart—for her purposes.

And yet, if she wanted a house, Montague was the best opportunity to cross her path. She simply needed to come up with terms they could both accept—and that would include allowing Richard to live with them. Really, she should have thought of a soldier sooner.

6

Blake would rather take a hot bath and fall between the sheets than change into dry clothes and venture out again, but his instincts warned him that preventive action was required. Curse and damn all interfering females! He couldn't believe a helpless twit like Miss Carrington could maneuver him into an unconscionable position, but he would take no chances.

Propensity for violence, be damned! He was no more violent than any other man he knew. Well, perhaps more violent than Ogilvie. Or Nick. Or . . . No matter. He had no desire to be *forced* into marriage because of a lot of twittering gossips, even if they included his family. And he had a strong suspicion that was precisely what Miss Carrington was set upon.

He suffered an appalling thought—had she learned that Carrington House could be his? There would be no stopping her, if so, no matter how his father tied up the deed.

If he was to be married, it would be on his terms and

no other's. He'd rather risk enlisting than fall under the thumb of still another nervous, smothering female who would take to heart his mother's foolish superstition about his impending death.

After finding Ogilvie's valet to help clean and bandage his toe, Blake winced while pulling on shoes. His boots were now unwearable. Breakfast was still not on the sideboard by the time he took the stairs and pounded on Hoyt's door.

Lord Quentin Hoyt was a younger son of the new Marquess of Belden. He'd come to London over a decade ago to make his fortune and had done so. The rest of his very large family remained in Scotland, where they continued to live modestly—because the dowager Lady Belden had inherited all of the late marquess's unentailed wealth. Fortunately, the Hoyts had little interest in society beyond allowing Quentin to provide for his sisters and nieces as they reached marriageable ages.

Scorning the traditional roles of the younger sons of society, Quentin had gone into shipping and secured funds of his own during his untitled years. Until his father had come into the marquessate, society had scorned Quent for his ambition. Now, he purported to act as his father's London liaison with the dowager marchioness. Blake assumed Quent had finagled an invitation to the house party just to annoy the lady because tradesmen wouldn't normally be invited to dirty a duke's parlor.

In Blake's cynical observation, his friend seemed to enjoy challenging the tart-tongued Lady Bell. At the very least, Hoyt knew her better than anyone, which made him a good man for the advice Blake needed.

Lord Quentin answered the knock himself. Dressed in a silk banyan, his jaw already shaved, he quirked a dark eyebrow at Blake, which told him Quentin had already been briefed on the morning's events.

Once inside, Blake limped up and down the chamber, organizing his arguments. "Lady Bell is matchmaking," he declared, still furious in so many ways he could not direct them all. "And this time, *I'm* Lady Bell's bait," he declared with disgust. "Worse yet, I'm discarded bait. She believes I am violent."

Quentin snorted and returned to the writing desk, where he was apparently working through a stack of documents requiring his signature. "I'm amazed she considered you bait at all. If Castlereagh is still here, he's even less likely to listen to you than before, if he hears of this latest escapade."

Blake winced, but it was far too late to appease the war secretary.

"I simply need to get my hands on more of that blamed French code before I can crack it," Blake argued. "I have to be in Portugal, where messages might be intercepted. To hell with Castlereagh, I need colors."

"You don't need a damned code. You need a woman, someone like that nice, malleable Carrington chit." Quentin's head jerked up, and a gleam appeared in his eyes as he finally caught the direction of the conversation. "Has Isabell rejected you as a match for her latest protégée?"

"So I understand. I was not even aware I was under consideration. I'm more inclined to shoot the birds Miss Carrington collects. It's not precisely an obvious match."

Quentin leaned back in his chair, crossed his arms, and sprawled his long legs across the carpet. Blake knew he ought to run and hide, but out of curiosity, he waited to see where his friend's mind would wander. For the sake of England and his future, he hoped Quent would find a way of returning him to the Continent.

Quent's large family had lived on breadcrumbs for decades and couldn't afford to be particular about their offspring going into trade. In contrast, Blake's conservative-minded father had a solid country income and no need for his sons to work anything except the fields. Unless he wished to completely alienate his family, Blake could not scandalize them by becoming a merchant. He wasn't the kind of cruel bastard who would jeopardize his sisters' chances in society, but marriage seemed an unnecessary torture to submit to for his family's sake.

"The Carrington wench possesses a fortune of a thousand pounds a year. You could do worse," Quent said thoughtfully.

"She shot me in the foot! What woman does that?"

"She carries a gun?" Quentin asked, raising a dubious eyebrow.

"It was my gun. She does not behave normally," Blake quibbled, his toe still aching from the incident. But he knew better than to belabor the point and went on to the next. "I just want your aid in diverting Lady Bell while I distract my mother before they concoct a scheme that will embroil us all."

"Considering the compromising circumstances in which you were found . . ."

Blake gestured dismissively. "She stole a bird! There was nothing compromising about our argument."

"Women do not necessarily look at things the same way we do. Does Miss Carrington express an interest in marriage?" Quentin asked, the dangerously thoughtful look still on his face.

"What does it matter? We would not suit," Blake argued.

Even he knew he protested too much. But he was

feeling trapped and harried and desperate, and wanted someone to tell him he had alternatives.

Quentin narrowed his eyes. "No woman would suit you unless she was a camp follower. And I suspect you'd be too fastidious to accept even that relationship."

Blast the man! That wasn't what he wanted to hear. "It hardly seems fair to leave a woman alone at home while I follow my duty to the Continent. If I had any other means of obtaining more of that code, I might consider marriage, but the army is my only hope."

"Admittedly, Miss Carrington is a trifle pale and delicate," Quentin said, staring at the ceiling. "She would no doubt dissolve with grief should you leave her."

"Pale and delicate? Are you mad? Are we talking about the same woman? She's a damned dangerous Venus!" Blake bit his tongue. He hadn't meant to admit that.

Quentin returned his gaze to study him. Blake felt like an insect caught on a pin.

"What if your marriage to Miss Carrington thwarted Lady Bell, bought your colors, and gave me the satisfaction of matching another of my friends with one of Isabell's protégées?"

Blake's foot ached and his soul rebelled. "You would make Miss Carrington miserable for the sake of annoying Lady Bell?"

"On the contrary," Quentin mused, smiling like a cat with a canary, "if I gauge her correctly, Miss Carrington would very much like a husband who will conveniently remove himself to the Continent."

Blake didn't like the sound of that at all. It had taken him years to admit that marriage might be the only solution to his perennial bankruptcy. He'd wasted additional time contemplating the best wife for his purposes. Harebrained and bird-witted weren't part of the qualifications he had considered.

But he had yet to find a wealthy woman with intelligence who was willing to accept an impoverished younger son, and Miss Carrington certainly did not lack in physical charm.

And Miss Carrington would not grieve should he manage to get his head blown off in Portugal, as long as she had the dratted house.

With Percy well fed and hidden safely in the carriage, Jocelyn changed into her travel gown and began a discreet search for her quarry.

Lady Bell would be down shortly, they'd be on the road soon, and she had not yet found any of the dratted gentlemen. They were no doubt all sleeping off the effects of last night's indulgence. She was almost relieved she did not have to face Mr. Montague again, but she could not seem to get the foolish notion of marrying him out of her head.

A masculine hand caught her elbow and dragged her from her search of the breakfast room. She recognized Mr. Montague's treacherously earthy scent of horse and leather. He'd found her first.

"If I might have a word with you, Miss Carrington." Without waiting for permission, he tugged her toward the library.

"Outside," she insisted. Heart pounding, she resisted his pull and hurried toward the carriage entrance for the second time that day. "I must keep Percy quiet."

"I hardly think a stable yard an appropriate setting for what I wish to say," he objected.

She cast him a startled look. Could he possibly have changed his mind? That would be a remarkable occurrence, if so. She studied him warily.

He'd shaved. She could still see a bit of moisture glistening on his square jaw. Blake Montague could hardly be called civilized by society's pretty standards. Still, with a blade of a nose and hollowed cheeks, and that very interesting bronzed coloring, his features were striking in a manner that stirred her interest far more than was safe.

The intensity of his gaze would have her blushing if she did not look away.

His limp was more pronounced when he limited his stride to match hers, and she felt an unusual warmth at his consideration. "On the contrary, Mr. Montague, given our inclinations, perhaps outside is the very best place for us to converse."

"Do you plan to screech like a parrot?" he asked with suspicion.

"No more than you intend to bellow like a bull," she said prosaically, hurrying down the outside steps. "It simply happens."

"I do not bellow. I am considered an even-tempered man." When she did not immediately object, he took charge of the conversational opening to continue listing his attributes. "I am ambitious, hardworking, and have access to a fine home in Chelsea, one I'm told has a conservatory suitable for birds."

Jocelyn almost laughed aloud. Among all his annoying character traits, Mr. Montague's cleverness was the most useful. Remarkably, he'd come to the same conclusion that she had, and he'd worked out all the benefits, disposed of the arguments, and was acting on the knowledge without hesitation. She liked a man of action—especially one who agreed with her.

A conservatory suitable for birds? Carrington House had a conservatory. . . .

She'd had Lady Bell's driver take her past her old

home and knew it was empty, but she could not be so optimistic as to believe Mr. Montague owned it now. It didn't seem possible that Harold would be so deep in debt as to sell it a mere six years after their father had died.

"You only have access to a fine home if your father approves of your choice of bride," she reminded him. "And while Lady Bell has no legal authority to deny me, I am very fond of her and would not hurt her feelings by ignoring her advice. She does not approve of you."

Still holding her arm, Montague checked the court-yard and the waiting carriage, and finding no one about, studied her face with cynical disbelief. "How can you be so blamed sure of what I want to ask?" he demanded. "We scarcely know each other."

"I may not be as learned as a man who attended Oxford, but I am well-tutored in matters of matrimony. After this morning's debacle, your decision is a simple matter of deduction. Society bears pressure, whether we like it or not. Gossip can ruin your chances as well as mine. Marriage might not be a palatable choice, but sometimes it's the lesser of all evils."

She had a tendency to prattle when nervous. She drew in a deep breath and changed the topic. It was time to learn if he could be trusted. "Will you take Percy back to London for me? I fear Lady Belden will not be in a receptive mood to my arguments should she discover I've purloined a duke's pet."

Incredulity darkened his icy eyes to nearly black. "You want *me* to steal the featherbrain?"

"He is already stolen. You need only transport him. I assume you have rooms where you may keep him until I can make other arrangements?" She checked to be certain the driver was still idling in the barn and opened the carriage door.

"Why?" he demanded. "Why would I possibly agree to this inanity?"

Well, if he was going to act all male and stupid . . . Jocelyn turned and batted her long lashes at him. Tapping a finger to her dimpled cheek, she smiled angelically. "Because you think you can tell Lady Belden about my parrot theft and blackmail me into marrying you so you can have access to my funds and join the army in the spring?"

"Of all the sapskulled . . ." He halted his insults and studied her through eyes darkened with interest and cynicism. "And I suppose you know this because you intended to blackmail me into marrying you so you could have my house with its aviary?"

His eyes turned a tarnished silver when he was angry. Jocelyn felt a dangerous thrill at the intensity of his focus. She was glad she had some experience in dealing with the results of risky behavior or she'd faint.

"Check and checkmate. I think we shall get along very well together," she announced. "Especially if we are a thousand miles apart."

She leaned inside the carriage and lifted the seat to produce a box with air holes. Percy squawked, *"Africa knows!"* and shifted his weight so she nearly dropped him. "He will probably travel easier pinned on your shoulder, but the cage can be tied to your saddle."

"You are not normal, you know that?" he asked, warily taking the box, which muffled Percy's protests. "Women do not marry for birds."

"Most men do not marry to get themselves killed, either," she said cheerfully. "We must get to know each other before making a permanent decision, I suppose. Consider this preliminary negotiations to see if we will suit. Feed Percy as many fresh fruits and vegetables as you can find. Apples are good as long as you do not let him eat the seeds. Turnip and dandelion greens are excellent. His diet affects his behavior, which is why he's been pulling out his feathers. Once he's eating better, he'll be better behaved."

Mr. Montague still looked as if he'd been struck by lightning. Perhaps she had pushed too hard, but they had little time, and he seemed a decisive gentleman who would not change his course once he set upon it. That could work against her in the future, but she already knew her choices were limited. And the possibility of Carrington House . . . she must investigate that. She couldn't expose her interest too early in the bargaining.

"If you've changed your mind, let me know now, and I will find another way to transport Percy," she said with a trace of sympathy. "Perhaps by the time the Season commences in the spring, all will have forgotten our little adventure."

"We were caught in a barn at dawn. You shot off my toe. I doubt we'll *ever* hear the end of the ridiculous tales that are sure to spread among the *ton*."

He glared at her, and she nearly trembled in her shoes until she gave herself another mental shake. He had proved to be an honorable man who would not harm a woman, even after she'd shot him. He didn't look too much a pirate now that he'd shaved and fastened his neckcloth. She'd survived cutting insults all her life. She could make this work—especially if they kept their distance. And if he accepted Richard's peculiarities. That part might be problematic. She didn't dare mention her mother's predilections. Besides, Mama might choose to stay in the country.

"I allow that we need further discussion before we can reach an agreement," he continued, much to her relief. "But my horse is already saddled. I can take Percy for now."

"If you think to strangle him if I disagree with you, do not underestimate my wrath," she said sweetly. "There have been times when birds were my only companions, and I am a loyal friend."

For the first time, he looked more intrigued than furious. Despite his superior education and brainpower, she thought perhaps there were a few things she could teach him.

"I trust you are as loyal to your human friends as to your feathered ones, Miss Carrington. I shall call on you upon my return to London. In the meantime, you might wish to convince Lady Bell that I am not a violent man."

He bowed and limped away, all stiff, noble pride and resolution—a valiant, terrifying man, indeed. She heard a muffled squawk before Mr. Montague disappeared inside the stable.

Could she really be thinking of marrying Blake Montague?

7

Could he really be thinking of marrying Jocelyn Carrington? No, he wasn't thinking at all. Not with his brain, leastways. Lower parts, very definitely engaged. She had only to turn those pansy blue eyes on him and all thought fled south. Words like *bewitching* and *beguiling* floated insanely in his empty head.

"Ride 'er 'ard, ride 'er wet, rider, rider, rider!" Percy squawked as Blake guided his gelding along the rural splendor of a lane bordering the Thames.

The damned obscene bird wasn't helping direct his thoughts down intelligent paths.

He had no intention of taking the creature back to London if he could possibly unload it elsewhere. He disliked taking advantage of friends, but Fitzhugh Wyckerly, now Earl of Danecroft, had an estate nearby that was large enough to hide a herd of horses. Harboring a mangy parrot shouldn't be a hardship for him. Blake had planned to visit anyway, although now he couldn't dally as long as he'd intended.

Miss Carrington would be waiting in London for his return—unless he managed to talk himself out of his decision to marry.

He enjoyed his independence. He didn't like the notion of having to dance attendance on anyone. But once the courtship period was over, he would be free to go his own way. Married couples did not live in each other's pockets. He'd keep his rooms in London. She'd have the pestilent house in the backwater of Chelsea.

Marriage meant he would not only have the wherewithal to buy his colors, but he might finally have peace from his parents' nagging.

The dome of the sprawling Danecroft mansion came into view as his horse cantered down the treelined lane and Blake contemplated Miss Carrington's moonlit hair, violet eyes, and taunting pink lips. She was gentle, soft-spoken, feminine—and a scheming bit of baggage. He detested deceit, but he had to admit, the lady certainly wasn't a whey-faced miss who sat back and waited for the world to come to her.

Percy squawking obscenities from his saddle was a firm mark against her.

He winced at the house ahead spilling children as he rode up—and he marked another firm demerit on the negative side of his marriage ledger. He didn't have any interest in children. Wives, of necessity, meant children—although most of these urchins were the countess's siblings and not Fitz's progeny.

Eyeing the gaggle of innocents, he entertained second thoughts about leaving the obscene bird with them—until a cat dashed into the drive. Avoiding damage to a family pet, Blake leaned back and pulled up on the reins. His usually steady mount whinnied, reared, and tossed him off. His backside met the hard road with an impact that stole his breath.

Well, blast, Blake thought morosely as he stared up at the sky and waited for pain to tell him what part of him had been maimed this time.

Audience to his incompetence, children and nurse-maids flew down the drive, screaming and crying. *Well, double blast.* Now he would have to stand up and pretend all was well. He glanced toward the gelding to be certain it would not stampede the little ones, but the irrational creature was calmly nipping grass. Blake grabbed a rein and hauled himself into an upright position while a shaken Percy caterwauled louder than the approaching army.

A stout nanny ran after the little hooligans, but she did not capture them before Percy burst into a seaman's chantey. Fortunately, the most intelligible verse seemed to be *hey-ho, and a nonny-nonny no.* Delighted, the children grabbed Blake's hands and tugged him up and toward the house, happily singing Percy's chorus and attempting to investigate the covered cage hanging from his saddle.

Limping badly, Blake could barely keep up with the short legs of the youngest toddler, but he seemed to have survived the accident without any broken ribs.

Blake let the oldest boy and Fitz's daughter fight over carrying the cage, while the oldest girl held the hand of a chubby toddler singing off-key as they returned up the long set of outside stairs to the portico. That left one solemn four-year-old proudly marching up alone, until Blake was forced to grab the boy's hand when the little one teetered and nearly fell backward.

At the sight of a tear of humiliation spilling down a grubby cheek, Blake sighed, threw the boy up to his shoulder, and, wincing, paraded up the stairs to meet the Countess of Danecroft waiting at the top, rocking the new heir to the earldom in her arms and staring at him as if he'd grown an extra appendage.

Really, if Fitz weren't his closest friend, Blake would have turned and fled back to London at the sight of all this domesticity.

"My father's willing to give up the house in Chelsea for the chit, but not provide funds to buy colors!" Blake protested, prowling the extensive floor of Danecroft's library later that evening. Every bruise ached, but he was damned lucky he hadn't broken his neck from his earlier fall. "He's doddering into senility."

The two stories of library shelves had been empty when Fitz had first acquired the title and estate, but despite the earldom's near bankruptcy, the shelves seemed to be slowly filling. Blake thought he ought to contribute his own collection before he marched off to war. Which brought his thoughts right back around to Miss Carrington. Could she even read? Considering the eyelash-flapping performances she'd given at the party, he doubted it.

"No more brandy for you, old boy. You're being churlish now." Fitz leaned back in one of the old cracked leather chairs and regarded him with amusement.

"Trapped animals snarl and bite. Churlish is my idea of being civilized." Blake glared at the finger Percy had bitten when he'd attempted to feed the wretched creature. He almost sympathized with the bird's plight. Parrots, like men, were meant to roam free.

As if he grasped Blake's reference, Percy stretched his neck, pranced along the perch of his cage, and began singing a dirty ditty. Blake put his fingers between his teeth and whistled sharply. Fitz covered his ears, but overwhelmed, the bird settled down to a mutter.

"Your father must realize that you will take Miss Carrington's money and buy colors," Fitz reminded him, pouring a finger more of brandy in each of their glasses.

"My father is notorious for adding stipulations to contracts. He'll wrap the settlement in chains that prevent me from doing what I want," Blake predicted gloomily. "But I won't know the terms until I make an offer, and Miss Carrington accepts. I'm hoping I can find alternatives."

"I wish I could offer to help, but all London knows the state of my finances. If Miss Carrington is as conniving as you say, she won't be too grief-stricken when you march off." Fitz offered up a nut kernel to the parrot. Percy pecked it neatly from his fingers.

"Why does the creature bite *me* when I feed it?" Blake glared down at the parrot's half-bare gray head. It really was a pathetic-looking excuse for a bird. He couldn't imagine what Miss Carrington saw in it.

"Because you don't like him. Very smart creature. Is the lady equally intelligent?"

"She hasn't bitten me yet." Blake returned to pacing.

Fitz snorted at the faint praise but wisely refrained from interrupting.

"I didn't come here to beg from you," Blake continued. "You've been an enormous help already. I just . . ." He frowned and tried to work out exactly what he did expect of his friend.

"You want to know if the leg shackles are worth it," Fitz finished for him. "I envisioned a golden chain on my pecker before I took vows. But our case is different. I admired Abby greatly even before we talked of marriage. You scarcely know Miss Carrington. I've met her only the once, when we visited Lady Bell a few months back. She seems a pleasant sort."

"She shot me in the foot and stole an obscene parrot!

That hardly qualifies as pleasant. And she's a bloody Carrington! That alone should be reason for caution." Blake glared at the offensive creature, which promptly flapped its wings and muttered, "Friggin' bloody 'ell."

Fitz chuckled. "I do believe he's captured your mood, Montague. Look at it this way—she rescued a helpless creature from an idiot. She can't be all bad."

"Society has rules for a reason," Blake complained. "One simply cannot steal another man's property because he isn't taking good care of it!"

"Perhaps we should," Fitz replied. "Perhaps the rules need changing. Isn't that what you want to do with our rules of war?"

"Rules of war aren't written in law books." But Blake knew what he meant. The rules of love and society weren't in law books, either. Could he set the rules to please himself?

"You've attempted every other method to get what you want." Fitz stayed with the point. "I've tried recommending you to the Home Office, but the Danecroft title impresses only the ignorant, and I have no connection elsewhere."

"It wouldn't matter if you did. Castlereagh has already rejected me. The prime minister is too ill to care if Canning and Castlereagh tear out each other's throats, and nothing gets done while they argue their differences. Admiral Nelson was correct when he called the ministry antiquated. The Foreign Office has encrypted documents left unopened since the colonial war!"

Blake spun on his heel and glared at his friend. "I wager you do not even realize the Post Office can send foreign letters to the Deciphering Branch to be opened without the recipient's knowledge. They're bloody well decoding some poor sap's foreign love notes, while they ignore the war situation. No one up there knows or cares what's happening beyond their own personal vendettas!"

Fitz shrugged. "Then it's a good thing you prefer war to civil service. At least shooting the enemy is more honorable than shooting government servants."

"I prefer dying honorably to being thrown by a horse," Blake muttered. "I cannot fathom how that burr got in the saddle blanket. I'm not in the habit of riding through woods where I might have picked one up. My horse would never have thrown me otherwise. My mother will have me locked in a room for fear her silly superstition is coming true."

Abby, the Countess of Danecroft, chose that moment to enter bearing a tray of assorted cheeses. She set the tray down on the library table and brushed a kiss on Fitz's head. "The children give you their good nights and hope you will ride with them in the morning."

She turned in Blake's direction. "And I know you will not ask my opinion, Mr. Montague, but if Lady Bell approves of Miss Carrington, then she must be a person of good character. Lady Bell does nothing without a thorough investigation."

The adorable little countess departed without expecting a reply.

There was the reason marriage would not suit him, Blake remembered. Women nested. They wanted houses and babies and gentle words and all those things that held utterly no interest for him. He required physical and intellectual stimulation, not cheese and children.

Fitz raised an eyebrow and smirked while Blake stewed over the decision he must make.

Two evenings after Ogilvie's house party had broken up, Isabell Hoyt, Lady Belden, stepped from her carriage in front of the London townhome of Lord Alvanley, one of the *ton*'s more sociable peers.

In front of her, Lord Quentin Hoyt was just handing his beaver hat to a footman. "Good evening, Isabell. You are looking delightful, as usual."

Isabell would swear the wretch had waited in the shadows for her carriage to pull up just so he could precede her into the house.

"And you are looking your usual smug self, Quentin," she acknowledged, taking his offered arm. "Tell me, does your father ever mean to take his seat in the Lords, or will he simply leave you to twist arms for him?"

"My, we are in a congenial humor this evening." He clasped his gloved hand over hers and led her up the stairs to their host's music room, making it seem as if they had arrived together. Isabell's superior position in the *ton* elevated Lord Quentin's simply by association.

Isabell would object, except she saw no reason to care what the gossip mill ground out. She had the wealth to buy half the people in the room, and they knew it. She smiled and made her curtsies as they progressed through the aisles looking for seats. "I did not think I had to be congenial with you, my lord. You claim we are family, so I merely treat you as such."

"That must mean you are growing more comfortable with my presence. Excellent. So, tell me, have you discovered where your protégée has hidden the parrot?"

"The parrot?" Startled, she made the mistake of glancing up at him.

Quentin was a very large, impressive man. His dark eyes twinkled, which meant he knew something she didn't, and she had the urge to smack him and tell him to quit playing games. At the same time, he stirred in her a long suppressed flirtatiousness—one that she failed to stifle.

"Ah, I take it Ladybyrd did not bring the creature home or you would have certainly noticed. Very clever of her," he commended.

Isabell scowled and took a seat next to a stout matron who would snore throughout the performance. Perhaps Hoyt would take the hint and find a more suitable seat so she need not resist temptation all evening. "Jocelyn's mother is a cousin on my late husband's maternal side. She was a Byrd before she married. Jocelyn's brother works with birds. Jocelyn may be called Byrd-Carrington, but she is a perfectly normal young woman. I have no idea why people insist on giving her that dreadful appellation."

"Do you deny she has established a bird haven in your garden?"

"We had an infestation of worms eating the roses. The birds keep the insects away. A few birdbaths and feeders are beneficial."

Undeterred, Quentin settled into the chair next to her, folding his arms across his formidable chest. "And I'm certain it was a lesson in education when in her youth she threw a tantrum until her father purchased the lovebirds from the Morrisons, and it was at her brother's behest that she wouldn't leave the Langsdales' front room until they gave her the macaw to be rid of her."

"She was a child!" Isabell straightened her skirts and looked properly toward the musicians taking their places at the front of the room. "She was an unhappy child with a reclusive mother, a jackass of an older brother, and a busy, politically active father who had little regard for family except for how he could use them. Her older sisters had married and left home, and she went unsupervised too often. She has a gentle, caring nature and loves animals."

"She stole the duke's parrot." Quentin, too, watched the musicians.

"Even if the parrot has gone missing, it originally belonged to her brother. And it was your beastly friend Montague who almost compromised her in the stable. Dueling! I vow, all of you should be sent to war. Why don't *you* buy his colors?"

"Because he's a friend, and I don't wish to see so valuable a mind lost to the senselessness of combat. Besides, his own officers are likely to murder him for preferring his sense of justice to their orders. The right woman could make him see the error of his ways and keep him home. He has a great deal to offer our country, just not on the battlefield."

"Balderdash. Montague's parents hold him on a tight string, and he's spoiling for a fight. So, let him fight on the Continent instead of instigating senseless duels."

"Blake is handy with his fists and with pistols," Quentin acknowledged. "But his mind is valuable to England. He and Ladybyrd could do worse than each other."

Lady Bell finally turned, if only to scowl even more fiercely at him. "He would take her money, buy colors, and get himself killed. You would make her a widow?"

"I thought you were enjoying widowhood," he said in mock surprise, raising his eyebrows. "Was I wrong?"

"No, but she is young and has done nothing to deserve a loveless life." The musicians struck the first chords, and she stared straight ahead, not acknowledging her own experience with a loveless life. "Jocelyn needs a family of her own besides her brother and his pets. Montague would most likely shoot the pets and get himself killed, leaving her with nothing at all."

Quentin leaned over and whispered in her ear, "Want to make a wager on that?"

His whisper produced a tingle in her earlobe, irritating her further. "I am giving my husband's female relations the inheritance he was too curmudgeonly to supply, but I am not providing an income for another of your impoverished friends. Just because Fitz turned over a new leaf doesn't mean Montague has the sense to do the same."

"Want to bet?" he taunted again.

A Mozart refrain poured through the room, and the audience quieted. Almost.

"Maybe you should provide your friends with dowries so they needn't look to my protégées," Isabell countered in an angry whisper that caused the stout matron beside her to frown.

"I earned my wealth. You didn't," Quentin retorted. "You inherited what belonged to my family. Fair is fair."

She'd known that retaliation for her inheriting the marquess's wealth had been his intention all along, the conniving rat. It was a good thing she'd learned her lesson after the last time one of his penniless cronies had claimed one of her charges. Admittedly, the match had turned out rather well, but there were no guarantees Quentin's other idle friends would inherit earldoms, as Danecroft unexpectedly had.

The dowry she had provided Jocelyn under the guise of an "inheritance" would not be so easily gained by Blake Montague if she had anything to say about it.

"I'll wager your new pair of bays that if Montague overcomes Jocelyn's good sense and they marry, he will not be joining Wellesley in the spring on my money," Isabell said complacently. Hoyt's matched bays were the envy of all London. He would despise losing them.

"And you will give my sister Margaret a Season as you did Sally if Miss Carrington gives him all that he wants before spring," he whispered boldly. "And you must give *me* a kiss."

Isabell narrowed her eyes and glared at the bold oaf. "If you think to humiliate me, you will lose. I accept your ridiculous wager."

She refused to think that it would almost be worth losing the wager to taste a man's kiss again, especially this man's. That was her foolish sentimental nature speaking. She would not succumb to it again.

8

Three days after the house party in Kent, Jocelyn sat in her hostess's parlor, dispiritedly watching the last of her callers depart. She truly did not wish to trust her precious funds through marriage to any of those callow youths.

"Do you have an interest in any of the other young men you've met this past Season?" Lady Bell asked, echoing Jocelyn's thoughts. "It would be better to quietly choose one than be pressured into marrying Montague."

"None are quite as interesting as Mr. Montague," Jocelyn admitted, although she hated to. She had spent every minute of these last few days comparing the gentlemen of her acquaintance with the irritable soldier and, despite her reservations, she found everyone else lacking.

"I'd not thought it possible for a gentleman to be both dashing and intelligent," Jocelyn mused aloud. Also contrary and dangerous, but no one was perfect.

Lady Bell sipped her tea. "Lord Quentin is both. I suspect Mr. Atherton is also, but he's a rake of the worst sort. I can name any number of dashing, intelligent men, but they are all flawed in one way or another."

Jocelyn did not think dignified Lord Quentin or indolent Mr. Atherton were dashing. They were admittedly fine-looking men, but she had little interest in pretty features or smooth manners. She wasn't at all certain what interested her about Montague except that he hadn't killed her for shooting his toe, hadn't returned Percy to Mr. Ogilvie—and he had a house in Chelsea and meant to march off to war.

"That is the problem, is it not?" Jocelyn murmured. "Most men are flawed. So we must look for the ones with the flaws that least annoy us."

Lady Bell laughed. "You are a very practical young woman. So, you do not dream of romance and love and being swept off your feet by a handsome prince?"

"Have you seen our princes lately?" Jocelyn countered. "*Spoiled*, *bigoted*, and *crude* come more immediately to mind than *handsome*. No, I do not dream of princes. It would be lovely to find a man who shares my interest in animals, but I assume horses and dogs are the most I can expect them to appreciate."

Lady Bell gave her one of her knowing glares. "And does Mr. Montague appreciate parrots?"

Jocelyn squirmed in discomfort and gazed out the large mullioned windows overlooking the street. "I hope so," was all the reply she gave, knowing her hostess would not pry too deeply.

"Despite having been in London for only six months, you have learned a great deal more than many misses who have lived here all their lives. Most young women dream of romance."

"I lived here until I was seventeen." Jocelyn shrugged. "I may have spent these last six years as unpaid nanny and servant in a rural wilderness, but before my father died, I'd been his hostess in political salons since I was nine, when my mother first withdrew from society. So I have observed far more than most girls my age. And I lost all romantic notions while watching my half sisters primp and simper and go into alts over men who possessed the exceptional wisdom to court the same level of stupidity as themselves."

Jocelyn thought her hostess sputtered in her tea, but she didn't much care.

"I see," Lady Bell said after regaining her composure. "And you do not mind that your suitors are more interested in money than society and animals?"

"I could have married the stable boy and had a man who worshipped at my feet. No, I do not mind a man's interest in bettering himself. I do draw the line at abusiveness, excessive drunkenness and gambling, and the other vices, but from all I hear, Mr. Montague is immune to vice. You must admit, he is far more exciting than a weak man like Mr. Ogilvie. And Mr. Montague has a house in Chelsea. Richard will be much happier in familiar surroundings."

She should have asked Mr. Montague where in Chelsea his house was located, but she'd been terrified of raising her hopes or giving him reason to believe he held anything over her. The dratted man would take every advantage he could.

Lady Belden nodded concession to the point just as a footman in royal blue livery appeared carrying a silver salver. She gestured for Jocelyn to take the note.

Jocelyn scowled at the name on the card. "Tell Lord Carrington we are not at home."

The footman nodded obediently and departed.

Lady Bell raised her eyebrows questioningly. "Are you not in the least bit curious about why your brother keeps calling?"

"I know why he keeps calling. He needs money, and he wants you to acknowledge his harridan of a wife. It does not matter that Antoinette is married to a once-proud title. Everyone knows she is a French actress with a vile temper. I'll not return your hospitality by recognizing the toady."

Lady Bell had just filled her teacup again when the footman reappeared. Jocelyn took the card with annoyance, thinking she needed a big dog to chase off Harold. But this time, after reading the card, she smiled.

"Mr. Montague is at the door," she said. "Are we at home to him?"

Not looking entirely satisfied with the result of their conversation, Lady Bell nodded. "You can do better. But if you insist on this one, then I must insist on asking the solicitors to find some way of tying up your funds so he cannot use them to get himself killed at war. Do not think in terms of a husband you will never see."

Jocelyn swallowed hard and nodded. The lady was much wiser in the ways of the world than she was, and Jocelyn respected her decision. Nevertheless, she hadn't given full deliberation to actually *living* with Mr. Montague and his black humors. They had spoken of a marriage of convenience, after all. And she didn't know how the lady could prevent him from buying colors and marching off to the Continent. He would never agree to less. "I understand, my lady."

The instant Mr. Montague walked into the parlor, she forgot everything she and Lady Bell had just discussed.

Her gentleman caller was not only clean shaven—he'd also had his hair cut. The silver streak was nearly hidden in thick black locks that waved enticingly around his ears, begging for feminine fingers to run through them. A single curl had fallen across Mr. Montague's noble brow, drawing her gaze to his intense gray eyes.

Oddly, his fierce look seemed to focus on her to the exclusion of all else, including the dainty, more sophisticated Lady Bell.

Jocelyn hoped that was because he admired the care she'd taken with her appearance and not because he wanted to annihilate her. She thrilled a little at the possibility that his efforts might be for *her* benefit. From Mr. Montague, that would be a genuine show of respect.

She did so adore square shoulders! His filled out the tailored cut of his blue superfine to perfection. His stiffly starched neckcloth looked as if Beau Brummel had arranged it for him. Not a spot of street dirt marred the mirror shine of his Hessians. He showed all the preparation of a man about to engage in battle.

And in his arms he carried not a bouquet, but a kitten with a bandaged paw.

Jocelyn didn't know whether to laugh or cry at the realization that she'd been outmaneuvered by a master strategist. He knew exactly what would please her most, the devil. Perhaps she did not hate him after all.

"Mr. Montague, how good to see you again. Wherever did you find this poor creature?"

"The cat belongs to a friend of mine. It ... er ... he had a bit of a run-in with a noisy ... um ... bird, and I felt responsible. I thought you, having some experience with birds, might know if there is danger of infection?"

He was exceedingly bad at lying.

Behind them, Lady Bell laughed. Mr. Montague instantly diverted his attention to their hostess, made a belated bow, and offered all the correct greetings. Jocelyn snuggled the kitten in her arms and wondered if she'd ever before noticed how a man smelled. Today, Mr. Montague had the most enticing woodsy odor. . . . Really, if she could just ignore his obstinacy and admire his physical attributes, she could be very happy.

Apparently during the exchange of pleasantries Jocelyn was ignoring while she and the kitten purred at each other, Lady Bell agreed to allow Mr. Montague to take Jocelyn for a walk in the park. When Montague raised an expectant eyebrow, Jocelyn woke up from her singular reverie and hurried to don bonnet and spencer. The kitten wasn't likely to stay long in her arms, so she picked up her knitting basket and hoped the lid would suffice to hold the creature.

"Permit me to say you look splendid, Miss Carrington," Mr. Montague said as they descended the graceful marble stairs of the dowager's mansion to the street. His flattery was as stiff as if he were practicing a foreign language.

"As do you, sir, although I begin to understand why you have worn your hair long until now," she said, refusing to let him think her an infatuated idiot. "It is difficult to be taken seriously with a curl in the middle of one's forehead."

He sliced her a dark look that produced an unexpectedly shocking thrill. It could be dangerous irritating this man—but for the first time in many years, she felt safe in speaking freely instead of hiding behind insipidness.

"I was told I looked a pirate and must change my ways if I am to seek Lady Bell's approval." He appropriated her hand to place it on his arm so they might stroll down the street.

"You are already so certain that you have *my* approval?" she asked, removing her hand from his arm and digging in the basket to untie the bandage and examine the kitten's paw.

"I'm not certain that I have *mine*," he said with deplorable honesty. "I cannot for the life of me see how we will suit. I may have to keep my guns under lock and key."

"An excellent notion," she murmured. "Better yet, toss them out."

That earned her another black look, but Mr. Montague was nothing if not determined.

"Nevertheless, I have been considering our discussion of marriage," he continued, "and must state my thoughts bluntly."

As if he ever did anything else! Jocelyn bit back her smile. Honesty was a fairly new experience for her. Most of her older siblings and certainly her father had never practiced it. Mama and Richard lived in their own worlds and wouldn't know how to lie, but neither did they communicate much.

He rested his broad hand at the small of her back and steered her through the gates of the little-used neighborhood park. Jocelyn had only a moment to bask in the protective masculine gesture before Mr. Montague assisted her to a bench in a secluded area behind some shrubbery, setting the kitten carrier in the next seat instead of taking the place himself. While she opened the lid, he crossed his hands behind his back and began to pace, for all the world like a general in his field tent. Jocelyn admired the view while pretending to study the kitten's minor scratch.

"I am nearly thirty years of age, fairly set in my ways, and have a household of my own that doesn't require a woman's touch. And I like it that way."

"You live in a pigsty with no valet, surrounded by books, and prefer to spend your evenings at cards and cigars instead of tamely squiring ladies to fetes and musicales," she interpreted. "Did anyone mention that I have three older half sisters and have lived in the households of my brothers-in-law these past years? Not that my father was much neater. I am well past romantic dreams of gallant knights in shining armor."

Mr. Montague nodded at her assessment of masculine behavior. Jocelyn hoped he did so with approval.

"I have my studies, but I understand you need the company of society, and the house will be a great deal of trouble. You will need servants, a companion," he continued.

He did not know the real problem facing them. With a home for Richard at stake, she was sure she could make everything right, given enough time—but first, how could she assure herself that he could accept Richard's habits? If she explained her brother's deficiencies, would she lose her only chance to obtain the home he so desperately needed?

She didn't want a husband who despised her for her deceit. Dare she risk being honest? She needed to know more of Mr. Montague first. "My brother and I grew up in Chelsea. Do you have any notion where in Chelsea the house might be?"

He grimaced and rubbed the back of his newly shorn nape. "I don't wish to ruin our pleasant interlude with unpleasant truths."

"That, sir, requires an explanation." She narrowed her eyes, watching with a nervous knot in her stomach. Was it a hovel and he was afraid to say so?

As if seeing her fear, he hurriedly corrected the impression he'd given. "I am told it is an excellent house in an excellent location or I would never have considered bringing a bride there. I suspect you would know its condition better than I. My father says it is Carrington House. I did not know if you were aware that your brother had . . . sold it."

Carrington House! Her home. Richard's home. The one Horrid Harold had thrown them out of six years ago. She wasn't daydreaming, but he'd really and truly sold *their home*? To the Montagues? Jocelyn could not quite take in this appalling, wonderful discovery.

To hide her shock, she concentrated on knotting a length of knitting yarn around the kitten's collar. How was she to react to the news that Blake Montague held the key to her happiness?

He took the seat beside her. He wasn't a bulky man so much as lofty and radiating strength. His greater size intimidated, especially after such a stunning surprise. She was accustomed to reacting to shock and disaster with vapid innocence, but her reaction this time was too confused for pretense. Fluttering fans couldn't hide it.

Despite Mr. Montague's attempt to conceal the ugly truth, she had little doubt of how her home had traded hands. Harold was a bad gambler and had never liked Chelsea. He would have been glad to exchange a large expensive house to cover his gambling debts. She should have realized it sooner. She took a deep breath and plunged into the unknown waters of honesty.

"You do understand that my entire purpose in considering your proposal is to obtain a home for my younger brother?" she asked. "And that the conservatory will become an aviary?" The conservatory! Richard would be ecstatic. She could scarcely catch her breath from the excitement filling her.

Mr. Montague didn't hesitate. "I hardly consider an aviary or your brother a problem. My family, on the other hand, will live on our doorstep if we let them. They will be far more nuisance than birds."

Jocelyn thought she might weep with relief. Perhaps he did not know of Richard's peculiarities, but he could not say he hadn't been warned that she meant for him to live with her. It wasn't as if she were capable of explaining what doctors could not. And Richard would fare so much better on familiar grounds!

Would he allow her mother to join them? Considering his opinion of his own family, she would not press the point just yet. "I enjoy Lady Montague and your sister. They are more loving and considerate than my own family." Well, than Harold's side, leastways.

"Does this mean you are seriously considering the proposal I haven't made yet?" Mr. Montague raised expressive eyebrows, and a dimple appeared briefly as he fought a reluctant smile.

Jocelyn thought maybe the birds in the trees were singing just for them, and she felt strangely breathless and lighthearted. *Carrington House!* How could she possibly say no? "Yes, I believe I am. Considering, that is. A few more meetings and I'm sure we will come to terms that might satisfy us both," she said with what she hoped was businesslike pragmatism.

"I'm sure we can, Miss Carrington," he said, glancing at her lips. "And since there is no one about, perhaps we can start now."

His smile turned wicked as he leaned down to place his mouth firmly across hers.

9

Blake hadn't meant to kiss Miss Carrington. He had developed a logical plan of action that involved proving he wasn't a violent man, followed by telling her that should they marry, they would each maintain their independence. He would keep his rooms in the city while she nested in rural solitude until such time as he could go off to the Continent. It was the only rational proposition he could offer, after all, since neither of them had a real interest in marriage.

But his infernal fascination with champagne blond curls and violet-blue eyes was his undoing. Her eyes had lit like a child's at hearing she could have Carrington House, and she had looked so delectable discussing marriage as if they were equals that he hadn't been able to resist reminding her that he was a man and she was a woman.

A very, very large mistake.

Now that he'd sampled her glorious mouth and the eager press of her luscious lips against his, it was difficult to stop. Rather like eating one of Gunter's ices. Blake hadn't known he was starving until he'd had a taste. He dived into the sweetness she offered and didn't want to halt until the dish was empty. Had there not been a basket and a kitten between them, he would have completely lost his head and reached for her—because the silly twit *wasn't stopping him.*

Unlike Gunter's ices, her kiss was warm and heated his blood clear down to his toes. Blake tried to turn her passion into a negative quality, but instead, he desperately desired to hold her closer and enjoy the pleasure of the firm, rounded breasts not inches from his grasp. . . .

He took a deep breath and pulled back since this dish was not one he meant to devour yet.

Miss Carrington stared up at him as if he'd just gifted her with the world's treasures.

And he, male imbecile that he was, all but crowed in satisfaction that he'd placed that expression of rapture on the face of the lovely, flirtatious Miss Carrington. He blamed the pleasure coursing through him on the novelty of kissing a lady. It in no way changed the matter at hand—which was Miss Carrington's dowry and his need to acquire it.

"I believe I am supposed to apologize for my inappropriate behavior, but I fear if we are to get along, you will have to learn that I'm not the civil sort of gentleman to which you may be accustomed," he said stiffly.

She smiled, and Blake noticed that Miss Carrington's lower lip was a trifle plumper than her upper, just right for nibbling. . . .

He rubbed his nape, glared up at the tree branches, and thought of the Union Jack and the code paper crackling in his pocket.

"That's fair enough. I'm not the civil sort of lady you seem to be expecting," Miss Carrington said pertly, standing up before he could help her from the seat. "How is Percy?" she asked, changing the subject.

Her cheeks were pink, so she was not quite so nonchalant as she pretended. Had he been anyone else, Blake would have thought her blush charming, but he did not have the patience to suffer the indignities of courtship. He was frustrated with himself for having taken things this far so quickly. He took the kitten's basket and tried not to glance down at the nicely plump breasts he'd wanted to squeeze.

How the devil did one bring up the subject of consummating a marriage of convenience? Did she even know what that meant? Should he even be considering it?

Yes, he most certainly should. Why should he accept leg shackles without some recompense? Besides, it would be hell attempting to ignore temptation. So much for logic and reason. He had the dread notion that consummation came with ties that bound too tightly, but it was not a topic suitable for discussion with a maiden lady. The choice must be his.

"Percy sings like a sailor and, inexplicably, is still being showered with attention and lavished with all the treats he can consume. His language is not fit for a household of children, however." There, now he sounded like his usual self.

Except now the word *children* floated between them. Marriage meant children. He couldn't afford them, wasn't even certain he liked them. He had never considered procreating. He had an older married brother who would inherit his father's title and estate, and another brother to be the spare heir. Did he dare hope Miss Carrington wished to raise only birds?

She flushed slightly, then glanced at him through her long lashes. "Where exactly did you leave Percy?"

"He is safe on Danecroft's estate, where no one can easily encounter him."

"Thank you." She squeezed his arm, apparently oblivious of the undercurrents he'd been conjuring in his head. "I know I owe you a debt of gratitude. Lady Bell is likely to send me home if I add Percy to the household."

"You are fortunate that I may be the only candidate for your hand who does not care if you fill his house with animals," he said dryly, relieved that the conversation had turned from the intimacies of courtship to safer avenues.

She frowned, and he feared he'd stepped over some invisible line. He had never been one to chase the ladies and so did not know where those lines were drawn. He really needed to learn the strategy of courtship if he were to succeed in this campaign.

"Marriage is a very odd sort of adjustment, is it not?" was all she said.

Which, of course, agreed with his own thinking. "As long as we enter into it sensibly, with no illusions, we should succeed at it."

As he guided Miss Carrington onto the street through the park gates, a woman's shriek split the air. The reckless rattle of wooden wheels against cobblestones and the shouts of passersby swung Blake to the left. A runaway horse and driverless open carriage were racing directly toward them.

Blake shoved the kitten basket into Miss Carrington's hand and pushed her to safety behind the park's wrought iron fence. She dragged at his coat sleeve, crying for him to follow. The horse was nearly upon them, screaming in terror at the carriage rocking behind it.

Blake knew his limitations. On a game leg, he could not hope to leap into the carriage seat and grab the reins.

But neither could he leave hapless pedestrians in peril. After prying Miss Carrington's grip from his sleeve, he hurried back to the street and grabbed for the harness as the horse bore down on him. The abrupt pull on the leather startled the animal into rearing. Blake avoided the hooves by mere inches but gained the reins, and applied all his strength to hauling the terrified animal to a halt.

Shouts and screams echoed up and down the normally quiet avenue of elegant mansions while he fought the bucking mare. What the devil had got into horses around him these days?

To his utter dismay, while his arms were in danger of being ripped from their sockets, Miss Carrington lost her common sense and raced from the haven where he'd left her. Leaving behind the kitten basket, she dodged into the street to retrieve a bunch of carrots fallen from a farm cart. She came within inches of the panicked mare's nose, waving the treat temptingly.

"I cannot hold her down much longer," Blake shouted. "Stand back!"

"Poor baby," Miss Carrington crooned idiotically in reply, reaching to pet the mare's arched neck. "Poor baby, somebody hit you, didn't they. Calm down, sweetikins, have a treat, and we will make it all better."

Murmuring in that same senseless manner, she distracted the mare as much as Blake's brute strength did. Maybe more.

"You're risking your damned life!" he shouted at her, furious as hell, then bit back his temper as the mare shied from him. He wrapped the reins more firmly in his fist so the damned animal wouldn't trample his almost fiancée.

"Oh, and you didn't?" Miss Carrington inquired, casting him an amused but admiring glance as the horse whinnied and seemed to settle. "There is logic in only one of us being maimed and killed?"

"Women are frail and more likely to be injured," he argued, insensibly apparently, since she'd survived. He hated having his logic disturbed.

"You have an injured toe and a game leg," she countered. "And you still leaped to the rescue." She flapped her ridiculously long lashes and beamed that vague smile he'd seen her use on her suitors. "I merely fed the poor thing carrots. You are above all gallant and brave, sir."

Blake wanted to roar his fury as the charming woman he'd just kissed affected society's facade of naïveté while a crowd gathered and the carriage's driver pushed through the throng, shouting. But he resisted, turning his anger to the man who must have lashed his horse to have caused the welt along the animal's flank.

But the driver did not carry a whip.

"Are you the owner, sir?" Miss Carrington called as the man pulled his cap and bowed to her. "She is such a lovely mare," she cried fatuously. "I cannot understand why you would need to whip the sweet thing!"

Blake scowled. Despite her missish behavior, she had drawn the same conclusion he had. He would rather punch the man, but he waited with foreboding for the result of Miss Carrington's less violent approach.

"My poor Molly has never known the sting of a lash," the driver protested. "I left her with the postboy but half a moment while I fetched the lady's boxes, and next I knew, she was off down the street!"

Miss Carrington continued to stroke the mare's nose while Blake took a second look at the painful welt across its flanks. The horse had definitely been struck. "Does your postboy carry a stick?" he asked.

"Tom?" The driver looked enraged. "Tom wouldn't raise a stick to a rabbit!"

"Someone must have pulled a prank," Miss Carrington murmured, glancing up the street with a frown. "We'd best let them go before we cause more of a scene."

Blake's gaze followed hers, but he recognized no one in the crowd. He would prefer to get to the bottom of the incident, but they were blocking the street. As long as the animal wasn't routinely mistreated, there was little more he could do here.

Except he'd just discovered there was far more to Miss Carrington than fluttering lashes and vacuous expressions. She was as suspicious of the incident as he, which ought to worry him. Instead, he was intrigued. Puzzles, after all, were his specialty.

In a flurry of gratitude for preventing the horse's harm, the driver led his carrot-chomping mare away.

Blake glared down at the dainty female who was now taking his arm as if they hadn't just courted death. "Do you generally defy common sense in dangerous situations?" he asked.

She patted his arm and offered him a devastating smile. "I do not generally encounter dangerous situations, sir," she said with a trilling laugh, before stooping down to retrieve her kitten basket. "You are the one who seems to attract them."

He frowned but did not take up that unpleasant observation. "Shall I drop my dangerous suit for the sake of your well-being, then?"

She laughed again, following his long strides without difficulty. "If I must marry to have a home, your ill humors and dangerous predilections are preferable to my other choices," she said with what sounded like good cheer.

Blake slanted her a suspicious look. "I do not have ill humors."

"You are a surly bear," she countered. "But fortunately I like bears."

He didn't know whether to laugh at her complacent tone or argue with her sentiment. "Must I escort you to fetes and musicales before I dare ask for your hand?"

He hadn't meant to say that. This whole episode had taken off on tangents that didn't fit his master plan. He'd thought her a fairly insensible young miss and meant to woo her with kittens and gallantry. He would prove he could be charming, escort her about town so everyone expected an announcement, speak with her solicitors and his parents, then ask to meet with whomever was responsible for her. That was the way it was supposed to be done.

But that was before she'd wooed a panicked mare with carrots, then laughed, calling forth in him another urge to kiss her. Or throttle her. Depending on the cause of the laughter, he supposed.

She shot him a smile so blindingly bright that Blake nearly staggered. He, who had stood courageously in three duels, four if the one with Bernie counted, floundered beneath a woman's enticing smile. He was damned glad his friends weren't here to notice.

"The choice of entertainment this time of year is limited," she said pragmatically. "I do not have a father with whom you might discuss settlements, and I am of age, so my pig of a half brother knows nothing of my business. I suppose you might consult with Lady Belden and the solicitor who handles my inheritance, if you wish to be proper—when you are ready, of course."

Viscount Carrington, as the head of her family, was a definite disadvantage that he must maneuver around. Guiltily, Blake wondered if he ought to tell her how he'd once shot Harold, but it would not reflect well on either of them. "Is there more I should know about the brother you call a pig?" he asked.

"Besides that he put my mother, my brother, and me out of our home as soon as he came into the estate? No, not particularly."

"Why would he throw you out?" Blake asked.

Miss Carrington shrugged. "The reasons are many, I'm sure. I believe the last straw came the evening I insisted that we go through with my come-out as planned, and Richard got into a fight with my sister-in-law over the birds. Harold intervened, and my mother swatted him with a broom. We are not a tight-knit family," she finished wryly.

"So you are estranged and that was not Harold I saw departing Lady Belden's when I arrived?" he asked, hating to doubt her honesty.

"Oh, no doubt it was," she said with a shrug. "He scarcely acknowledged my existence until I came into my inheritance and moved in with a marchioness. He's been calling regularly since then. I daresay his wife is eager to cozy up to me now that I have funds and connections. I have had my revenge by giving them the cut direct and refusing to accept their calls."

"Vicious little viper, aren't you?" Blake said without thinking, rather enjoying her feminine idea of vengeance on a man he detested.

They were almost back at Lady Belden's, and Blake was oddly reluctant to let Miss Carrington go. He supposed he would overcome that weakness with time. "The name Jocelyn is unusual. Is it a family name?"

"In a way," she said dryly. "My mother is something of a historian. There was a knight named Jocelyn on the Byrd family tree somewhere back in the fourteenth century."

He was amused by her chatter. And the blond wisp blowing against her cheek. She laughed, and the infectious sound pushed him over the edge and into the abyss.

She had money and was beautiful. Did it matter if she was related to a treacherous bastard like Carrington? "So, Miss Jocelyn Byrd-Carrington, will becoming a Byrd-Montague suit?"

Blake couldn't believe he'd said that while standing on the front step of Belden House, in full view of half a dozen carriages, a street sweeper, and two stout matrons. He'd resisted this moment for nearly thirty years—if one didn't count their discussion at the house party—and now, a simple brush with death had reduced him to acting on impulse.

Perhaps it was better this way, rather like yanking an aching tooth immediately instead of suffering days of agony fretting about it.

Long lashes framed the tilt of her exotic eyes as she turned them upward to peruse his face. She wore a rose bonnet with pink ribbons that nearly concealed all her silken tresses. He had to resist brushing that one wisp from her cheek.

She actually looked intrigued by his question, as if they hadn't been dancing around it this past half hour. "I hadn't thought of being a Montague. I fear, in the past, I did not give much thought to the wedded state. But I do relish the thought of having my very own home. And you are the most interesting man to have asked me."

He wanted to growl and inquire how many fools she had rejected, but his intellect overruled his impulse this time. She thought him *interesting*? He waited.

"It's possible that we might suit, Mr. Montague, if you do not mind Richard or his birds. And possibly my mother, although she does not like being moved about."

Her brother was of little consequence. In his experience, sisters were far more irritating. And mothers—but an invalid parent would keep to her room. He minded keeping the wretched bird, but not enough to take back his offer. Portugal, deciphering the French code, and saving England prevailed over a rude fowl.

"Percy will inhabit the conservatory," he said dismissively. "I would not let a mere bird stand in the way of my acquiring the most beautiful woman in England."

She gave an elegant little snort. "You need not gammon me, sir. I thought we were to have no illusions between us. I am feckless and irritating, but my lineage is as good as yours, and I can provide what you want, if you will provide what I want. It's the other details that I have not thought of that worry me."

"You are far from feckless, but if you will consider my suit, allow me to deal with the details that worry you. Husbands should be of some use."

She blinked, apparently startled by the concept of a man being of use. Her expression was so endearing that Blake bent and planted a kiss upon the frown forming between her eyes. "Is that a yes, Miss Carrington?"

She nodded, her eyes almost round with wonder. "Yes, I do believe it is, Mr. Montague."

10

Blake Montague single-handedly stopped a panicked horse!
Jocelyn thought as she slipped upstairs. Most gentlemen
would have preferred to keep their boots dust-free and
leave the livestock to servants. They certainly wouldn't
have risked their lives for the safety of strangers. She had
never known a man with so much courage. And foolhardi-
ness, she must admit. He could have been crushed.

So could a lot of other people, plus the poor animal.

She pondered the possibility that she'd seen Harold
walking away from the frightening scene with the runaway horse. It wouldn't have been the first time her half
brother's temper had turned to retaliation, and she had
insulted him by refusing to accept his calls. He could
have followed her. One would think age might have
mellowed him, though.

Lady Belden arrived in the doorway as soon as Jocelyn reached her chamber. "Well? Was Mr. Montague
arrogant enough to bypass my consent and ask you
directly?"

Jocelyn welcomed the distraction. Casually, she dropped her bonnet on the bed. "He is a man who plans ahead. If I do not mistake, first, he will consult with his father about the house. Then he will ask to speak to you and my solicitor about my inheritance. And then we will discuss the announcement. But yes, I do believe we have an understanding."

Jocelyn patted her chest and tried to breathe again, as she had not been quite able to do since Mr. Montague had kissed her. Her head had been spinning even before the carriage incident. He'd *kissed* her. Deeply. Profoundly. She had not thought the stern Mr. Montague contained such passion. She, herself, had never experienced the like. It had been *marvelous*. She shook her head, trying not to let sentimentality interfere with her thinking, but the fact remained, Mr. Montague was overwhelming.

She was frightened that in marrying him, she might be doing the wrong thing for the right reasons.

But Mr. Montague was a tactician. He would ponder and study every possible detail before committing to this marriage. That was both reassuring and wholly terrifying. She had no reason to trust men, but she was trusting this one with her future.

Lady Belden tilted her head and regarded Jocelyn with curiosity. "You are not singing his praises? Dancing with eagerness? You have apparently just received a proposal of marriage, and you do no more than take off your hat? Is there no heart in your chest?"

Jocelyn beamed her happiness at her hostess. "You are a gem among women for allowing me the benefit of your sponsorship and for enduring my crotchets for as long as you have. I am eternally grateful and wish that there was some way in which I could return the favor. I have never been happier than I have been these past six months. Forgive me if I regret giving up that freedom to a man who will control my fortune and my future."

Lady Belden nodded her acknowledgment. "I keep forgetting how much good sense you conceal beneath that blond artlessness. If Montague follows the proper course, as you say, and you are agreeable, then I will not stand in the way of the match. But I will see that he does not control all your fortune," she said with a determination that did not bode well for Mr. Montague.

Jocelyn hoped a marchioness had the power to flout English law, which treated women as if they were little more than mindless pets. In the meantime, she must find some way to see what state Harold had left Carrington House in. The very thought of owning it again provoked dizzying happiness.

Surely, once she married, Harold would not bother her again.

As was her experience, Jocelyn's happiness lasted only a short while, until that evening at the theater. While Lady Belden lingered to gossip in the corridor with her cronies at intermission, Jocelyn curtsied to a gentleman who had provided her with lemonade and brushed aside the curtain in order to enter Lady Belden's box and regain her seat.

Harold, Viscount Carrington, and his pestilent nuisance of a French wife awaited her on the other side. At forty, Harold hid his receding hairline beneath his hat, but even a good girdle could not conceal his expanding waistline, and no amount of neckcloth could conceal his jowls. Antoinette, on the other hand, retained her slender, childless figure, luxurious dark locks, and taut jaw— made more so by her forced grimace of a smile.

Jocelyn glanced about for her maid, but they'd apparently sent the silly twit on an errand. Most maids did not know to fear brothers. Or sisters-in-law, even if they were sleek, sharp-edged, and very French. And smirking unpleasantly.

Resenting that the pair must once more force themselves into her life, Jocelyn smiled vapidly and fluttered her fan. She had learned that it served her well to let the enemy underestimate her, but now that she had come into her independence, she was having difficulty pretending she was still a foolish child. "Why, Harold, how vastly entertaining that you must seek me out instead of the other way around!"

"We are family," he said stiffly. "We should look out for one another."

She tittered and batted her fan against his cheek. "And how very well you have done that, too! I suppose, in return for all the thoughtful care you have provided over the years, you have come to ask for a favor."

In her heavily accented English, Antoinette replied for him. "You and your useless family drained the estate until it was little more than a fraction of what Harold should have inherited. You owe us."

Jocelyn covered her mouth as if in astonishment at her thoughtlessness. "Oh, my, yes, I'm sure. Why did I not think of that? Papa simply wasted *fortunes* in feeding us, did he not? Such a shame. And clothing! Why, Mama must have spent all of forty pounds on her round gowns over the years. But surely Harold regained that amount when he sold Percy." She added spitefully, "I have retrieved him, you know."

She didn't know why she'd taunted them with that bit of news, but she enjoyed watching the pair grow pale with rage. She didn't like the way Antoinette's eyes narrowed, but she couldn't seem to stop her malicious chatter. "Perhaps you thought I should repay the forty pounds for Mama's gowns?" she asked mockingly.

"Let us say four hundred, and we will call it even for now," Harold retorted.

Jocelyn blinked. After paying for her wardrobe and Richard's caretaker, that was almost all she had left of this year's funds. What on earth was going through the maggot's head that he dared believe she'd give him such a sum?

Direct confrontation had never worked for her, though. Rather than push him over the balcony, she offered a blank expression. "I cannot imagine why you think I'd call that fair."

"Because without it, I won't sign over Richard's guardianship papers to you. Our brothers-in-law have petitioned me to take him off their hands. If I do, he can rot in an attic or break his neck on the stairs for all I care, and you won't be able to do a damned thing about it."

They shoved past her and walked out, not giving her time to think, much less argue.

"You did not tell me you'd sold the bird! I thought you said the duke promised torture and punishment if anything happened to it," a man's voice murmured angrily in the alley beside the theater.

Waiting for his carriage, Quentin remained in the shadows and strained to hear more. Sometimes knowing what was flowing through the currents of London could make his pockets richer. Sometimes knowledge just made life more amusing. He had reason to recognize Viscount Carrington's furious voice and was prepared to be amused.

"She stole it! Your blamed idiot sister stole the bird! And the duke thinks I ought to marry the thieving tart!"

Quentin had no difficulty identifying this speaker as Ogilvie, the Duke of Fortham's not-so-charming lump of an heir. If the duke thought Miss Carrington was nodcock enough to marry Ogilvie, His Grace seriously underestimated the lady.

Interestingly, the viscount did not defend his sister's honor. Instead, he merely replied, "I told you Antoinette has made my life a living hell since I got rid of the creatures. She wants them back. And you let one go, damn you! Where is it now?"

"Your sister and Montague have been thick as thieves. He probably has it. I was hoping the know-it-all would break his neck so I would have a chance to turn her head, but I haven't a hope against a Corinthian. If he's got the bird, too, I might as well kiss my allowance good-bye."

Quent had to strain to hear this last. The men were moving away. He glanced around the corner and down the alley, but they were disappearing into the drizzling rain, heading away from him. He glanced up, saw his carriage approaching, and didn't follow. But he frowned thoughtfully all the way home.

The next day, Jocelyn borrowed Lady Belden's carriage and set out for Chelsea. She had a terrible decision to make, and she needed confirmation that she was making the right choice. Last night's encounter with Harold had kept her tossing in her bed all night. With her nerves on edge, she needed reassurance before she could commit so base an act as defrauding a good man to pay off a rotten one. Clenching her gloved hands, she peered around the hood of the landaulet, anxious for a sight of the prize for which she was considering surrendering her life— and Blake's.

She adored the quaint cottages lining the road between London and Chelsea, and she'd almost forgotten the enormous estates ornamenting the countryside. She caught glimpses of the Thames River through the trees and breathed deeply of the clean air. The flowers alone were enough to have her sighing wistfully.

Perhaps if she lived out here, Harold would never cross her path. Perhaps once she was wedded, he would not dare interfere in her life. And if she had Richard's guardianship papers, Harold could never harm him again.

Except—if she gave Harold all her money, Mr. Montague would have no reason to marry her. She would lose the house and have no funds with which to take Richard elsewhere.

She would not even consider the loss of a fine husband. She could not lose what she did not have, and after Mr. Montague discovered her treachery, she could never hope to earn his respect. She would lose him whether they married or not.

That saddened her more than she'd anticipated. She was rather accustomed to being thought of as a nuisance. She could scarcely expect Mr. Montague's esteem, if only because he had principles and she had none. Or very few. They'd been brought up differently. But she had enjoyed seeing admiration in his eyes yesterday.

She would have her semiannual allowance in January. She feared it wouldn't be enough to buy colors and live on as well. But she could not even begin to consider leaving Richard in Harold's clutches.

She was staring in longing at her childhood home when Lady Belden's driver halted the carriage in front of the forlorn estate. With a basement kitchen and an attic and two entire stories in between, the house had more than enough room for all of them to live together without being under one another's feet.

Well, her mother might be a trifle underfoot if she decided to follow Richard, but her mother was always an unknown factor. The dowager Lady Carrington did

not enjoy society. She preferred living in rural isola-
tion as long as her stepdaughters ignored her existence,
which they did. Unlike Richard, Lady Carrington was
perfectly capable of making her wishes known.

As much as Jocelyn would prefer to have her mother
with her, she had a strong suspicion that Blake was not
fond of having family about, so she would discourage
visits until she'd found some way of making reparations
for the dowry she wouldn't have.

Heart beating in agitation at the enormity of the deception she meant to perpetrate, Jocelyn accepted the
driver's assistance down the carriage steps. The dilapidated gate and overgrown hedge prevented her from
seeing much of the yard. Promising to return quickly,
she left her maid behind.

She was halfway up the walk before she recognized a
familiar horse tied to a post on the other side of a mul-
berry tree. Mr. Montague was here! She didn't know if
she dared face him just yet. Besides, there would be no
servants, so it would be more proper if she stayed outside, which was all she'd intended anyway.

She followed a brick path around the corner, wondering how one went about hiring gardeners to trim yew
hedges when one had no money.

"The rabbit hutch is still here!" she exclaimed, then
covered her mouth at her silly excitement over the
weathered, screened cages. She'd had to leave all her animals behind when Harold had selfishly cast her family
out. She knew better than to become attached to childish pets anymore, but perhaps she could safely keep her
kitten. And Percy.

She shouldn't be thinking of her own pleasure when
she was considering depriving a noble gentleman of
his—for a little while. Not forever. Just until she had
funds again.

She strolled to the rear grounds, gathering her muslin skirt and lifting it above her ankles so she might step past a muddy bit. She stopped at a gate to peer into the backyard.

She did not see Mr. Montague. Taking a deep breath, she followed the path until she could see through the alley of espaliered fruit trees to the conservatory.

A man's threatening shout startled her into dropping her skirt and looking for a weapon. Before she could so much as locate a dead branch, a mangy mastiff burst past the fruit trees, followed more slowly by a tottering pig.

The curses smoking the air were all too familiar.

11

Blake burst through the hedge, wielding his walking stick to chase off the damned animals. He halted just short of bowling Miss Carrington into a weed-infested ornamental pond.

She tilted backward to avoid collision, and he recovered enough equilibrium to grab her waist and steady her—not precisely the gallant, courtly behavior of a gentleman, but as close as he could execute under the circumstances. He was too furious and disgusted by the condition of the house to be polite. Feral pigs in the yard!

"Mr. Montague!" she scolded.

"Miss Carrington!" He bit his tongue on his sharp tone and tried to recover his aplomb while holding her fair form dangerously close—in a secluded garden. His brain instantly decamped to the wrong part of his anatomy. "What the devil are you doing here?" *Damnation.* He obviously lacked the ability to control his lust and be civil at the same time.

He glanced around for a garden bench where he

could deposit her, but there was nothing except weeds and deterioration everywhere he looked. In that froth of muslin and lace, she was a dewy rose among the thistles.

He'd had some foolish notion that he had something worthy to offer in giving her back her family home, but this was a hovel of the worst sort—with livestock rooting around unattended. How could he expect a wealthy young lady to accept rural decrepitude?

He wouldn't blame Miss Carrington for fleeing in horror. As he feared, she withdrew from his grasp and offered him the frosty look he deserved. "It appears I'm doing the same as you, checking on the condition of what might be my new home."

All Blake's hopes crashed back to reality. She had changed her mind after seeing the pig. How the devil did other fellows marry? And *why*? He resisted the first cutting response that reached his tongue and bowed as he should have done in the first place. "My apologies, Miss Carrington. I am appalled by the sad neglect of the estate."

He heard the walking bacon snuffling on the other side of the boxwood. Chelsea was so rural it still had *pigs* rooting through the streets? As if in reply, a rooster crowed from what might be the rear of the property.

Instead of looking horrified, Miss Carrington's face lit with delight, and she hurried deeper into the weed patch. "Do you think the chicken coop might still be here? I once had a red hen I raised from a chick."

Chickens? Here? Blake ran a hand through his hair and tried to reorient his thinking. It was *him* to which she objected, not the hovel? "The place is a pigsty," he couldn't help noting. He refrained from mentioning that he had originally abandoned the rural environs of his family's Shropshire estate because he could not carry on intelligent conversations with livestock. He needed intellectual stimulation. "You cannot possibly be thinking of moving in."

Her foolish delight slid away, and she cast him a startled look that oddly affected his breathing and made him want to say anything to bring back her earlier joy.

"No? Your father has rejected our marriage, then?" she asked with disappointment.

Disappointment! She *wanted* to live in a pigsty? She *still* wanted to marry him? And reside in rural decrepitude? She was a most unusual woman, if so. But if it would return that rapturous smile . . .

"You would actually consider living here?" he asked warily.

"Of course!" she cried in satisfaction, abandoning the feral pig and crowing rooster to follow a walkway toward the conservatory with its cracked panes. "Someone should take care of the poor animals before winter comes. Will it take very much work to repair the conservatory glass?"

"I fear it will take a great deal of work just to restore the main portion for habitation, much less any barn or stable." More work than he had time or she had money to accomplish.

"The gardens merely need a bit of mowing and trimming," she declared. "But I know nothing of repairing barns or conservatories." She found the garden entrance and appeared to be hunting for a key above the doorframe. "We cannot bring Percy here until the glass is repaired."

He'd already unlatched the door before the pig had rushed him. Since she'd disregarded both pork and mastiff, Blake assumed his valor in protecting Miss Carrington from wild animals went unappreciated. The *house* was the key to her happiness. Strangely disgruntled to be reminded where he stood in the scheme of things, he shoved open the rusty iron and glass panel and gestured for her to enter. Her smile challenged the sun as she stepped over the threshold.

Blake suffered a chill of foreboding. In a few weeks, this hovel could be his home. The bewildering Ladybyrd could be his wife. He'd rather face a duel. At least in a duel the outcome was straightforward. Wives and houses promised an entire array of uncertain tortures, like rampaging pigs and inconvenient demands for attention.

Perhaps he could fortify the study and lock out intruders. Or better yet, hope her income would allow him to maintain rooms in the city. Perhaps he could demand his father provide a greater allowance for agreeing to the settlements. That prospect cheered him considerably.

"Isn't the ironwork marvelous?" Like a beam of sunshine, she whirled between rotten wood tables and gazed upward at filthy, cobweb-encrusted fretwork.

Blake didn't know Miss Carrington well enough to decide if she was crazed or joking, but she seemed genuinely pleased. Warily, he crossed the moss-covered ancient stone floor to the house proper. "If you love this spider-infested filth, you should be in alt over the rest of the place."

Her eyes widened. "Really? We can see the rest of the house? It is not improper?"

He hesitated. Of course it was improper. But at his shrug, she grabbed his arm, stood on her toes to press a kiss to his stubbly cheek, and reminded him of why he'd agreed to consider giving up his bachelor freedom. He had to steady himself after that brief inundation of lavender, powder, and feminine pulchritude.

He was developing a depressing—and swelling— awareness of why men married. Ah, yes, that was it. The flesh was very weak indeed.

"Oh, look, the study is still in excellent condition!" she said as they entered. "You would have a place for your books. And your friends. And your cigars. You should be very happy here," she exclaimed heartily, as if reassuring herself. She whirled briefly around the walnut-paneled chamber to verify her observation before dashing off to an adjoining room.

A study of his own . . . seemed dismayingly staid and ho-hum. Perhaps he could set up a boxing ring in the carriage house for the winter months when he was not on campaign.

"A working fireplace would be more useful," he complained, smelling damp ashes and running his hand over the smoke stains on the marble.

"A chimney sweep will solve that," she called from the next room. "Oh, the velvet draperies are still on the bay window!"

Following her to the parlor, Blake shoved aside the moldering fabric to better see outside the filthy glass. Dust billowed into the air. He fought a cough by gripping tighter, and the panel tore with rot, crumpling at his feet in a cloud of dust. Obviously, Carrington hadn't wasted money on renovation. How damned long had he left the place untended?

"Oh, well, the velvet was too heavy anyway. An airy muslin, perhaps." She flitted from the window to examine the peeling fireplace mantel. "This was carved in the style of John Adams. Isn't it exquisite?"

Blake narrowed his eyes and regarded his bride-to-be's behavior with suspicion. She seemed a trifle anxious, where before she'd been all fluttering lashes and giddy laughter. Was she actually trying to convince him that he would enjoy living in this hole?

Perhaps she was nervous about being alone with him. It wasn't as if he had any skill at putting ladies at ease.

He bumped his leg on a low table that served no purpose other than to bruise shins. "We will have to hire someone to haul all these abominations out of here," he declared in disgust, finding a topic he could expound upon. "Apparently, the furnishings have not been changed since the first King George."

"Don't be silly. Let's see what condition the attics are in. We can move a few of the unnecessary pieces up there, if there's room. Some new fabric and a good polish on the rest, and it will be like new."

The woman was definitely nicked in the nob if she thought anything short of a magic wand could restore this place. Would she attempt to refurbish him, too?

Not until he watched Miss Carrington's dainty feet dancing up the stairs did Blake fully comprehend the danger of being entirely, inappropriately alone with her. If anyone walked in on them now, their fates were sealed. He might call witnesses to dismiss and override the house party gossip, but he was fully responsible for his actions at this moment.

He was courting fate. Unfortunately, living dangerously had its appeal. He followed the swaying temptation of her nicely rounded derriere.

"The guest rooms are in excellent shape!" she cried, flinging open doors right and left on the next floor. "Your family could stay with us whenever they're in London."

"I'd rather they not," he growled, knowing he sounded surly as he peered into furnished rooms draped in faded flowered fabrics, laces, and frippery. The enormity of what they were doing was finally sinking in. He'd spent his life plotting and planning, but marriage was a foreign concept. He knew how to face pistols at dawn, but not *lace*.

He propped his arm on the doorjamb and leaned over her shoulder to examine the next room. Her lavender scent seeped into his brain, and he was exceedingly aware of the vulnerability of her bare nape beneath her foolish bonnet. Pale blond wisps adorned her neck, and he no longer noticed the dusty chamber she was admiring. He wanted to wrap those wisps around his fingers and pull her toward him. . . .

"It's an *enormous* house. We won't even know your family is here." With a happy cry, she whirled to kiss his cheek again, oblivious of his wayward thoughts.

This time, instead of letting her flit away like an exotic butterfly, Blake slid his arms around her waist and lifted her to him, meaning to teach her the consequences of flirting with danger.

Or so he told himself.

She gasped, and he took advantage to ravish her soft lips as he'd been dying to do since the first time she'd opened them in his presence. This was what mouths were made for—taming, taunting, and melting resistance. Her tongue eagerly met his, and his doubts fled, replaced by the certainty that he could teach her pleasure and offer her more security than any of her other suitors could do.

She clung to his shoulders, and *finally*, her perfect breasts were pressed into his coat front as she responded eagerly to his plundering. A woman who enjoyed kissing would suit him well.

Blake adjusted his stance to fully support her, then lowered one hand to press her bottom until her skirts and his trousers were all that separated them. She didn't seem aware of the impropriety but returned his kisses with gratifying enthusiasm.

He, on the other hand, was stiff and ready to roger her against the damned wall. He was actually maneuvering her in that direction, nuzzling her throat, lost in her moans of pleasure, when feminine voices broke through his cloud of bliss.

"Blake Anthony Montague, what is the meaning of this?" His mother's horrified voice rang loud and clear, tolling clarions of doom.

"Oh, it is Miss Carrington," his married sister Agatha chirped.

Keeping his back to his family, Blake wondered if it might be possible to sink through the floor. Miss Carrington's small hands slid from his shoulders to burrow into his coat as she tried to disappear behind his bulk. Not for the first time in her company, Blake wanted to howl with rage, except this time it was at her distress. He didn't wish her humiliated by his deuced intrusive family. He'd learned to deal with them, but Miss Carrington shouldn't have to endure their constant nosy smothering.

He couldn't spin around and confront them quite yet. Willing his unruly cock into submission, Blake tucked a wisp of hair behind Miss Carrington's ear, rather glad that her bonnet had fallen back on its ribbons so he could finally see the glory of her silver-gold tresses. "You see why I do not anticipate housing my family?" he muttered.

"I'm sorry," she whispered back.

He couldn't ascertain if she was sorry he had a meddling family or sorry that they'd been caught. Possibly both.

"Well, Miss Carrington," his mother said from the end of the hall, "I see my son meets with your approval."

Blake drew his bride-to-be in front of him and finally turned to nod a greeting at his mother and sisters. Damn, but even Frances was here to witness his downfall. "Miss Carrington has agreed to make me a happy man, Mother. I would have announced the news this evening."

"Miss Carrington, may I say how delighted we are

to welcome you to our little family?" Lady Montague cried, rushing forward to grab her hands.

"If you call my two brothers and four sisters a *little* family," Blake murmured in her ear. "And each one nosier than the next, which is why they're here now."

Like him, she did not express dismay at being trapped. Unlike him, she donned a smile of delight and accepted his mother's hand in greeting. "Lady Montague, how good of you! Frances, such a delightful bonnet! Did you find it at that shop on Berkeley I mentioned? And, Agatha, I'm so pleased to see you. . . ."

She caught his mother's arm and turned Lady Montague toward the stairway, chattering and behaving as if it were the most normal thing in the world to be caught *in flagrante* in a filthy corridor.

Surely, she could not have set him up to be caught?

Horrified to think that Miss Carrington's pretty head could conceal a tactical skill greater than his own, Blake gave himself a minute to cool off before stomping down the stairs after the women. He should have questioned why she was out here alone. He damned well should have done a lot of things besides have his way with her. Not that he'd fully done that yet, which was probably why he was feeling so hostile.

"Mr. Montague believes a chimney sweep is required, and a glazier to repair the conservatory."

Mr. Montague thought no such thing. That was pure Miss Carrington talking. Mr. Montague would rather be in his rooms, drinking a glass of brandy and pondering the blasted French cipher instead of shepherding chattering females about a filthy house, inhaling their sweet perfumes. Atherton, the rake, belonged here, not him.

He despised the kind of social conniving Miss Carrington was currently engaging in.

"Have you set a date, dear?" his mother asked eagerly.

"If you had not interrupted," Blake curtly intercepted his *intended's* response, "we might have set one by now. Come back next week and perhaps I'll have had time to make arrangements."

Blake knew it no longer mattered how his father drew up the settlements. They were trapped. He had to accept whatever bones were thrown at him. He'd compromised a lady in front of his family. For better or worse, his carefree bachelor days had ended.

"A special license would be romantic but would probably cause too much gossip," Miss Carrington replied gaily.

Blake wanted to clap his hand over her mouth before she offered to elope to Gretna. "I need time," he warned. "Banns take three weeks, and we haven't even chosen a church."

"Lady Belden lives in a lovely parish," his mother corrected. "If Miss Carrington's banns are called there, the church will be perfectly suitable. I'm sure the house can be ready in three weeks."

Three weeks! He wasn't sure *he* could be ready in three weeks. Planning a courtship was all he'd been prepared for. Suddenly, he seemed to have boarded a runaway mail coach.

"Don't rush us, Mother. We'll do this at our own time and pace. You can scarcely expect me to bring a bride to a home in this sorry state."

His mother looked hurt by his cold reply, but he was too furious with himself to care.

Letting his mother and sisters wander into the next room, Blake caught his betrothed's elbow and held her back. "I won't be manipulated, Miss Carrington," he said in a low voice. "Our decision to marry may have just been removed from my hands, but I am in no hurry to turn my life inside out because my family—or you—wishes it so."

Frost whitened the deep blue of her eyes to gray. "You, sir, are the most rude, unsociable, difficult man I've ever had the misfortune to encounter. It was not my fault or your mother's that you were caught kissing me and now have no choice but to marry. Do not take your anger out on us!"

Which was what he'd been doing, admittedly, except it wasn't his lack of choice that was the problem. The problem was that he would break his family's hearts no matter what he did, so it was better if he kept them at a distance. As it would be better for any wife to keep hers. They may as well lay down the terms of their arrangement now. "I have spent my life avoiding their intrusive manipulations. I do not intend to let them take over now. You may endure their managing ways, for I will not."

"Fine, why don't you just keep your rooms in the city," she said scornfully, providing him with the escape he'd already considered. "I will entertain your family here, in this *sorry state*. I think I like them better than I do you."

"You like the *house* better than you do me. Just so long as we both recognize where we stand, we'll march along fine." He was almost relieved to have this tiff aired now.

Her smile was forced. "Excellent. We'll lead our separate lives and be happier for it."

She tugged her arm free of his grasp and swept from the room.

Although she'd said exactly what he wanted to hear, Blake felt a cold draft upon her departure, as if the sun had just gone behind a cloud.

12

That evening, Jocelyn was still confused by Mr. Montague's imperious behavior and was almost relieved that a decision had been taken from her hands. She had to marry him now. She couldn't precisely pay off Harold with a clear conscience, but she would do it. Richard was helpless, but Mr. Montague was not. The dratted man could wait a few months before becoming an officer and rushing off to Portugal. It would serve him right for being so insufferable.

Dithering over money was preferable to fretting over her inexplicable reaction to the annoying Mr. Montague's kisses, and the astounding fact that she'd *loved* them. Their first kiss had been delicious, but the next . . . His arms, his caress, his *mouth* had stimulated such excitement that she'd been giddy with foolish anticipation. Her pulse still beat too fast just thinking about it.

She knew better than to expect anything from a man. She should have resisted.

Except—after she'd seen her home in such disrepair,

she had been fighting tears and wanting to murder Harold. Blake's kiss had wiped away the dismals and offered enticing promises, dreams she'd never dreamed, ones of true love and real marriage.

He had kissed her as if she might really be *important* to him. Her heart stirred a little more than it should at the seductive possibility. She had never been of much value to anyone. Still, it would be wonderful if she could matter to so eminently accomplished and self-sufficient a gentleman as Mr. Montague. . . .

Stop thinking like that. He would more likely throttle her than appreciate her once he discovered what she was about to do, and justifiably so. She'd already sent a note around to Lady Bell's lawyer to arrange for Richard's guardianship to be irrevocably transferred to her. She would have that paper signed before she paid Harold the preposterous, horrendous sum of four hundred pounds.

Once he'd learned what she'd done, Mr. Montague might never kiss her again.

She dared not think about that too hard, either. Preparing for the evening's entertainment, Jocelyn raised her hair from her neck so her maid could fasten the buttons at the back of her bodice. "I am having second and third thoughts about this marriage," she announced in a fit of pique at her own spineless vacillation.

Lady Bell looked up from the correspondence her secretary had just delivered. "He has made improper advances?" she asked dryly. "Men will try, you know. If you do not like intimacy, then you most certainly should reconsider."

"You are a very broad-minded person," Jocelyn said grumpily, taking a seat at the vanity so the maid might pin up her hair. "Most women say that side of marriage is a cross they must bear."

Not that she knew anything of the familiarities they were talking about. But she had listened to her married sisters when she shouldn't have and asked questions when she could get away with them. And she'd hinted that she knew more than she did so that people like Lady Bell would open up and explain. Because she really wanted to know what would be expected of her.

Why in the name of all that was holy would anyone object to what Mr. Montague had done to her this afternoon? Really, it had been the most delectable experience. . . . If she could have the kisses without putting up with his irritable humors, she'd be thrilled with marriage. She had never known a man's chest could be so very hard, or his lips so demanding. Or that his tongue could produce such intimate sensations! She suffered the most delicious tingles simply thinking about what they'd done.

"Most women are fools." After sorting through her mail, Lady Bell tossed a letter to the vanity in front of Jocelyn. "Or they're so desperate to marry that they accept the first man to ask, without consideration of the physical side of marriage. You have alternatives."

Not anymore, but Jocelyn didn't tell Lady Belden that. What she really wanted to know was if her husband's kisses would continue to be exciting or if he would stop them altogether once he learned how she'd betrayed him.

"Decisions are difficult." Jocelyn tried to see the writing on the letter Lady Bell had just tossed at her, but her maid tugged her hair to keep her from twisting. "When Mr. Montague is on his best behavior, he can be very . . . charming."

Perhaps *charming* wasn't the correct word, but she liked talking with him when he wasn't growling. Sometimes, she even liked his cynical attitude. She'd learned smiles more often got her what she wanted, but men had the freedom to be themselves. They could afford to be unpleasant if they wished—as Lady Bell could when she felt like it.

"But?" the marchioness inquired, looking up with interest.

"He hates his family," Jocelyn responded with a sigh. "He bristles like an angry cur whenever they're about. He doesn't like parties. He's even more unsociable than poor Richard. I do not understand it, because he has gentlemanliness ingrained in him. Even when he is shouting at me, he helps me past mud puddles, and he protects me from falls when I'm trespassing and he's chasing pigs. But he's the most disagreeable man I have ever met."

"Chasing pigs?" Lady Bell asked faintly.

As the maid finally released her, Jocelyn waved away a reply and picked up the letter. She stared at the elegant handwriting with astonishment. *Richard!* Richard all but lived in their sister Elizabeth's barn. He never wrote letters. He hadn't even sealed this one. She pulled the edges from the fold and straightened the badly crumpled paper.

He opened the windows and let them all out were the only words on the page.

Two fat tears ran down Jocelyn's cheeks, and she grabbed a handkerchief to blot them before more spilled over. She covered her mouth to hold back a sob that threatened to escape, but she couldn't prevent the shudder racking her.

"Jocelyn?" Lady Bell asked in concern. "Is it bad news?"

She shook her head, unable to explain clearly what those few words meant to her, much less how devastating they were to poor Richard.

Apparently her brother-in-law had tired of Richard's aviary and had freed all the new specimens her brother had carefully collected these past few years. The monster may as well have taken a hatchet to Richard's family. For the second time in his short life, Richard had lost all he loved. How could he survive such a blow?

Jocelyn had to give him hope. No one understood Richard as she did. They had shared a nursery and the bullying of their older half siblings, who'd resented them. Their mother lacked nurturing instincts and failed to protect her offspring. Richard had been scorned and pushed aside, until Jocelyn was old enough to imitate her father's sister Matilda and use her looks to deceive and distract until she had what she wanted.

Richard had no conception of how to deceive. He would never learn how to survive in the real world. If Jocelyn had any say in it, he wouldn't have to. She hoped and prayed that an intelligent man like Mr. Montague would recognize and accept her brother's eccentric intellect, because really, she had no other choice.

Jocelyn tucked the precious paper into her bodice. Richard wrote so seldom, she might never see another letter from him again. "My sister's husband has tired of my family, I believe," she said with brittle gaiety. "I must marry Mr. Montague with all speed."

Perceptive as she was, her hostess frowned but refrained from questioning the despair in her guest's voice.

Having no valet, Blake ungraciously allowed Atherton to fold his neckcloth in some knot he'd never succeed in unfastening without ripping the aging linen to shreds.

"Bernie was here earlier," Blake said, twisting his neck so he didn't feel as if a rope was being tied about it. "He thinks because I'm courting Miss Carrington that I know where to find his damned bird."

"And you don't?" Nick asked wryly, knowing better.

"He insults me by questioning my integrity." Which had left him feeling more surly than usual. "It's all *her* fault. And now I have offended her and can't even say why," he complained.

It had been very well to agree to rooms in the city, but that left him without a woman in his bed. Miss Carrington had him practically slavering for the altar for that reason alone, and he'd be damned if he got leg-shackled for nothing. If he was to take a wife, he needed to learn what made one biddable. "How can I repair what I don't understand?" He glared at his cravat knot in the mirror and deliberately loosened it.

"And do you want to?" Atherton asked affably. "She's a bird-wit. She'll drive you mad."

"I doubt that she's a bird-wit, but she's already driving me mad," Blake grumbled, hunting behind a towering stack of books for his hat. "Every time I see her, I have the urge to either throttle her or kiss her. It's deuced annoying."

Atherton laughed. "Then you must marry her, by all means. No other woman has ever roused you to such passion. It's healthy for you, old boy. Stirs the blood, y'know."

Blake sent his friend a jaded look. "Says the man whose blood is ever stirred. I doubt it's healthy if a husband shoots you or a spurned lover takes off your head." He pounded his hat onto his head and opened the door.

The rooms he rented were in the upper story of an ancient town house. The narrow, crooked corridor had only a single lamp and no window to light the stairwell. Blake had taken the stairs thousands of times without mishap.

Which meant he was unprepared for his foot to hit a solid lump on the top step. Before he could right himself, he tumbled head over heels to the landing, breaking his fall with only the training he'd received in the boxing ring, by twisting his torso so his shoulder took the blow.

Atherton grabbed a lamp from inside the rooms and held it aloft. "You still alive down there?"

Beyond furious now, Blake grabbed a banister and hauled himself to his feet, heedless of whatever damage he might have done to his bones. "What the devil did I trip on? Someone will hang for leaving it lying about, whatever it is."

Atherton gave him a cool once-over, hiding any relief before examining the floorboards. "An andiron, I believe, with the yoke caught between the stair rails so it cannot move. Are you in the habit of losing andirons, old chap?"

"I have a coal stove, not a fireplace." Limping worse than ever, Blake climbed the stairs and attempted to dislodge the heavy iron piece. "I must have a talk with my landlady."

Atherton finally had the grace to look concerned. "She was leaving just as I came up. Is there any chance that could have been placed there on purpose?"

Blake's rooms were on the top floor. If the andiron had been left intentionally, it was for his benefit alone. "It makes no sense. I have nothing anyone could want. I think we'll find Mrs. Beasel had it in her hand for some reason when she cleaned my rooms and she simply forgot it."

Atherton's usually affable expression replaced his earlier frown. "Of course, that's bound to be it, unless you have French spies following you, searching for that demmed paper that half London knows you possess."

Blake almost laughed. "Since it came from a battlefield, one assumes the French already know what's in the message. Besides, it's too late for them to try to hide the code. My version is but a copy. The original is somewhere in Whitehall, being pored over by experts—provided anyone has bothered to look at it at all."

"Well, then, batty landladies and not French spies. How boring your life is, old chap." He handed Blake his stick. "You might want to use this. Looks to me as if you're in more danger of losing your head than I am."

"Your conquests—and their husbands—are more dangerous than andirons. One of your jilts or their irate spouses is likely to take a knife to your neck one of these days." Blake returned to their previous topic while his mind quietly worked at the puzzle of who might want him dead—or if the family curse was more than superstition. Neither possibility seemed credible. A string of bad luck made more sense. Still, Bernie had just been here. Could he have . . . ? No, that made even less sense. Killing Blake wouldn't get the bird back.

"Wealthy widows are more my taste these days." Exhibiting no shame at the admission, Atherton ambled down the stairs after Blake. "If it were not for Quent's eagle eye, I should go after Lady Bell. Now there is a lady ripe for dalliance."

"Dragon Lady would bite off your foolish head. Leave her to Quentin. They deserve each other," Blake said dismissively. "I should have studied the strategy of courtship instead of chess. How do I make Miss Carrington speak to me again?"

"I almost hate to see another friend caught by ball and chain," Nick said mournfully as they left the house. "But Fitz seems to have done well, so perhaps there is something agreeable about the wedded state."

"Money," Blake said succinctly, striding down the street in the direction of the soiree he knew Miss Carrington would attend. "An ability to pay one's bills leads to happiness."

Nick snorted. "An ability to dip one's wick at will also leads to happiness, not that a monk like you would appreciate that."

Blake would certainly appreciate it if the malleable wax he dipped his wick into was the beautiful Miss Carrington, but he knew there was nothing remotely wax-like about Ladybyrd. "The pleasures of the flesh dilute one's concentration," Blake argued. "You're a fine example of that. I swear, you have a different female each week. You cannot even concentrate on one or two."

"There are so many stars in the sky to admire, how can I choose just one? Come along, crosspatch, let us plan a strategy for pacifying the lovely Miss C and wooing her into your bed and her money into your coffers."

"Do not lecture us on what Wellesley should do when he returns to the Continent," Sir Barton begged. "We'd rather hear how you mean to tame Ladybyrd." An impoverished baronet from the Lake Country, Barton had been in search of a wealthy wife for the past year or more.

"If I told you how it was done, then you would all be after her." Surrounded by other bachelors at the buffet table, Blake leaned against a Grecian column and ground his teeth at the overfamiliar appellation used for his intended. He would prefer that only *he* had the right to call her by that name.

"Montague yells at Miss C," Nick explained, nibbling on a pâté-covered wafer.

Only because Atherton was his friend did Blake refrain from shoving the meaty wafer into his face. Besides, he was too bruised to move.

"You yell at her?" Sir Barton asked with interest. "And this works?"

"Don't recommend it with other ladies," Nick warned. "It only seems to work with Miss C."

Since Nick was the expert at winning ladies, several of the idiots nodded at his wisdom and slipped away from the buffet table the instant Miss Carrington entered the parlor. *There* was one reason for making the announcement of their betrothal public, Blake thought grimly. It would drive away the boneheaded gallants flocking around the woman he intended to make his own.

He'd at least like to have Miss Carrington speaking to him before he did so.

He cleaned his plate—the only proper meal he'd had all day. He would need his strength shortly. Nick's manipulations were so obvious, a five-year-old could have discerned them.

"They're off to yell at your betrothed," Atherton offered genially.

"So that I may rescue her? Quite thoughtful of you, I'm sure." Blake handed his plate to a passing servant. Still taking support from the column, he twitched his shoulders in the confining coat. He supposed he *had* shouted at Miss Carrington more than once, but how else was one to converse with the woman? That didn't mean he wished anyone else to shout at her.

"Miss Carrington, I insist that you accompany me in this duet," Barton demanded loudly in the next room, grasping her elbow and tugging her in a domineering manner that Blake rather painfully remembered employing with her himself.

He didn't relish being the leader of a dog pack, but he could not in good conscience allow Miss Carrington to be nipped at by puppies. With a wince, he pushed himself off the wall. If he had any more accidents, they'd be carrying him to the altar on a stretcher.

"Pardon me, sir, have you quite taken leave of your senses?" Jocelyn's laughing voice carried across the room, and heads turned. Society thrived on drama. "I don't sing."

"Of course you sing, Miss Carrington," one of the older ladies called out. "You used to do so when you were out and about with your papa. You were ever so precocious."

Blake refrained from rolling his eyes as he crossed the room. From what little he'd gathered about the eccentric Carringtons, this was not the incentive to encourage the lady.

Miss Carrington looked up at Blake's approach and bestowed a smile on him that could have frozen candle flames. "Have you come to order me to sing, too?"

She flirted with that damned fan as if she hadn't a care in the world, but he'd learned her smiles were deceptive. If there was a gun about, Barton was in danger of losing a toe.

"Do I look like a nodcock?" Blake asked, raising a disapproving eyebrow before turning to Barton. "I believe Frances would enjoy playing your duet."

Disregarding Barton's offended look, Blake offered his arm to the lady. "A stroll around the room, or am I still in your bad graces?"

"You did not shoot Sir Barton, so you are momentarily reprieved. I'm sure you will find some other means of annoying me before the evening's end." She took his arm while Blake's sister and Sir Barton began bleating a popular refrain to the accompaniment of the poor pianoforte.

Promenading senselessly about the room as etiquette required, having no conversation to make with Miss Carrington, Blake attempted to occupy himself with the puzzle of the "accidents" that had left him bruised and aching. Had he annoyed his acquaintances so much that they'd go to such extremes as murder to save them from his company?

Of course, he could scarcely think clearly while Miss

Carrington's delicate floral scent wafted around him and her skirts brushed against his legs, reminding him of what he could have if he minded his manners. Her kiss had burned a hole straight through his skull, and he feared if he didn't bed her soon, his gray matter would seep out the cracks—a rather humbling development.

"Then let us shorten the evening by my annoying you now and coming straight to the point," Blake said in resignation. "My family will not forgive me if I do not do the proper thing and have the banns called. Would you rather marry me or see me cast from the nest?"

The glance she gave him contained the mysteries of the universe. Against his better judgment, she fascinated him. Another woman would have already hit him over the head with the nearest hard object.

"It is interesting that your family's opinion concerns you only when you do not have to speak with them," she said. "You were extremely rude earlier today. Is that how you mean to treat me should we marry? With the contempt of familiarity?"

Blake thought he might have fared better had she used an inanimate object with which to beat him. He winced and finally admitted the embarrassing situation. "My mother is superstitious and lives in dire fear that I will die before thirty. Frances and my father do not wish to be in London at this time of year, but my mother will not leave until she's satisfied that I'll stay alive. It is more than embarrassing to be followed about by one's mother."

"Die before thirty?" Miss Carrington repeated with appalled curiosity.

Blake swiped at his temple, lifting the darker curls to reveal the silver streak underneath. "A family curse that comes to everyone with this streak in his hair. It is superstitious nonsense, naturally."

Although Blake's favorite uncle, who also bore the

silver streak, was swept away in a flood at the age of twenty, victim of a bursting dam. Still, freak accidents were just that, accidents.

"My father is not so much concerned with superstition as the fact that my brothers have yet to produce heirs," he continued, more sensibly. "Hence, my parents' desire to marry me off. I have little patience with their stifling attentions. Do not hover over me, and I will worship the ground you walk on."

She laughed. He had been serious, but he enjoyed the full-throated music of her laughter. At least she was not a woman who scolded and nagged. At least, he hoped not, because every person in the room was watching them and gossip would fly by morning. He was unaccustomed to being the subject of speculation.

"I can assure you, sir, that hovering is the very last thing I will do. But I'd rather you worshipped *me* than the ground. No one has ever worshipped me before, unless you count Richard."

Blake halted their progress in a dim corner, where he could stare down at her in surprise. "Surely you jest. You were meant for adoration."

An adoration he couldn't provide. Damn, but she deserved better, he realized, much to his great dismay. He ought to shove a more deserving fellow in her direction, but he was selfish enough to refuse to let her go. So much for believing he was sacrificing himself for a noble cause.

Her eyes widened in startlement at his declaration. She raised one of her expressive hands, started to speak, then shook her curls, as if unable to find words.

Puzzled, he studied her. As far as he was aware, the lady never lacked for words. How had he surprised her? By saying she was adorable? She had to know that she was everything appealing . . . most of the time.

She shook her head again and a pale curl danced with her earrings. Recovering from her momentary uncertainty, she replied, "You must meet my family someday to understand. We do not do adoration well. If you require worship, be sure that we will not suit."

Relief swept through him, and he almost got down on one knee right there. "Then you are the woman of my dreams, Miss Carrington. Let me make the announcement."

"You must speak with Lady Belden first. And perhaps my solicitor?"

"In the morning, then?"

She stared up at him with a concern that matched his own, but her gloved hand was warm and vulnerable and wrapped trustingly in his.

"If all goes well with Lady Bell and the solicitor in the morning, Mr. Montague, then yes, I suppose we might make the announcement."

By tomorrow, the noose would be firmly fastened around his neck. Blake tugged at the knot of his neckcloth and resisted dragging her somewhere private to reassure himself this was what he wanted.

"You honor me, Miss Carrington," was all he managed to say.

13

Mr. Montague thought she deserved adoration! Jocelyn was not at all certain how to take that declaration from a man she'd thought honest but whom she knew wanted her money.

She tugged nervously at the ribbon of her pocket and wished she could pace Lady Bell's study as her intended was doing. His father's solicitors and Lady Bell's were poring over the settlement papers, harrumphing, and whispering to their clerks.

She didn't want to be here at all, except she had no father to conduct the negotiations, and Viscount Pig would fly before she let him represent her interests. She'd persuaded Lady Bell's solicitor to carry out the diabolical exchange Harold had demanded for Richard's guardianship. She was almost penniless again, but Richard was safe. She'd made certain of that. The responsibility was both terrifying and satisfying.

She would owe her new husband a great deal when

he discovered what she'd done. She hoped she could find some way to make up for her deception.

Living from one calamity to another made planning difficult. She'd spent her childhood hiding Richard from Harold's abuse, lost her father at seventeen, been thrown out of her beloved home not long after, and spent these last six years trying to prevent Richard's occasionally hysterical behavior from getting them flung from their half sisters' homes. Without great success. Her impulsive acts, like the bird-snatching, often had far-reaching, unintended consequences. Who would have thought stealing Percy would lead to marriage?

Sitting in the window seat, she glanced at the street below. Since receiving Richard's cryptic note, she was heeding her instinct for trouble. Ogilvie might even now be stalking her, looking for his parrot. The house in Chelsea could be on fire. Her mother could arrive on the doorstep with Richard in tow. Her life was such that it made sense to plan for disaster and disruption.

In comparison, deciding to marry seemed an exercise in serenity.

"This is outrageous!" Lady Bell's man uttered in rage, shaking one of the papers at his counterpart across the table. "This says the house reverts to Baron Montague should his son die within the next year. Miss Carrington cannot place all her funds in the hands of her husband, only to have the roof snatched from her head if he's inconveniently run over by a carriage!"

Jocelyn raised her eyebrows questioningly to Mr. Montague. At the solicitor's outburst, he stopped his pacing to glance at her with what appeared to be concern. She knew the lawyers would not heed her, but she was interested in her intended's explanation of the outburst. Madly enough, she was learning to trust his cynicism.

"I warned you of my family's manipulations," he said

for her ears alone. "I was afraid there would be a catch to my father's generosity. This is my parents' attempt to prevent me from going to war." He squeezed her hand in reassurance.

Returning to his pacing, he spoke to the table of lawyers. "Perhaps a clause might be entered that the property revert to my child if I suffer a sudden, injudicious demise," he suggested.

He was being sarcastic again. Apparently, his parents were playing the superstition card and hoped she might keep their son from dying before thirty. Would his father accept an heir in return for his expensive property?

An heir. She'd never once considered children. She needed to start considering them. She suffered an urge to run far, far away. She'd thought this was to be a marriage of *convenience*, but his family, naturally, had different ideas.

"Then perhaps the lady's funds should be kept in *her* family as well," Lady Bell's attorney responded matter-of-factly. "I suggest she be allowed complete control of her income until such time as the house is legally hers."

Smart man. That would prevent Mr. Montague from learning she had no funds until the beginning of the year. Better yet, if he did not go to war, she was less likely to lose the house due to his *injudicious demise*.

The attorneys returned to muttering among themselves, but Mr. Montague set aside his copy of the papers to loom over the seat where she was perched.

"You are worried," he stated flatly. "Second thoughts?"

"I'm on my hundredth and one thought by now. Remind me why I am doing this?"

"Because your parrot is teaching Fitz's innocent children how to curse?" he suggested. "I thought it was because you would like to return to your home."

"But if I am understanding the argument, your father will not let me have the house should you die in battle over this next year." She threaded her fingers to prevent herself from fraying her ribbon.

"I have Wellesley's promise of a staff position if I can buy in by Christmas. If I tell you that I'm unlikely to be at the front, will you feel less anxious?" he asked.

Christmas. She gulped. He wouldn't be going anywhere at Christmas. "What is the point of our marrying if I do not have a house and you end up dead?" she asked instead.

"I do not intend to end up dead," he pointed out, "but they are merely negotiating at the moment."

"It is all very cold, is it not?" she asked wistfully. "I am sorry I shot your toe. You are still limping. Is it healing yet?"

"It was only a scratch. I bumped my knee the other night. If you are sorry we must marry, we should find a way out of our impending vows now, before it's too late."

Perhaps he was right. Perhaps that was exactly what they should do.

A sharp rap sounded on the study door, jarring Jocelyn from wondering if Mr. Montague was having second thoughts, too. Before a footman could formally announce the visitor, Harold sauntered into the room. Or perhaps *waddled* was more accurate.

Jocelyn gazed heavenward and wished for a stout stick. The tedious conference had just become more perilous. What if Harold revealed to Blake that she'd spent this year's income? She clenched her fingers into fists and donned her best insouciant mask while studying the brother she'd done her best to ignore since returning to London.

She'd heard Harold had injured his shoulder in a duel a year or two ago, but she'd been in Norfolk at the time and did not know the details. Besides having grown fat and bald, he did seem to be favoring one side.

"As head of the Carrington family, I should have been informed of this meeting," the viscount announced to the startled company. "I believe I am entitled to be included in any business that affects my sister's welfare."

"Half sister," Jocelyn murmured under her breath, wondering what on earth the leech wanted now, after he'd already drained her coffers. "I have more than enough competent representation, but thank you, Harold, for thinking of me." She winced at the sarcasm in her voice. The last thing she needed was to irritate the vicious wretch.

Recognizing Quality, if not the viscount himself, the lawyers all respectfully rose from the table and looked to Lady Bell for leadership.

"Carrington House must be settled on Jocelyn," the viscount continued, ignoring her as usual. "She will need the aviary if she is to collect Richard's birds."

Harold *hated* Richard's birds. Only with extreme restraint did Jocelyn prevent her jaw from dropping in disbelief.

"Arrangements should be made so Jocelyn's income is not left to a barnacle like Montague, but to Richard and any offspring," Harold announced.

Where it might come under Harold's guardianship as head of the family, Jocelyn realized, finally grasping the purpose of her brother's sudden interest.

The marchioness glanced at Jocelyn to see how she would like to handle the intruder. Mr. Montague did not wait for her suggestions. Her personal warrior stepped in front of Harold, towering a good head and shoulders above him, Jocelyn noted with satisfaction.

"My lord, I believe you are mistaken," Mr. Montague said with what sounded like pleasure. "Miss Carrington is of legal age, and she has the ability to hire her own solicitors and make her own decisions. You are unnecessary and unwelcome."

Her half brother puffed up like an enraged rooster with a crooked wing.

She ought to inquire about the details of the duel. Harold and Mr. Montague seemed at daggers drawn already, and her intended *did* have those much-lamented violent tendencies. Now she would have to wonder how they knew each other.

Jocelyn had a vague childhood memory of Harold in his adolescence, stomping about in heels, powdered wig, and a beauty patch. She'd thought him silly then. He was equally silly now, looking like a pouter pigeon in his double-breasted coat.

She couldn't imagine why a woman as beautiful as his wife would have looked twice at him, but the French had strange notions. He'd brought Antoinette back from that rebellious country along with a case of brandy when Jocelyn had been in the schoolroom. Their father had detested Antoinette and her cloying mannerisms, but at least she had taken an interest in Richard's birds.

"And who the devil do you think you are, Montague, to claim my sister without my permission?" Harold demanded. "I will not see her naïveté taken advantage of!"

"Quite generous of you, I'm sure," Mr. Montague answered with ominous affability. Without further warning, he forcibly twisted the viscount's good arm behind his back in a move so swift, Jocelyn could not quite follow how he did it. "But I do not believe Miss Carrington has requested your aid."

She admired the fierce gleam in her intended's eyes as he defended her against dragons. Poor Harold was a reptile but scarcely a dragon. Still, she appreciated his effort.

Mr. Montague hauled Harold over to the window seat. "Miss Carrington, do you wish to have your brother view the settlements?"

She didn't think anyone had ever asked for her opinion. Every person in the room watched her to see how the drama played out. Since Richard's guardianship papers were secure with a solicitor, she had no more to fear from her bully of a brother. It would be lovely to have revenge for all his depredations, but probably not wise.

"Don't let this cradle-robbing, money-hungry poltroon rob you of your inheritance!" Harold protested.

"Cradle-robbing?" Jocelyn tilted her head. "Just how old do you think I am, Harold? Or perhaps you think time stands still outside the city, so I must still be the age I was when you threw me out of my home?"

"I could not let my wife live in a house full of loose screws!" he protested. "You were barely out of the schoolroom then."

She had been seventeen and prepared for her formal come-out. She'd been a young woman grieving her father's death, but scarcely a schoolroom miss. And Antoinette was an actress who had lived with the worst sorts of people, those far less conventional than any Byrd-Carrington. Although it strained her practiced nonchalance, Jocelyn refrained from shouting, *Balderdash!*

Mr. Montague growled something irascible that made Harold blanch. Or perhaps her warrior jerked harder on the arm he was twisting. "As much as everyone is enjoying this spectacle, I'd prefer that you simply tell me what I should do about him."

"I'd rather not consider the viscount at all," Jocelyn said in what she hoped was a bored tone that did not reveal how much she despised her father's heir. A lifetime spent hiding what she thought gave credibility to her act. "I trust hired solicitors more than I do him."

"Jocelyn, that is ridiculous!" the viscount sputtered. "I should have been consulted about these proceedings. You have no idea what manner of disreputable scoundrel you are marrying. I must file my objections. Lady Belden, surely you—"

Before Harold could annoy the marchioness with his appeal, Mr. Montague marched him toward the door. Jocelyn did her best not to gape. Harold might be of medium height, but he was heavy. Even so, she wasn't at all certain that under Mr. Montague's encouragement Harold's feet so much as touched the carpet.

Her betrothed flung the fuming viscount into the arms of a strong young footman, then shut the door and turned the key in the lock. Jocelyn waited for the audience to stand up, applaud, and cheer so she might do the same.

Lady Belden merely nodded and turned back to the solicitors. "Please return to your seats, gentlemen, and let us finish our business."

Mr. Montague came to stand beside Jocelyn as if he had done no more than call for tea. Really, life lacked the climactic drama of a good play.

"I rather think I shall enjoy having a soldier for a husband," she said thoughtfully, still stunned by the encounter. For years, she'd dreamed of flinging Harold off parapets, and Mr. Montague had nearly fulfilled her fantasy. "Could you drive him out at the point of a sword next time?"

"Blowhards and bullies are not worth the trouble," her gallant knight said dismissively.

She'd accept this as a sign that Mr. Montague would protect her and hers, even after he learned of her deception. She would do her very best to make it up to him at the first opportunity.

It was time to stop fretting and move forward. "If you do not mind, I shall ask the solicitors to keep my dowry in my control until your father's terms are met and we know the house is ours. Then we both will have what we need."

He bowed. "You have made me a happy man, Miss Carrington."

Blake paced the cluttered floor of his narrow rooms, rereading the settlements he'd finally agreed to sign, against his better judgment.

Although he and Miss Carrington were free to live in Carrington House, his father's attorneys had insisted that the deed would not be signed over to him unless Blake was still alive in one year. Given the law's reluctance to acknowledge that women had the ability to handle their own fortunes, that did not leave Miss Carrington's side much room for negotiation.

Lady Belden's attorneys had eventually quit arguing with his father's over the control of Miss Carrington's fortune. Instead, they had inserted a devilish clause preventing his spending any of his bride's dowry for purposes *that might lead to his wife losing her home.*

He could legally fritter away her fortune on gambling, but he must have his wife's permission to buy colors—since going to war might lead to his death, thus leading to the loss of Carrington House. His father's stubbornness was the real problem here.

Should he annoy his bride into giving him permission? He had a far better chance of that than sweet-talking her into it.

Now that the banns had been placed, he had no choice. Blake sighed and flung the papers to his desk.

A ferocious squawking interspersed with cries of "Roger the wench!" echoed from the stairwell, and Blake groaned. Since he'd encountered Miss Carrington, his well-ordered life had turned into a Punch and Judy show. Had her half brother been half a man, the viscount would be pounding on the door by now, demanding satisfaction for his earlier insult. Instead, Blake was cursed by birds.

The messenger carrying the box swore along with the parrot all the way up the narrow staircase. Blake let the man into his small rooms after verifying there were no stray andirons lying about.

The landlady had been bewildered over how her parlor piece had ended up on his landing, causing his tumultuous fall. Unless he wished to believe Carrington meant to kill him to prevent his sister's marriage, Blake had to blame the andiron on his landlady's absentmindedness.

He had no evidence that Ogilvie was stupid enough to murder him over a purloined parrot. And surely the nodcock had no notion of putting Blake out of the competition for Miss Carrington's hand by crippling him for life. Although Blake twitched uncomfortably remembering Quent's report of the conversation between Ogilvie and the viscount. The duke had apparently promised torture if the bird was lost.

"The earl says as how you'll need to take the bird back," the footman said, scowling at the shrieking package and handing over a note.

Blake searched his pockets, then among the litter of paper on his desk, until he found a coin to hand the man. It was scarce fair recompense for being cursed at during the journey from Sussex to London. "Have a tankard at the tavern on the corner and put it on my tab," he told the messenger. "It's the least I can do."

The footman tapped his hat and departed, leaving Percy screeching, "All dicks on deck! Avast ye mateys, it's mutiny."

Blake unfolded Fitz's note and read, *Sorry, old chap.*

Abby just figured out what the song meant after Jeremy called his sister a cunny, not a bunny. Did you know the creature speaks French? Heard you're owed congratulations. Marry her and let her send Percy to her brother posthaste.

Blake thought he ought to send the foul fowl to kingdom come, but he supposed the creature shouldn't be shot for repeating what he'd been taught. Made one wonder about the old duke, though. The parrot had learned his colorful vocabulary somewhere. Or had Percy acquired the vulgarities in Carrington House? If so, Blake hoped it was after Jocelyn had departed.

He pried open the packing case and removed the cover protecting the parrot from chills. The mangy African Grey squawked and grew silent. His beady black eyes regarded Blake with suspicion.

What had Miss Carrington said the creature ate? Preposterous things like fruit and greens. He rummaged around in a desk drawer until he found a box of sweetmeats that Agatha had sent for his birthday. Remembering the bird's vicious beak, he dropped a sugared fruit into the cage and let Percy peck at the floor.

"Keep a civil tongue in your head and there's more where that came from," he promised. Not that he expected Percy to understand. He just believed in fair warning.

Clearing off his desk, he applied his mind to Jefferson's thesis on the wheel code and the one example of the code he had at hand, while occasionally throwing Percy a crumb for his continued silence.

He had time. He could strategize how to woo and win a bride into buying his colors even if she feared it might ultimately cost her the home she wanted.

14

The next morning, Blake stopped at the library club to which Danecroft had introduced him. Like Blake, Fitz had few funds and an inquisitive mind, so sharing books made sense. Blake had heard there was a new treatise on Jefferson's wheel and similar codes.

Engrossed in the plate showing an example of the wheel, he wasn't aware of being approached until Bernard Ogilvie belched the stench of ale in his ear. "The duke says even if I can't win the lady, I'm to get the parrot back," Ogilvie said, his words slurring only slightly. "Since you are the lady's betrothed, I have no choice but to demand that you make her return Percy."

Blake wasn't certain how an oaf like Ogilvie had found him here, or how he even knew a library club existed, but he supposed a duke's nephew had sources at his disposal. The real question was what the devil the duke wanted with a blasphemous parrot.

He closed the section he was reading on cryptography and glared at Ogilvie. "Isn't it a trifle early in the day to be foxed?" he asked coldly, not bothering to disguise his annoyance. If he was fortunate, the pest would take fright and fly away.

"He says I should challenge you and winner take all!" Ogilvie expounded belligerently. "I'm in line to a dukedom, and you are nobody. I can marry Miss Carrington *and* have the bird."

"I suggest you talk to Miss Carrington before making any challenges," Blake said. "I rather imagine she'd have a word or two to say about being thought a prize to be won, especially since you cannot provide the estate she has her heart set on."

Ogilvie hiccupped. "She has an income. We could live anywhere."

"She has a younger brother in need of an aviary. Be a man. Stand up and tell the duke that getting shot won't solve your problems."

"I demand satisfaction!" Bernie smacked his fist on the table so hard that the books jumped. The blow caused him to list to one side.

A footman ran up and caught him before he fell. "I will see him out, sir." He bowed to Blake, then led the inebriated Ogilvie from the room.

The library's other occupants stared briefly, then returned to their books, declining to interfere in what wasn't their business. Perhaps in ducal circles challenges were tossed about for amusement, but here they were a mere annoyance, Blake mused, opening to the passage he'd been committing to memory.

With the information firmly in his head, he left the club, pondering who he could find to build a wheel cipher for him. Even if he could not get his hands on the French code key, he thought Wellesley could use the machine for his own reports.

The late September day had grown considerably

cooler and damper since he'd been outside last. Blake stepped briskly into the breeze, bending and holding his hat to his head as he hurried toward Bond Street. Remembering Quentin's admonition about Ogilvie and Carrington conspiring, he was already on the alert when he heard a shout. Quickly, he glanced up the street in the direction of the warning and saw an ale barrel tumbling directly toward him. And a damned puppy darting in front of it.

A brief image of Jocelyn's horror was all it took to send him dashing into the path of a hundred-and-fifty-pound keg. Scooping the pup from the cobblestones, Blake almost escaped the barrel's path, but he had to twist abruptly to prevent toppling under the wheels of a coach, and his lame leg brought him down.

The wooden keg cracked against his ankle, bounced off a mounting block, and shattered as it hit the corner of a mercantile. Ale spewed across pedestrians, coaches, horses, and Blake's freshly pressed coat.

Grimacing at his ruined clothes and his newly crippled leg, holding the wriggling puppy safe in one arm, he pushed up on his elbow to scan the street from whence the runaway keg had come. The ale wagon had halted at the intersection, causing an immense traffic jam as the driver climbed down to run after his lost barrels. Nothing suspicious in that, except in considering his earlier contretemps with Ogilvie and yesterday's fracas with Carrington. It was hard to pin an accident on no evidence.

The puppy licked his ale-splattered nose.

Cursing, Blake set the foolish animal down. A gash in his boot gave evidence of the damage the keg would have caused had it struck him broad on, as it might have had he not moved so swiftly.

He could have been killed.

Blake distinctly remembered the helpless horror he'd suffered as he'd watched his uncle wash away in a raging current. He had not known the two older Arbuthnot uncles who had died in battle, but the one death was sufficiently emblazoned on his memory.

If he was meant to die, he preferred that it be while performing a task more purposeful than rescuing a puppy. It would appear he might be safer on a battlefield than on the civilized streets of the city.

Someone in the crowd helped him to his feet. A few fellows recognized him, and before long, Blake was assisted back to his rooms, sopping with ale, his foot swollen inside his boot, and a happy puppy trailing at his heels.

He'd either damned well have to start believing Ogilvie was trying to kill him or that he really was cursed.

"It is such a sadness, yes? Your betrothed is wounded and cannot make his vows?"

Jocelyn nearly dropped the length of fabric she was examining at the sound of the snide nasal voice behind her. She considered whipping around and "accidentally" smashing Antoinette with the bolt of linen, but the old habit of caution died hard. She pinned a vacuous smile on her face, turned slightly, and nodded acknowledgment.

In bland tones, she replied, "Blake has only minor injuries. The wedding will go on as planned." At least she hoped Blake's injuries were minor. She'd spent these last days stewing because the blasted man wouldn't let her visit him to find out. His friends had assured her he would be fine.

"Ah, that is excellent," Antoinette replied. "Then you will move the poor boy and his birds back to Chelsea. It is a terrible place, Chelsea, but one must play the hand one is given. There is much to be admired in you, little sister." Antoinette tapped her garish red parasol on Jocelyn's shoulder while examining the shop crowded with wealthy ladies and clerks bustling around them.

Jocelyn noticed her sister-in-law's gown was furbished in ruffles and frills a woman of her age and large bosom should never wear. It was also cut in an indecent manner for daytime, but that was the actress in her.

"You will allow us to come visit when you are settled in?" Antoinette asked.

Jocelyn nearly fell over in astonishment. "You don't like Chelsea, me, or Richard. I can't imagine why you would." Although she recollected her sister-in-law cooing over the Greys on occasion, presumably to agitate Richard. Antoinette's mean streak was more subtle than Harold's.

Antoinette tilted her head in a birdlike manner. "When you are married, you will understand. Your clever husband-to-be, he talks to the birds?"

"There are no birds," Jocelyn replied in irritation, setting down the bolt of linen and edging toward the door. "Ogilvie is all about in his head to think we have the duke's parrot." She escaped the shop, leaving her sister-in-law to frown after her.

What the devil had that been about? Antoinette hadn't even asked for money.

"Dear Blake has never been accident-prone," Lady Montague said worriedly as she stretched a fabric sample across the bay window of the Chelsea house. A workman she'd hired was scrubbing the window on the outside. "I simply cannot fathom how the barrel came loose at just that moment, when he was the only person in its path."

Jocelyn held up the other end of the muslin and did not comment. She'd had nearly a fortnight to ponder the incident without direct information from the main participant beyond his impolite notes concerning Percy's diet.

Upon first hearing of Mr. Montague's encounter with an ale barrel, she'd anxiously planned to visit him, until she'd remembered her betrothed did not like hovering. So she had patiently waited for him to send for her. She would have gone, too, especially after Antoinette's odd inquiries at the dressmaker's, but Blake's brief missives had merely brushed off her concerns and queried Percy's behavior.

Following the example he set of cool distance, Jocelyn had entertained him with solicitous replies, then had their marriage announcement framed and sent to his rooms—just in case he forgot.

"I hope he is healing well?" Jocelyn asked his mother now, hiding her anxiety.

"He is on the mend, all gruff and snarling and working on one of his infernal puzzles, but I have insisted that he not leave Lord Quentin's house until his ankle heals. I am most grateful his friends are looking after him, but really, I wish he had chosen a special license so you could settle down in the countryside, where kegs do not tumble down the street."

Jocelyn knew the folly of believing Blake would be content in the country, but she did not correct Lady Montague, who was paying to repair much of Carrington House simply to keep busy while she fretted over her son. Apparently the lady's superstition about her son's eminent demise extended to assuming marriage would end the curse.

Personally, Jocelyn believed Mr. Montague's determination to court death was more of a problem than any curse—he had stopped a runaway horse with his bare hands and run in front of a full keg of ale to save a *puppy*. He was obviously incapable of thinking of his own safety.

She had heard about her intended's heroics after forcing Mr. Atherton to explain why Blake was sending her a wiggling baby mutt. The poor thing had followed Mr. Montague home after the accident. The creature was all hair and eyes and waggling tail, more terrier than Pomeranian, she thought, and beyond adorable. If Mr. Montague kept sending her gifts like the puppy and kitten, she just might become attached to the impossible man.

She really shouldn't be collecting pets, but how could she refuse such admirable presents? Releasing the muslin once Lady Montague decided it would make suitable curtains, Jocelyn crouched down to tickle the dog she'd named Bitty. During visits over these past weeks, Bitty had christened every floor in Carrington House, marking his territory. Lady Belden had wisely insisted that the puppy stay outside. A maid and a footman had already been hired to tidy up Carrington House after the workmen left. Perhaps she could leave the dog with them. It was a good thing Jocelyn would be moving here before winter set in.

As a married woman. This was Wednesday. The wedding was on Monday.

"Men dislike confinement," she said in answer to Lady Montague's complaints about her son. She really could not argue with the lady who was so generously providing the funds to repair her home.

"I may have insisted that Blake stay at Lord Quentin's until the wedding, but it can hardly be considered confinement," the lady objected. "He has a very large house littered with servants to deliver meals and guard against falling ale kegs. Keeping to his meager rooms would be *confinement*."

Lady Montague was a plump, busy hen who pecked away at her large family until they fell in line or fled. Jocelyn had the urge to hug her, if only because she was so patently oblivious of her effect on her offspring.

She had hoped she and Mr. Montague would have had more time to work things out between them, but she couldn't express her fears in her notes. She needed to see him in person.

Before she and the baroness left Carrington House later that day, Jocelyn took one more look at the newly repaired conservatory to reassure herself that she was doing the right thing. If she had her way, the glass house would soon be filled with lush plants and exotic birds, and Richard would be settled in and happy again. And so would she—

For a fleeting moment, she had a horrifying notion that perhaps someone meant to keep her from returning to Carrington House by murdering Blake, but that was patently ridiculous. She was just overset with worry.

"This is ridiculous!" Blake protested, discovering Atherton blocking the door of his bedchamber in Quentin's town house, preventing his escape. "You cannot keep me here one instant longer! The sprain is nothing." He stomped his foot to prove his point and hid a wince of pain.

"It is not the sprain that worries us." Nick shoved his way inside and closed the door after him. "You're not likely to live until your wedding day at your current rate."

His friends' fear that Blake was incapable of defending himself was more an aggravation than the so-called *accidents*. Quentin had told everyone about Ogilvie's argument with Carrington over the damnable parrot, and the duke's threats to torture him if he lost it.

Blake had not been able to convince his friends that no bird was worth murder. That the incidents had stopped once he was out of public sight had not escaped their notice, however. Still, he detested being cosseted, even by his friends.

"Ogilvie has not only been hunting all over town for you, he's been seen in the company of Carrion while doing so," Atherton warned.

Nick had taken to calling Carrington by that revolting term years ago, after Harold had stolen Acton Penrose's money. Penrose had been a particular friend of Nick's from school, another younger son who had to make his own way. Blake trusted Nick wouldn't let the appellation slip in Miss Carrington's presence. It was very well for family to call the viscount names, but Blake would rather not explain to his bride why outsiders insulted the head of her family.

"You really don't want to be forced into a duel before you bed your bride, do you?" Nick continued, dropping into a wing chair and draping his boots over the arm.

"With Ogilvie?" Blake asked in incredility. "I'd shoot off his fingers before he could aim the pistol. His petty revenge is no reason to keep me from my bride."

"We thought perhaps you were a bit too distracted by the lovely Miss Carrington to believe the accidents might not be accidental," Nick admitted.

"I'm suspicious, not superstitious. I'm not planning on dying before thirty. But if I have to listen to this damned bird any longer, I may have to kill it. I need to get out of here for a few hours."

The maligned parrot glanced up from his perch and muttered, *"Damned parrot,"* before pecking at his feed tray. He looked a little less mangy than he had before his rescue, and with nothing better to do with his time, Blake had taught him not to emit some of his more salty phrases. The creature responded well to bribes of food.

"The physician said you must not put weight on your foot for a full fortnight," Atherton argued. "It won't hurt you to listen to good advice for a change. Your bride will appreciate not having to carry you down the aisle."

His *bride* had weaseled her way so far into his family's affections that they would probably take her in without him. At least he didn't have to worry about another man competing with him for her attention. From the reports he'd received while he was moldering away, she was apparently lavishing the bloody house with her adoration.

So much for seduction, or entertainment of any sort. He'd naught to do but study the French cipher and carve a block of wood into a set of code wheels. In doing so, he realized inking letters into the edge could jumble them in any manner, so his set of wheels wouldn't replicate the French one. Still, it was an intriguing process. Each of the thirty-six wheels were given numbers. One would need to know the order the wheels were inserted on the spindle before decoding the message. Impossible.

He wouldn't go so far as to admit that he missed Jocelyn's attentions. He didn't like women smothering him, after all. But he did miss her soft scents and the potential of soft curves and lusty kisses. He might almost endure her hovering in return for those kisses.

"I have never been so inactive since I broke my leg when I was nine," Blake complained, pacing the room to prove he was no invalid. "I had thought to take Miss Carrington on a picnic."

"Why, to give her one more chance to cry off?" Nick asked cynically, leaning back to grab the code spindle from the desk behind him.

To taste her kisses. And more. Blake had spent weeks lusting for a woman who held his future in her hands.

He was rapidly losing his mind. "I am healthy. I can kick Ogilvie's brains out his ears. I don't need a keeper."

"You'll have one soon enough," Nick said cheerfully, spinning the lettered wheels and studying the jumbled alphabet they created. "She is growing a little anxious, though, so I suppose you might venture out of town to some pastoral idyll with her."

"She'll want me to see the damned house," Blake said, eyeing the parrot and suddenly brightening at the prospect of visiting Chelsea. "I believe I was told there are servants now?"

"And a repaired conservatory," Nick agreed with amusement, following Blake's thoughts as Percy burst into one of his noisy refrains. "The other night your mother entertained my sisters with stories of the restoration. There are beds and fresh linens awaiting your wedding night."

Blake flung a pillow at him, then sat down at his desk to pen a note to his betrothed. Nick was right. Given that he'd become so *accident*-prone lately, the house might never be hers. He must give Miss Carrington one last chance to cry off. And if she did, she could take the mangy parrot with her.

If she didn't wish to cry off, then an intended bride was fair game for seduction.

15

Returning to Lady Belden's home after nest feathering in Chelsea, Jocelyn flipped through the invitations that had arrived in her absence and unfolded a rare note from her intended. She glanced at the sparse words and swore he was worse than Richard. At least Richard's handwriting was more legible.

Picnic tomorrow? Noon. Best, Montague.

Despite his lack of affectionate phrases, he hadn't forgotten her! She'd never been on a picnic. It seemed a trifle silly to be this thrilled over a childish pastime, but she was delighted that he understood and courted her, even though it must seem foolishness to an intellectual gentleman. Besides, she was eager to see that he truly was all right, and that he did not regret their impending nuptials.

She'd spent these last weeks in a stew of guilt, worrying that she'd made a very bad decision, that she'd simply imagined the wonder of his kiss, that she'd talked herself into believing he was an honorable man. And if he really was all that she believed him to be, how could she possibly make up for her deception about her money?

She lifted the kitten he'd given her and rubbed it against her cheek, no more certain of what she should tell him than before.

At a sharp rap on the bedchamber door, her maid opened it.

"There is a lad to see you, miss," Lady Belden's footman intoned with an odd emphasis on *lad*.

"A lad?" Jocelyn asked in puzzlement. "Does he have a card?"

"No, miss, just said as to tell you he's here."

No one but Richard could be so rude. She could imagine her brother saying, "Tell Josie I'm here," then settling into the chair nearest any available book. A thrill of excitement and disbelief shot through her.

But it wasn't possible. How could Richard be here, so far from Norfolk?

With a crashing sense of disaster—and rebellious delight—Jocelyn followed the footman ... to Lady Belden's study, of course. Richard might only be seventeen, but in his head he was sole owner of the world. Normally, Richard avoided people, but Belden House had no library to hide in. Anything resembling a book was in the study—which was always occupied.

Jocelyn knew what to expect before she entered. She'd lived with her brother in any number of different households, so she was well aware of the various reactions people had to his odd behavior. At least Lady Bell wasn't of the hysterical sort.

Jocelyn drew a deep breath, summoned the smile of welcome her brother deserved, and breezed into the study as if the situation were completely natural.

When Richard actually rose from his chair at her entrance, set aside the book on finance he'd been perusing, and awkwardly accepted her hug of greeting, tears filled her eyes.

"Richard, however did you get here?"

"Gerry didn't like Norfolk," he said simply. "Neither do I. So we came here."

Gerry was the servant she'd hired to keep an eye on Richard while she was in London. She had hoped the man might survive the chaos of her sister's household until she'd found a home. Foolish of her. Well, at least he'd delivered her brother safely.

"I think you've grown even skinnier." She patted Richard's rumpled waistcoat and brushed his mop of light brown hair from his brow. Once upon a time she could have leaned her cheek against the top of his head to disguise her sniffles, but he'd shot straight up this past year until he was taller than she was. She didn't feel quite comfortable crying on his shoulder.

"Have I?" He looked down at himself to verify what he would never notice on his own, just as he did not notice her tears.

At seventeen, Richard was tall, gangly, physically clumsy, and, somewhat similar to their mother, detached from the real world in a manner no physician had been able to explain. He did not travel well. His vest and rumpled neckcloth were food-stained, and his boots and breeches appeared as if he'd wallowed in a stable yard.

While he was momentarily distracted checking the size of his waistcoat, Jocelyn turned to her hostess and her man of business. "I beg your pardon, my lady, but I invited my brother for the wedding," she prevaricated, attempting to cover her brother's peculiarity as best as she could, "and I had no word of his arrival until this moment. Lady Belden, may I introduce you to my brother, Richard Carrington. Richard, this is my friend and hostess, the Marchioness of Belden, and her assistant, Mr. Maynard."

She pinched her brother's wrist to remind him of what was expected. With only a slight delay while he worked out her signal, he bowed and parroted, "Pleased to make your acquaintance," as he'd learned to do.

Richard could perform all the social niceties. It simply never occurred to him to do so on his own. He'd been sitting here in the company of his hostess and her employee for at least ten minutes, and Jocelyn knew he had not said a word to either of them.

Since strangers didn't normally barge into her study and pick up a book on finance without greeting or introduction, Lady Bell rightfully looked at both of them with curiosity. "It is good to finally meet you, Mr. Carrington," she said cautiously. "And how is your aviary?"

"Gone now," Richard replied with a scowl that could easily lead to a frantic tantrum if he had time to consider his loss.

"If you don't mind, my lady," Jocelyn said, "I'll take Richard to the back parlor, where we may talk." Grabbing her brother's arm, she steered him to a quiet room, where the reactions of strangers wouldn't disturb him.

What would she do with him until the wedding? She hadn't expected to introduce Richard into her new home until she knew her husband's intentions. If Mr. Montague decided to keep his rooms, she would have sent for Richard immediately. If he decided to stay in Chelsea—she needed to be more cautious.

Her betrothed was to arrive tomorrow to take her on a picnic.

The precipice of disaster loomed closer. Her life had ever been thus.

Fearing that witlessness ran in the family, any suitors she'd had over the years had been scared off by Richard's idiosyncrasies. Mr. Montague didn't seem the fearful sort, but once he saw her brother in a rage or shrinking into a corner and refusing to come out, what would he think? She didn't want to frighten him off.

Or alternatively, perhaps she didn't wish to know if Mr. Montague was as craven as her other suitors had been.

"Where is Gerry?" she asked. She supposed she needed to reward the man for bringing Richard safely to London.

Richard looked around as if he'd just missed his companion. "Gone," was all he reported. "Can we go home now?"

How had he heard that she would soon acquire their former home? She'd been very careful not to raise his hopes. She hadn't even invited her family to the wedding, because her mother hated leaving her books and her half sisters would have complained of the travel— and because the news about Carrington House would have them cackling enough for Richard to hear. Gossip must have reached them despite her precautions.

The black cloud of worry that had been hovering over Jocelyn since she'd first read Richard's cryptic note dissipated, and was replaced with a whole new set of concerns. She considered his demand to go home. Carrington House was his real home. Richard needed familiar surroundings to feel safe. He wouldn't know the new servants, but perhaps . . . Did she dare? She had already cheated Mr. Montague of the funds he was expecting. Once he learned about that, how could he become any more angry?

"Would you mind staying in Chelsea without me?" she asked her brother.

Richard shrugged as if he understood, which he might. He would simply forget the problem a moment later. "You found Percy?" he asked.

Jocelyn almost laughed. Richard could remember birds better than what he ate for lunch. She had told him she'd found the Grey, in hopes it would keep him happy for a while longer.

"Percy is with Mr. Montague, the man I mean to marry."

He looked at her blankly and waited for her to say what he wanted to hear. His obliviousness could be most frustrating at times.

"Everything will be fine shortly," she assured him. "I cannot replace all you've lost, but we can look for new specimens, just as we did when we lived there last." Before their father died, she meant, but that loss still bewildered Richard, so she didn't mention it.

He still looked baffled and unhappy. "I don't know what to do, Josie."

"I know. Sometimes I don't either," she admitted with a sigh, letting down her guard with this one person she trusted. "That's when we just do whatever we must and hope for the best. Have you eaten?"

He frowned. "I don't think so."

"We'll find you something to eat first. Then we'll worry about the next step."

It was a pity all men weren't so easy to maneuver as Richard.

16

On Thursday, Blake steered his father's cabriolet around an oxen cart and sent the horse trotting down the open road toward Chelsea. It was damned good to finally be out of confinement. Autumn had begun painting the leaves, and the carriage hood was required to protect against a brisk wind. But with Miss Carrington by his side, he was inordinately warm. Her smile could heat an empty chamber, and she beamed like sunshine on his dark world.

Seduction was all that had occupied his mind for these past weeks of enforced idleness. He couldn't easily turn off his lascivious thoughts now that she was about to become his bride.

"Lady Belden is quite certain you mean to ravish me, you know," she said with such innocence that Blake knew she had no idea that was exactly what he was inclined to do. "I had to persuade her that you are a gentleman, and my reputation is secure."

"We have a postboy and an open carriage." Both of

which he had intended to lose, but as usual, she was diverting his plans.

She would be his *wife*. It would be his duty to protect her with his life. So he supposed ravishing would be wrong. "I would never do anything to harm you," he added gruffly, cursing his inbred honor.

"Except throttle Percy and shoot my toe in retaliation," she agreed, bursting his bubble with her usual perception. "You have already told me you are not a domesticated man. You do not have to pretend you are what you are not for my sake. Shall we see how the house progresses?"

Perhaps wooing Miss Carrington involved houses and family instead of kisses and gifts. How the hell would he know? Someone really ought to write a textbook on the minds of women.

Blake realized his seduction plans had been anticipated and outmaneuvered by a supposedly naive miss. He didn't know how he felt about that. "We will picnic in the barnyard then, with the pigs and dogs and roosters."

"I like pigs and dogs and roosters," she countered.

"I like books and cigars and Scotch, but that doesn't mean I'll make you endure them." So much for wooing. He was better at irritating.

She tilted her head and regarded him with interest. "That doesn't mean I wouldn't like to try things that you like, although I must admit, cigars sound particularly nasty."

"How do you do that? How do you take everything I say and turn it around so that you seem sweet and appealing, when I know you are simply skewering me?"

For a change, she looked startled, but she recovered admirably. "You don't wish me to be sweet and appealing?" She flapped her thick lashes at him. "Or you dislike being skewered as you skewer everyone else?"

"Now, you intrigue me." And she did. She looked like a flaxen ball of fluff in her ridiculous blue bonnet and nearly see-through muslin gown adorned with bits of silk flower buds. He felt as if he ought to pet her like a kitten and listen to her purr. But the kitten had claws.

He stopped the cart in front of the carriage house and let the postboy handle the horse while he helped her down.

"I am very adaptable." She took his hand and stepped down to the newly mown grass. "But no one has ever called me intriguing. I think I like being mysterious, and I wager you prefer your ladies to be a bit of a puzzle you must conquer. Am I right?"

"I have never conquered a lady," he pointed out as he lifted the hampers from the back of the seat. Apparently Lady Belden's cook had thought to show off her picnicking skills. A delicious aroma of meat pie drifted from her basket.

"Your interest in me is puzzling," Miss Carrington acknowledged. "Aside from the money, of course."

"Apparently I like having my toe shot just as you like being shouted at. Either that, or we make a handsome pair."

She laughed and tripped happily along beside him as he led her to a secluded area out of sight of the house. Admiring the overgrown brambles, she swung in happy circles in a grassy place concealed by shrubbery. Blake had to admit he enjoyed the puzzle she presented almost as much as he admired her lovely figure.

"I have been shouted at a great deal and tend to ignore blustering threats, so I shall settle for being a handsome pair." She untied her hat and let it fall, then tilted her head to smile provocatively at him. "I also like kissing."

A man could resist only so much. Setting down the

hampers, Blake reached for the beauty tempting him. Somewhere in the recesses of his mind, he knew that she wanted something and this was her way of getting it. But he wanted the same, so he was happy to oblige.

She was so slight against him that it was almost like holding a feather, until their mouths met, and passion exploded. Blake sank into the plushness of her lips and breasts and drove his hand into the lovely silver-gold tresses he'd been dying to unravel.

She moaned and crushed closer, enthusiastically wrapping her slender arms around his neck and standing on her toes to better reach him.

The damned woman had no idea how close he was to ravishing her, just as her hostess had warned. He deepened their kiss.

Mr. Montague's masculine scent of bay rum and whiskery skin aroused and tantalized, while his kisses taught Jocelyn the mysteries of desire. A shocking thrill rose in her midsection when his muscled arms lifted her and his mouth took possession.

His tongue hungrily probing at her lips made her actually feel wanted, *needed*, for the first time in her life. She craved more of these heady promises of happiness.

She dug her fingers into his coat and allowed him to pry her lips apart. She was glad for his support when his tongue touched hers. The sizzling thrill caused her to doubt her ability to stand on her own. His broad hands grasped her more tightly. He was to be her *husband*. With the freedom to do this every day—

She gasped when her betrothed abruptly set her feet back on the ground. Covering her tingling lips with her hands, she watched in surprise as he grabbed the checked cloth Cook had used to cover the hamper.

He flicked the cloth open, threw it across the grass, and reached for her again.

She knew she ought to stand firm, but she was still too dizzy to think. She had wanted reassurance, and he was offering it.

Now, she wanted more of his amazing kisses, much, much more. She'd tried to keep her teasing and taunting to a minimum, knowing he was already a smoldering fire ready to burst into flame. But she hadn't counted on her own desires.

She willingly tumbled to the cloth with him, loving the hardness of his pure masculinity as he leaned over to resume their explorations. Recklessly, he nibbled her ear and down her throat, until she was certain she would be consumed. His knee pinned her gown between her legs, and her hips strained upward, aching to press against him.

Heat encompassed her breast through the thin fabric of her bodice where his fingers cupped her. His moan of pleasure aroused her own. She ached. She longed. She desperately needed more....

And she remembered marriage meant babies.

Before her formidable betrothed could take what she so recklessly offered, Jocelyn shoved him off, rolling breathlessly out of his reach. She scrambled to her feet, shook out her skirt with trembling fingers, and tried not to look at the big man lying sprawled on the cloth, propped on his elbows while jabbing his hands into his hair with frustration.

"I want to trust you," she said, crouching down and hiding her blushing cheeks by poking around in the hamper. "I really do. But it would be much easier to trust after we have said vows."

Mr. Montague didn't answer, and Jocelyn steeled herself for a furious male tirade. She had hoped and prayed that if she could cajole him into a reasonable mood, she would find some way of working Richard into the conversation, but that would not be practical now.

"When it comes to women, men are never to be trusted," he finally replied, in a pure male rumble that sent a tingle up her spine.

"Really?" Fascinated, she set out the bottle of wine and glasses Cook had provided and dared look at him again. "Are you saying men are little better than animals? I like animals."

He continued to lie prone on the tablecloth while he gathered his obviously thunderous thoughts. "Thank you for that insight," he grumbled. "Would you care to scratch behind my ears?"

She laughed. She almost fell over laughing. It was such a relief to know that he didn't hate her, and that he could see the lighter side of his dark nature.

He turned on his side to watch her with an odd expression. He was all masculine strength and muscle, a large cat stretching in the sun. She averted her gaze from the powerful play of muscular thighs revealed by tight pantaloons.

Seeing the wine, he grabbed the corkscrew and put his energy into a practical task. "I suppose if you can find amusement in our strange predicament, I can learn tolerance. Some," he admitted reluctantly. "I am not, on the whole, a tolerant man."

She located the wineglasses. "I, on the other hand, am very tolerant and simple. You are doing your best to confuse me and succeeding. I am not accustomed to that."

"You are accustomed to outwitting every man who crosses your path," he argued, popping the cork and pouring the wine. "You may do it with artlessness and beauty, but you use your wiles deliberately. Men can fight with words and fists, but they cannot fight winsome looks."

He thought her beautiful? Jocelyn touched her sorry excuse for a nose and hid her smile of delight. He thought her *beautiful*. And that she could outwit men! Well, maybe she did that a bit. But she would not let his flattery go to her head.

"Men fight women's wiles all the time," she argued. "Viscount Pig was never swayed by tears or pity. I think it may only be gallant gentlemen who are swayed by wiles. Not that I admit to having any," she added hastily.

"Then let us simply say you are a formidable opponent." Mr. Montague lifted his glass to hers in salute.

Fascinated by his perception of her, she finally dared to settle on the ground when he gestured for her to sit opposite where he lay.

"I fear I was spoiled by my father's political salons. I acted as his hostess because my mother would not, but I was only a child. So I curtsied greetings and sang if my father asked it. I was not allowed to speak, but I learned a great deal from listening," she explained, now that they had reached what she hoped was a higher level of understanding.

"Politics," he said in disbelief, as if she'd suggested running nude and strewing feathers through the queen's chambers. "I cannot imagine your interest."

Well, she supposed understanding went only so far.

She tried not to stare too hard at broad shoulders bulging in tight superfine as he rested on one arm, but it was hard to drag her gaze away. She had a vague understanding that normal wedding nights involved sharing a bed and more than kisses. She tried to envision him without his clothes, and her cheeks heated.

It was very difficult staying affixed to her decision to tell him about Richard and the money.

"You are an enticing opponent," he said with amusement when he saw her rosy cheeks. "Food?" he suggested. "I believe I smell a meat pie."

Yes, that's what she meant to do! Entice him with Cook's savory offerings until he was in a good humor and willing to listen. Glad to be offered the opportunity to return to good sense again, she began spreading the wealth from the hamper across the cloth.

"I suppose it is too soon to return Percy to the conservatory?" she asked.

Instead of flirting, they really needed to be talking, but she wasn't much accustomed to serious discussion. When her wiles didn't work, she usually did what she wanted and let the shouting fly over her head. Which inevitably led to those disasters that plagued her path. Really, she ought to learn a better method, but if she was too honest, she was terrified Mr. Montague would call off the wedding.

He nodded while chewing his pie, then took a sip of wine to wash it down. "If nothing else, the bird's curses could chase off the pigs."

Jocelyn hid her delight that *talking* had actually got her one thing that she wanted. She pinched a crust off her pie and flung it to a noisy sparrow. "Shall I send one of Lady Belden's footmen to retrieve Percy?"

And then the servant could bring the parrot and Richard to Chelsea. She would have one small part of her family safe and happy.

"You have to ask?" Mr. Montague said dryly. "The creature raises a racket every time I leave the room."

"I know, but I thank you for not making him into parrot pie. You'll be amazed at how well Percy adapts once he has a home. Why on earth did the duke ever acquire him? I wonder."

"I've never exchanged more than a few words with

His Grace, so I can't say," Blake said with a dismissive wave of his wineglass.

She moved on to the next idle question floating across her mind. "Would you really have shot Mr. Ogilvie in a duel if he hadn't chased after Percy?"

Watching the sparrow bob about, she flung bread crusts, and a squirrel peered from beneath a blackberry bramble, his tail quirking.

"Duels don't necessitate killing." Mr. Montague shrugged and sat up to inspect the dishes she'd set out. "I only meant to terrify Ogilvie and shoot the bird to impress the ladies."

"A little hint," Jocelyn said dryly. "Women most generally do not appreciate violence."

"Men hunt," he declared. "We are nothing if we cannot provide for and protect our families. I cannot promise I won't shoot birds, because I do. Partridges are particularly tasty."

"Fair enough. I can't promise I won't scare the birds from your guns if I have the opportunity," she replied pertly, hiding her trepidation. They truly did hold opposing viewpoints.

That their marriage might be the worst disaster she'd ever willingly entered into loomed ever more certain. Perhaps she did not need to tell Blake of Richard just yet, not until the vows were said and there was no backing out.

17

Jocelyn watched anxiously out the window of Lady Belden's carriage as it pulled up to Carrington House on Friday. Blake had gladly surrendered his house key and Percy to the footman she'd sent to fetch them. He did not have to know that the servant did not go straight to Chelsea with the items, but back to her. She couldn't possibly send Richard out here with only servants to introduce him to his new/old home.

"You and Percy will be in charge until I can move in," she told her brother as the carriage halted and he reached for the door.

She knew better than to expect Richard to compliment the house's newly polished front entrance and trimmed lawn. Still, she was a trifle disappointed when he simply said, "Harold cannot have Percy. He is *ours*."

He leaped out before the steps could be lowered. He was already halfway up the front walk, carrying a whistling Percy, before the postboy could help Jocelyn down.

Having Blake treat her like she was a spun confection all yesterday had been rather intoxicating. She had to remember that *this* was her life—watching out for her brother. His love and trust were all she really needed. She wasn't foolish enough to believe Blake would appreciate her concern.

"This is better than before," Richard said approvingly after touring the conservatory and kitchen. "I wish I could have Africa back."

If Harold had sold Percy after he'd lost the house, might he have done so only recently? In which case, tracking Percy's mate might be possible once she had the time to focus on the search.

"I will ask around and see if we can find Africa. And the cockatiel twins." The rare Australian birds had been ordered especially for Richard's tenth birthday. She still cried when she remembered their special whistle as she entered a room.

Richard nodded in agreement. He did not express emotion well, but she thought it was a happy nod. "I will start building perches," he said.

Jocelyn breathed a sigh of relief. Once Richard was suitably occupied, all would be well. "You must choose your bedchamber while we're here."

"I have already noted appropriate hiding places," he answered.

Of course he had. They'd spent a great deal of their childhood hiding. Before their father's death, their ability to sit quietly out of sight had also made them good at scouting wild birds.

Their experience in making themselves invisible had been useful later, during their years of dodging annoyed brothers-in-law and furious older sisters. They'd lasted about two years with each sister before exasperation had set in and they'd been asked to move on to the next.

They only had three sisters, so now it was Jocelyn's turn. This time, they were staying.

"We won't have a cook until Monday," she warned her brother. "You must be careful with the money I gave you. Don't spend it all on Percy's feed. You must buy food for yourself. There is a very nice pub up the street."

Richard nodded. She knew he was only half hearing her, so she hoped some of what she'd said stayed with him.

She followed Richard around the conservatory as he checked out the dilapidated tables and repaired panes and examined the broken birdcage she had refused to throw out. "I've sent Mama a note asking her to forward your trunk," she added. She'd also sent a note to her half sister in case Mama buried her request in a book and forgot about it. One never knew for certain what information might divert Mama from any appointed task. Many of Richard's oddities replicated their mother's behavior, which was why people often looked askance at Jocelyn. The Byrd-Carrington line was not precisely normal.

"She has reached Charlemagne," Richard said. "Will we have palm trees?"

Jocelyn easily followed the wandering path of his thoughts. "Charlemagne, my, my. So we are of royal lineage. How amazing." And totally useless, but tracing the family genealogy made their mother happy. "I am sure we can find palm trees to buy, but you must be the one to keep them watered. I don't think I can afford a gardener."

"I can do that. My bird books?"

"I will send for all your books. We will build shelves just for them."

Richard turned abruptly and squeezed her in a clumsy hug. "Thank you!"

The times when Richard was comfortable enough to show his appreciation could be counted on one hand. Rejoicing, Jocelyn hugged him back. "I love you, Richie. I promise, we're going to be happy here, and no one will ever take this home away from us!"

As long as she could keep Blake alive for a year.

18

Monday morning, Jocelyn tugged nervously at the slip of lacy veil she wore over her hair. Entering through the church's side door with only Lady Belden and Richard as company, she listened to the silk crepe of her short train rustling across the cold stone floors. She was well versed in what etiquette required of her, but given her lack of experience, she was not so certain about her moral choices.

Which was why she was worrying about silk and not the man waiting for her on the other side of the transept.

Lady Montague had happily agreed with the marchioness that silver was the latest rage in wedding gowns, although Jocelyn thought the silk wasn't very practical. If she did not freeze for lack of underclothing, she'd no doubt have wedding cake staining it before the morning was done. But she loved the little slip of lace threaded with gold ribbons pinned to her hair. It had taken the maid an hour to curl her hair into shiny ringlets. She hoped the result would leave Blake as speechless as he made her.

The priest in Lady Belden's parish had cried the last

of the banns yesterday. Since no one had objected to their marriage—or really, scarcely cared—they were free to perform the ceremony today. Jocelyn was torn between wanting the exchange of vows to be over and wishing she could wait forever.

She had seen her groom only in church since the picnic. She'd held her breath and introduced him to Richard, but they'd done no more than shake hands. Blake hadn't seemed to notice anything amiss with her brother's asking if he liked birds.

Actually, Blake had seemed to be nursing an aching head, probably from bachelor frivolities with his rather intimidating friends. His neckcloth had been a little more askew than usual, and he'd been staring at her bosom more than listening to the sermon after they'd taken their seats. She wasn't certain that he'd paid much better notice when she'd said her brother would give her away, but he couldn't say that she hadn't warned him that Richard had arrived. Surely he understood that meant he would be living with them.

Blake still hadn't told her if he meant to keep his rooms in the city or if he intended to live with her and Richard. She was too nervous to think past the next few minutes.

She jerked her thoughts back to the moment as the door on the south side of the transept opened. A rustle of skirts and chatter warned her that the groom's party was arriving. Jocelyn clutched her bouquet of hothouse roses bound with gold and silver ribbons. She would have the ribbons undone from nervousness if she must stand there much longer.

She took a deep breath as Blake entered, his sharp gaze sweeping the aisle until he found her in the shadows. She thought maybe his wide shoulders relaxed slightly before he turned to escort Frances in. He'd chosen to wear formal black trousers and an elegant gray cutaway coat that she'd been told was a gift from his parents. And he wore his silver vest. She smiled, inordinately pleased that he'd not only remembered the color of her gown but also matched it to make her happy.

Baron Montague had been reluctantly kept from the fall harvest for the occasion. Jocelyn studied him, seeking some resemblance to his youngest son, but Lord Montague was half a head shorter and quite a few stone heavier, with a ring of silver hair. He lacked Blake's straight, square-shouldered posture.

The baron seemed content with the short, stout Lady Montague, though, and led her in with quiet pride.

Jocelyn wished that Blake would someday look upon her that way, but it didn't seem possible.

One of Blake's older brothers attended. He was a little more like Blake, without the silver streak in his dark hair, or the proud, broad-shouldered stance that Blake naturally assumed. Jocelyn had merely sent announcements to her family, knowing they would not come. Her mother was easily confused and did not like being rousted from her studies, and her half sisters would not leave their children to accompany Lady Carrington to see that she arrived safely. Jocelyn was thrilled just to have Richard.

The vicar stood at the altar, gesturing them to come forward. Lady Belden stood up with Jocelyn. Mr. Atherton stood with Blake while his family settled in the pews. Jocelyn thought she'd nibble her nails through her gloves if someone didn't say something soon.

In the light from the rose window, Blake looked more stiff and solemn than usual. Beneath his thick dark hair, his gaze was steady when he met her eyes, but she could read nothing in it. She prayed he did not regret agreeing to this marriage. It was so very *permanent*.

But people married all the time, on far less basis than they were. She tried to stay smiling as the vicar announced matrimony was for the procreation of children and a remedy against sin. She was far more ready for sin than children. The part about *the mutual society, help, and comfort* they were supposed to provide each other was a little dubious as well. Shooting Blake's toe was probably not helpful. Hiding an addled brother might not be comforting. And the *mutual society* might be angry and cold once her groom learned she had no ready cash.

She needed to concentrate on the vicar's words. At the proper phrase, she tapped her brother's shoulder, reminding him to say "I do" and sit down. Richard seemed a bit distracted by his surroundings, but he performed his duty well. As long as he didn't see any pigeons, he'd be fine.

Now that Richard had given her away, Blake captured her hand and held it firmly, as if he had no intention of letting her go. She breathed a little easier. They were two adults with an *understanding*. She was swearing it before God and Church, after all. She had to make it work.

If only there had been time to ask Blake what they would do after the wedding breakfast. Their kisses were lovely, but this was a marriage of convenience. Surely he could not expect more than kisses? She really should have made that clear, but such a topic had been too embarrassing to talk about.

Blake startled Jocelyn out of her reverie by placing an old and lovely band of gold inset with tiny diamonds on her finger. Jocelyn held her breath as the ring slipped over her knuckle, and she fully grasped the reality of this moment. Nervously, she glanced up, and caught the flare of heat in her groom's eyes as he stared at her ... only her. *Oh, my.*

Those whom God hath joined together let no man put asunder were the last words that she actually heard. The vicar prosed on in a monotonous tone for some while after that, but all she could do was look up at Blake looking down at her and hope her knees didn't give out.

The ceremony did not allow for kisses, but Blake's warm gaze and his appropriation of her hand had the same effect. She wasn't entirely aware of how they returned to Lady Belden's house afterward. There was much murmuring between the men, and jostling about, and arranging of carriages and who would walk and who would ride.

She and Blake ended up in Lady Belden's closed coach so Jocelyn's hair wouldn't come undone in the breeze. She was so nervous, she didn't know what to say to him as he sat across from her. She didn't know why he sat across instead of beside her, but she soaked up the view. Her new husband was so very incredibly ... stern and masculine. Overwhelmingly so.

In a few short hours, she would have to go wherever he wanted her to go and do whatever he wanted her to do, and she hardly knew the man.

Blake didn't dare take the seat beside the ethereal goddess he'd just married. Until this moment, he'd convinced himself that Jocelyn was a bit imprudent but self-reliant. Today, she appeared helpless enough to blow away like a piece of dandelion fluff, and so beautiful his heart ached. How did he dare touch her with his rough hands? How could he possibly keep her safe?

He wasn't a sentimental man, Blake reminded himself, straightening his shoulders in the confining coat and trying not to worry about the way his bride fretted at her lower lip. As the coach rumbled on, he attempted to recall Shakespearean quotes on marriage with which to entertain her, but Shakespeare had been a romantic. Or a licentious rogue, depending on how one looked at it. He wrote more of love and romance than marriage.

He felt a right silly fool not being able to make conversation with his own wife. They'd been able to converse easily while discussing business or simply arguing. Maybe he should argue with her.

Not before bedding her. There was the real mountain between them. He desperately wanted her, but the idea of leaving a pregnant wife behind while he went to war gnawed at his conscience. Especially when she looked so delicate that he feared his touch would harm her. It seemed devilish cruel to marry and walk away. He'd never had to concern himself with others before and was apparently very bad at it. But now that he had a bride, devil take it, he had to think about such things.

The coach halted outside Lady Belden's town house, and Jocelyn was the one to break the silence. She leaned forward and placed her hand on his arm. "Did you invite Ogilvie to our wedding breakfast?"

He glanced out the window and saw the duke's nephew and a stranger conversing at the next street corner. He'd not seen the nodcock since the incident at the library club, but Blake had been staying with Quent, and duke's nephews did not visit tradesmen. Something would have to be done about Ogilvie's persistence in demanding the cursed parrot. Surely a wedding had disabused him of any notion that he could have Jocelyn!

Ogilvie was a task he could handle. "I do not threaten to shoot a man and then invite him to break fast with my bride. I'll not let the cur ruin your day."

Before the footman could lower the step, Blake

swung out the door and ventured forth to confront his nemesis. Bernie took alarm at his expression and, nodding farewell to the stranger, vanished around the corner, swinging his walking stick as if he just happened to be passing by.

Deprived of a victim, Blake cursed in frustration and turned to see his bride poking her head from the carriage interior. He offered his hand, and Jocelyn beamed at him as if he were Sir Lancelot.

"I do adore your scowl, sir," she said pertly as she clasped his hand, held up her gossamer skirt, and floated to the walk beside him. "Could you teach me to scowl like that?"

Tension flowed out of him, and with just her ridiculous suggestion, he was himself again. "And have you practice scowling at me? No, thank you. You are the expert at smiling at your enemies until they succumb."

She laughed. "We do make an excellent pair, do we not? Dark and light, scowl and smile, scholarly and untutored."

"Oil and water," he agreed, leading her past a parade of smiling servants into the dining room, where a buffet had been laid out.

Breathing in the heavenly scent of his bride, drinking in the trill of her laughter, Blake was more than famished. He was crippled with lust. Addled beyond all reasoning that this woman was *his*, to do with as he wished.

He groaned as Jocelyn performed the seductive act of peeling off the glove of her left hand to display the gleam of her wedding ring to their guests. The pale fine hairs on her slender arm reminded him that he could have her naked before the day's end. He grabbed a glass of champagne from a passing footman and struggled to keep his thoughts on this moment rather than on those ahead.

"The ring is so lovely, Blake. And feels very heavy." His bride lifted her devastating eyes to him. "I think women ought to be allowed to pin rings through their husband's noses."

He spluttered and nearly lost his champagne at the absurdity of the image and her manner of reminding him that she wasn't thinking romantical thoughts. Only her giggles prevented him from making a total ass of himself.

"Check and checkmate," she murmured, as she had the other day. Offering a sly smile that said she knew what she'd just done to him, she accepted a glass from the servant.

If she'd meant to check his lust, she'd succeeded brilliantly, but he wouldn't let her think she had the upper hand. As Lady Bell lifted her glass of champagne for a wedding toast, Blake caught his bride's elbow and murmured in her ear, "Chess requires strategy, my dear. Royal tennis is your game. And we're at fifteen love."

"I'm better at golf." She stood on her toes and kissed his cheek. "I do believe I've scored a hole in one."

Uneducated, his bride might be, but dull she was not. Blake spent the rest of the reception deciding which piece of the bold wench's wedding gown he would divest her of first.

19

Jocelyn twisted her wedding ring and fought back a burp of champagne. She had perhaps indulged a trifle more than she should have. The daunting man beside her on the carriage seat was only half the reason. The reception had ended, and they were headed into the future, or utter disaster. Which in her case was usually both. She did not know how much longer she could smile and tease and pretend she wasn't terrified.

"It was thoughtful of Lady Belden to lend us her carriage, was it not?" she heard herself saying.

"Either that, or she was anxious to have her house to herself again," Blake said thoughtlessly.

He sat beside her, making her dreadfully aware of his size compared to hers. Or deliciously aware. Her scrambled mind could not quite sort the difference.

It was only a little after noon. There was time to travel any number of places. Could she hope that he would merely deposit her at the house in Chelsea and go on? She really hadn't had any choice except to put

Richard in a carriage and send him back to Percy after the ceremony. She hoped Blake would not mind that they wouldn't be alone. There would be servants, and perhaps visitors come to congratulate them on their nuptials. Really, if he wanted privacy, it would be best for them to go elsewhere.

"Is this the direction to your rooms?" she asked, not daring to express the basis of her nervousness.

Her new husband glanced down at her in surprise. "Why would I take you to that hovel? If you're in such haste to have me pounce on you that you can't wait an hour's ride, we'll have to hire a hotel room."

She gulped. There was an opening she must heed.

"That sounds an excellent idea," she said brightly. "If you must pounce at all," she added. "It is not entirely necessary, you know. The vows finalized the settlements. We could have ices at Gunter's and stroll around, and then you could send me back to Chelsea while you go about your usual manly business."

Blake scowled. She could almost feel the fierceness burn through her lace cap. Well, she'd had to try. Life would be much simpler if they went their separate ways now.

"Are you saying you do not wish to have marital relations?" he growled ominously.

"I'm not entirely certain a house is fair trade for the enormous responsibility of a child I might have to raise alone," she declared. "Alone and with no roof over my head should you die in this next year." The champagne had dangerously loosened her tongue.

"You should have thought of that sooner." Blake crossed his arms and stretched his long legs across the carriage, taking up her space as well as his own. The lovely gray frock coat and satin breeches might give the appearance of civilization, but they did not disguise his manliness. "My father offered the house in hopes I would give him an heir. We took vows declaring fidelity. I have no desire to be celibate. Do you intend to renege on our bargain now?"

Definitely a challenge. Jocelyn finally dared look up at him and felt her soft heart lurch. His fierce expression was much like the one he'd worn when she shot his toe, and she still adored looking at him. There was no accounting for taste. She wanted to kiss his square jaw, tease away the frown, and return the pleased look he occasionally exhibited when she said something with which he agreed.

She knew how to make herself agreeable to men, but sometime over these last months of freedom, she had decided she didn't intend to spend her life making sacrifices for one. "We *agreed* that I would have the house in return for buying your colors." Although she couldn't fulfill her part of the bargain as quickly as he hoped. "I would be far happier if we lived separately until you marched off to war," she said in all honesty.

"No," he replied without hesitation.

Before she could put forth any further argument, her dark and forbidding husband gathered her in his arms, dragged her onto his lap, and proceeded to kiss her until the sheer force of his desire made her more dizzy than the champagne.

At first, Jocelyn simply clung to his shoulders and succumbed to the enchantment of her husband's mouth on hers and of his powerful arms supporting her, while they engaged in a sensual duel of tongues and soft murmurs. Blake's masculine scents provided a headier brew than ale, and she responded with boldness to the muscular hardness enveloping her in safety.

Encouraged by his ardor, she wrestled with his starched neckcloth, while Blake blessed her ear and nape with hungry kisses that made her lower parts hot and tingly.

By the time she could happily stroke her bare fingers over the base of his throat, her gallant gentleman had located the laces at the back of her bodice. She gasped as the silk fell loose. The modiste had insisted the delicate fabric have no bulky undershift. Jocelyn wore only a very thin silk chemise beneath her small corset— daringly naked for her groom's depredations.

At discovering the accessibility of his prize, Blake kissed her in gratitude before lowering his mouth to the upper curve of her breast. She nearly swooned at the heat of his mouth in so intimate a place.

She hadn't been aware the coach had stopped until the door abruptly opened. She didn't have time to rearrange her clothing or cover herself. Blake simply swept her against his chest and carried her out—up the walk to Carrington House.

That's what giving in to a man did to her—she lost track of her intentions. And her dignity also, apparently.

Praying Richard had the sense to stay out of the way cooled her ardor somewhat. With her arms around her husband's neck, and the train of her wedding gown wrapping about his trouser legs, Jocelyn buried her face in his shoulder.

Rather than politely greeting their newly hired servants, Blake carried her past them to the stairs, limping only slightly. She thought the maid and footman bobbed and curtsied properly, but she refused to face anyone while being hauled about like a sack of flour.

"Put me down," she whispered as they reached the steps. "You will break your back or your neck carrying me up."

He snorted most inelegantly while ignoring her admonitions. "I can pin Gentleman Jim to the mat. You are no heavier than a box of books."

A box of books, indeed! She should take umbrage,

but still giddy from his kisses and his strength, she giggled at his unromantic outlook. "Try a box of flowers next time," she suggested, "or lighter than a fairy. More pleasant images, if you please."

A low vibration rumbled in his throat as Blake bumped open the door to the master bedchamber with his shoulder. "'I'll say she looks as clear as morning roses newly washed with dew,'" he quoted, carrying her to a crocheted coverlet and laying her down, before sitting on the bed's edge and pushing off his shoes. "'In thy face I see honor, truth, and loyalty. My heart is ever at your service.'"

Even though she knew he didn't mean a word, that he merely repeated Shakespeare as cynically as he had on the night of the duel, Jocelyn thrilled with the warmth of his deep baritone. Just his voice could excite her. When he leaned over to remove her unfastened gown, he quite possibly incited her to madness.

"It's broad daylight," she protested as he lifted her and tugged until her lovely gown pooled on the floor. She pushed at agile fingers stripping her down to her corset and the thin chemise over her breasts. "The servants will be scandalized."

"And why should I care?" Triumphing over the corset hooks, Blake kissed the curve of her breast again.

Before she could think of a suitable reply, his mouth closed over her nipple, and Jocelyn gasped at the exciting new sensation. A strong tug of desire reawakened her lower parts, and she hastily gripped Blake's biceps in hopes of deterring him. Or herself.

He suckled deeper and fondled her other breast. She squealed with delight. In that moment, if she'd had any hope of a marriage of convenience, she gave it up. She ought to be terrified, but she was thrilled that his kisses wouldn't end now.

Her groom was more powerful and determined than a line of cavalry storming the bastions, whatever bastions were. And he did things to her that undermined her defenses. The moisture of his mouth on her breast was a seductive sin. Jocelyn tried to speak, but Blake stopped her with kisses. Just as she settled into the welcome familiarity of his mouth and tongue, he lifted her breast free of confinement, and caressed the aroused nub.

Her traitorous body arched into his hands. In return, he groaned against her mouth and hastily untied her chemise, until he could fully cradle and caress her breasts. Jocelyn nearly wept with the wonder of his touch. His hands weren't smooth, but tough and hardened, yet still gentle as they explored what was his to take.

"I am no gentleman waiting politely for the night. I think I might explode if I wait," he warned against her lips.

Just the depth of his hunger heated her insides like liquid fire. She could hardly believe a man of the finest quality like Blake could desire someone of her weak fiber in such a way. He made her giddy with hope and terrified her at the same time.

Sun streamed through the open drapery. She covered her bare bosom with her arm when he halted just to gaze upon her nakedness.

Blake's big hand stayed her, and his heated gaze scorched through her middle to the place where she burned for him. "No, I want to see all of you, know all of you. You are the most beautiful prize I have ever won."

The lure of his passionate declaration was strong. No one had ever thought of her as a prize, beautiful or not, but still, she registered a protest for decency. "The draperies are open."

"Do you think someone hangs from the roof to look in?" he asked in amusement.

It was all happening too fast. She didn't know what to think. She hardly even knew what he was doing. She wasn't shy and missish. She'd undressed in front of dozens of maids and modistes and even Lady Belden. But never for a man who touched her flesh as boldly as he did.

"I thought . . . ," she started to say, but he leaned over and swept his tongue over her nipple again, and moisture pooled between her thighs.

"Don't think," he suggested, lifting her and pulling the coverlet off to lay her against the sheets. "Lovemaking isn't for thinking. It's for doing."

There was a philosophy after her own heart.

He stood and finished unwrapping his neckcloth, revealing the full brown column of his throat. Jocelyn scrambled to her knees, determined not to be a passive contender in this battle of wills. Painfully aware that her chemise gaped open, leaving her breasts bare like a wanton's, she wrestled with the buttons of his waistcoat while he struggled from the tight fit of his cutaway.

"You are supposed to have a valet help you with that," she scolded, hiding her shiver of excitement at the way he admired her breasts. "This is what comes of such havey-cavey haste."

He heaved the coat over a chair and adeptly finished the waistcoat buttons. "I do not consider tupping my wife in broad daylight in the least questionable. And if I wished to be hasty, I'd have flipped up your skirts and ravished you in the carriage."

Jocelyn gulped, suddenly aware that she wore nothing except garters and stockings beneath her chemise. She pounded her fist against his shirtfront, refusing to be intimidated by his greater experience. "That is crude, sir. Go back to quoting Shakespeare."

She untied his shirt and tried to tug it from his tight

breeches. She had no earthly idea what she was doing except it seemed unfair that she be the only one undressed.

Blake enveloped her hand in his fist and gently pushed her backward to the bed, so that her bottom met the mattress and she had to hastily unfold her legs, leaving them dangling over the edge—with his rather intimidating size looming over her.

"You'd rather have Shakespeare's words than my own?" Stripped to his shirt and trousers, he studied her recumbent position with satisfaction. Or perhaps her breasts. He seemed to like her overly plump bosom. Jocelyn clapped her arms over her front, and his eyes lit from within at the challenge she presented. Her position was indecent, and she briefly considered pulling her legs to the mattress and rolling to the other side.

But like the idiot she was, she relished having his full attention. She pushed her breasts up with her arm, daring him to take what she offered. He moved closer, crushing the thin silk of her chemise while standing between her knees. He aroused her woman's place to demand a satisfaction she could not envision. Yet. She eyed his button flap with interest. The fabric scarcely seemed sufficient to confine the bulge it concealed.

She forgot his question. So did he, apparently. Parting her knees farther, Blake leaned over to pin her arms to the mattress. Neutralizing her ability to provoke him more, he suckled hard on her breast until she stifled moans of pleasure and gave up any pretense of decency.

"You first," he murmured, trailing kisses down her middle as he shoved the skirt of her chemise up to her waist.

Jocelyn had no idea of his intentions until he stroked her stockings with tantalizing caresses, untied her garters with agile fingers, and eased her thighs apart, then stroked her in a place she scarcely dared touch herself. He held her down when she almost came up off the bed.

Before she knew what he intended, he was kneeling between her thighs, kissing, nibbling, doing all those things that he had done to torment her lips. She bit back a shriek as his tongue swept her . . . there. She needed to sit up, stop him, not let him dangle her knees over his shoulders so he could . . .

Moisture spilled as he suckled at a delicate part. She wasn't certain if her screams were in her head or if she uttered them. His depredations shocked her from her senses, shooting her high into the ether, where she learned true mindlessness and a raging need that must be satisfied. Now.

And her gallant husband obliged, returning to her side to push his fingers deep and caress until she burst apart into a million tiny pieces of Jocelyn and her screams echoed against the bare walls.

Before she could recover her senses and float back to the room, a frantic cry echoed from outside the bedroom. "Jooooossssie!" Heavy feet clumped down the uncarpeted hall, followed by another call. "*Josie*, where are you?"

Jocelyn turned her head and bit the pillow to hold back a sob.

20

Rolling over to trap Jocelyn between his arms, on the brink of *finally* having his way with his audacious, heaven-sent bride, Blake did his best to shut out the uproar rising from the rest of the house. Her cries of ecstasy still rang satisfyingly in his ears. His cock strained eagerly at his buttons, but even though his mind had sunk to his lower parts, he couldn't ignore Jocelyn's inexplicable outburst of tears.

Why was she crying now that he'd given her pleasure? He'd planned this moment with as much care as was possible, given his state of mindless lust.

Uproar. In an empty house. Some of the blood returned to the thinking part of his brain. *Uproar* had yet to equate with danger, not in rural Chelsea. Befuddlement slowed his reactions.

Fists beat against the bedroom door. A parrot shrieked from a distance. A dog yipped in alarm. Glass broke and a maid screamed. A howl of fear accompanied the pounding. Blake wanted to beat something, too, but the only object within reach was his beautiful sobbing bride. Nearly nude and within a hand's reach of being ravished ...

Her tears finally unmanned him. Stunned, he didn't know how to respond to this display of feminine weakness, except to murder whatever had caused her grief. Surely *he* hadn't ...?

Before his wits could completely relocate from lower parts to his head, Jocelyn brushed at her eyes and recovered her aplomb with remarkable rapidity, as if she had practice in controlling bouts of weeping. "I believe you will have to get up now, sir."

"Can't," he muttered, inches from the swirling champagne tresses he'd loosed and had meant to have brushing his skin in another moment or two. Leaning over her, with both hands trapping her on the bed, he listened to judge whether the knocking indicated reason for alarm, but in his bones, he knew who it was. The rest of the cacophony raised his hackles, though. "Give me a few minutes. What's that racket?"

"Percy?" she asked hesitantly.

Blake frowned. Percy did seem to be squawking more than usual. The door began to rattle in the frame. Damned good thing he'd locked it.

"That's not Percy at the door," he argued.

"Ummm, that might be Percy's keeper. If you would move just slightly to your left ..." She wiggled under him, trying to escape.

She was nearly naked. He wasn't close enough for skin contact. He wanted to keep stripping.

The chaos below did not diminish. In fact, the dog howled as if it were being beaten.

"Close your ears. I'm about to swear." Cursing under his breath while Jocelyn stuck her fingers in her ears, Blake shoved up from the bed.

As soon as he started dragging on his waistcoat, Jocelyn sat up and began fastening her fallen chemise with shaking fingers.

Another crash of breaking glass cut off any protest he might make. With shirt gaping, Blake opened the door and caught sight of a skinny back and mop of hair racing down the service stairs, toward the back of the house.

After years as a bachelor, he was not prepared for married life resembling the chaos of war. Perhaps he should acquire a cannon.

Below, Percy broke into a rapid spate of French about wheels of fortune and rogering rakes. Cries and shouts and the decided thud of a blow followed. This time, the warning of peril smothered Blake's lust, and his instincts leaped to the fore. Waistcoat unbuttoned and flapping, still in his stockinged feet, he ran toward the commotion, wishing he had weapons close at hand.

Jocelyn clamped down her fears as her trembling fingers refused to fasten the ties of her chemise. Fearing Blake would keep on running and never return while she wasted time dressing, she hunted for a robe.

He'd turned her world upside down, and she was too shaken to think. What had he *done* to her? Was that what lovemaking was about? It had been wonderful, beautiful, but . . . not quite complete somehow. She didn't have time to ponder like a lovesick fool.

Finding her robe, she gathered it around her and left the room where she'd learned the sweetness of marriage and felt so briefly loved and wanted.

She longed for more of that sweetness with all her heart. But Blake's admiration would not last. She knew the panic-stricken voice at the door had been Richard's. Once Blake realized the turmoil in which she lived, her experience with Harold and her brothers-in-law told her that he would be furious. His resentment would mount and before long, arguing, screaming, and flung objects would ensue.

But this time, *they could not be tossed from their home*. She repeated that reassuring refrain as she hurried down the back stairs.

She arrived in the conservatory to discover Bitty cowering under the bench and Richard racing wildly in circles, clutching Percy's cage while the bird screamed in several languages.

Richard must have spent these last few days repairing the big cage. The last she'd seen of it, it had been left in a crumpled heap on one of the plant tables after a cleaning crew had swept out the debris.

The cause of her brother's panic lay sprawled across the mostly empty stone floor, shaking his head as if to regain his wits. Judging by his clothes, the intruder was a ruffian. A stout stick that Richard may have been carving for perches lay on the floor beside the prone man. That her harmless young brother might have struck a thief shocked her into silence while she tried to reorient herself.

"Mine!" Richard cried frantically at Jocelyn's arrival. "Mine!" Clutching Percy's cage, he whirled in a frenzy, as if searching for hidden enemies.

Looking puzzled, her new husband collared the intruder and jerked him to his feet. He raised his eyebrows in question. Or in expectation of answers. Either way, Blake was not smiling.

He wasn't shouting or pounding Richard into the ground as Harold might have, either. Jocelyn took a deep breath to calm her rattled nerves.

"Richard," she said in the firm voice that sometimes penetrated her brother's panic attacks. "Richard, it is all right. You are scaring Percy."

She crossed the conservatory to break his pattern and force him to acknowledge her presence. "No one is taking Percy," she reminded him soothingly. "Did you stop the ruffian?"

"Tony, bad," Richard shouted, hugging the cage against his thin chest and retreating into simpleness, as he sometimes did when he was frightened.

Tony? Harold often called Antoinette *Tony.* And Richard used to argue with Antoinette whenever she came near the birdcages. There had been a dreadful drama right before Harold had thrown them out, after Richard had discovered Antoinette fiddling with the cages in the middle of the night. But that had been six years ago. Richard must have mixed up something in his head.

Jocelyn glanced nervously at the ruffian but she could not see the connection to their sister-in-law. Bitty had come out of hiding to growl now that Blake held the stranger.

Her little brother was no longer the cherubic toddler she'd cradled when he'd had nightmares. He stood taller and was probably stronger than she. But in his befuddled head, she was still the big sister he trusted. While Blake interrogated the thief—oddly enough, in French—Jocelyn pried the cage from her brother's fingers. She set it on a worktable, then soothed Richard with words. Once he calmed down enough to realize no one would hurt his pet, he sank to a workbench and rocked a muttering Percy while crooning softly.

She was afraid to turn and see if Blake had walked off in disgust. For a few heavenly moments, she'd been an object of desire and had felt as if she might actually have a life with a good man in it.

Blake's furious cry of pain caused her to swing about in alarm.

To her dismay, the thief had sufficiently recovered from his blow to attempt escape. He held a bloody knife in his hand while Blake clutched his wrist. She didn't understand the words, but from Blake's actions, she assumed the Frenchman was ordering him to stand back. Where were the damned servants when she needed them? Probably hiding in the cellar.

Blake's shirtsleeve was soaked with blood. Before Jocelyn could think, or even panic, her ferocious husband kicked the knife from the man's hands, and it skittered across the floor.

Shouting French curses, the ruffian fled the room, running toward the front of the house. Holding his wounded arm, Blake chased after him—in his stockinged feet!

Torn between the need to calm her little brother and assist Blake, Jocelyn could do neither. Aware that she was barefoot and walking on glass, she returned gingerly to the hall in hopes of dragging the maid and footman from their hiding places. The blood drops staining the newly waxed floors caused her heart to rise up in her throat and impede her breathing.

The sound of a horse galloping away warned her that the thief had escaped. Shaking, she stood at the top of the kitchen stairs and shouted at the useless servants to bring bandages and lend a hand. Finally, they came running.

She met Blake at the front door with a basket of medical supplies, hoping to offer some succor in return for his not yelling. She wanted to start off on the right foot.

He scowled, rejecting her offer of aid, and stalked past her toward the conservatory. Too shaken to argue, she followed, leaving the maid to wipe up the blood.

At discovering Richard senselessly rocking a now

quiet parrot, Blake glowered at her, waiting for explanations. As if she had any.

"What happened?" he demanded of her incoherent brother.

Richard shook his head and hugged the parrot cage tighter.

"Did someone harm Percy?" Jocelyn asked, seeing nothing else in the room worth stealing.

Richard reluctantly nodded.

"The thief spoke only French. He refused to say who sent him. Why would he want a parrot?" Blake demanded.

Jocelyn had no answer. "Perhaps Ogilvie sent him to steal the bird back?" She set the basket of bandages down on a bench and waited for her husband to sit so she might dress his wound.

Blake grabbed a cloth and wrapped it around his arm.

Irritated by his rejection, shaken by the emotional and physical upheaval, she fell back on her usual habit of blithely ignoring all conflict. She sat beside Richard and rubbed his arm until he stopped rocking so hard. "Can you tell me what happened?" she asked as gently as she could.

"I hit him," he attested. "I hit him so he could not steal Percy."

"Good job," Blake acknowledged, tying a knot in his makeshift bandage. "I'll have to teach you to fight with your fists so you don't nearly cosh his brains out next time." He nodded to indicate the bloody stick Richard had used on the intruder.

Jocelyn wanted to throw something at him. *Next time!* What did he mean, next time? As if Richard needed to go about punching people. She huffed but bit her tongue. Her heart was still thudding too hard for her to speak coherently.

"Do you think Mr. Ogilvie sent him?" she asked again, not knowing how else to explain a thief stealing a parrot. Or could he have been trying to murder Blake for some reason? She tried not to consider that.

"Ogilvie may have followed your footman the other day when he fetched Percy, then hired someone to break in," Blake acknowledged grudgingly.

Or followed Richard from the reception. Panic clutched at Jocelyn's heart at the notion of anyone attacking her little brother for his silly bird.

Blake continued thinking aloud. "Ogilvie is a little obsessive about the bird. The duke must be leaning on him." He glared at her meaningfully.

But Jocelyn wasn't about to return Richard's pet to a man who hired vicious thieves! She might not always be very clear on what was right or wrong, but she was quite clear on the necessity of taking care of innocent creatures that couldn't defend themselves.

"I suppose we can warn Ogilvie we'll tell the duke what he's done if any harm should ever come to Percy," she suggested.

"That's certain to stop a desperate man," Blake said dryly. "Your brother had better take Percy back to his room until we can find a better way of securing the conservatory."

Relieved that he did not question Richard's behavior more than that, Jocelyn did as she'd been told.

She didn't think it necessary to explain that her brother had probably left the conservatory unattended in the first place because he'd heard her screams of pleasure. That would not only be embarrassing but would also lead to lengthy, unpleasant explanations.

She suspected there would be plenty of those in the next few hours.

It had been a pleasant fantasy, believing she finally

had someone to stand at her side, but the reality was that she had a brother who required constant attention and a husband who was determined to get himself killed.

Once again, she stood alone, and her heart ached.

"Don't!" Blake ordered, entering the bedchamber to discover his bride pulling a plain round gown over her head.

He was frustrated on too many levels to be polite. He needed a horse to chase after the thieving wretch. He needed to send for a magistrate. He needed *explanations*. What the devil was that scene below all about? Why had there been a Frenchman in the house stealing a damned bird? What the devil was wrong with her brother? And what had he done by marrying a woman who apparently accepted this madness as normal?

Jocelyn left her wedding dress on the floor and struggled to pull the day gown into place before he could so much as glimpse the bare flesh above her stockings. He had been granted a glimpse of heaven and was slavering for more. He'd even allowed a thief to go free because he'd been in a hurry to return to his bride. Despite the pain from the knife wound, he was ready to rip off her gown. His lack of control shocked him.

Crossing his arms in a semblance of composure, Blake studied Jocelyn. Her brother's tantrum had not flustered her, but *he* seemed to do so. She was deliberately not facing him, but fumbled with the drawstrings of the morning gown rather than look at him. He had only to think of his own sisters and couldn't bear to berate her. If he could not have what he wanted, he would at least get some explanations.

"What are you not telling me, *Josie*?"

"I had rather hoped we would stay elsewhere for our

honeymoon," she said with forced nonchalance. "I did not think you liked it out here."

"I thought you *preferred* to be in Chelsea," he said with caution, attempting to discover if she objected to his lovemaking or was simply anxious about the intruder.

She sent him a quick glance over her shoulder, and at his scowl, returned to her dressing. "That was generous of you to think of my preferences."

"Are you pacifying me?" he asked. He really couldn't challenge his wife to a duel or a bout in the ring—his usual choices when he had the urge to throttle someone.

"I do that when men scowl. I'm really trying to cure myself of the habit." Finally satisfied that her dress was secure, she shoved strands of hair behind her ears and swung to face him. "I can't do this," she said stiffly, glaring at his bandaged arm.

He'd been interrupted in making love to his wife by a howling adolescent, stabbed by a bird thief, and was damned if he could make any sense of events, and *she* couldn't do this? "Do what?" he asked stupidly.

"I can't watch you bleed and not want to help. I can't watch my troubles become yours. And I bloody well can't keep you alive when you are determined to get killed! You attacked an armed thief while in your bare feet! I want a *home*, a safe home, a place that is mine so the only person I have to care for is Richard. He's all I can manage. I can't do any more! And you are determined to lose my home by getting yourself killed!" His smiling, sweet-voiced bride ended her tirade on a shrill note that would make a fishwife proud.

Below, the door knocker rapped, and a moment later, familiar feminine voices drifted up the stairs. Blake groaned.

Before he could so much as walk out and roar at his

mother to get the hell out, Jocelyn swept past him, head held high, saying carelessly, "I'll dispose of them."

Shocked, Blake watched her sail out like a ship to battle, as if she hadn't just been putty in his hands before all the commotion ensued. What in hell manner of woman had he married?

One who intended to *dispose* of his interfering family? For *his* sake?

Aware he was half undressed and unable to follow her down, he caught only a glimpse of the top of his wife's blond head as she descended the open staircase. He halted at the upper handrail to look below, and sure enough, there was his mother's beribboned bonnet. He heard Agatha and Frances nattering frantically, he trusted in apology. Jocelyn's voice sounded warm and reassuring and very, very firm. He'd like to hear what she was saying, but he had no particular desire for his mother to see him with blood staining his shirt. She would post guards and never leave.

In resignation, he watched Richard emerge from a chamber at the end of the corridor. The boy joined him in leaning over the balustrade to watch the proceedings in the foyer below. Really, he should have known marriage to Jocelyn meant—at the very least—living in a circus. She had mentioned her brother living with them. She had not mentioned Richard was . . . temperamental?

"Percy faring well?" Blake asked with a sense of fatality.

"He has almost stopped plucking out his feathers," Richard said solemnly. "You should visit him. Greys become attached to their companions."

"I don't suppose you know why my family is here?" he asked idly.

That question apparently took some thought. Finally Richard replied, "I don't know."

"Women are a confusing lot," Blake said. To his amazement, the voices below seemed to be saying farewell. "Jocelyn is very good at manipulating people."

Richard nodded. "She takes care of us."

That said it all, Blake decided. That's what she'd been shrieking about. Beneath that vacuous, doll-like look she often hid behind, his wife took care of everyone and everything within her range. The bird, the house, her brother—*him*.

That wouldn't do at all. But *taking care* of him was what she was damned well doing downstairs now. He'd objected to his family, so she was getting rid of them. For him. Because, on her own, she would have welcomed them with open arms and probably invited them to dinner and made a match between Frances and Richard and then given them all kittens for presents.

Cursing at his observation, Blake shoved his hand through his hair and stalked back to the bedroom. He hadn't married to acquire another mother. And she'd made it plain that she hadn't married for more than the house. She'd accommodate him because that's what she did—please people to get what she wanted.

He had the strength and the right to demand marital relations. But demanding her reluctant obedience went against all his principles. He'd deal later with the humiliation of knowing his wife didn't want him, when he had a wall to bash his head against.

Except he damned well couldn't leave Jocelyn alone when knife-wielding bird snatchers were around. So, she considered him another responsibility, a liability to the safe little nest she wanted to create. Outrage welled where lust had been. To hell with women. He had no intention of spending the next thirty years in the same henpecked manner as the last thirty.

He'd lost sight of his purpose for a while, but he

knew from experience that even lust could be conquered if he applied his mind to it. *Money, officer's colors, code, and England.* Priorities. He'd visit the bank in the morning and start the process before he was distracted again.

He didn't have to pack. He'd never removed anything from his rooms except a few of his clothes. *Of course* his wife had thought he hadn't meant to stay.

By the time she returned to their chamber, Blake had tucked in his shirt, donned his waistcoat, and was tugging on his coat.

Jocelyn looked at him with bewilderment. "Where are you going?"

"After notifying the magistrate of the intruder, I'll take the room over the carriage house. Unless you care to give up the parrot, I can't leave you alone. I'll have to give up my rooms in town."

"But . . ." She glanced at the rumpled bed, and Blake felt a tug of despair.

"There are ways to make love without making babies," he told her, hoping that would relieve at least one of her fears. "But I will give you more time," he conceded grudgingly. "In the meantime, I'll endeavor not to drop dead over the next year. In case I do, let me apologize in advance. I believe we agreed on the sum for an ensign's colors. I'll go up to town in the morning and arrange for the papers. Under the terms of the settlement, they'll need your signature agreeing to the expenditure."

She looked so crestfallen, standing there, that Blake was reminded that she was very young. He bent and kissed her cheek, placed his hat on his head, and strode out without farewell.

21

There were ways of making love without making babies.
She really, really didn't want to think about that just
now. Left alone in her wedding chamber, Jocelyn forced
her knees not to buckle and angrily rubbed the moisture from her eyes. He'd given her the most amazing
experience of her life and then just walked out as if it
meant nothing. Her fault. It was always her fault.

After a lifetime of keeping her desperation to herself,
why had she shouted at Blake now? She had so hoped
that she could at least make him like her.

But when would she ever be allowed to do and say as
she wanted, and not what everyone wanted of her? All
she'd sought to do was see that he wasn't bleeding to
death. But the man was so prickly he might as well be a
damned hedgehog.

She'd known this was the way it would be. She couldn't
expect a few minutes of exquisite pleasure to change the
habits of a lifetime. She kicked her beautiful wedding
dress, then picked it up and angrily folded it over a chair.

She wished she knew what precisely had set Blake off—Richard, the intruder, his family, or her shrieking like a banshee.

She would be fine on her own. That's all she'd ever wanted anyway. Throwing back her shoulders, she marched into the hall—after the downstairs door slammed in the wake of her departing groom.

The house was hers—unless the bloody fool got himself killed. He might die of septic poisoning if he did not treat that wound.

If she didn't think about what she'd just done or what might be next, she could simply enjoy the wonder of having a whole entire house of her own—with no sister nagging at her to marry stuffy farmers and no brother-in-law threatening the kittens with a hatchet or Richard with Bedlam.

She took a deep breath of her own fresh air and nearly let despair swamp her again. She'd so hoped Blake actually enjoyed her company. . . .

He didn't even like the company of his own family. She should have invited them to stay instead of her husband.

She didn't need his friendship, she told herself. She could find her own friends.

She swept into the conservatory and admired the large palm that Lady Belden had sent as a wedding gift. Someone had cleaned up the glass and blood and covered the broken panes with boards. Richard had apparently felt safe in letting Percy loose. The Grey had taken a perch among the palm fronds. She whistled at him, and the parrot hopped sideways.

"Ack! Bugger off, looby."

"Oh, and I love you, too, Percy," she countered, holding out a walnut kernel from the covered bowl Richard kept nearby.

Percy whistled like a teakettle in reply.

"He does that to make me come running," Richard said, entering the conservatory behind her. "He must have seen a cook hurrying for a teakettle."

"In the morning I shall start making inquiries about our other birds," she promised.

"A man in the village said he could find them." Richard gathered up his tools and settled on the floor to repair one of the wooden benches. "Did I make Blake go away?"

Jocelyn wished she could comfort her brother with hugs, but she would only be comforting herself.

"No, his family drove him away. For some reason, he resents their interference, and he gets irritated and goes off on his own. I suppose I must send someone out to the carriage house to see that he has a bed and linens."

"He does not mind if I stay here?"

Jocelyn huffed and settled on one of the newly repaired benches. "This is *our* house. He agreed. That is why *he* left."

Richard nodded as if he understood. Or was actually listening. "Bitty piddled in the kitchen again. Cook has threatened to make soup of her."

Of course, listening and responding were not necessarily the same thing in Richard's world. "I'm glad you're here, Richie. You make me happy."

"Birds make you happy," he pointed out. "And kittens. And parties. And Blake."

"Then I must be a very happy person," she said sadly.

Deciding she needed to reassure the cook that the puppy was only marking territory after being terrified, she hurried to the kitchen. It was always easier to be doing than thinking. The world was a daunting place when one thought too hard.

*   *   *

The next morning, with a feeling much like despair, Jocelyn watched her soldier husband ride away. She should have told him that he was wasting his time seeking her nonexistent funds, but she thought it might be better if he worked out some of his rage in a long ride before he confronted her.

Knowing she was a horrible disappointment to him, she had spent the remainder of her wedding day sending over to the carriage house a fresh mattress and linens—and bandages—and hoping Blake would at least join her for supper. He hadn't. She'd sent food over to him instead. He'd not appeared for breakfast, either, and now he rode away without word or explanation.

She knew he would have a few words for her, not pleasant ones, when he returned.

Using a hoe from the shed, Jocelyn chopped at the weeds in the neglected rose garden. She'd only wanted the house, not a husband, she told herself. Except now that she had her home, it was rather lonely with only Richard's conversations to enliven her day.

Worse yet, she'd spent the entire night longing for the lovemaking Blake had only begun to teach her. Could he really turn off his lustful thoughts and desires as if she did not exist? Or did he mean to use her money to find a more satisfactory mistress? If so, he really would be furious when he learned the bank was empty until next year. She shivered in her shoes.

Jocelyn had almost accidentally snapped off the last lingering autumn rose when a familiar "Yoo-hoo" beckoned from the garden gate.

Eager for any company at all, she drew off her gardening gloves and turned to greet Lady Montague. "Good morning," she called, hiding her unbecoming megrims. "I thought you would be off to Shropshire."

"Not without seeing how you are faring." Looking a

little relieved to be welcomed, the baroness enveloped Jocelyn in a cloud of perfume and tugged her to a garden bench. "Marriage is a very large step, and you have no mother here to give you advice. I wish I did not have to leave so soon."

Jocelyn patted her mother-in-law's plump hand. "Your family needs you. You have granddaughters who must miss you. And I confess, I'm quite accustomed to getting along on my own. But it is very kind of you to think of me."

Lady Montague nodded absently, a worry wrinkle settling over her nose. "I saw Blake in town this morning. It seems rather early for newlyweds to be parted. I hope you two did not have a falling out."

Jocelyn forced a smile. "Of course not. You mustn't fret so. He has business in the city, and I wouldn't think of interfering." She'd only contemplated hitting him over the head, trussing him like a thief, and storing him in the cellar for a year.

Lady Montague's frown deepened. "I suppose you were brought up to believe that, dear, but really, despite their many strengths, men cannot be expected to look after themselves."

Jocelyn coughed to cover a laugh. When she recovered, she patted her chest. "Pardon me. A small tickle. But truly, Blake has been taking care of himself for many years. I do not expect him to fall into a decline any time soon."

"Yes, he is quite a force of nature sometimes." The baroness leaned over and plucked the last rose and began shredding its petals. "I have often wondered how my husband and I could have bred so stubborn a creature, but there it is. I believe sheer obstinacy keeps him alive."

"Excuse me?" Jocelyn masked her surprise at that odd declaration. "The man fights duels, races Thoroughbreds, and goes off to foreign wars." And attacks thieves in his stockinged feet, but she thought better of mentioning that. "I rather think it's the grace of God that keeps him alive."

"That, too, which is why we thought he'd make an excellent vicar. The good Lord has saved his life so many times, it must be for a purpose."

To annoy me, would be Jocelyn's guess, but she supposed it was a selfish thought. Not that Blake was any less selfish, fretting his mother with his careless attitude. "I'm sure we all have a purpose. It just isn't necessarily what others expect of us."

"I've accepted that," Lady Montague said with a heavy sigh. "But that does not mean he must go off to deliberately get himself killed. Anyone with a modicum of good sense could see he might solve his silly puzzles right here, without going to war."

"A modicum of good sense might prevent wars in the first place," Jocelyn said. "But I have not seen men exercise such qualities when a good fight will do. You do not think it honorable to defend our country?"

"I lost two brothers to war!" Lady Montague cried in anguish. "Both wore the silver streak in their hair. I am relying on you to keep Blake home, persuade him to the vicarage, where we can watch over him. His clever mind is sufficient force without need of guns."

Jocelyn most heartily agreed with the latter, if not the part about a vicarage, but she did not dare mention that the point was moot. She had no funds left with which to buy his colors. She was simply waiting for the ax to fall when Blake found out.

After speaking with the banker handling Jocelyn's funds, Blake stormed in the direction of his city rooms. He was still too stunned to be coherent.

She had *deceived* him. His lovely, wide-eyed *Carrington* bride had led him to believe she could buy his colors when, in fact, she was practically penniless. How could he have ever believed all that blond innocence hid a character any better than her scapegrace brother's?

He wanted to howl and punch something. Which could also have something to do with the fact that he'd been left unsatisfied on his wedding night. He'd spent a lonely, aching night on a damned cot while his *wife* luxuriated in their bed. Now, of course, her betrayal had turned all hint of lust into bloody-minded anger.

What could she have done with a *thousand pounds*? She'd only been in London half a year, with naught on which to spend her coin but frills and furbelows. Had she somehow poured the money into the house when she'd said his parents were paying for the repairs? Why the devil would she lie to him about that? And what else might she have lied about?

He despised deceit above all else, so why had he married the sister of lying, conniving Carrington? Lust and silver-blond tresses had infected his brain.

He supposed now that he was legally in charge of her funds, he could control Jocelyn's expenditures once her semiannual income arrived, but that wouldn't be until January.

He only had until Christmas to fill the position Wellesley was holding for him. An ensign was the cheapest post he could obtain. How would he find four hundred fifty pounds in three months?

He had the most beddable wife in the world, and he couldn't in all conscience bed her, not if he meant to leave. He was as penniless as he had been before he married. He was no closer to solving the code now than he'd been before. And he was now responsible for a house, a demented brother-in-law, and an obscene parrot. What in hell kind of twisted trap had he fallen into?

The first damned thing on his agenda was to let his rooms go. Carrington House was hardly the center of London, but it was spacious enough to hold his books. He could save his own modest income, although even with the increase his father had granted upon his marriage, his available funds wouldn't pay for an ensign's position.

When Blake reached his rooms, Quent was waiting for him at the top of the stairs.

"What the devil are you doing back in town?" his towering lordship demanded. "You'll owe me a pair of bays at this rate."

"I didn't make that wager. You did." Blake unlocked his door and entered rooms bereft of a screaming parrot and already smelling empty in comparison to Jocelyn's beeswax-polished nest.

"Carrington and Ogilvie had dinner together last night," Quent informed him, heaving his hat at a document-strewn table. "You'd better tell your bride to give back that bird before the vultures start circling."

"I've already been attacked by one of Ogilvie's minions." Although now that his lust-hazed mind had cleared, he wondered if Bernie was capable of speaking French well enough for the thief to understand his orders. He needed to ponder that. Why would a thief be in the conservatory except to steal back the bird?

Blake searched an empty cabinet and found nothing worth serving his guest.

Which made him wonder if Jocelyn had enough funds for food and if her other brother, the demented elder one, would leave her be. Or if they must fight off intruders on a regular basis.

"It's hard to believe the duke would have that much

interest in an obscene bird," Quentin mused, pacing in front of Blake's overflowing desk. "Perhaps His Grace is just punishing his nephew for being a twit."

"Or perhaps there is more to the bird than we know." The moment he said that, Blake wanted to pound his head against the wall for having ignored the obvious. "Percy once belonged to the Carringtons. There is no knowing what's in its beady little brain."

Quentin looked up with interest. "Something a duke would want?"

"Or something His Grace wouldn't want known," Blake concluded grimly. "And that Carrington might know. Ogilvie is in deep if he's playing both sides of the board."

"Unwittingly," Quentin suggested. "You'd best warn His Grace."

Blake snorted. "Even should a duke allow me in his exalted presence, he's likely to laugh in my face if I give him no more than supposition. I'd best get to the bottom of the puzzle first."

Which meant confronting his bewildering wife. Without bedding her. Now there was a challenge he might not be prepared to face.

22

From the garret over the carriage house where she'd gone to ascertain that Blake had everything he needed, Jocelyn watched out the window as an oxcart rolled up the overgrown drive. She had not ordered anything delivered. All her trunks were already here, emptied and stored away. So what was in those towering stacks of crates?

She shook out her dusty skirt and glanced about the room Blake had made his own the night before. She'd had the footman carry over a spare table and chairs this morning, but she wouldn't tear apart a perfectly good study to accommodate the irritating man. If he meant to live in such crude surroundings, he'd have to find his own shelves and desk.

She deliberately blocked out any thought of what Blake was learning from the bankers. She wasn't even entirely certain she'd ever see his face darken her door again. The possibility hurt more than she wanted to admit.

She hurried down the rough ladder to discover what the new arrival meant.

She almost ran straight into her husband as he opened the carriage house door at the same time she shoved at it. Wearing a caped greatcoat against the damp, his hat pulled over his eyes, and his arms full of books, Blake stepped backward at her abrupt appearance.

"Madam?" he said coolly, juggling the books and looking upon her as if she were a mongrel caught rummaging in the trash. "Were you looking for me?"

"Of course not. Why should I?" she responded as haughtily as he, then moved aside so he might enter out of the rain. "I had the servants carry in some furniture, but if you wish to install your books, I fear it must be in the study. There are no shelves out here."

He muttered something irascible and set his stack down on the dirty floor. He glanced about at the large empty space and the stalls that would house only his gelding. "Since we have no carriage, this space is wasted. A pity we cannot afford a carpenter."

His voice dripped scorn, and Jocelyn flinched. He'd been to the bank, of course.

"I am sorry," she said with more defiance than apology. "But Richard is more important than sending you off to war. Now that I've paid off Harold and I'm Richard's legal guardian, my next allotment is yours. Harold was insistent. I had no choice."

Blake took off his hat and shook it to shed the raindrops. "What the devil does Harold have to do with your damned dowry? I thought we disillusioned him of the notion that he had any claim to your income."

"Come in and have some tea before you catch your death of cold. There is no sense talking out here when we have a perfectly good fire in the house."

"Quit mollycoddling me and just tell me what your

damnable brother has done!" he shouted. "I have a cart of books outside getting wet and I detest tea!"

"Of all the irrational . . ." Jocelyn shut up at the fire leaping to Blake's eyes. She had learned long ago that stating her point of view was useless. Really, she didn't know what she'd thought to accomplish by losing her temper and expressing her fears yesterday. Rather than bicker, she pulled her shawl over her head and hurried down the path to the house. If he wanted answers, he'd get them when *she* was warm.

Perhaps walking out was another act of pacifying an angry male, which she'd vowed never to do again—especially since she sent Molly the maid for *coffee* as well as tea, and the footman to help unload the cart. She couldn't help it, she liked being useful. And she hated confrontation. When Blake arrived with his arms full of books, she hurried to unlatch the study door, glancing anxiously at his wrist. No blood stained the bandage.

"The shelves have been dusted and polished," she told him. "I did not disturb anything more than that since I thought you might like to arrange the study to your taste."

"I want to know what Harold has to do with my not being able to buy an officer's colors—*as we agreed*." Still wearing his damp greatcoat and dwarfing the room with his masculine presence, he slammed the volumes onto the desk.

She ought to be terrified of his fury, but oddly, she wasn't. Instead, she hurt for him. And she didn't want to. Richard had to come first.

Jocelyn waved him out of the way so Molly might enter with the tea tray. Teddy, the footman, arrived carrying a crate of books, and she gestured for him to light the coals in the grate. She took several of the volumes off Blake's stack, saw they were in Latin, sighed, and set them on a shelf at random.

Blake shoved the others next to them, coming so close to her that she could smell wet wool and the enticing male scent she recognized as purely his. Desire curled inside her, and she hated that he could make her want his kisses simply by his proximity.

Once the servants had departed, and Blake had shrugged off his wet coat so he didn't look quite so menacing, she poured coffee and handed a cup to him. "Harold threatened to lock Richard in the attic if I did not pay him four hundred pounds in return for signing over the guardianship papers. I saw no other choice."

"You could have told *me*! That was one choice. Hiring a lawyer was another."

"Hitting Harold over the head was still another," she agreed mockingly. "I doubt any of them would have gained me what I wanted. I thought it an excellent bargain. Now Harold may never threaten Richard again."

"Of course he will threaten Richard again. Every time he needs money he'll find a way to challenge any documents held by a *woman*. And you *still* went through with this farce of a marriage, even though you knew I needed the funds now!"

"I *hired* a lawyer. The papers are irrevocable! I'm not a dunderhead," she said, with more anger than she'd intended. "And you will *have* the funds," she protested. "It will just be a little later than anticipated. If Wellesley does not mean to leave until spring, I cannot see the harm."

"The harm will be that he cannot leave a position on his staff open until spring! I will be out on the front lines with all the enlisted men instead of decrypting code behind the lines. If you wish to keep me alive, you might want to consider that."

Blake took another swallow of his coffee and stalked out.

Jocelyn nibbled her fingernail and wondered how she would repair this new catastrophe. She didn't want Blake killed because of her!

Like it or not, she was now responsible for keeping him alive. Measures must be taken. Her shoulders bent beneath the burden of yet one more duty for which she was not qualified.

Blake had crated and carted his entire library by himself, borrowing a cart from one of Quent's businesses in which to haul the boxes. His healing leg protested and his wounded wrist ached as he lugged the books into the study, but it was easier than hauling them into a loft. At least he had the help of his footman's broad back.

He had a *study* and a *footman* and coffee on tea trays, but no damned officer's colors. He wanted to gnash his teeth, but in all fairness, he could not argue with his bride's choice. That she had been smart enough to hire a lawyer and demand an irrevocable custodianship had caught him by surprise. And even he wouldn't want any of his family in the clutches of Viscount Pig, as Harold would always be termed in his mind after hearing Jocelyn's name for him.

Which only made Blake want to howl louder. It was only a day after their wedding and she had *deceived* him already. Yet he'd known all along that she wasn't to be trusted. He had only his blind lust and greed to blame for accepting this arrangement. And his desire to have what was Carrington's, he admitted.

Except, as usual, Carrington had walked off with the money. How did the fat bounder always manage that? Blake was as furious with himself as he was with Jocelyn.

He dropped a crate on the floor, taking satisfaction in the slamming of wood against wood. With his luck, the floor would give way and he'd end up in the kitchen stew pot. What the devil did he do now? Talk to a parrot? Investigating why the duke wanted Percy had made sense in his rage, but he'd lived with the damned bird for weeks and had not heard anything useful out of its mouth except a new French curse or two.

Could he make leaps of assumption and wonder if Percy speaking French and Harold's wife being French had any connection to a French thief? He was grasping at straws if he thought bird-wits were spies. Besides, hadn't Harold sold the bird to the duke?

Blake ran his hand through his already disheveled hair and glared at the empty—polished—shelves. He'd never adapted well to domestication, but he had to admit that an entire room of shelves instead of overflowing tables and stacks of tottering books had appeal. The top of the massive, *polished* mahogany desk would provide more space for his research.

The wine-colored walls . . . He rummaged through one of his boxes and produced the chart of possible alphanumeric equations that could be employed through Jefferson's version of the code wheel. He could pin the chart on the wall where he could view it more easily.

He was rooting through the crate of code books when his young brother-in-law wandered in. Immersed in what he was doing, Blake ignored the lad. Blessedly, Richard made no greeting, but began perusing the shelved titles. When the boy found the crate of wire mind teasers people had given Blake over the years, he settled into a leather chair and began to take them apart.

Blake forgot he was there. Had his own brothers been so silent, he would have thought them dead, but Richard was obviously cut from a different cloth. The fluffy pug-nosed puppy wandered in and fell asleep at Richard's feet.

Blake had all the books shelved, his work organized on the desk, and was sipping the last of a brandy he'd found while packing when Jocelyn reappeared.

By all that was holy, even knowing she was a deceitful minx, Blake couldn't help admiring his wife's stunning loveliness. She still wore her dowdy morning gown, and strands of ivory hair had fallen loose from their pins, but her rose lips begged for kissing, and her lively eyes danced upon taking in the domestic scene.

Something in her expression caused Blake to glance toward Richard. The boy had systematically dismantled all his cleverly designed puzzles and had them spread across the floor. He was studying them as if he could find some new means of putting the jumble back together again.

It had taken grown men *days* to undo just one of those pieces.

The wretched puppy was chasing escaped parts under the chairs. Blake would never find and match all the right pieces and return them to their original state again.

His bride waited with an expression of expectation.

If she waited for him to bellow and shout—Blake shut down that thought. Of course, she thought he would yell and threaten. She had only Viscount Pig as an example. And maybe her brothers-in-law. He'd have to meet the louts someday, but he damned well wasn't following in their footsteps.

"You had a message?" he asked in a tone of irritation he couldn't conceal. He had Venus for a wife, an enormous roof over his head, a place to work in peace, but he still didn't have what he most wanted. Because she'd *lied*. He wasn't certain he'd ever forgive that.

"I thought we might have a bite to eat before we attend Lord Cowper's soiree."

Blake scratched his ear and wondered if his mind

had wandered while she was saying something he hadn't quite caught. "Cowper's soiree?"

"Yes, of course. I accepted the invitation some time ago, and I'm certain that as my husband, you will be welcome. The Cowpers were married only a few years back. The earl is too busy buying estates to be helpful, but Lady Cowper knows everyone. She has been reintroducing me to all my father's old cronies."

"Old cronies?" He would sound like the parrot shortly.

"Lord Melbourne, the Duke of Devonshire, Lord Castlereagh . . ." She waved her hand vaguely as she reeled off the names of some of the most powerful political figures in the country.

"Why would you wish to bother men like that?" he asked warily.

"Originally, I'd hoped they might know to whom Harold had sold Richard's birds, but now I think there might be other ways of obtaining your colors besides money. Knowing people can be very beneficial. It will not hurt, and you cannot bury yourself with books every evening. I have had Teddy lay out your gray coat, but you must be peckish by now. Let us see what Cook has prepared. Richard, go wash up."

"Will you order me to go wash while you're at it?" Blake shoved aside his papers and rose, still staggering under the knowledge that his wife had inside access to the highest realms.

She showed no indication that his looming size intimidated her. She merely smiled and fluttered her lashes outrageously. "Why, I assume a big strong man like you must know whether you're dirty or not. We'll be served in the dining room."

She spun around and slipped away, leaving him to stew or comply, as he would. He'd be damned if he knew what to do about her.

He supposed if they were to live together in some form of peace, he should be polite. He didn't have to take orders from anyone, but she was right, damn her. He was starving—for far more than food. Would he have to seduce the damned woman to get her back in his bed?

Cowper's soiree was another matter entirely. Why the devil should he waste time toadying to a bunch of toplofty aristocrats who had already expressed their disdain for the penniless younger son of a rural baron?

Which was good enough reason to defy them, he supposed.

23

Jocelyn watched her new husband wander the periphery of Cowper's elegant salon, examining the objets d'art.

Blake was the most physically commanding man in the room. Whispering behind their fans, all the ladies remarked upon it. He did not return the favor by admiring their bountiful charms. She selfishly felt relief. She wanted him to notice only *her*. Foolish, she knew, but she wasn't good at lying to herself. She loved having her formidable husband's attention.

Even when it meant he scowled at her, which he was doing now. Her insides fluttered at realizing he knew where she was even when he didn't seem to be watching. Flashing him a smile in return for his glower, she continued her path to her next target, who had finally been abandoned by his sycophants. Blake was an arrogant, intelligent man. He would not tolerate fools, and even she must admit that there were a great many fools present. Aristocracy did not guarantee intelligence. But a prime minister and former chancellor of Oxford could not be a fool.

She approached the elderly Duke of Portland with a fresh glass of his favorite beverage, presenting an elegant curtsy and the glass in the same graceful motion—a trick she'd learned to amuse her father's guests.

"Your Grace, how good it is to see you again. I don't suppose you remember so humble a servant as myself?"

The prime minister snorted in what would have been derision had not his eyes danced with amusement. "Forget such impudence and grace? I think not. Your father's wit is sorely missed."

"'Tis a pity he did not pass it on," she agreed, most solemnly. She waited until he chuckled at her self-deprecation before adding, "But I have found someone who is his intellectual equal. Have you met my husband, Blake Montague, the baron's son?"

She gestured toward the intimidating man bearing down on her as if he meant to heave her over his shoulder.

"Montague, hmm?" The duke perused Blake as he arrived to take his place at her side. "Tipped off the dean's deviant proclivities some years back, did you not?" was the duke's opening volley. "Honor and honesty above personal gain I believe was the refrain when you made the accusation that the dean favored his . . . ahem . . . some students over others?"

Jocelyn hid her interest as Blake scowled—at a *prime minister*! She must apologize to turkeys for comparing her husband's social graces to theirs. His were worse. But he obviously knew how to make a name for himself if a man as busy as the duke knew of him.

"If a man does not have honor, he cannot be called a man," Blake declared, "although in all honesty, had I known I'd be thrown from the university for my actions, I might have been more discreet."

"The righteous outrage of youth," the duke agreed with a nod. "I assume you have gained more caution with age and more sense if you have married Carrington's daughter. She is not of the common cut, but an eminently useful young lady."

Blake bowed as if he agreed, delighting Jocelyn even though she knew it was an act.

"We are newly wed and just learning the extent of each other's charms, Your Grace," Blake said diplomatically.

"I have yet to dissuade him from rejoining Wellesley," Jocelyn purred, seeing one of the duke's ministers approaching and knowing they would soon be dismissed from his company. "Blake is most insistent on returning to the Continent in the spring, once his wound has healed."

Blake's strong grip crushed her elbow at this presumption. He did not understand that a woman could accomplish with a smile what a man could not with words. She had learned that at her father's knee.

The duke looked interested, but the chancellor of the exchequer diverted his attention, and they had to make their bows and move on.

"What the devil are you about?" Blake roared— quietly—in her ear. "You cannot go about airing our differences to men who have no interest in us."

"It is a pity your parents are not political or you would know otherwise. Men in power always have an interest in people who might be of use to them."

"How can *you* know that?" he exclaimed. "I thought you'd been abandoned in Norfolk these past years."

She bobbed a curtsy to her toplofty old friend Lady Jersey but avoided her by turning in the direction of their more congenial hostess, Lady Cowper. "I have known these people since infancy. I played spillikins with Emily before she was a countess, when she was still a Lamb living at Melbourne House. I have run in and out of the parlors of wealthy and powerful families since childhood. My family may have a reputation for eccentricity, but my father knew how to make use of my precocious social talents."

Blake looked appropriately appalled. "Where the devil was your mother? Shouldn't she have been the one catering to his cronies?"

Jocelyn shrugged. "My mother is much like Richard. She prefers staying in her study with her books. As long as Harold wasn't about, we had a very carefree childhood, and I returned the favor by standing in her place as needed."

"What about your older sisters?"

Jocelyn laughed. "Half sisters. I must assume their mother was a stupid cow, for they haven't a brain among them. They were married and gone by the time I was nine."

Lady Cowper enveloped Jocelyn in a cloud of French scent as she and Blake approached to offer their gratitude for the evening. "My dear, it is good to see you back in town. And married! It is so hard to believe! I am delighted you brought your groom!" She turned with interest to Blake, who made his bow.

"My lady, it's a pleasure," he said gruffly.

Jocelyn would like to elbow him into expansiveness, but she understood that was not his nature. He could flourish polite phrases as required. Blake did not lack understanding; he was simply too proud to ask for help or use flattery to obtain it.

She supposed she ought to appreciate his complete lack of deception, but sometimes a little charm and honey opened doors.

"Mr. Montague has the extreme good sense to recognize that I no longer belong in the nursery," Jocelyn told her childhood acquaintance. "But now that he has restored Carrington House to me, I fear he grows bored and looks for new challenges. If I am not careful, he will be off with Wellesley in the spring. I am hoping to find him better occupation."

The countess laughed and eyed Blake's stoic expression with interest. "Ah, new love, I remember it well! We cannot lose you now that you have returned, Jocelyn. Let us apply our minds to finding your husband suitable occupation."

"You are all graciousness, my lady," Blake said stiffly. "But I would not bore you with my interests. My bride is overeager to please. If you will excuse us—" He bowed again and tugged Jocelyn into making her departure.

Giddy with delight at this opportunity to sharpen her skills in her natural habitat and at having escaped the insipid marriage mart set, Jocelyn didn't know whether to spin in happy circles or be irritated that Blake had cut off her fun so soon.

"What was the purpose of that nonsense?" Blake demanded as they stepped into the cool night air and called for their hired carriage. "Could you not renew old acquaintances without humiliating me by letting everyone know that I need a position?"

Jocelyn settled onto the worn velvet squabs and pulled her wrap more snugly around her so Blake did not sit on it when he swung into the narrow seat. In this close confinement, the scent of his shaving soap was enticing enough to make her wish she could lick him, but she must not give in to his kisses again. Not for at least a year. Although his promise that they could indulge without making babies roused an insistent hum of interest that prevented her from thinking clearly. Surely he did not mean to come to her bed tonight. . . .

"Your future is now mine," she reminded him, and herself. "I have a vested interest in keeping you from becoming cannon fodder. If it is Wellesley's staff you crave, these people have the prince's ear and can place you there with merely a word."

Blake's greatcoat rubbed her arm as he ran his hand through his hair. Jocelyn had the urge to smooth the thick locks back again, but she rolled her gloved fingers into fists and resisted. She liked *touching* far more than she ought.

"I appreciate your consideration," he said, although he did not sound grateful. "But I prefer not to ask for favors, and I certainly don't want a wife fussing over me. I will earn my place with my knowledge and abilities, not through the people I know."

"I *know* people, all sorts of people, influential and otherwise. That is my area of expertise." He'd finally reduced her to irritation. "Do not disdain my knowledge, and I will respect yours, whatever it might be. I'm sure there is more to your prowess than fighting drunken duels."

He leaned his glossy black hair against the seat and closed his eyes. "Let us agree on mutual respect and leave it at that."

"You don't respect me," she countered testily, "so don't start pretending you do. You see me as no more than a bank account, one that is currently empty."

She didn't know what had got into her to state things so bluntly. She could practically feel his scowl scorching her hair. She suspected his anger was more because of this . . . awareness . . . between them than because of her words. She doubted she could say anything that would disturb Blake's implacable demeanor, but she had felt the heat of the passion he kept bottled up inside. She had a notion that she could unleash those desires, should she wish to do so.

Not a good idea.

"I do not know what kind of men you have known until now, but do not place me in the category of idiot," he said. "You are a beautiful, desirable woman with the ability to sway men's thoughts with a flutter of an eyelash, and what is worse, you know it. That does not make you knowledgeable of the needs of dukes or politicians. And I refuse to use your wiles as a means to achieve what I want. We had a deal, and you reneged on it. I cannot imagine how we can renegotiate it."

Jocelyn crossed her arms and simmered. No one had ever refused her very obvious charms, or so much as hinted that they might in some way be . . . unethical. That was nonsense. Human nature was what it was. She knew she wasn't beautiful so much as *noticeable*. She designed her gowns and wore her hair and flirted outrageously to achieve that effect.

"You're wrong," she declared. "Men can wield power and authority that I don't possess. I see no harm in using what I *do* have to achieve what I want. That's what you do, only you seem to think your much-vaunted intellect is preferable to my *wiles*. And I disagree. You have apparently spent years attempting to gain colors and failed. If you can explain why you wish to become cannon fodder, then I'll wager I can arrange for one of my father's friends to send you to war." She said this last with mockery.

"I do not wish to enlist as cannon fodder," he protested. "I would much rather keep all my body parts. I simply wish to have access to French codes so I might decipher them. I'm better than most at it, and despite the thickheaded oblivion of the War Office, the war could be won or lost on England's ability to know what the French mean to do next."

"And you can only do that as a member of Wellesley's staff?" she asked, not entirely understanding how such things worked but thrilled that he was willing to discuss them with her. "If all you wish to do is decipher code, why not do so from your study?"

She met his glare with equanimity until he relented and attempted an explanation.

"A department of the Home Office deciphers codes found in diplomatic pouches and the like. They're good at what they do. They don't need me. But the French are far ahead of us in battlefield communication and espionage. They've been using semaphore towers on land for years, while Whitehall dithers over the necessity of following suit. When I was in Portugal, Wellesley's men captured a sophisticated French code that no one on his staff, including me, could decrypt. I have since decided it is an example of an advanced form of cryptology for which I need a machine."

"A code wheel," she said encouragingly, as if she knew what one was.

"I have explained the theory to Wellesley, and he agrees, but the War Office is stuck in feudal times. They refuse to even think about modern gimmickry like Jefferson's code wheel for intelligence communication. They're so hidebound that they still inform the enemy of troop movements by advertising the date new battleships set sail. If I'm to find the key needed to set the wheel spindle, I must have more missives like the ones intercepted when I was in Portugal. Wellesley is more forward-thinking than the stuffed old birds in the War Office, who have yet to realize this is no longer a gentleman's war. The French *beheaded* all their gentlemen. We're up against rabble who fight with tooth and nail now. Those codes are the key to winning."

"Thank you for explaining it to me," she said stiffly, aware that he spoke more out of frustration than in any belief that she could help him. "Most gentlemen would not, and I appreciate your patience."

He slanted a suspicious glare in her direction. "I do not know how to treat you any differently than I would a man."

Jocelyn giggled at the notion of being treated like a man. "That's a lie, unless you're in the habit of kissing men."

He seemed to relax at her foolishness. "Hardly. Although now I think on it, since I'll not be heading for the Continent any time soon, there are other ways I might occupy my time. Having a wife ought to have some benefit," he said in a meaningful manner that shivered her toes.

"It has given you a roof over your head, a stable for your horse, and three hot meals a day," she retorted, knowing where his thoughts had strayed. It heated her all over to know he was still interested in her in *that* way.

"We'll not have three meals a day for long if we have no money," he reminded her.

He didn't slide an arm around her or crush her closer, for which she told herself she was grateful. It was very difficult sitting so near to a man who stirred her desires as no other did—and resist him. Still, she did not object when he lifted her gloved hand and began drawing absentminded circles on the back of it with his fingertips. She needed that tactile connection to keep her thoughts focused on something other than kisses.

"Don't be silly," she said. "The pantry is stocked and the grocer will extend credit until we receive January's income. I am not entirely certain how I will purchase Richard's birds or the trees for the conservatory, but I will think of something."

Blake gripped her hand a little more fiercely. "I have a small income, and now that I've given up my rooms, some funds to spare. I will see you are taken care of. That is what a husband does."

"Not in my world," she said with laughter, although it warmed her even more that he'd said such a thing. "I have gone without for so long that I have developed excellent bartering skills."

Blake groaned. "No bartering, either," he muttered, leaning over her so she could see his face against the darkness.

Before she could argue, he kissed her.

24

After a tedious evening of society, Blake decided he deserved some recompense. His wife had been the most enchanting woman in the room, devil take her deceitful soul. He needed to vent his frustrations, but he could not yell at a woman who was still—despite all his protests—attempting to make a pet lapdog of him.

So he sought the one solace he longed for—her beautiful mouth. Jocelyn's sweet, eager kisses sang songs in Blake's misbegotten soul. His wife had become like a drug in his veins, one he could not resist. He despised weakness and would work to overcome this one—later, when he was less frustrated.

She briefly shoved at his chest—no doubt still peeved at him. But in moments her lace gloves slid around his neck and her light fragrance of lavender enfolded him. He took advantage of her proximity to nibble her earlobe and press kisses down her slender throat until she wriggled closer, nearly sitting on his lap. He loved that, despite all her reservations, she snuggled willingly into his arms.

Even knowing better, Blake still had the urge to carry her to bed. His normally competent wits rang clarion warnings, but her kisses had wiped out the reasons why. He wasn't meant to be a monk. She was his wife. He almost persuaded himself that they'd learn to rub along better once they satisfied their lust.

As the horses jerked to a halt in front of the house, Blake glanced up from ravishing his wife to see the blaze of lamps lit in every window.

Jocelyn peered around him, saw the lights, and nearly climbed over him to reach the door. "Something is wrong!" she declared. "Hurry."

Remembering French intruders with broken heads, Blake kicked open the carriage door, jumped down, and hauled Jocelyn out before a postboy could let down the stairs. He had to grapple for his coin purse to pay the driver while she flew through the gateway and up the walk.

Duty performed, he strode rapidly after Jocelyn. In his experience with his own family, domestic crises were usually resolved without his aid, but perhaps if he settled this one swiftly, his wife might be returned to a receptive mood—

He forgot that pleasant thought upon entering the narrow foyer and cracking his shin on a large wooden crate. He could hear the maid and footman shouting at each other in the back of the house, out of sight. Jocelyn's usually unruffled tones were sharp and anxious in response. But he could not rush forward to end the dispute without falling over a few dozen containers and the unfamiliar woman bent over them, obliviously unpacking books and papers and stacking them across the floor.

Giving up any hope of sweeping Jocelyn off her feet and into bed, Blake politely removed his hat and bowed. "Good evening, madam." He could not be faulted for ending on a questioning note. He was fairly certain he'd never met the woman before.

With strands of long gray hair slipping from beneath a cap that oddly sported a quill tucked into a ribbon, the rail-thin lady studied him for a moment. "Tony's brother is back," she announced before gesturing at an unopened box. "I'm sure it's in that one. If you would be so good?"

She handed him a crowbar.

Before Blake could decide if he was disarming a lunatic, aiding a trespasser, or rescuing someone locked in a box, Jocelyn reappeared. "Mother, what did you say to Richard? He is not anywhere about, and he *promised* he would not leave without me."

Mother? Blake suffered a foreboding that warned him to head for his loft *now*, but proper etiquette had been ingrained in him since birth. He waited expectantly for an introduction.

"I merely told him that Harold boasted he'd sold Africa to the greengrocer in town. He would have found out anyway. We need to remove these crates to the study, where they belong. I think I should like the rose bedroom, if you do not mind. It has a good view of the river in winter." She took the crowbar from Blake and attacked the container she'd ordered him to open.

"You told Richard where to find Africa *at this hour*?" Jocelyn cried.

Blake had had just about enough of being ignored. He grabbed the crowbar and stopped the destruction of the crate. Both women turned to stare at him in bewilderment.

"Lady Carrington?" he asked in a voice heavy with irony.

Jocelyn stepped upon a container between them and flung her arms around his neck. He'd be gratified except he knew she wanted something and that it would be directly opposed to his own desires. But her breasts pressing against his chest had a way of distracting his wits. If this was her method of settling arguments, he might grow used to it.

"I'm so sorry, Blake. I did not mean to immerse you in our family dramas so soon. I'll take care of it, I promise. Shall I have Molly bring you a brandy and light a fire in the study? Please, ignore all this—"

Damn it all! She would never learn he did not want coddling like the rest of her harebrained relations. He cut her off by squeezing her close, stealing a quick kiss, and setting her back on the floor. "I do not want brandy if Richard is missing. Africa is his bird, I take it?"

He refrained from rolling his eyes at the family squabble that ensued—joined by the maid's protests—and applied himself to keeping the crowbar from Lady Carrington, who evidently meant to take squatter's possession of his home by emptying her treasures in the front foyer. And everyone called the lady an *invalid*? He'd hate to see the dowager viscountess in full health then.

Once Blake had sorted through the recriminations and had the story, he assigned the footman to carry the boxes to the carriage house, ordered the maid to douse the lamps, and donned his hat again.

"I'll find Richard. You settle your mother," he told Jocelyn, who looked ready to follow him out the door.

"Richard won't go with you," she said worriedly, twisting her hands. "I'm the one he trusts."

"Then he needs to learn to trust me. You cannot go

out at this hour." He glared sternly at her. "Remember, I told you, I have my uses. And I don't need *coddling.*"

Blake stalked out, and Jocelyn nearly wept in panic. In the past, Richard's wanderings had caused hysterical arguments in every home they'd ever lived in. His disappearances—and the ensuing search and anxiety— were one of the many reasons Harold had threatened to lock him up and her brothers-in-law had thrown them out.

She couldn't be thrown out of this home. Blinking back tears as she repeated that refrain, Jocelyn steadied her shaking fingers on the newel post. This home was *hers.*

And instead of shouting and complaining like the rest of her family, Blake had stepped in to help. She hadn't asked him to accept responsibility for her burdens—he simply had. That raised a very odd sensation in her neglected heart.

She regarded her mother with resignation. "You could have given me some warning, Mother," she said with a sigh. "I thought you were happy with Elizabeth."

"Nonsense, dear, this is home. You've chosen a fine young man, but really, we can't put my papers outside. We've always kept them in the study. If you'll help—"

"No, Mother, the study is Blake's. He does important work there. We'll figure out something in the morning. Did they carry your trunks to the rose bedroom? Let's see if they've been unpacked. How was your journey? You look well."

With each sentence or question, she steered her mother away from the crates and up the stairs. She desperately wished to go in search of Richard, but Blake was right—again. Even a simple village could be dangerous at this late hour. She prayed Richard was safe and would not hide if he saw Blake coming.

She settled her mother in the rose bedroom at the back of the house, had Molly bring up hot tea and start a fire in the grate, while listening for the sound of Blake and Richard returning. She didn't know how many nights she'd spent fretting over her brother while soothing her mother or sisters. It felt extremely odd to have someone sharing the responsibility that had been solely hers these last six years, and longer.

"It is very hard to trace Charlemagne's origins," Lady Carrington complained, settling into bed with her tea tray. "It is quite unfair that Tony's brother might come and go from France when I am the one who must talk with scholars there."

Antoinette's brother was French and probably had not visited in years. With a war going on, a journey back in time would be just as likely as one to France, but Jocelyn bit back a retort. At least she understood her mother. Lady Carrington was a historian who took comfort in a past of medieval courts and kings. Would Blake comprehend her mother's peculiarity?

Jocelyn could appreciate that dealing with family eccentricities might make Blake cynical, but her case was the exact opposite of his. While the Montagues huddled together, chirruping sympathetically to one another over any disaster, the Carringtons followed their own independent interests to the exclusion of all else, including one another.

She'd unwittingly followed that familiar path when she'd paid off Harold without consulting Blake. In her experience, trusting others was a road to ruin. How would she ever explain that to her white knight? Or learn to change her ways?

If Blake would just bring Richard safely home and not threaten to throw her out on her ear, she would figure it out.

Blake returned in the wee hours of the morning with a weeping Richard and no parrot. If he hadn't suspected something wasn't quite right about the boy before, he knew it now, although he could not quite analyze the difficulty. He just knew no normal lad of seventeen would ingeniously determine the best way of breaking into the greengrocer's at midnight without causing alarm, then do nothing more than wander about, calling loudly for a bird.

It had taken powers of persuasion Blake had not known he'd possessed to prevent the grocer from waking the magistrate, and to convince Richard to come home. Having to leave the bird behind once it had been discovered had compounded the difficulty.

As Blake guided Richard into the now empty foyer, the sight of Jocelyn asleep in one of the ancient chairs in the front room added to Blake's aggravation. Rationally, he understood that none of this situation was her fault. He would like nothing better than to shake every member of the Carrington family until what little wits they possessed fell out their ears for leaving Jocelyn, their next to youngest, to deal with her addlepated brother and mother.

But in every other way, Blake was reduced to the towering fury of a tantrum-throwing toddler. His life was meant to be sane. Orderly. Following the path of intellectual pursuits. Cryptology appealed to him because it made perfectly logical sense.

People didn't.

"You made Jocelyn cry," he scolded Richard. "You promised you would stay home, and you scared her when you weren't here. I don't want you to do that again, do you understand?"

Richard nodded miserably, although Blake suspected the boy did not fully comprehend and might not even remember in the morning. He needed to have a little talk with his *wife* about Richard's limitations.

"Go up to your room. We'll talk about Africa in the morning."

This time, Richard nodded a little more eagerly. As the lad hurried for the stairs, Blake sighed and turned to his sleeping bride. She hadn't changed out of her elegant evening gown, but her hair was tumbling from its pins, and red creases marred her cheek where it had been pressed into the rough fabric of the chair.

He turned the lamp down to its lowest setting, placed it on a stand so he could see the stairs, then lifted Jocelyn into his arms. She stirred and snuggled close to his chest, murmuring, *"Richard?"*

"He's safe," Blake assured her.

That was apparently all she needed to hear before curling up against him and falling back to sleep. Blake had to wonder how exhausted she must be to sleep so heavily no matter where she lay. The second day of their marriage had admittedly been wearying. He couldn't take advantage of her exhaustion.

He had to keep reminding himself that behind his wife's delicate beauty lurked a deceptive mind. He shouldn't feel sorry for her. Instead, he was wondering just what kind of life she must have had with a dotty mother, a felonious older brother, three apparent harpies for sisters, and a younger brother with wits to let.

That didn't mean he had to encourage her deceptive practices or allow her to work her sticky web around him. He had a purpose that ran counter to hers.

Carrying his sleeping beauty up the stairs, he nearly

tripped over a wandering kitten, came down hard on his weak leg, and cursed before righting himself again. He ought to be awarded medals for surviving the combat zone he now called home.

He wasn't thirty yet. There was still time to get himself killed by kittens, stairs, and French thieves before his next birthday.

25

Jocelyn woke with her corset crushed into her breast and a man's heavy arm around her waist. She inhaled sharply and went from groggy to wide awake in an instant.

Beneath the covers pulled up to her shoulders, she was still wearing her evening gown, although it and the corset had been loosened, exposing a scandalous amount of bosom. She squirmed, and the arm at her waist tightened.

"Don't move. I'm not awake yet," Blake grumbled from behind her.

"Then you need to do a better job of unfastening me," she countered, wriggling to adjust the corset stay that was cutting into her flesh.

A male hand instantly tugged at her back laces, loosening them before she could scarce take a breath at his audacity.

"You found Richard," she said, seeking confirmation

that she had not dreamed hearing him last night. Or dreamed of being carried up the steps.

"And we need to waylay him before he attempts to sneak out again this morning."

The hand around her waist slid upward, pushing aside silk and loosened stays to locate her breast, clothed only in frail linen. Jocelyn suffered unseemly urges as her husband's fingers found her nipple. She shifted in discomposure, not knowing how to deal with the physical needs he aroused.

"Then shouldn't we be getting up?" she asked testily.

"I am," he mumbled, pulling her closer.

He was wearing only breeches. Her nearly bare back pressed into Blake's bare chest, and Jocelyn swallowed hard at the intimate contact. The bulge pressing against her bottom added to her alarm.

"No time," she stated flatly, pulling away from the fascinating shelter of his arms and throwing back the covers to let the morning air cool them.

He rolled over and buried his face in a pillow after she slid from his grasp. "I cannot take much more of this."

She tumbled from the bed before her husband decided to assert his marital rights. He had every legal and moral right to do so, she knew. It was just a matter of time before he claimed her. And she wanted him to show her more of the pleasure he'd taught her. But in her experience, pleasure seldom lasted long and usually ended in disaster. She had better things to do than tempt fate.

She wanted to resent Blake for breaking her happy bubble of believing he despised her and would be delighted to live elsewhere. But if she was honest with herself, she knew Blake had never hidden his intentions. She had known from that first kiss that he was a man of passion. And her heart fluttered at the thought of having a *real* marriage, one that involved kisses and caresses and more. If only she could believe in happiness . . .

Retreating behind a dressing screen, Jocelyn shed her crushed gown, washed, and tugged on a simple morning dress with drawstrings instead of hooks. She hadn't dared take on the expense of a personal maid. Molly had helped fasten her hooks last night, but the housemaid had more important duties, like stoking fires in the morning.

Now that her mother was here, they could help each other dress, as before.

Or—Blake could help her.

The images of such intimacy shivered Jocelyn down to her toes, so she mentally shut them out. She tugged on stockings, tied garters, and listened to her husband grumble and the bedpost squeak as he rolled out.

She hadn't braided her hair last night. Blake must have removed the pins because it tumbled in heavy lengths down her back. She hastily rolled it around her hand and pinned it to the back of her head, covering the mess with a cap.

Taking a deep breath, she dared step from behind the screen.

Silhouetted against the dawn light coming through the lacy curtains, Blake stood bare-chested and rumpled. A river of dark hair flowed down his broad torso to his partially unfastened breeches. He was all magnificent male animal, glaring at her blearily while rubbing his whiskered jaw.

She gulped, but before she had a chance to escape, he strode around the bed and ripped the cap off her head, flinging it to the dressing table, and bringing all that raw masculinity entirely too close for comfort.

"Why do women hide their hair?" He yanked out her

pins until the tresses tumbled to her waist again. "You were gifted with all this glory and you hide it under abominable gewgaws. I'll never understand."

Before she could even think of a stunned reply, he dragged her into his arms and kissed her.

It was a kiss of possession. One that laid claim to her soul and warned he would not be put off much longer. It was a kiss that weakened her knees and her will and would have her pulling him down on the bed if she did not have the nagging reminder of family impressed upon her brain.

She pushed free, her palms encountering broad, muscled flesh and freezing there for just a moment before she could step away.

She couldn't meet his eyes. "There are things I—"

He grabbed a clump of her hair, preventing her from fleeing, while reaching for a brush on the dressing table. "Let me braid it until your maid can see to it. I told Richard we will speak properly to the grocer this morning about Africa, so I suppose we must be ready, or like a child on Boxing Day, he will be anxiously wandering the halls."

Jocelyn sighed, gave up her fretting, and succumbed to the pleasure of Blake running the bristles through snarls and tangles, gently working them loose. "Richard is not entirely a child," she said. "He's simply been allowed to behave like one since it's easier than dealing with his hysteria. He's capable of quite complex thought."

"He put all my puzzles back together, so I gathered that last part," Blake said dryly. "Do the physicians know what's wrong with him?"

His strong hands holding her steady while gently teasing her tresses apart distracted her thinking no end. She kept waiting for his fingers to stray— She caught her breath imagining his hands on her breasts and tried to stay with the conversation.

"My father called in the best physicians when it became apparent Richard was not normal. Their treatments only made him worse. He is not a moron, as Harold calls him. He can learn and probably knows more than all of us put together. He just does not do well with people."

"Does he analyze numbers and letters as well? I may give him the wheel and let him work out the cipher." He gently massaged her head as if he needed to be *doing* while thinking.

"He is obsessed with birds," Jocelyn said with a sigh of pleasure at his stroking. "He has written scientific treatises on the behavior of wild water fowl, then pitched a fit and shut himself in a wardrobe after we've removed chicken eggs from under his pillow. His interest in your puzzles is surprising, but he'll read anything set before him until his birds distract him. I cannot predict what will arouse his curiosity."

Blake's hands on her acted as a catharsis for all the fears locked up inside her. It was a relief to finally speak of her brother's troubles to someone who was not shouting to have Richard locked in an attic like a madman. "His behavior was much more amenable when we lived here."

"Stability," Blake suggested. "He lived here all his life and knew what to expect from one day to the next."

Jocelyn nodded. "Most likely. We've moved from house to house since then, and he does not adapt well. He needs his birds as you need your books."

She waited, holding her breath as Blake silently and expertly parted her hair while pondering her conclusions. His strong hands sensually worked the brush through the long strands, stimulating longings she feared to acknowledge. He caressed her hair, pulling it through his fingers before pinning it, showing that his thoughts were not all on the problem at hand.

He was a man of many talents. With four sisters. She could imagine him as a youth straightening out his siblings' ribbons before their nanny yelled at them. He was a man who knew how to take care of whatever needed doing.

If she allowed herself to believe in good fortune, he was the man she'd searched for all her life. The one she hadn't believed existed.

She couldn't allow him to go off to war. Wellesley would simply have to find another officer. If she was to have babies, she needed a husband at home. Fair was fair. Perhaps they could negotiate a new deal. Not that she had learned to speak her thoughts aloud yet. She was too accustomed to being laughed at and ignored. She needed to find just the right presentation.

After braiding a length of hair, Blake finally spoke. "I saw Africa last night, when I was prying Richard out of the greengrocer's. The bird is nearly identical to Percy. If we buy back Africa, it might confuse Ogilvie and his thieves to find two similar birds."

Caught by surprise at this response so wildly divergent from her own, Jocelyn coughed to hide her laugh. Here she'd been thinking romantic, sentimental thoughts while he'd been plotting against Ogilvie! In this instance, she heartily approved.

"Perhaps it would be better if I went to His Grace and offered to buy Percy," she offered. "Then he might leave poor Mr. Ogilvie alone."

"It would be simpler to send 'round a note. The duke is a busy man." He tugged her braid. "And your wiles will not work on him. He is not like simpleminded Bernie."

Jocelyn scowled but conceded the point. "I have no

idea how much a parrot costs," she warned. "And if you use your money to buy him, it will be months before I can repay you."

"Your money is mine, remember? Save your wiles for wooing me."

She elbowed him, but that was akin to punching a solid wall. Blake didn't even grunt. He released her after he finished tying her ribbon.

By the time he was done, her skin felt hot, her heart raced, and her thoughts tumbled. After his declaration that he wished to be wooed for his money, she felt like Richard, needing the reassurance of familiarity. Woo her husband, instead of the other way around? It was too much to consider.

Unable to speak, she left the room, closing the door quietly after her. She might explode if she tried to decipher all her conflicting emotions. Much better that she find a practical activity.

The greengrocer would not sell the blasted parrot.

Blake watched in frustration as Richard stood beneath the cage hung high on the ceiling, whistling to the pathetic creature bobbing its molting gray head. In daylight, Africa looked even more pitiful than Percy had when Jocelyn stole him.

"It's the lad's pet," Blake tried explaining. "As I understand it, birds mate for life, and this one is pining for her mate." He doubted if he'd said anything more asinine in his life. The things a man would do to persuade a woman into his bed!

Just remembering Jocelyn in his bed this morning, all warm and sleep-tousled and available, was not conducive to his sanity. To hell with being honorable. He wanted a wife.

The stout, balding grocer shook his head in refusal.

"My customers like the creature. The boy already has one bird. He don't need another."

A month ago, Blake would have agreed. Before Jocelyn had smashed into his life, he would have scorned the wretched creature. At least this bird wasn't spouting obscenities, but its unhappy whistles were almost worse.

But now—he'd seen how Percy had grown healthier and happier simply from a little attention and proper care. Even Richard was looking less skeletal and sallow, although whether that was from better care or happiness at being back home wasn't easily discerned. Still, it was obvious that all creatures needed love and care to flourish.

Besides, wasn't the bird's health and the lad's happiness more important than the few extra coins the bird might draw? Given the size of the grocer's paunch and the value of his silver buttons, the man wasn't on the brink of starvation.

"I'm offering enough to cover any loss of business," Blake asserted. "You can find a less expensive bird and make a profit on the deal."

"Nope, they like this 'un. It does tricks and sings."

At the moment, Africa was hanging upside down and muttering.

He wanted Jocelyn back in his bed tonight. He was pretty damned certain that recovering the bird for her brother would do the trick. Courting her didn't work. Making her family happy did. And aggravating this smug bastard in the process would add to the pleasure.

Stealing the bird back was becoming a temptation, if straightforward bargaining and honesty didn't work.

"Come along, Richard. We'll go to the river and look for swans." In disgust that he couldn't accomplish this one thing for the woman who was driving him mad with lust, Blake turned on his heel and started for the door.

Richard didn't follow. He'd climbed up on a flour barrel and was now unhooking the cage, as if he'd been granted possession. Africa flapped her wings and emitted cooing sounds that sounded incredibly like encouragement.

"Richard, you can't take Africa with you."

"Won't," Richard responded promptly. "I'll stay right here." To prove his point, he sat on the barrel, wrapped the cage in his arms, and, whistling happily, rocked back and forth. Africa pecked Richard on the nose as if kissing him.

The greengrocer turned purple with rage.

Blake nearly laughed aloud at how easy it was to manipulate one stubborn old man. Maybe—just maybe—Jocelyn had a point. People were not necessarily swayed by logic and reason.

"Fine, then, old chap," Blake said cheerfully. "Come along home at lunchtime or your sister will come looking for you."

"All right." Richard nodded agreement, pushing a walnut kernel through the cage bars.

"You can't leave the nodcock here!" the grocer shouted. "He'll drive off my customers!"

"He won't leave without the bird," Blake said with a shrug.

"I'll call the magistrate, I will!"

Blake polished a button on his coat before reaching for the door. "Good luck with that. I'll send his sister down later. She has an affinity for useless creatures."

He stared up at the ceiling and whistled, as if just realizing something, which in a way he had. His eminently social, clever wife would know precisely the best way to approach his plan. "I daresay she knows a lot of your customers. Used to live here, you know. Wonder what she'll say when she learns you won't let her little brother have his pet. Send word to Carrington House if you change your mind. I think my offer for the bird may have been too generous, after all."

He strode out, leaving the grocer shouting and cursing.

26

After Blake had returned and explained his newly hatched plot, one that so eminently suited her gregarious nature, Jocelyn had been thrilled by the excuse to visit all their neighbors. Raising a crowd of mothers and children to save a pet was hardly difficult. She was even more thrilled that Blake understood how her social skills could do what his keen mind could not. There was hope for the man yet.

Laughing in delight, Jocelyn watched the neighborhood women and children crush into the grocer's shop and gather around Richard and Africa to watch the bird do a parrot dance to the tune Richard whistled. Unmindful of the crowd, concentrating on his beloved pet, Richard looked as if he were in heaven. All the mamas nodded in approval at his bird training abilities and agreed that the bird belonged with the lad. The children cheered him on.

As the tide turned against him, the grocer scowled even blacker than Blake on a bad day. Jocelyn threw him a cheerful smile. "It is so very kind of you to return Richard's pet," she called over the mob.

The grocer muttered something she thankfully couldn't hear. "Come along, Richard, we must take Africa home. Then we'll look for a lovely pair of canaries for Mr. White, shall we?" She gestured for Richard to cover the cage with the linen she'd brought, then called to the grocer again, "This is incredibly kind of you, Mr. White! Thank you so much for looking after Richard's bird for him."

Then, without paying the man a penny, she took Richard's arm and stepped into the brisk autumn day. A few of the children followed, hoping to hear more of Africa's nonsense, but the bird had wisely shut up.

Two birds and her home back. This was beginning to look like the start of a very happy life. And she owed it all to her brilliant husband.

Whoever would have thought the arrogant, insulting Blake Montague would enjoy thwarting a greedy grocer for the sake of her younger brother? She really must not be so hasty in passing judgment from now on.

She arrived home to an oddly silent house. Bitty wasn't chasing the kitten. Molly and Teddy weren't flirting or fighting in the back hall. Blake wasn't shouting at her mother for scattering her genealogy books across the parlor. Her mother . . .

Where was Lady Carrington?

Watching Richard murmur to Africa while carrying the Grey back to the conservatory and Percy, Jocelyn stood in the corridor and listened. And heard nothing. A house filled with people and pets ought to give some evidence as to their presence. She'd been gone only a few hours. What could they be about?

She tiptoed down the dimly lit corridor and pressed open the study door. Within, her mother had covered every inch of the carpet with her family tree charts. Teetering stacks of books lined the edges of the floor. Engrossed in her research, Lady Carrington sat inelegantly in the window seat, furiously marking up documents, leaving a trail of ink across her person as well as the paper.

Terrified that the hero of the hour may have fled for the Continent in a fit of pique for being banished from his study, or in search of more peace than he'd find in his own home, Jocelyn hurried toward the conservatory, aiming for the exit to the carriage house.

"Africa knows!" Percy squawked when she entered. He bobbed happily on the one tree in the room.

"E pluribus unum," Africa sang, nuzzling the mate she hadn't seen in months. "Seventeen seventy-six."

Shaking her head at their nonsense, lifting her skirts off the stone floor, Jocelyn started across the room until she realized Richard wasn't inside the conservatory, but outside. She stared out the glass panes, trying to make sense of the odd scene in the backyard.

Blake sat on an old garden bench, feeding kitchen scraps to a feral pig, while Richard scattered corn to the flock of abandoned hens, and Bitty raced through the weeds, yapping after rabbits.

Blake had on a shapeless tweed coat and a cap against the October breeze, instead of his usual elegant attire. Was he wearing a disguise? Was he attempting to tell her something? She wasn't much at puzzle solving. She'd rather he just said what he wanted.

Jocelyn hurried outside. The pig and chickens scampered the instant she appeared, but Bitty ran up to be cuddled. Jocelyn happily obliged.

"We'll need a better fence to hold them," Blake said as Richard started after the fleeing creatures. "They'll be back."

"I thought you hated pigs." Suspicious, Jocelyn nuzzled Bitty's head while taking the seat beside her husband. "And why is Mother in your study while you're out here?"

"It's too cold in the carriage house for her. I'm accustomed to the cold, so I can work out there. And pigs make good bacon."

She elbowed his arm. "You'll not make bacon out of pet pigs. I won't allow it. And Richard will come after you with a pitchfork if you eat his chickens, so don't even think of it. You might smuggle an egg or two upon occasion, especially if he's occupied with the parrots, but I wouldn't set my heart on custard."

"I've married into a family of crackbrains." He leaned back against the bench and sprawled his boots across the barren kitchen garden, apparently unconcerned. "What did the parrot cost us?"

"Nothing," she said, pleased. "Or a pair of canaries, perhaps. Sally has a pair she wishes to be rid of. I'd rather keep them, but I suppose it's only fair."

"Sally, as in the Countess of Jersey?" he asked without inflection.

"She's a year younger than I and trying much too hard to be higher in the instep than her mother-in-law these days, which is to my advantage. Canaries are apparently no longer fashionable and thus beneath her dignity."

"You can socialize with earls and their wives. You are familiar with dukes. Why on earth did you marry me?"

"Hmmm, let me think. . . ." She pretended to ponder as she leaned her head against his shoulder. "Aside from the fact that I don't own a bank as Sally's family does, or that my only family connection is Viscount Pig, and I have no estates of my own, or anything that an earl could conceivably want, I simply cannot imagine why I chose you."

He made a rude noise but circled her waist. "Fine, then. Who is Tony?"

"Tony?" she asked in puzzlement. "Antoinette? Harold's wife?"

"She has a French brother?" he asked casually.

"My mother has been talking about Albert again," Jocelyn surmised. "She disliked him, but we have not seen him in years."

"Tony's brother is mean," Richard acknowledged, returning with a chicken in his arms.

"Mean, like Harold?" Blake inquired with interest.

"Harold is stupid," Richard said scornfully, before heading for the battered chicken coop.

"What is this about?" Jocelyn demanded.

"I am deciphering a puzzle," Blake said, without explanation. "What do we have to do to find me a position in the War Office? I cannot guarantee that will be sufficient to obtain the information I need, but it might at least give us an income until I find another situation."

She gazed up at his stubborn jaw with amazement. He did not look happy to concede to using her social connections, but at least he admitted he needed her aid. "You don't mind escorting me to salons and soirees? There are not many other events this time of year."

He glared at the crumbling garden wall. "I'd almost rather attend balls and dance the night away with you than listen to people natter mindlessly. My leg has begun to heal, so dancing I might do. Gossip . . . I don't suppose they'd appreciate Shakespeare."

Of course, that was the way into his heart! Her boy thrived on action. Blake was a very physical man, despite all that activity buzzing around in his brainbox. He needed one or the other—physical or intellectual exercise. Preferably, both at the same time.

"One day, we'll hold our own galas, have dancing, and only invite people who like Shakespeare," she said dreamily. "But for now . . . I'll send a note around to Lady Belden. She'll know which gatherings will be best for our purposes and will help us obtain invitations."

He looked down at her. "You are very sure of yourself."

She beamed up at him. "You are the one who believes only you can crack this mysterious code. Our mutual arrogance is boundless."

"I think you terrify me," he said with what appeared to be sincerity. "Let us both get to work then, and see if we can at least turn London upside down, even if we cannot save England from itself."

"We are a little frightening together, aren't we?" she murmured, as much to herself as to him. If he would truly accept her as helpmate, they would be a very dangerous pair, indeed.

In the parlor after luncheon, writing notes offering to buy Percy from the Duke of Fortham, and to Lady Belden inquiring about which invitations they should accept, Jocelyn looked up at the discreet knock of the footman. She had her own *footman*. She could only marvel at her good fortune.

"A lady to see you, miss," the young man intoned dutifully.

"Did she present a card?" she asked, hoping one day Teddy would learn to ask for one.

Since they did not employ enough servants to guard the door and carry messages at the same time, it was no surprise when the *lady* appeared in the doorway before Teddy could reply.

"My dear Jocelyn!" Antoinette gushed, pushing past the startled servant. "How happy it is to see our home restored so excellently!"

"Teddy, I am never at home to Lady Carrington," Jocelyn admonished. She did not worry about insulting her sister-in-law, who had insulted her so many times over the years that it had become a way of passing time. "Please fetch Mr. Montague from the carriage house, if you will."

"Ah, can we not put the past behind us?" Antoinette cried in her best demonstration of regret as the footman departed. She'd barely covered her thick dark tresses with a tiny indigo bonnet lined in white frills. Her matching spencer was cut to emphasize her splendid bosom. "We were very young before. I am only come to see that the poor birdies are safe. I was devastated, so crushed when that beast of a husband of mine sold them! I told him he had no right, but would he listen? No, he does not listen!"

"Then you are well matched," Jocelyn replied disagreeably. "The birds are fine, and no, you cannot see them."

"But I can tell you where to find the other birdies," Antoinette declared in triumph. "You may have all manner of them twittering in your lovely birdhouse. If only I might have the pretty pair of Greys back. They are special to me in my loneliness, you see."

"No, I do not see. They are Richard's birds. Harold sold them. I cannot imagine you have a place in town that would suitably house them. And I can find the others without your help. If the birds are all you want, you have wasted your time."

Tears appeared in the woman's eyes. Jocelyn had seen Antoinette produce tears at will, twisting stupid Harold and any man in her company to her pleas. She was not impressed when Tony began patting the corner of her eye. In fact, she was fairly certain the lace-edged, monogrammed handkerchief Tony wielded had once belonged to Jocelyn's mother. Her brother and his wife must be deep in debt, indeed, if they could not afford new linen.

"I have tried so very hard to be the good English-woman," Antoinette wept. "But the English are so . . . how you say? Bigoted? The ladies will not accept me. I have only the birdies for company. If you would see fit to forgive me, perhaps we can help each other."

The act almost had Jocelyn convinced she had treated Antoinette harshly—until Blake arrived, looking rumpled and annoyed and covered in dust. He waited patiently for an explanation, jarring Jocelyn back to reality.

"Lady Carrington, may I introduce my husband, Blake Montague? Blake, my sister-in-law. I believe she was just leaving."

Antoinette patted her teary eye and peered up at him from beneath her bonnet. "You would not deprive a poor lady from seeing her pets, would you?"

Blake shot Jocelyn an inscrutable scowl, caught Tony's elbow, and steered her toward the door. "The pig and roosters are in the yard, my lady. I will be happy to let you pet them. You might take them with you, if you prefer."

Jocelyn nearly choked on laughter at the dismay in Antoinette's expression. She did not know what her brother's wife meant to steal, but a pig was apparently not on the agenda.

After Tony had left in a huff, Blake returned to his carriage house office to work on the one coded message he possessed. He spun his homemade wheel to note the next combination of letters. Twenty-six letters and nine numerals had an almost infinite number of combinations.

Just as he was thinking he would perish of hunger and ought to see if supper was far off, Jocelyn poked her head through the trap door in the floor. "Thank you for removing Antoinette."

Trying to avoid further distraction, he noted the sequence of numbers and turned the next wheel. "It was my pleasure. Is she demented?"

"No more so than the rest of us. Did she have more to say after you dragged her out?"

"Only that she would ruin us, and she will have her vengeance," he repeated, attempting to concentrate on his work while the loft filled with the scent of lavender and his mind conjured images of his bride's magnificent, naked breasts.

"Hmm," she murmured, climbing into his apartment and glancing around.

Blake lifted his head at her odd reticence and watched her chew her lovely bottom lip in thought. Something was on her mind. Prurient images fled when faced with real problems. "What did the duke say?" he demanded.

"He didn't," she answered. "Lady Bell says he's at his hunting box in Scotland. Unless you are interested in traveling north to discuss Percy's price, we are left to deal with Mr. Ogilvie on our own."

"He's a twit. It's Ogilvie's choice of companions that concerns me. Can you arrange to send Harold and his wife to perdition?"

"Harold? Harold is a twit, too. A good stout stick should take care of him."

Blake suspected his gentle wife had never had the physical courage or ability to defend herself or Richard. She must have spent nights dreaming of wielding cudgels and swords. He believed she'd mentioned stout sticks in reference to Harold in the past.

She did not putter or natter or do anything more than fill the vast empty space with her beauty. That's all it took to distract Blake from his work. With a sigh, he set the wheel and his pen down and let himself enjoy his wife's charms. It wasn't as if he had a chance in hell of breaking this code without more information than he possessed, and it was obvious she was chewing on a dilemma of her own.

"Have you ever taken a stick to Harold's hide?" he asked, trying to imagine his delicate wife attacking a stout pig and deciding she was far more likely to damn one with smiles. Jocelyn hated confrontation, he realized. Her small deceits were a manner of self-protection against bullies like her wretched brother.

"Not as I should have," she said absently, lifting a kitten that had followed her up. Blake wasn't certain he'd seen this creature before.

"Then you should learn to fight back," he suggested. "He'll think he wins otherwise.

She shrugged. "Staying out of the pig's way is safer."

"You insult pigs by calling him one. Pigs are quite clever. Cows are stupid."

She rewarded him with a golden smile. "At last, the country boy emerges! I am not so careful with my nomenclature. Perhaps I should call him Viscount Steer."

Blake laughed. "That's vicious if you know what a steer is."

Her batting lashes and false smile told him she was perfectly aware that a steer was a neutered bull.

But she had not come here to discuss Harold's beastliness. "What else does Lady Bell have to say?"

"That Harold is spreading rumors that he has loaned

Carrington House to his witless sister and her impoverished husband out of the kindness of his heart, to keep us off the streets. And Mr. Ogilvie is claiming you stole his pet and cheated in a duel. I daresay Antoinette is also offering her fair share of scandal broth."

"All lies," Blake said with a shrug. "Why do we care if nodcocks tell lies?"

Jocelyn sighed in exasperation. "Because it becomes exceedingly difficult to obtain important invitations when one's reputation is being smeared by a viscount and the nephew of a duke," she stated in a voice that reflected her hurt. "We have not been invited to Lady Jersey's soiree."

Harming Jocelyn in any way riled Blake's anger. "Why in damn . . . Why would they do that?" he demanded, keeping his voice below a thunder blast so as not to terrify her.

Ogilvie might be childishly spiteful about losing the duke's favor, but Carrion had no cards in this game. Or did he? What did Jocelyn's brother have to gain by cutting her off from society? Or from undermining Blake's reputation?

There hadn't been any more incidents that had threatened his life. Would Harold think he could get his hands on Jocelyn's money if her husband went to war? Very likely, since Harold knew her weakness—that her family would always come before money. Perhaps he thought Blake would have no choice but to join the army if London society turned its collective back on him.

Except the peculiarity of a French thief and Jocelyn's mother mentioning the arrival of Antoinette's French brother, followed by Lady Carrion's odd visit, didn't fit the puzzle.

"Harold does these things to be mean?" Jocelyn suggested, falling far short of his theories. She was not much inclined to suspicion.

Blake rose from his makeshift desk, crossed the room, and took his slender wife into his arms. He rested his chin on her hair and recalled pulling the silken strands through his fingers that morning. Somehow, her softness eased his need to beat up bullies.

"And you have a suggestion that you're afraid to propose. How can I convince you to trust me?"

Letting the kitten escape, she leaned against his shoulder and shook her head. "You are a man. Men generally do not understand what women must do to get their way, as you call it. Men can pound freely on the doors of all society. Men can shout and argue and beat their enemies with fists. Men can hire lawyers, buy bullies, gather wealth, and use it like a club. Women can only smile and whisper among themselves."

"Smiling and whispering accomplish a great deal, then," he said dryly. "We might not be married were it not for smiling and whispering. So what have you and Lady Belden conjured between you?"

"A masquerade," she murmured into his shoulder, tensing as if expecting his reproof.

"Will there be dancing?" he asked.

She lifted her head then and met his eyes with laughter. "Yes, of course. I would keep you busy while I work my wiles. I have never danced with you. Are you very good?"

"Of course. Dancing is a matter of patterns and athletic skill." He bent and claimed the kiss he deserved for suppressing his need to strangle odious bastards.

To hell with decorous masquerades. If Carrington and Ogilvie aimed to harm his beautiful wife with their malicious rumors, they were going to die—or at the very least, wish they were dead.

* * *

Familiar drunken laughter filtered through the walls from the gaming room to the quiet smoking room. Nick Atherton curled his lip in distaste. "I say, the quality of this club's membership is deteriorating. Really, we must find better accommodations."

Lord Quentin snorted and puffed on his cigar. "You can't afford better. Who is offending your delicate ear now?"

Nick eyed his companion with disfavor. "Someday, my lord, someone will take down your arrogance a peg. Meanwhile, I intend to determine why Carrion is allowed in my place of leisure."

"Carrion?" With interest, Quentin imitated Atherton and rose from his comfortable chair. "I assume you mean Carrington? He's been up to something with our friend Ogilvie for some time now."

"He has his piggy snout in the air about his sister snaring the estate he lost, I daresay, but I can't imagine what he thinks he can do about it," Nick commented.

He ambled into the gaming room and settled in a dark corner, partially hidden by an antique room divider painted with nubile, naked maidens. Pulling a deck of cards from his coat pocket, Nick distributed them on the green baize table. Quent took a chair beside him where he could observe the room better.

But Nick needed only his ears to determine the participants at the table on the back wall.

"My stepmama has wits to let, as do her offspring," Viscount Carrington claimed. "I control Jocelyn's inheritance, so it's not as if that scoundrel Montague can run off with it. I've let them use the old place in Chelsea in hopes they'll stay out of trouble, but I don't put much hope in it."

Quent's eyes narrowed dangerously, but he was smart

enough to listen rather than engage. Nick clipped the end of a new cigar and leaned back in his chair. "What does he hope to accomplish?" Nick asked the other man quietly.

"Destroy their social credibility is the obvious. Possibly establish that he has funds with which to wager." Quent picked up the cards he'd been given while watching the back table. "Carrington isn't clever enough for much more than the obvious. So if there's more to his insults, someone else is behind it."

"They stole the duke's bird," Ogilvie was saying petulantly. "His Grace says if I don't get it back, he'll cut me off without a shilling. You promised to retrieve it for me."

"I did not," Carrington retorted. "I said I'd pay you back as soon as I get my hands on them. My wife wants the blithering things returned. Don't know what His Grace wants with the noisy creature anyway. I was glad to have them off my hands, but Tony is pouting."

"Montague meant to shoot the bird," another player said. "It might be dead by now."

Nick snorted and studied his cards, but he wasn't paying attention to the hand he held. The speaker was Viscount Ponsonby, who was connected to every noble family in the *ton*. Carrington was playing in deep waters.

"Or he could be using it to catch French spies," another lordling said with a chortle. "Montague has even been bothering Castlereagh with his mad theories."

Nick scowled, recognizing one of the secretary of state's minions.

"Ho, your wife is French, Carrington," Ogilvie shouted drunkenly. "Montague can catch her!"

"That ain't funny, Bernie. Tony's brother is offering a reward to get the birds back. You'd better be thinking of a better way to do that than by insulting my wife."

Nick and Quent exchanged glances. Carrion's French brother-in-law wanted the birds?

The drunken argument descended into insults. Nick dropped his cards on the table, picked up his snifter of brandy, and rose from his chair. Quent merely sat back and puffed on his cigar, willing to be entertained.

"I say, old chap, did I hear you're offering a reward for birds?" Nick inquired, swaying drunkenly toward the back table, cigar in one hand, brandy in the other.

Carrington glanced at him in annoyance. "Not just any birds. My wife's birds."

Nick frowned as if pondering the deeper meaning of birds. "Your sister has your wife's birds?"

"My sister is a bird-wit! And her damned husband is poking his nose where he shouldn't. He's as nocked in the noggin as the rest of them!"

Nick nodded wisely. "Got sisters like that." He leaned forward confidingly, getting into the viscount's face and puffing smoke in his direction. "Get a bailiff," he whispered, drunkenly tipping his snifter.

Carrington shoved him out of his face. The snifter jerked, slopping golden brandy into the viscount's lap.

"Oops, sorry about that, old chap," Nick blustered, pounding his victim on the back as if that would help the alcohol dousing his breeches. "Have a cigar."

He dropped his smoking tobacco on Carrington's lap and staggered off, leaving the table of sots screaming as flames immediately licked from the alcohol up the cloth covering the table.

"Doeskin," Nick murmured in disgust as Quentin caught his elbow and steered him away from the shouts and flames. "Was really hoping for silk."

"Silk breeches in a club?" Quentin asked, hiding his amusement. "One would think you've done this before."

Nick sighed heavily. "A regrettable regression to

youthful failings. Forget you saw that and send a word of warning to Blake." Nick straightened as they stepped into the chilly autumn evening. "Carrion is a dimwit, but there's more here than meets the eye when he starts offering a reward from a Frenchman."

"You know the Frenchman in question?" Quent asked.

"That I *don't* know him is the problem," Nick responded enigmatically.

27

Feeling very mature and responsible after leaving instructions with the servants for the next day's menu and duties, Jocelyn wandered into the parlor in search of company. Blake had followed her inside after agreeing to the masquerade, and she didn't think he'd left the house after dinner.

He had slept in her bed last night. Would he do so tonight? More important, would he finally demand his husbandly rights? Did she want him to? Restless, she practiced not thinking about it. There was only so much maturity she could manage in a day. She'd hoped to find her husband alone, but the parlor was oddly empty.

Her mother and Richard gravitated toward books and were likely in the study. On top of everything else, now she must feel guilty about putting Blake out of the room he deserved for his work.

With trepidation, she traversed the corridor and peered around the study door to see if anyone was there—and blinked at the scene within.

Lady Carrington sat in the window seat with Africa on her shoulder—the female Grey was easily differentiated from Percy by one nearly bald wing and the pattern of white on her face. Her mother was feeding the bird bits of lettuce while perusing what appeared to be one of Blake's cryptography texts. Bitty lay sleeping at her feet, her furry legs jerking in dreamland.

The sight of the bird outside the conservatory was cause for alarm. Men did not like birds messing on their books and papers. Jocelyn had horrible memories of all the times she'd chased Richard's birds to save them from Harold.

But this was her home now. She would chase any man who hurt Richard's creatures. She relaxed and took comfort in the rest of the warm family scene. Richard had Blake's code wheel scattered in discs across the desk, apparently amusing himself with lining up the letters in order. She would pray Blake didn't kill him for taking apart his work, except a pair of dirty boots sprawled across the carpet gave evidence that Blake was present.

She had to push the door open more to observe what her toplofty husband might be doing on the floor.

Percy pranced up and down Blake's back while Blake added a notation to her mother's lengthy genealogy chart. Jocelyn had to grasp the door latch to keep from falling into the room with shock.

When Percy squawked an obscenity, Blake absently replied, *"Fermez la bouche."* The parrot then retorted in French. Jocelyn had forgotten most of what she'd learned from her brief time with a French tutor, but the elegant Gallic for *Close your mouth* had been one of her favorite phrases to toss at her older sisters. Percy's garbled response was a little less translatable.

She scrubbed at a tear of joy as she realized how well her new husband fit into her eccentric family. She had expected him to decamp to his apartment immediately after dinner. Instead, he was apparently enlisting her family's help in his efforts to decrypt the code, while applying himself to their endeavors in return.

Blake didn't really hate people—he simply despised his family's cosseting. And he disliked fools. He wasn't a saint by any means. But her family was intelligent and so self-absorbed that they didn't waste time fussing. He could be his curmudgeonly self in their company, and they didn't even notice, much less complain.

She slipped in to peruse the bookshelves in the vague hope she might find a volume on costumes. She didn't like to go into debt for the elaborate ones sold by tailors and modistes for masquerades. She'd have to concoct them on her own.

"Ma belle épouse," Blake murmured as she entered, proving he'd known she was there, even though his back was to her.

"Belly up to the bar, boys," Percy countered.

"Blake believes his lineage also traces back to Charlemagne, dear," Lady Carrington said, directing her comment to Jocelyn. "He is looking for our common ancestor."

"How very . . . useful," Jocelyn said, hiding a smile. "An eminent cryptographer tracing English ancestry to France. Very original employment of your skills."

"Eminent. I like the sound of that." Blake turned on his elbow so he could see her. Percy hopped to his head, and he swept the bird off before it could feed on his nose. "But brushing up on my French is helping with the code. Vowels are the most common letters in both languages, but consonants differ. I am trying to think like a Frenchman."

"A," Richard said, apropos of nothing.

Blake glanced at him. "What was that, Rich?"

"Neuf," Africa chirped.

"Seventeen seventy-six," Percy countered.

Richard shrugged. "Nothing, just something the birds like." He began stacking the discs back on their spindle.

Blake's gaze narrowed as he glanced to the French-speaking Africa. "Richard, do me a favor, will you? Keep track of what your birds are saying. See if there's a pattern."

Her brother nodded and happily withdrew a sheaf of paper from a desk drawer.

Jocelyn was thrilled at Blake's patience, even though Richard would understand little of her husband's obsession with war and codes. "Richard, do you know French?" she asked, wondering if he could even write out Africa's nonsense.

"Antoinette talked in funny words," Richard said with a shrug. "I learned them."

"Antoinette?" Uneasy, Jocelyn glanced at Blake, but he seemed lost in thought. Surely . . . No, he could not think her brother's wife had anything to do with codes. "That's ridiculous. Antoinette always irritated the birds. I think she is using them as an excuse to see the house."

"Maybe so," Blake said with a shrug. "But you've given me an idea."

She hoped it was about Charlemagne and not her sister-in-law. "I take it that the birds and present company keep your brain leaping about like a frog until, ultimately, you hope to cross the pond?" Jocelyn asked, not expecting him to follow her nonsense any more than she did his.

"It's the reason I work the mind teasers," he agreed, sitting up and propping his shoulders against the shelves, draping his arm over a bent knee in a purely masculine pose that took her breath away. "It takes an agile brain to stay out of ruts."

"I don't suppose you could apply your agile brain to costumes we might make for the masquerade?" Jocelyn plucked Percy off Blake's hair and placed the obnoxious bird on his perch, feeding him a nut kernel to persuade him to stay put.

"Ghosts, and we put sheets over our heads?" Blake asked hopefully.

She threw a walnut meat at him.

"Saint Francis of Assisi," Lady Carrington murmured. "Although I believe Jocelyn would then have to dress as a dove or a donkey."

"A soiled dove," Jocelyn said mischievously.

"Virgin Mary, more like," Blake countered, shoving to his feet and towering over her. "Saint it is, thumbing our noses at the anti-Catholic bigots. You may wear feathers on your wings." He plucked a gray one from his coat sleeve.

"Saints don't have wings," she protested uneasily as he took her elbow and turned her toward the door.

"Saints, angels, who knows the difference? Either one is likely a bore." He bowed to her mother. "I beg your leave, my lady. We have plans to pursue."

He steered Jocelyn out of the study and closed the door behind him without waiting for any reply, apparently already accepting he wouldn't get one from her less than social family.

"My brothers-in-law pitched fits when Richard let his birds loose in the house," Jocelyn murmured nervously, as he maneuvered her toward the stairs.

"I might protest a chicken on my head, too," Blake pointed out. "Percy, however, I've grown used to. He's easily trained and responds to various signals. Quite fascinating, actually. Who taught them to speak French?"

"Not Richard. We had a French tutor but she fled after about six months in our mad household. Antoinette, perhaps. She's had them these last years."

Blake seemed lost in thought after that comment, but he led her inexorably up the stairs. Jocelyn considered fighting him off. But her heart fluttered in anticipation, and she knew everything worked against her, including herself.

"Did you wish me to prepare a room up here for you?" she asked, refusing to let him push her any farther than the door. "The carriage house must be difficult to heat."

His eyes were shadowed as he gazed at her, and she had to look away from the knowledge in them. And the desire.

"I've slept alone all my life. Cold doesn't bother me. If you want me to sleep outside, I will."

He waited. This was where she should smile vacantly, tap him on the chest, flap her lashes, and tell him good night.

She swallowed back the falsities. Blake had been nothing but honest with her. It was time her new mature, responsible self learned to be honest as well. She simply didn't know how to begin.

"You have given me everything I've dreamed of," she murmured, hoping this one truth would prime the pump. Forthrightness did not come easily to her. "And all I've done in return is shoot your toe and spend your money so you cannot have what you want."

"I am not looking for payment," he said in a tone that could have reflected annoyance—or hurt. "I have made my choices deliberately. You owe me nothing."

It was hard to imagine such a large, self-assured man feeling insulted, so she sought other meanings. "I . . . I thought we had a business deal." She picked nervously at her gown, still too frightened of herself to face him. "I didn't keep my end of the bargain."

Blake traced his finger along an escaped lock of hair

resting against her jaw. Jocelyn shivered at the tenderness of his touch—and the yearning he stirred inside her. She had never known tenderness and had not realized how she craved it.

"It's not as if there are any guarantees you will keep the house," he reminded her. "So my end of the bargain has not held up, either. I regret that I could not give it to you free and clear. But I think . . . I hope that we have gone beyond that bargain, haven't we?"

She wanted so desperately to believe that—but she could not trust dreams and wishes. Jocelyn hugged herself and dared to look up. The light of a single candle wasn't sufficient to see more than the deep sockets of Blake's eyes and the flash of silver in his thick hair. Her insides heated with desire with just those brief glimpses.

"I haven't been honest about my feelings for so long that I cannot know how I feel anymore," she admitted. "It has always been easier to smile through adversity, tease people out of their rage, and look uncomprehending when they ask too much. The only thing I know right now is that I'm frightened. Fear overwhelms all other emotion."

"You sheltered your mother and brother from reality as your father once did." He nodded acknowledgment of her reasons for hiding. "And now you fear I will add to your burden."

She bent her head in shame. "I'm sorry. I know I'm being selfish. But I'm so tired—"

He tipped her chin up with his finger. "You are one of the least selfish women I know. I had hoped I had given you enough time to trust me, but I can see where you might have doubts." His tone was wry. "I want to beat my fist against the wall and kick something right now. You have a right to be wary. I am not always civil."

She laughed shakily. "Or civilized. But you are a good man. I trusted you enough to marry you." She took a deep breath, straightened her shoulders, and met his gaze. "It is the future that frightens me, not you. I have suffered one too many disasters in my life, and I keep waiting for the next to hit."

Blake reached past her and opened the bedroom door. Warmth and the delicious scent of lavender emanated from the chamber. "My mother keeps expecting me to die, and in consequence she would wrap me in batting and store me in a wardrobe if she could. Living in fear is not living. The world is made for exploring."

Enticed from the drafty hall, Jocelyn drifted into her room. A blazing fire lit the grate. In front of it, water steamed in a large hip bath. Candles illumined every surface. Her kitten had curled into a fuzzy ball and fallen asleep in her chair.

The bedcovers had been turned back, and a bouquet of late autumn roses dropped their pink petals on her pillow.

He'd set the scene for seduction.

28

Blake clenched his molars and wished he was a praying man. His lust for his wife was so powerful that he'd been tempted throughout the day to heave her over his shoulder and haul her off to bed. Any bed. Or sofa. Or patch of grass. He ached with need. He just might conceivably die of lust, humiliating as that might be.

But the more he knew of Jocelyn, the better he understood that while pouncing on her might give him momentary respite, it would not generate the future he wanted. She might acquiesce because she thought she must, but devil take it, he wanted her to *want* him. He might as well shove a knife between his ribs and carve out his heart as to admit such a weakness.

He was praying that a modicum of patience would achieve his goals. Solving puzzles was one of his favorite things to do, and his wife was a puzzle he might explore forever, if he took extra care while she was still skittish.

She trailed her fingers through the hot bathwater and gazed at him with such wide-eyed doubt that Blake knew he had to study the situation carefully. She'd revealed some of her true self tonight. She wasn't the blithe, confident sophisticate that she portrayed to the world. She was barely more than a terrified girl who carried too much weight on her slender shoulders.

Oddly, that didn't reassure him as it ought. He'd never taken care of anyone but himself.

"There's . . . a dressing screen, if you would like a bath," she said hesitantly. "I had not thought how cold it would be for you to wash in the carriage house."

Blake bit back a groan of dismay. That she mistook any offer of comfort as belonging to someone else told him enough of her upbringing to make his heart ache.

"The bath is for you," he said. "I think it's time someone looked after you for a change, instead of the other way around."

Her eyes widened even farther. "We have servants to look after me," she said in puzzlement.

"And you would not order them to fetch a hot bath because you know how much work it is," he pointed out, beginning to understand her even more. "Even though I assume we pay them well and they are happy to do it."

She looked startled, began to say something, then shook her head. He prepared for a vociferous argument. Which was foolish, because she never argued. She presented her back to him.

"Unhook me, please."

She didn't have to ask twice. Still wary of such unexpected success but unable to resist the opportunity to stroke her velvet skin, Blake crossed the room in two strides. His fingers felt large and clumsy on the frail fabric and tiny hoops. He wasn't a rake like Atherton. His women of choice had been bored matrons and paid prostitutes, women who came to him in dishabille. He was almost as much a virgin at this seduction business as his wife.

With a lifetime of sensual delight as the prize, he would learn this lesson as well as he learned all others and enjoy it a thousand times more.

He eased the bodice sleeves off, then pressed a kiss to her bare shoulder as he untied the ribbons of her outer chemise. Blake burned to carry his kisses lower, to nip and taste and arouse, but he restrained his building passion. Unwrapping his wife was far more absorbing than solving a puzzle, and she deserved his attention.

When she did not object to his ministrations but merely held the sagging folds of cloth to her bosom, he unknotted the laces of her stays.

The ache in his loins demanded that he shove all the hampering fabric to the floor and claim what was his, but once the laces were unfastened, Blake fisted his fingers to prevent further depredation. "Tell me what you would like," he said hoarsely.

"The . . . dressing screen, I believe. To keep the heat in."

He'd rather break the screen into kindling if she meant to put it between them, but he dragged the heavy frame over to the fire and set it around the tub.

By the time he returned, she'd dropped her garments and stood only in a gossamer shift, with her back to him. Blake's cock swelled against the restraint of his buttons. *His*, primeval instinct cried. Delicate skin, sumptuous curves . . . His. And he daren't touch. Yet.

"Shall I wash your hair?" he suggested politely, slamming a mental fist into his primeval instincts and knocking them down.

She cast him a startled glance over her shoulder. Firelight danced shadows over her bare slender back, silhouetting her curves beneath the linen. Strands of light locks tumbled to her shoulders, and he fought the urge to fling her hairpins into the fire.

"Take off your coat," she whispered, rewarding his patience. "It will get wet."

Blake eagerly complied. By the time he'd peeled his arms from the sleeves, she'd dropped the shift and climbed into the tub. Before she sank into the water, he was given a heavenly glimpse of smooth, fair skin, a shapely back that narrowed, then curved in perfect globes below the waist.

He was a lucky, lucky man.

She covered her bosom with her arm and kept her back to him but did not demand that he leave. After all, he'd seen most of her in bits and pieces. Just not whole, like this, like Venus rising from the sea. Blake swallowed hard.

"My hair?" she inquired cautiously.

He would trade his right hand to touch that glorious mane of silvery gold, but she already owned too much of him, so he kept that sentiment to himself. Kneeling beside the tub, he gently sought and removed each pin, digging his fingers through thick silk and trying not to groan too loud with pleasure.

"Perhaps you should take off your waistcoat and shirt so they won't get wet?" she suggested once her hair tumbled to cover her back and shoulders.

In a surge of delight that his wife wasn't shy—and that she didn't object to where he hoped this was going— Blake threw his old leather waistcoat across the room, then unwrapped his neckcloth.

She peeked daringly over her shoulder to watch. Pretending not to notice, he peeled his linen from the band of his trousers and slowly drew the shirt upward, revealing his bare chest one rib at a time, stretching his arms over his head so she could see all of him.

He feared his trouser buttons would pop when she gasped and hurriedly returned to splashing in the water. Inordinately pleased that she seemed to appreciate what she'd seen, he let his shirt join her gown on the floor and reached for the pitcher beside the tub. "Duck and let me pour this over your hair."

She obeyed, probably for the first and last time, Blake thought with a mental smile as he soaked handfuls of flaxen tresses.

"Are you staying warm?" he asked, taking the scented soap she handed him.

"Yes, very," she said in a husky voice.

He wasn't a man who smiled often, but he thought he might crack his face with the grin spreading across it. He had her hot and naked. One step at a time. . . .

"Will you bathe when I am done?" she asked as he pressed suds through her hair.

And terrify her with his great throbbing rod? He didn't think so. "Another time."

She pondered that, or kept her mouth shut so soapy water didn't drown her. Blake applied all his vast concentration to removing every bit of soap from her hair. And still his gaze drifted over her shoulder, to the wet globes of her breasts. Suds ran down the curves, lingering at aroused nipples, and he didn't know how much longer he could withstand temptation.

When she bent her knee and propped her foot on the tub's edge so she might run a soapy cloth over her leg, Blake learned the limits of his restraint.

Rubbing the cloth over her knee, Jocelyn didn't think she'd teased her husband on purpose. She was many things, but a wanton was not one of them. It was just . . . Blake was behaving with such composure that she needed to know if their passionate wedding afternoon had been a fluke or if he truly desired her.

She didn't have a great deal of experience with desire.

She simply knew she was naked, and he wasn't touching her. And she wanted him to. Very, very much, she wanted his hands on her skin. Her body seemed to require it, even though she suspected she shouldn't encourage him or herself. She leaned over farther to scrub her toes.

She was a simple woman with simple hungers. Perhaps just this once . . .

No. For many reasons, that was a very bad idea.

At his hungry growl, she hastily returned her foot to the water.

"The towel, please," she said stiffly, having no idea how she would smile her way out of this predicament.

She was about to oppose a very angry man. One justified in his anger. She felt guilty that she had not opposed him from the start. He'd offered her this lovely bath and been all that was kind and said wonderful things—for Blake, anyway. And because he said them, she knew he meant what he said. It wasn't polite flattery.

She had wanted to please him. But she couldn't.

What she was about to do was unconscionable. And she had to do it, for her family's sake as well as her own.

Instead of handing her a towel, he began drying her hair with it. Jocelyn wanted to weep at his attentive care. Blake had the ability to apply his entire concentration to what he was doing. It would be so wonderful to give herself up to his ministrations. . . .

"Please, Blake," she murmured helplessly. "I cannot do this. I simply cannot."

His comforting strokes froze, then resumed, a little more cautiously. "Do what, precisely?" he asked without inflection.

"Anything!" she said in exasperation at her inability to express herself. She smacked the water, splashing droplets onto the rug. "It doesn't matter what I *want.* It's just that I *cannot.*"

"You're afraid I'll hurt you?" he asked in that professorial tone he adopted when addressing a problem. "Has someone else hurt you?"

That last sounded a little more explosive, and Jocelyn waved her hand to dismiss whatever he had in his head. "No, never. Just give me the towel, please. We've discussed this. I thought I could, but I simply can't. I have to think of my family first. *You* may not want me to look after you, but *they* need my care."

He stopped rubbing her hair, and Jocelyn refused to glance over her shoulder. She had blatantly asked that he strip to his trousers, and now she would have to suffer the consequences if she looked or touched. Her husband was a powerful male animal, and she didn't have the willpower to resist him. Although if he was scowling at her . . . she might simply die of heartbreak.

Instead of handing her a dry towel, Blake abruptly wrapped the cloth around her and hauled her, dripping, out of the tub.

Jocelyn bit back a shriek.

He turned her around until only the thin towel was between her breasts and his bare chest. Effortlessly, he held her off the floor so she couldn't even touch her toes to the ground. She squirmed, but learned the danger of that quickly enough. Blake's muscled arms tightened, and she simply wanted to curl up in his embrace, rest her head on his powerful shoulder, and submit.

"Let me clarify," he growled in her ear, since she wouldn't look up at him. "You won't go to bed with me because I won't let you take care of me?"

That didn't sound right. She shook her wet hair. "You don't *need* me, but Richard and my mother do. And a baby would. What happens if you die and I lose the house and have a baby to raise with no roof over my head? I cannot do it. I just cannot."

"I am not going to die," he said most emphatically. "Look at me," he added. When she still did not, he ran a hand downward, cupping her nearly bare buttock.

Jocelyn gasped at the river of heat flowing through her midsection with that intimate touch. She turned a glare upward to his scowl. "Put me down!"

"No. Not until we have this out. We are married. I am not a monk."

She offered him a sweet smile and fluttering eyelashes. "Perhaps I wish to be a nun."

"Stop that!" he roared.

She blinked and stared. "Stop what?"

"Pacifying me with simpers. Now that I know you have a brain in your head, it won't work." He let her feet touch the ground so he could begin rubbing the towel over her rapidly cooling skin. "Simper at idiots, if you will, but if we're to live together, we have to *talk.*"

She gasped again as his big hands rubbed the linen over her breasts, then downward, to places where no man should stray. "Stop that." She grabbed the towel and tugged, but he wouldn't release the cloth that was the only thing halfway covering her.

And he wasn't exactly decent, either. She tried not to stare at aroused male nipples or the way his muscles rippled across his chest when he tugged the towel—and her—toward him.

She gazed in fascination at the line of darker skin above his half-unbuttoned trousers, where the stripe of hair disappeared downward. Then jerked her attention back to the stubborn set of his jaw. "What is there to talk about? I tell you no, and you say I can't. That rather limits conversation. *Simpering* is far easier than arguing with mule-headed men who won't listen."

"I'm listening. You're not." He picked her up again and dropped her onto the bed.

The bed with roses on the pillow—both peace offering and seduction. Jocelyn thought her heart really would break as she rolled up in the coverlet. Concealment didn't help as much as she hoped. She still had to look at *his* nakedness and feel the desire nagging at her to give up, give in, and learn more of those mysteries to which he'd introduced her.

"What else can you say that will make any difference?" she cried in both anger and desperation.

"Good. Now you're being honest. Scream at me if you will. Hit me, if you must. I can take it." He sat down on the bed and began removing his shoes.

She hit him. She smacked him hard on his broad brown back. He didn't even flinch. Nor did he protest or hit her back. He merely dropped a shoe and glared over his shoulder.

"I don't know how to make you trust me," he said. "I have told you there are ways of reducing the chances of babies, but if you won't believe me, then what else can I do?"

She wanted to fling her arms around his neck and say, *Yes, yes, I believe you! Make love to me. I want babies, beautiful babies.*

Instead, she wept. And smacked him again, just because it felt good to express frustration over what she felt and couldn't say.

His other shoe hit the floor. She eased to the far side of the bed. He grabbed her arm and turned to face her, but he wasn't scowling.

"Give me tonight. Give me our wedding night. The odds of creating a child in one night are very slim. Take a chance, Jocelyn."

29

"I'm tired of taking chances!" Jocelyn shouted, jerking her arm from his grasp. "I'm the one who must deal with babies, not you. Why can I not have security for a change? Certainty. Just a minute to breathe without wondering whether I'll be thrown from my home tomorrow? Do you have any idea how many times I've found our trunks sitting on the doorstep and the unwelcome sign hung on the door? *Four!*" she shouted. "Four times I've been thrown from my home. In *six* years!"

"Very good." Her overbearing, impossible, much-too-handsome husband swung around and captured her wrists, pushing her back to the rose-petaled pillow. "Now you're being honest."

She fought futilely against his greater strength, more out of frustration and fury than any fear that he might force her to do what she didn't want.

She'd married an honorable gentleman. She wanted to weep, torn between her desire to love and adore him and her need to be safe.

"You could die tomorrow!" she shouted.

"So could you," he pointed out with infuriating logic. "We all must die someday. Is that any reason to stop living now?"

"Quit being so blasted reasonable." She hurled herself upward, attempting to unbalance him and push him over.

He merely caught her arms and rolled onto his back, carrying her with him so she stared down at his stubbornly set jaw. Blake might be honorable, but he was the most obstinate man alive. Surrender wasn't in his nature. And she couldn't pound the stuffing out of him while wearing nothing.

"One night," he insisted, "and I will do nothing that causes babies."

She glared down at him. "How is that possible?"

"I've already shown you one way. Trust me."

He wouldn't plead, but there was an urgent passion behind his words that she seldom heard from this self-possessed man. She longed with all her heart and soul to respond to it. He needed *her*. Flighty, useless, silly *her*. It seemed impossible. Improbable. And he was admitting it! Almost.

What he had already shown her had been so glorious . . . she was terrified of knowing more. Of trusting.

"You're not afraid of me, are you?" he asked when she said nothing.

She shook her head vigorously. "Not of you. I married you because you're a man of honor." But she wasn't ready to back down. "That doesn't mean you're any more useful than any other male on the planet."

He chuckled deep in his throat, an erotic sound that sent ripples up and down her skin. Before she could resist, he rolled her back to the bed, and his powerful torso pinned her to the mattress. And still, she wasn't afraid. Just wary. Only a thin sheet and his trousers separated them.

"I can be immensely useful, if only you will give me a chance," he informed her. "Don't be like those mummified corpses at Whitehall, refusing to accept new ideas. Somewhere beneath all the pretty hair you conceal a very smart mind. Open it up for me."

"I do?" she asked in wonder, hiding the inane urge to touch her hair as if she could detect what he saw. He'd said something similar earlier, but she had dismissed it as flattery. But Blake didn't flatter. She studied his face to see if he was laughing at her and saw only desire in his eyes. "You think I'm smart?" she whispered.

"You're smart enough to catch me," he returned, although he grinned as he said it. When she tried to punch him again, he pinned her wrists to the pillow. "Neither your brother nor your mother are witless, just eccentric in their knowledge. You're no different. You've simply chosen to specialize in people, as I do puzzles. That does not make you stupid."

"I know I'm not stupid," she said irritably, wiggling beneath his greater weight, unable to think straight while all her senses were filled with raw male power. "But I'm not schoolbook smart."

"Do you want to be?" He leaned over and kissed her cheek, then nibbled her ear.

Jocelyn closed her eyes against the strength of desire flowing through her. "I can't *think* like this," she protested.

"Thinking isn't required. Feeling is. What you need to learn isn't in schoolbooks." Keeping her pinned, he continued kissing and nibbling down her throat.

What he was doing to her certainly wasn't in schoolbooks or she would have studied her lessons more willingly. Jocelyn fought the urge to arch closer. Her husband's handsome—bare—chest was temptingly out of her reach, but his hips pressed hers into the downy mattress. She ached where they met. "I hate it when men know more than me," she muttered, foolishly, since he knew so much more that it frightened her. And made her feel safe at the same time.

"I have a notion that you'll learn this lesson so fast that I'll come to regret it later." Finally, he pressed his mouth to hers.

As always, she was lost once Blake began kissing her. His kisses turned her inside out and reduced her to mindless rubble. She knew she should be strong and resist, but she wasn't strong and she didn't want to resist. She wanted her husband with a desire so deep she couldn't deny it.

She wanted the freedom to be herself, to claim what *she* wanted, and Blake was giving her that chance. When he finally released her wrists, she wrapped her arms around his neck, arched upward, and flung herself fully into the thrill of kissing.

He groaned and propped himself on an elbow to circle one breast with a big hand. His thumb playing against her nipples caused her to writhe against the confinement of the linen separating them. She parted her legs and curved her hips upward, desperately wanting what he'd given on their wedding day.

Blake lifted his solid weight enough to peel off the sheet and apply his kisses to her bare breasts. Jocelyn fought a scream of desire and grabbed his muscled arms while he turned her into molten jelly. His thumb pressed into her belly, until he slid his hand over her hip, then lower, digging his strong fingers into her buttocks until she rose helplessly upward to offer him the access he sought.

"For now, let us repeat lesson one," he murmured,

carrying his kisses downward, lifting her legs to rest on his shoulders.

Cool air flowed over heated moisture, and she jerked involuntarily, but he held her safe.

He was kneeling between her bare legs.

He bent his head, and his mouth covered the place between her thighs.

Jocelyn bit back a shriek as his tongue lapped at oversensitive tissues. She couldn't think, so she had to trust him. And because she trusted her educated, experienced husband, she took what she wanted for a change, and surrendered to the feelings to which he had introduced her. She stuffed a corner of her pillow in her mouth to quiet her cries as the pressure built inside her until she thought she'd surely burst.

Just when she thought she must grab his hair and scream from sensations she could not control, Blake inserted his fingers, and she came apart, crying and quaking and reaching to pull him back, to hold her, while her whole world erupted in joy.

He obliged, taking her in his arms and kissing her tears and her cheeks, and, before long, she was kissing him back, kissing him so thoroughly that the giddy pressure was building all over again.

"Now," he whispered, "you do the same for me."

With pleasure, Blake let his daring wife take charge and explore at her own pace. He had the willpower to fight his animal urge to possess and plunder, aided by his primitive instinct to protect what was his. And Jocelyn was *his*, he knew with pride and no small degree of wonder.

Rationally, he knew he did not own her, but instincts weren't rational. He'd never owned more than his horse and his books, but in some fashion, he owned his wife. And she owned him. With her glorious, flaxen hair brushing his chest as she pressed exploratory kisses down his throat, he figured he could adapt to being possessed by this wanton, gorgeous creature.

Jocelyn was not shy. Given permission to do as she wished, she kissed him in places he hadn't known needed attention, giving far more than he'd ever received, introducing him to a voluptuous sensuality he could get used to quickly. She imitated his earlier caresses, sucking at his nipples until he thought he'd have to roll her over and take what he wanted.

He dug his fingers into the sheets and lost all power of thought the moment she finished unfastening his trousers. Just the anticipation of her warm, soft hands cupped around him had him on the verge of losing control. When she traced a tentative finger down his erection, he had to fight to lie still and not frighten her by spreading her flat against the bed.

No babies, she'd said. He had an expensive condom, but sheep guts weren't perfect. He'd promised her security. He would give it to her, even if he must die in the process.

When her mouth covered his cock, Blake came very close to dying.

Before he could explode with bliss and joy, he pulled out and spilled his seed across the sheets. Shaken by a lust for his wife so strong that he couldn't last longer than a schoolboy, he hauled her into his arms and squeezed her to show his appreciation and relief.

It wasn't nearly enough, but it was a beginning. The firm mounds of her breasts pressing into his side would stimulate him into readiness again in a few minutes. In her bed, he could easily become a rutting bull.

"Thank you," he whispered into her hair. "Thank you for trusting me. I will try very hard to justify your trust."

She snuggled against his chest, and he thought he felt her tears wetting his skin.

"I want all the rest," she cried. "I want the lovemaking and the babies, but I just *can't*."

"I understand," he said, even though he really didn't. Blake stroked her hair and settled her more comfortably against his shoulder. "I cannot make promises, so neither should you. It's all right. We'll muddle through."

He wasn't entirely certain how. He knew better than she that once they started down this path, there was no turning back unless they slept in separate beds. And those wretched instincts of his didn't want to let her out of his sight, much less out of his bed.

But Blake couldn't do that. Saving England from the French was more important than making love to his wife.

He needed to solve the damned code before he could move forward.

30

Blake scowled at the note from Nick waiting for him at the breakfast table the next day. Judging from the missive's contents, Jocelyn was right. Taking a stout stick to her brother would make everyone feel better. He was still scowling when she sailed into the room, dressed for an outing.

She hesitated, then, pushing back her bonnet, she leaned over to kiss his cheek. "Your lessons last night were very . . . memorable," she whispered. "You should not rise so early."

He immediately grew hard and lost track of his thoughts, until the paper in his hand crumpled. He waved it under her nose. "Your brother is conspiring with Ogilvie."

"I told you that yesterday. It is the reason I'm going to Lady Bell's today." She removed Nick's note to peruse it.

Blake tugged her onto his lap, encompassing her slender waist with his arm and kissing the hollow at the base of her throat as she read. He'd had to get up early so as not to tup his eager wife too soon. He needed a plan of action and couldn't think with all her luscious curves within easy reach.

"Richard and I will spend the day trying to determine why your brother, a duke, and a Frenchman want those wretched parrots," he said when she returned Nick's note to the table.

"Money," she said succinctly. "Money will be at the bottom of it. You are crumpling my gown, sir. You had your chance this morning. It is too late now," she said pertly.

He kissed her throat until she was kissing him back.

"Africa laid an egg," Richard announced, entering the room with his idea of mealtime chatter. He strode immediately for the sideboard dishes without regard to what was happening at the table.

"An egg," Blake echoed, choking as Jocelyn laughed and slid from his grasp.

"I'm pretty certain Harold doesn't want an egg," she said, pulling up her bonnet. "But if you two will set the snare, Lady Bell and I shall bait the trap, and with any luck, prove to all the world that Viscount Pig is the dimwit in this family."

Lady Bell had apparently emptied her attics into the parlor before Jocelyn arrived. Enormous French silk gowns from a prior century spilled over the sofa. Powdered wigs left drifts of white flakes across the polished floor. An elaborate bejeweled raja's costume decorated a wing chair. And Lady Bell was holding up a harem gown of fine, nearly translucent silk embroidered in gold thread.

"What do you think? Am I too old for this?" she asked as Jocelyn entered.

"Certainly not, my lady. Men would be wallowing at your feet should you wear such a creation," Jocelyn told her. "Only—such a gown lends no air of mystery, and this time of year, you'll freeze, raising ugly goose flesh. Besides, the pink doesn't flatter you. You want reds or blacks or blues with your dramatic coloring."

Jocelyn rummaged among the gowns strewn about until she found a stunning ice blue silk and a black velvet, spreading them both out on the carpet. "Wear the black with a red lined cloak and dripping with diamonds and come as a countess of Transylvania. Is that not where the vampire monsters are reported to live?" She lifted the gorgeous velvet and spread the wide skirt out to sweep about the room.

"The blue has all the lovely lace, though," her hostess said wistfully. "Can I not just go as myself in a prior era?"

"You weren't even a gleam in your mother's eye when this was worn." Jocelyn set aside the black and lifted the blue. "Wherever did you find this? You could go as Anne Boleyn."

Lady Bell laughed. "The Belden ladies never threw out good fabric. These gowns have probably been wrapped in linens for a hundred years. I don't fancy being a victim like Lady Anne, though. That color is gorgeous with your ice blond hair. You could be an ice queen."

Jocelyn swept the gown about her, admiring the yards of silk. "Blake says we must go as monks in homespun and ropes. That may suit him, but . . ."

"You belong in silk," Lady Belden said firmly. "I will wear rubies with the black, and you must wear the diamonds."

"But ice queens aren't real."

"Masquerades aren't real," Lady Belden said, adjusting the gown's bodice to Jocelyn's waistline. "Our purpose is to prove the rumors aren't true, that you and your husband are blissfully happy and well set for funds. Diamonds are perfect."

"I can't imagine why anyone would conspire and spread lies to harm us." Jocelyn fretted at a worn bit of lace while thinking of the note Blake had received that morning. "I have written the duke about his parrot to say we will pay him for it with my next allowance, which should satisfy Ogilvie. What purpose does lying serve?"

Lady Bell patted her shoulder. "If money would help, I could give you the price of the bays I'm about to acquire from Lord Quentin. Just the pleasure of winning is worth every penny."

"But if you gave me money, I'd have to buy Blake's colors," Jocelyn objected, willing to be distracted from Horrid Harold. She already knew the details of her friend's wager. "And then you'd lose. Although I must say, Lord Quentin's half of the bet is very murky. If I give Blake *all he wants* by spring? Who is to judge what he wants?"

Her hostess laughed. "Oh, I mean to bring out his sister no matter what the outcome. She's a Hoyt, after all, and deserves the benefit of my late husband's wealth. It's merely the winning that counts. Quent is much too sure of himself."

"I'm inclined to agree if Lord Quentin's wager means that he believes Blake can talk me into buying colors and sending him off to be shot at. It's the honorable thing to do, I know, but no one has ever claimed that I am honorable. I can't help hoping there are other means of accomplishing what he wants."

Especially if she could keep him home so they could continue what they'd shared last night! She blushed every time she thought of where Blake's hands and mouth—and her own—had been, so she tried not to think too much.

"We'll never get him into the Foreign Office if Ogilvie and Carrington persist in their slanders," Lady Bell said fretfully. "I don't know why that would be their intent, but your husband already has a curmudgeonly reputation that works against him."

The marchioness tapped her chin in thought. "If we are to overcome the slanders, it might be best to arrange an exclusive entertainment, so exclusive that it requires traveling outside of the city to Chelsea."

"I'm not sure Carrington House"—or her family—"is ready for a masquerade," Jocelyn said worriedly. She had vaguely hoped Lady Bell would offer to host it.

"Our purpose is to show the proper people in Whitehall that Mr. Montague could be valuable to their goals, is it not? Can you think of a better way of discrediting Carrington and his lies than by opening your home with an elegant entertainment to prove you have nothing to hide?"

"An entertainment that does not include Viscount Pig in the home he claims is still his own," Jocelyn said. "The perfect bait to snare a conniving rat."

"The women are scheming," Quent said with unconcern, watching Blake tack an alphanumeric frequency analysis chart on the carriage house wall. "You're about to lose me my bays, aren't you?"

"Your cattle are scarcely my concern," Blake reminded him. "But if the women are scheming, it's over Carrion." He hung an analysis of the coded message beside the larger chart.

Quentin glanced at the charts and dismissed them. "I'm more concerned with what the ladies are about."

Blake gave up on work. "The invitation list is inside. Do you wish to see it?"

"Wouldn't hurt." Quent rose from the desk chair and brushed straw dust off his hat. "I don't suppose you care to explain why you work in a carriage house instead of in your study like a civilized man?"

"You'll see." Blake backed down the ladder stairs to the barn, where he'd installed his father's cabriolet and carriage horse while his father was out of town, thus saving stable rent. Living out here had several advantages it seemed.

He led Quent inside the house through the conservatory door. Percy shouted, *"Fermez la bouche,"* from his perch in the palm tree, and Africa retorted, *"Seventeen seventy-six."* At the sight of Blake, Percy began singing his *hey-nonny* song.

Blake put his fingers to his mouth and whistled sharply. At the sound, Percy quit singing his obscene ditty—as Blake had taught him to do. The birds learned very quickly.

Richard looked up from whittling a code wheel that would match the one Blake had made. As Jocelyn had predicted, the lad was settling down now that he felt safe. He'd even lost his haunted look. He still stuffed eggs in every nook and cranny and got frantic if one was out of place, but then, no one was perfect. It just necessitated looking under cushions and pillows before sitting on them.

"You have a way with birds," Quent said as he followed Blake into the house.

"Animals are easy. It's humans who are complicated." Blake pushed open the study door, hoping he'd see Jocelyn engaged in her party planning.

But only Lady Carrington occupied the room, filling a table with her books and papers. She looked up, wiggled an ink-stained finger in greeting, and returned to her scholarly pursuits. The puppy lay on its furry back, legs curled, snoring before the fireplace, oblivious of intruders.

Blake found it hard to believe he had an entire household teeming with irritating complications and that he suffered their presence without annoyance. He needed to study that anomaly, but he suspected it had much to do with having a wife he lusted after and more important things to occupy his mind than worrying over minor nuisances. As long as he was *doing* instead of *stewing*, he could tolerate almost anything. It was idleness that frustrated him. He'd not suffered a dull moment since his wedding day.

Blake rummaged through the papers Jocelyn had left scattered over the desk and produced a list of names, and handed it to Quent for his perusal. "As I understand it, since this is the off season, the company was limited."

Quent raised his eyebrows and chuckled as he studied the list. "She's even invited the Duke of Fortham! You have acquired an exceedingly devious bride, Montague. If you had the funds to join White's, you might reach some of these men on your own, but most of them are semiretired, with young wives who will adore the idea of a masquerade. You'll despise most of the lot, but they have the connections you need. A martyr to the cause, you'll be."

"There you are. A masquerade of stuffed mummies."

"The duke isn't back from Scotland," Quentin reminded him, returning the list.

Blake shrugged. "We owe him for the bird. I assume Jocelyn considers the invitation a social obligation. If the masquerade is a success, I daresay she will gladly throw any number of parties for the younger set like your sisters to attend. She isn't a high-stickler."

Blake admitted this last with approval. His wife would be far more likely to discriminate in favor of *interesting* people over wealthy, aristocratic ones.

Blake thought his mental ledger was leaning heavily on the approval side of a woman he'd once thought a bird-wit. He ought to punch himself out for blind stupidity.

Quentin laughed at Blake's stunned expression of discovery. "If I lose those bays, I'll make your wife oversee my sister's come-out next Season."

"Marry and have your own wife do it," Blake replied in disgruntlement. "The cost of gowns alone would break us. Are we standing here cackling like hens or studying Richard's bird talk list to find any connection to Carrington or Ogilvie?"

"Me? You're asking me to solve your puzzle? I'm just checking on my investment." Still grinning, Quentin donned his hat and headed for the front door.

Blake threw his friend a black look and returned to the conservatory, where Richard was happily looking for patterns in the birds' nonsense calls. Despite the intellectual distraction, Jocelyn preoccupied Blake's mind.

He wasn't yet ready to admit his obsession with his wife, but his every thought these days seemed to be connected to her. He couldn't even remember why he'd once wanted to remain a bachelor.

31

Blake watched Jocelyn flutter around the bedchamber they'd shared this past week. They'd done more than share a room and a bed. They'd shared their bodies in every way but one. He knew now that she was a generous woman, willing to shower him with all the devotion she offered her family and animals, if he would only let her.

But not knowing his future, he couldn't let her, and he suffered pangs of . . . emptiness . . . in consequence, needing something he could not quite define. He blamed it on the fact that they'd done everything except consummate their marriage—his wife was still a virgin. And he knew she ought to remain that way if he must enlist as a common soldier, which was an increasingly likely event.

He had no right to rob her of the security she prized so much, but he was no further ahead on solving the code than before. Unless they performed miracles at Jocelyn's masquerade and convinced powerful men that he was capable of working with others, so he could find employment at Whitchall . . . He was more likely to learn bird talk.

Despite applying his analytical mind to the problem, he'd not been able to put together all the pieces of the other puzzle that lay tauntingly out of his reach. Carrington, his French wife, the birds, and a mysterious intruder could very well be a danger to Jocelyn. He feared he was missing a significant piece of the riddle. He'd had Atherton keeping an eye and ear open for the Frenchman offering a reward for the birds, but even Nick had uncovered no trace of him.

Blake's patience almost unraveled when Jocelyn appeared from behind the dressing screen wearing a diaphanous night shift. He flung his neckcloth across a chair while she let down her hair, cautiously watching him in her mirror.

The tension between them could not continue much longer. Thanks to his own greedy stupidity, Jocelyn was now as aware of the pleasures of the flesh as he. An eager student, she kept pressing for more, unaware of how much his restraint cost him.

"I am nervous about tomorrow night," she admitted, ignoring his pacing. "What if no one comes?"

"It's a masquerade, and there is little entertainment in the city until society returns over the next month. Your guests will show up, if only to satisfy their curiosity and be the first to carry the gossip." Blake shrugged out of his coat and resisted reaching for her hairbrush. He'd tried stroking the tangles out of Jocelyn's silken tresses the other night, and they'd ended up naked, rolling across the carpet, inches away from doing what he'd promised not to do.

Closing his eyes and thinking of duty and England wasn't helping much anymore. He walked about in a permanent state of arousal. He clutched his fingers into fists and willed his body into submission.

"I'm afraid Harold may attempt trouble," she said in a voice so low, Blake wasn't certain he was meant to hear.

"I've prepared for it," Blake replied curtly. "I cannot imagine what he and Ogilvie hope to achieve except a bit of birdnapping."

"It does not make sense," Jocelyn fretted, slamming her brush onto the dressing table. "I can see that Mr. Ogilvie might be peeved because I stole Percy, but Harold must know that he cannot squeeze blood from a turnip. What does he have to gain by helping Mr. Ogilvie steal Percy back or by spreading lies about us?"

Blake feared he knew the answer. "The duke wanted Bernie to marry you. So Bernie's now in disgrace not only for losing the parrot, but also for losing you and your funds. When I refused his challenge the second time, he took insult. Worse yet, I shot Harold in a duel some years ago," he admitted. "He may want retaliation, too."

He waited for a storm of accusations about his violent ways and how he risked lives—and how their current predicament was all his fault.

Instead, Jocelyn looked up at him, nearly glowing with approval. "Did you really shoot Harold? I wish I could have been there. I'm utterly sure he deserved it, whatever the matter was."

Blake thought he might laugh and fall at her feet in relief that she did not hold him in contempt. He ought to kiss her, but that was dangerous territory. "What kind of sister approves of a man shooting her brother?"

"One who has spent the better part of her life hiding from that brute of a brother. He used to hit anyone who crossed his path."

"He *hit* you?" Blake thought his rage would explode the walls.

"He never got near enough to hit me after the first time. I learned to be very good at staying out of everyone's way," she said, as if men striking women and women hiding from men were a perfectly natural occurrence. "What did he do to cause you to duel?"

Blake could scarcely keep his mind on the conversation while fury boiled his blood. Jocelyn didn't deserve a display of temper. He'd reserve that for Harold when he caught him.

"Harold encouraged a good man to invest his last ha'penny in a fraudulent shipping scam. Your brother pocketed a commission for the bad investment and walked away free. My friend merely wanted to better his lot so he could court his childhood sweetheart. Instead, he is serving in the army just to put food on his plate, and the woman he loved married someone else. I thought Harold ought to pay his fair share of the pain he caused, so we dueled and I shot him."

Jocelyn rose from the dressing table to envelop him in lavender scent and sensual silk. She pressed eager kisses to his newly shaven jaw. Blake hugged her bounteous curves against him, resting his chin on her moon-gold hair. Just having her in his arms served to reduce his rage, if not his lust. She tore him in two with emotions he had little experience in fighting.

"I'm *glad* you shot him," she said fiercely. "It is a pity he did not rot from the wound. I do not know how he could have grown up so vile."

"I suppose he was a pampered only son and heir for many years," Blake suggested, letting her head on his shoulder calm the beast inside him. "He no doubt resented your mother and her babies and having your father's attention diverted to a second son. It happens."

"Or he could have been born a pig," she added, stepping away before he was ready to let her go. Her expression was fierce. "He was out of university and on his own by the time Richard arrived. He had no reason to resent him, but he *did*, most horribly."

"He hurt a baby?" Blake asked, incredulous.

"Every time Harold came home, Richard had some dreadful accident."

Temper stained her cheeks with pink, and Blake realized she hid her emotions as well as he did. And she was trusting him enough to let him see who she really was.

"Poor Richard simply never understood what he was doing wrong," she said tearfully. "I finally took to hiding him until Harold left again. The pig usually only came home for money."

"Accidents?" Blake asked, processing this confirmation of his suspicions. "What kind of accidents?"

She looked at him with curiosity. "Richard would fall down entire flights of stairs, or his pony would throw him off, things that Harold could not possibly be blamed for. But it simply happened too often when he was home for it to be a coincidence."

Rage rose in Blake's gullet at a coward who would harm the helpless. His hands itched to form fists, but he merely tugged her back into his arms and hugged her. He had a family to protect now. He could not go about challenging Harold to duels any longer.

"That reminds me, I must teach Richard to defend himself," was all he said while his mind fit this puzzle piece into the bigger picture.

Random events began to connect. Harold and Ogilvie had gone to the same public school as boys, a public school where they might learn the same ugly "accidents" for tormenting each other. That first burr under his saddle—that may have been Ogilvie's idea of retaliation for the duel. The andiron had been placed immediately after Blake had argued with Ogilvie over the parrot. The runaway horse had occurred after Jocelyn had turned Harold away and gone out with Blake.

He wasn't clumsy and fate wasn't trying to kill him. Ogilvie and Carrington had been behind at least some of his earlier accidents, motivated by spite, rage, and frustration. That's how the small minds of bullies worked. Ogilvie could have hoped to marry Jocelyn if Blake was out of the way. Carrington might have hoped to gain control of his sister's inheritance. And the birds? They didn't fit—yet.

"Teaching Richard to hide worked when he was little, but he's almost a man and must learn to fight back," was all Blake said aloud.

Jocelyn nodded against his shoulder. "Since Harold has no children, Richard is his heir. If he may someday be a viscount, he needs a man to help him grow up. Viscount Pig is not a man."

Blake smiled into her hair at her ferocity. "I have learned not to get on your wrong side, my deadly queen. And I shall keep pistols away from you until you have learned to shoot them properly."

"I don't think I should like shooting anyone. I think I prefer stout sticks."

"No, you prefer hiding. Perhaps I'll teach you both to fence."

He was about to carry her off to bed when the unmistakable pounding of teenage male feet on the stairs echoed through the corridor outside.

"Blake!" Richard shouted. "Blake, come see!"

Jocelyn froze. "Richard, what is wrong?" She rushed for her robe before Blake had time to protest.

He caught her arms, preventing her from donning it. "I'll be there in a minute, Richard. You needn't alarm your sister like that."

Holding his fretting wife steady, Blake met her glare.

"He is not a little boy you must cosset. He is capable of learning to respect other people's privacy and not think only of himself."

"He thinks only of his birds," she corrected. "He is the very opposite of Harold. And for that, he must be shielded."

"Until I teach him to fight back. Take my word for it, cosseting does not help. Stay here. I'll see what he wants."

She nodded reluctantly.

If what she said about Harold was true, it was a miracle the boy was still alive—a miracle and the intelligence of a good woman. She did not give herself enough credit.

Garbed in only shirt and trousers, Blake strode into the corridor to find Richard pacing up and down, rubbing his arms as if to keep from flying off like one of his birds. "This had better be worth it," he warned.

Richard nodded and hurried for the stairs. "I have found the pattern."

Blake had already learned that with Richard that could mean anything from a swan's mating dance to an arrangement of duck feathers that allowed fowl to swim. He could not hope the boy had learned to read code.

But he could hope that encouraging Richard's talents would someday give the lad a future as something more than Harold's heir. The devil only knew that it was difficult enough in this world to find outlets for nonconforming brains!

He followed Richard into the conservatory, where Percy swung on a perch in his newly repaired birdcage. Richard had been as meticulous in restoring the cage to its original grandeur as Blake's mother had been in refurbishing Carrington House.

"Where, Africa!" Richard called to the mangier creature nibbling at a stick dangling from the cage bars.

Head tilted, the female Grey eyed him skeptically through beady black eyes. "Where, Percy!" she called back.

Or perhaps they said '*Ware!* Blake doubted either bird knew what the words meant. They simply repeated what they heard.

Percy squawked, "Here," and began pecking at his perch as if he were a woodpecker and the perch was a tree.

"B," Richard added to the bird-witted conversation.

"Huit," Africa called happily, before returning to stick nibbling.

"They do that every time," Richard said in satisfaction. "I say a letter, and they say a number. The same number and letter each time after I say *where*."

Blake rubbed his hair and tried not to roll his eyes. *Huit?* French for eight. He'd already suspected that the parrots had learned the language from Antoinette. But why in this order? When Blake had first noticed the pattern, Richard had said *A*, and Africa had said *neuf.* Nine.

The birds were speaking in code.

Earlier, he'd suspected Ogilvie of having a grudge over the bird, or even over Jocelyn, but now that he knew *Harold* was also in the habit of causing murderous incidents, a more serious pattern was developing.

Had Harold conspired with Ogilvie, thinking he'd be able to steal Percy if Blake was incapacitated? Why would Harold suddenly want to reclaim the noisy parrot?

For money, as Jocelyn had predicted. Quent's note had said a reward had been offered for the birds. What was so important about them that they were worth a reward?

Blake examined the cage Richard had restored. The perch on which Percy pecked was thicker than the others. *Where. Here!* And then the bird pecked his perch. Blake studied what appeared to be an ivory cylinder instead of a wooden stick. "Richard, can that big perch come off?"

"It all comes apart to be cleaned." Richard stuck his hand in and moved Percy to another roost, pulled fastenings on either side of the ivory stick, then detached it. "See?"

"May I see it?"

Not believing that the obvious had been right before his eyes all this time, Blake examined the notched rod. Definitely ivory. As he studied the fastenings that held the stick to the chains, his gut lurched. "Where did you find this?"

Richard shrugged uneasily. "It's pretty. Percy liked it."

"That's not what I asked. You won't get into trouble. Just tell me where you found it."

Richard hung his head and shuffled his foot. "I stole it," he whispered.

"From whom?" Blake examined the numbered notches and carried the cylinder out of the conservatory, checking to be certain that Richard followed.

"From Tony. She would not let me see the wheels."

"What wheels?" Blake asked, coming to full alert.

"The ones like you make. She let her friends use them, but not me. They took Percy's perch when he was sleeping! So I stole it back."

Blake thought his heart might stop ticking. He tried to act casual as they reached the study. "So you've had this for how long?"

"Before they sent us to Kate's," he said defiantly, still not meeting Blake's eyes.

"Six years? You stole this six years ago? While you still lived here?"

"Percy liked the perch, and Tony wanted to keep it. It wasn't right!"

The perch—the spindle—was essential to the code wheel only for holding the pieces together and allowing them to turn. It was replaceable. But the loss of an important component of spy equipment would have terrified anyone guilty of treason—terrified them into banishing any young witnesses whose curiosity could lead to trouble.

Blake sat down at his desk and located the wheels he'd carved. *Neuf. Nine. A.* Antoinette's code key was unlikely to be the same key used on a battlefield, but if it was being used right here in London . . . *Eight. B.* If the numbers were the key . . . There were only nine of them on Jefferson's wheel. If he worked his way through alphanumeric combinations of nine, he could see if any worked with the coded message he wanted to decipher.

His hands almost shook as he attempted to insert his version of the wheels over the ivory spindle. They didn't quite fit. It didn't matter. Jefferson's spindle was metal. Blake's was wood because he couldn't work metal. Ivory was just gilding the lily. "After you stole the stick, Harold sent you to Kate's?" he asked.

"Yes," Richard said sullenly. "Antoinette yelled and Harold hit her and she hit him back. And then we all went away."

Antoinette had yelled. Antoinette wanted the birds back. Her brother had offered a reward.

Harold's wife had been hiding a spindle from a code wheel in a birdcage. A spindle she removed from the cage—when she or *others* needed it. A spindle she needed to stack the wheels on to encrypt messages—using a designated pattern that started with a number matching a letter.

If any of his suspicions were true, it would look very

bad for Jocelyn and her family. The government destroyed traitors, and in consequence, their families, removing their titles, their lands, anything they possessed. He should burn the spindle and sell the birds.

He could not. He held evidence of Carrington treason in his hands, and also, possibly, the key to the French code that could save Wellesley's troops. He wondered how spies without birds would communicate the key to the code.

"Who knows you have this stick?" he asked, looking up to watch Richard pacing before the empty grate.

Richard shrugged. "Mama. Josie. A man."

Blake swallowed bile. He firmly rejected the notion that either Lady Carrington or Jocelyn was involved in treason, if treason this was. To them, a stick was a stick. Harold and Antoinette were the ones who had fought over losing the ivory. "A man?"

"He asked if he could buy Percy. I told him no. He tried to take Percy's perch away while I was fixing the cage." Richard finally looked up, frowning at the memory.

"When was this?" Blake tried not to cause alarm. Richard panicked easily.

"When I moved here. Before you did. He helped me hold a wire on the cage, but I didn't like him. He smelled funny."

"Was he short and fat?" Bernie didn't smell funny unless he was drunk. And Richard would recognize Harold or the knife-wielding thief.

"No, he was big like you."

The prior intruder had not been large, but Blake asked anyway, "The man you hit before?"

Richard shook his head. "No, but he talked like Antoinette. Funny."

French. Another damned Frenchman had been in his house. Looking at Richard's birds. And the cage. And the spindle—damning evidence of a code wheel to anyone who knew about them. As Blake did. As he'd stupidly made apparent to any who had listened—not realizing the French could actually have spies in England already.

A French thief had broken the glass and attempted to steal the cage. It couldn't be a coincidence. French spies might fear Blake would put two and two together.

Blake gazed at the slender piece of ivory, glanced toward the ceiling where Jocelyn waited, and decided he might hold both their fates in his hands. If he solved the code, he might earn the commission with Wellesley. If he reported Antoinette's treason, Jocelyn's reputation and that of her family would be ruined.

A pall of desperation descended as he spoke. "I'd like to borrow Percy's perch, if you don't mind, Richard. I'll give it back as soon as I'm done. Will you tell Jocelyn I'll be upstairs in a little while?"

Richard nodded. "I'll tell Percy, too."

Blake nodded absently, already working out a chart in his head. Puzzles were easier than dealing with the rampaging screams for justice in his head.

He could only pray the trap he had planned for tomorrow would catch French spies and not Jocelyn's relations.

32

Jocelyn fell asleep waiting for her husband to return to bed.

Blake still wasn't there when she woke at dawn.

Had the newness of their marriage bed worn off already? Not for her, it hadn't! She had learned to love waking in Blake's arms, feeling his arousal pressed against her, knowing he desired her. Wanted *her*, flighty little Ladybyrd.

He actually *listened* to her and made her feel special. And best of all, he heeded what she wanted! In bed, at least. She'd thought that might be important.

She kicked off the covers, and rather than wait to call on her mother or a maid to help her dress, she found her robe and wandered out in search of her errant spouse.

With any other man, she might descend into despair and fear that he had tired of her refusals and sought other outlets for his lust, but she knew Blake a little too well. He would never give up a challenge.

She found him asleep at the study desk, his dark hair

resting on his arms and scribbled papers scattered across the surface. Wood shavings dotted the desk, certain to leave ugly marks on his jaw. He'd let his hair grow overlong again, and she stroked the blue-black strands.

Blake stirred. Her emotions spun in a whirlwind she didn't understand and wasn't prepared to accept. Even in beard stubble and shirtsleeves, he was an immensely attractive man. She didn't know what she would do without him if he must go to war.

"Coffee?" she asked as he rubbed his eyes.

"I'll get it," he muttered, his eyes widening as he discovered her dishabille. "What the devil are you doing down here dressed like that?"

She smacked him over the head with one of his papers. "I could ask the same. I'll have the coffee sent upstairs so you may dress properly."

She whirled around and marched out to summon a maid, leaving the exasperating man to his work.

The exasperating man arrived in their bedchamber right behind the coffee tray, slamming the door shut after the departing maid and sweeping Jocelyn into his arms. Before she could utter a squeak, Blake kissed her so thoroughly she thought she might swoon from lack of air.

"What was that for?" she asked when they were both forced to breathe.

"For not hitting me with something harder than paper." He set her back down and grabbed the coffee, swallowing it black and boiling.

She knew him well enough now to recognize he was seething with some suppressed passion. Really, her husband might appear calm, but beneath that composure Blake Montague was a steaming cauldron that could scald on the slightest provocation.

"What did you find?" she asked, consumed with curiosity about what he'd been doing with his papers and books that so fascinated him.

He set the nearly empty cup down, raked his hands through his hair, and practically glowed with energy and excitement. "I have broken the code."

Jocelyn dropped to a chair in astonishment. "You've found the answer? How?"

He shook his head and looked as if he regretted having said anything. "Every code has a pattern. I found this one."

She sensed he was holding back, screening his words, but codes were military matters she did not understand, and he possibly thought she should not know. She would not press him. She was simply delighted that he was sharing his excitement.

"I must write Wellesley," he continued. "And persuade the War Office to see me."

That jerked her back to reality. "You cannot go into London today!" she said in alarm. "The masquerade is tonight. There is far too much to do. Send a note asking for a meeting. You can speak to a few of our guests this evening and ensure that whoever needs to hear your news will grant you an audience."

Beneath his mop of hair, Blake developed that mulish expression she recognized too well. She stood and poked him in his linen-covered chest. "Respect my knowledge of social codes, please. You cannot barge about London, demanding that important people see you. It is not done. Society is not a battlefield."

She stopped and thought about that, then shrugged. "Well, maybe it is, but not one in which traditional warfare wins out."

When he would have shrugged off her warning, she threw her arms around his neck and pressed against him, smiling as he developed that dazed look she loved so well. "I don't want you to go to war and die when you could save more lives by working here. If we are ever to have babies, you must trust my expertise in this matter."

Blake pressed her tight against him and watched her through smoky eyes. "Are we to have babies?"

"Oh, yes, I fear so, no matter how hard we may try to delay them."

She amazed herself by saying that. He amazed her even more by not arguing.

A grin tugged at the corners of his weary mouth. "I like it when you're being perfectly clear."

The heat of his kiss seared her straight to her toes, and Jocelyn vowed to be honest forevermore if this was the result.

"I thought we were wearing sackcloth and ashes," Blake said in puzzlement, watching his bedazzling wife descend the stairs that evening to greet the guests they'd invited to dinner before the masquerade. He was wearing a monk's cowled robe over his shirt and breeches. Given what he was about to do to his wife and her family, he probably ought to be wearing a hair shirt.

Jocelyn was wearing a Renaissance costume so spectacular he could scarcely tear his gaze from the plump mounds of her breasts, which he feared would pop from the corset. She wore her hair in a glorious mane of silver curls supported on a diamond tiara that resembled no sixteenth-century portrait he could recall. She glistened.

That might be because Jocelyn was wearing a fortune's worth of diamonds—in her hair, around her throat, dangling between her ripe breasts, on her wrists and fingers. He wagered she even wore them on her toes. This hadn't been part of his plans.

"Ice queen!" Fitz, the Earl of Danecroft, crowed. "Ice blue velvet, glittering ice, snowy froths of lace. . . ."

"You are far too familiar with ladies' costumes," Abigail, the Countess of Danecroft, noted. She wore a Queen of Hearts attire to match her husband's Knave.

"I chose yours, didn't I?" Fitz inquired cheerfully, gazing with affection at his red-haired wife. "Does it not suit?"

"Belden's diamonds," Quentin asserted, when Jocelyn bobbed a haughty curtsy before them, acting out her ice queen role by not deigning to reply. "I knew the late marquess possessed buckets of them, but I had not realized the extent of the largesse. I sense a plot behind the choice." He had not bothered with more than a black domino, the mask and cape of which currently adorned a chair so that he stood in his black evening attire.

"You had some doubt, milord?" Jocelyn inquired coolly. "Perhaps you thought ladies do not have the wits to plot?"

Nick Atherton, dressed as a dandy from a prior century in red heels, clocked stockings, and acres of lace and velvet, leaned against a doorjamb and admired Jocelyn's costume. "A man would have to be mindless to miss the fact that the ladies run the world. I bow to your greater grandeur, my queen." He made a leg and bowed so low his powdered wig threatened to fall off.

Feeling decidedly out of place in his homespun monk's robe, Blake grabbed the back of his friend's velvet coat and jerked him upright. "No peeking under skirts."

Nick placed his hand over his heart and adopted a humble pose. "Would I do such a thing? Really, I only sought to see if there were diamonds on your lovely wife's toes."

Since that was precisely the question he'd pondered, Blake considered punching his best friend in the snout but let it go when Jocelyn snickered.

"I'm hoping she's wearing a knife strapped to her ankle to fight off the hordes," Blake grumbled. "Jocelyn, don't you believe I have enough to worry about tonight without also having to beat off jewel thieves?"

Lady Belden swept down the staircase, garbed in a revealing black velvet gown, rubies, and a black cloak lined in garnet red. She wore her black hair stacked high and wrapped in more red jewels that framed her white powdered face and kohl-lined eyes. "We are not in the city. Jewel thieves are the least of your concerns," she declared in a low, throaty voice.

Blake noticed Lord Quentin came to attention at the sensual purr, but the Scotsman refrained from joining the banter, merely bowing over the lady's hand without comment.

"If you're dressed like that simply to provoke lying gossips, then the rest of us should be wearing weapons to prevent warfare," Blake said, convinced he should have found a musketeer's costume so he might wear a sword.

"No violence," Jocelyn warned. "We are all civilized, mature citizens with a healthy desire to satisfy our curiosity about Harold's peculiar behavior. There is no call for violence."

He had not told her of his suspicions about Harold's wife and French codes. Jocelyn still thought they were trying to stop birdnappers and her brother's lying gossip. If, after tonight, she took up swords and killed him, he could hardly blame her.

"Shall we have sherry and brandy in the parlor?" she suggested, leading the way.

"What peculiar behavior are we curious about?" Lady Danecroft inquired.

"Peculiar thieves," Nick said with deceptive joviality, already having been apprised of Blake's plot. Behind his blithe insouciance, Nick was on full alert tonight.

"Birds are peculiar," Quentin replied, entering the parlor to discover Richard and Lady Carrington hanging Percy's cage to a warning bell Richard had concocted to protect his pet. The dowager viscountess was looking distinguished in a velvet gown from her youth, with her hair elaborately coiffed. Richard had dressed in a proper jacket and trousers, but his neckcloth was already awry.

Jocelyn had not been happy when Blake had insisted on setting the birds up where they could be seen. He couldn't explain his plot without making her even less happy. The ice queen hauteur was probably for his benefit. She still hadn't learned to express her anger well, which was probably for the best.

"Awwwk, Percy want a canary," the parrot called, preening the fluffy new gray feathers he'd grown since being rescued.

"Fermez la bouche," Blake told the creature, reaching for the brandy bottle.

"Africa knows," the Grey replied happily, doing a little jig on his new perch and inspecting the guests gathering around him.

Africa knows. The birds repeated anything they heard. *Africa knew* the code key. How often had Percy heard the phrase? Blake's stomach soured at the treason hanging over their heads.

"You're training the bird to be a courtier," Nick decided. "Teach him flattery and we'll take him to Prinny."

"Nick doesn't really mean that, Richard," Blake reassured the boy, who looked alarmed. "Nick says a great deal of meaningless things, just like Percy."

Jocelyn sighed and took his arm. A rich perfume more potent than her usual lavender enveloped him, rendering him momentarily speechless. Which was probably her purpose, since she took charge. Lady Bell was correct. Jocelyn was meant to lead society.

"You are all here because you are our friends and would not spread the ridiculous rumors my half brother is perpetrating about town," Jocelyn blithely declared. "Blake has important information for the War Office, and we must make our guests aware that Harold's vicious rumors are untrue so they will take Blake seriously. I don't think that kind of plotting requires weapons, only common sense and your support."

In the light of new knowledge, even Harold's rumor-mongering pointed to evil intent—he, or his wife, was hoping to discredit anything Blake should discover. If Jocelyn's party did not cement Blake's reputation as a respectable citizen, the War Office might laugh off his spy theory as Castlereagh already had.

"Hear, hear!" Fitz cried, lifting his glass in a salute. "Well said. Am I allowed to fleece your guests in the game room, just a little?"

"Fleece them all you like," Blake agreed, "as long as they come away thinking you're a jolly good fellow and they ought to heed you when you tell them I'm not a desperate cad preying on my impecunious bride, as Carrington is spreading about."

With the bird secured, Lady Carrington smiled vaguely at their guests and drifted away. Richard stayed to monitor his pet. They'd divided the parrots in hopes of confusing any thieves. Now that Blake had a facsimile of the original spindle and the key to the code, he didn't need the ivory perch. Percy swung on it now, taunting villains, as planned.

"This isn't just about Carrington's rumors, is it?" Quentin murmured to Blake as the general conversation took a more lighthearted turn.

"Squelching rumors is what the ladies hope," Blake replied, watching Jocelyn as she charmed his friends with laughter, gentle touches, and an adept word or question here and there.

"But you think Carrington will show. Why? Was he added to the invitation list?"

"Hardly. Richard would run for the hills if the viscount showed up. Jocelyn would take a fire iron to Harold's head. But Carrington has a reason for maligning my name and for conspiring with Bernie. And I think I know what it is."

"Do you intend to tell me or remain enigmatic?" Quent asked in disgruntlement.

"I have Jocelyn's mother and brother to consider. You've seen them. They're helpless as babes in the woods. Jocelyn has stood between them and the real world for years. She's very good at it because she enjoys attention and diverts it from them. If Carrington is what I fear he is, his treachery could ruin them."

"I'm not following," Quentin admitted. "Carrington is a termite, I understand, but I don't see how that can harm your wife or her family."

From across the parlor, Jocelyn sent Blake a knowing glance. He lifted his glass in salute, as if he wasn't being torn by powerful forces. Even the suspicion of treason would destroy Jocelyn's social standing. He needed proof first. "Just keep an eye out for Carrington and Ogilvie. I expect them or their hired scoundrels to be lurking."

"Fitz and Nick are watching for them also?"

Blake nodded. "I'm hoping we can catch the cads without an audience, but the chances aren't good. Jocelyn's invitations have all been accepted, and she's expecting a crush. You should find yourself a wife like her. She'd erase the stench of trade and have half of society believing you're heir to a kingdom."

Quent snorted. "Apparently love infects the brains of even the smartest men. I hope she's worth it, old chap." After pounding Blake on the back, he wandered off to annoy Lady Bell.

Leaving Blake to ponder his words. *Lust* might be affecting his brains, but love? That would indeed be dangerous.

And might explain why he was oddly reluctant to catch a traitor and blot the name of Carrington.

33

Jocelyn sighed happily as the house filled with laughing, cheerful people—just as she'd once dreamed, and all thanks to Blake.

Because of the crowd, it wasn't obviously noticeable that the surroundings were a little shabby. The company was too busy preening in their costumes, drinking Lady Bell's fine wine, and exclaiming over one another to care if the sofa was outmoded or the draperies were muslin. She'd purchased some greenery on credit, and Lady Bell and Lord Quentin had contributed more, so the heated glasshouse looked both spacious and elegant.

The diamonds she wore were having an amazing effect. All her father's old cronies patted her on the back and murmured about knowing her father had taken care of her and that the rumors clearly weren't true. Their wives hummed with envy and assured Jocelyn they'd be sending invitations to dinners, the kind of invitations Blake needed to make his way in government. It was amazing how much society judged on appearance.

She was astoundingly fortunate to have found the one man who saw *her*, and not just what she wore. A man who could even see beyond what she said to what she meant. Someone probably ought to slap some sense into her, but she was giddy with happiness. Her brilliant husband thought she was clever and useful and not a burden!

She sought a glimpse of Blake across the conservatory and hoped he was succeeding in meeting the men he needed to impress.

Because so many of these people were old friends of her father's, they accepted Richard's peculiarities without the usual maliciousness. Well, most of them just ignored him, but Richard preferred to be ignored. She watched as he showed Lady Jersey how to feed Africa. The lady might regret giving up her canaries if birds became all the rage again.

Blake had found local musicians to play country dances—nothing sophisticated, but a pleasant diversion for those so inclined. She had hoped to join Blake in the dancing later. She'd spent this first hour memorizing costumes as their guests arrived. If their ploy worked and drew out the miscreants who were causing them such grief, she needed to differentiate between guests and intruders.

Jocelyn narrowed her eyes as an unfamiliar domino wove through the colorful costumes in the center of the conservatory. That domino hadn't been among those she'd greeted.

"Lady Danecroft, may I impose upon you?" she murmured to the countess, who had stopped beside her at the buffet table.

With the ruff of her Queen of Hearts costume slightly askew, Abigail Wyckerly paused in her contemplation of the tarts. "Gladly. Fitz has deserted me for the gaming table, and I do not know half these people, so any task will amuse me."

"I will be happy to introduce you to any and all, but right now, I need my husband or one of his friends to keep an eye on that man in the domino, the short one, not Lord Quentin. Whoever you find, tell him I'll be in the parlor. I suspect that stealing Percy may be the intruder's purpose in coming here."

"You will tell me the story sometime?" Lady Danecroft asked, picking up on Jocelyn's urgency.

"It could easily become the evening's entertainment," Jocelyn promised grimly. It would most certainly be diverting to punch Bernie in the beak if he meant to steal Percy back. She didn't understand why Blake had insisted on placing Percy in plain sight.

The Queen of Hearts nodded and dived into the crowd.

Clenching her fingers into fists, Jocelyn wended her way toward the conservatory exit, stopping to chat when she was approached while keeping an eye on the figure in black.

Instead of aiming for the front parlor and Percy, the unidentified guest gravitated toward the greenery where Richard and Africa were entertaining a small group. Was she wrong? Was that not someone attempting to retrieve Percy for the duke?

She hesitated, then noticed the Queen of Hearts and the formidable Lord Quentin striding toward Richard, and sighed in relief. Blake's friend would make mincemeat of the intruder. Still, she'd feel better if she checked on Percy.

A few ladies asked for the retiring chamber, and she directed them to the top of the stairs. In the foyer, she noticed that the front door had been left open. Her footman was nowhere about. She supposed some of the gentlemen might have stepped outside to smoke. That was the trouble with a small house. There was never enough room for everyone's bad habits.

Blake's study had become a gaming room, routing her mother from her usual hiding place. Jocelyn saw that Lord Danecroft had amassed a stack of coins in front of him. She waved when he winked at her, but she continued on. Blake had said his friend was short of funds, with a costly estate he hoped to return to profit. She liked his countess and wished the earl well, but she was glad Blake was not in the habit of gambling.

A few elderly ladies had congregated in the parlor, away from the dancing and music. They had set up their own card table and scarcely glanced up at Jocelyn's entrance. Lady Bell was there, chatting with several of her friends and feeding Percy. The bird was safe for the moment.

The only male present was Teddy, the footman, offering a round of punch to the ladies. The man in the domino would look exceedingly out of place if he charged into this chamber.

Relieved, Jocelyn swept across the parlor to speak with Lady Bell. The billowing old-fashioned skirts and panniers she wore made her feel like a ship rolling across the sea, and the diamonds felt like an anchor around her neck. She'd be happy to divest herself of them soon.

She noticed someone had opened a casement window overlooking the side yard. The heavy stench of perfume and candle smoke required fresh air, but it would be better if one of the windows away from Percy were opened. She could fix that.

"Jocelyn, there you are," Lady Bell called as she approached. "I was just telling Lady Ann that you designed this brilliant costume for me."

Jocelyn curtsied to the Duke of Fortham's daughter.

"That is an amazing watered silk, my lady. Angelic, with all the lace and petticoats. I do believe your fashion style suits Mr. Atherton's costume."

Tall with dark hair that set off the ivory silk of her gown, Lady Ann did not smile. "I believe Atherton chose his costume to outdo me on purpose. His sisters knew what I would be wearing."

"I cannot imagine why he would—" Jocelyn paused, seeing movement outside the window. Perhaps it was just one of the smokers. She hurriedly finished her sentence— "do such a thing, unless he seeks your attention."

"Atherton? I hardly think so. My father would cut Nick's throat."

"Your father is one of the many reasons you are not married," Lady Bell said with a laugh. "Is His Grace here? We sent him an invitation in case he'd returned from Scotland."

"He's home. He mentioned an impudent woman and putting her in her place, but I doubt he'll show. In any case, you needn't worry. Mostly, he's all bark and no bite, though the bark is terrifying enough."

Jocelyn laughed. "I shall have to correct His Grace's notion of me if he deigns to put in an appearance."

"Which just proves your impudence," Lady Ann pointed out with a smile. "No one corrects my father."

"He's not met Mr. Montague then," Lady Bell said. "He and Jocelyn are two of a kind."

Trying to determine how she and Blake could possibly be alike, Jocelyn didn't immediately reply. Before she could, the sounds of an escalating tumult reverberated from the conservatory.

Blake was already halfway through the crowd, pursuing Jocelyn, when Richard cried out in outrage, and Quent nearly knocked over a prancing Egyptian in his effort to reach the boy. Blake cast a hasty glance after his wife's swaying skirts, but a struggle involving overturned greenery ensued as Richard dashed after someone hiding behind the potted palms. Blake changed course to follow the lad.

Before Blake could cross the crowded room, a pudgy man in a domino climbed from under a fallen palm and snatched Africa's cage from Richard's arms. The boy shouted, waving his hands and causing a commotion. Cursing the throng of costumed guests, Blake fought his way toward the back and the nearest exit—the thief's apparent goal. Women screamed as the birdnapper stepped on the trains of their gowns. The musicians halted their playing in uncertainty.

Africa's squawks rose above the screams, matched by Richard's frenzied yells as the boy stumbled after the thief. Deciding the assemblage was too dense for him to elbow his way through, Blake turned back toward the empty corridor into the house with the intent of reaching the street to cut off the thief. Quent and Nick were closer to the rear and could block the back.

By the time Blake reached the parlor, the ladies at the card table had leaped up to see what was happening. Skirts and feathers and petticoats filled the corridor as Lady Bell and her friends raced past him, toward the conservatory.

Where was Jocelyn?

As the women's gowns foamed around him like sea froth about a boulder, Blake fought to see if his wife was guarding the other trap Richard had set. He relaxed as he arrived at the door and saw Jocelyn reaching to shut the window near Percy's cage. As if she was expecting him, she turned and lifted questioning eyes in Blake's direction.

Alarm punched him in the gut at a sight just past his wife's shoulder.

At his expression, Jocelyn whipped around.

A cloaked figure leaned through the open window, wielding a wicked knife and reaching out to slash the ropes attaching the cage to Richard's makeshift alarm system. The bells rang a clarion, but the noise was drowned out by the crowd's uproar in the conservatory.

Shouting his fury, Blake raced into the room and nearly died a thousand deaths as he watched Jocelyn grab a fireplace poker and whack at the wrist holding the cage.

The thief screamed in agony, grabbing his arm and dropping the cage, but not the knife. Apparently intent only on rescuing the bird, Jocelyn caught and cradled the immense cage against her chest, nearly coming unbalanced from Percy's terrified flapping.

To Blake's horror, instead of fleeing, the cloaked intruder cursed and climbed over the sill, into the room. Before Blake could pull Jocelyn out of harm's way, the villain had her in a stranglehold and was pressing the knife to her throat. With her arms full of cage, she couldn't easily struggle.

One swift stroke, one wrong move, and Jocelyn could lose her life.

"Stand back, Montague, or I'll make my pretty sister a little less attractive."

Jocelyn thought her knees would give out, but Harold jerked her chin up so she couldn't see Blake's expression. The horror she'd glimpsed in her husband's face as he'd entered was sufficient to make her regret that she'd involved him in another of her family's disasters. She did not want him to regret marrying her, but for the first time in her life, she intended to fight back. Blake had shown her the meaning of courage.

Heart thudding, she clung to Percy's cage, praying for

a distraction before either man did anything rash. The commotion in the conservatory seemed to have grown in volume and had spilled into the yard.

She and Blake were alone in the parlor with Harold.

"It's the bird or her life," Harold said maliciously. "I'd hate to see a bastard like you gain her inheritance if I have to kill her."

Setting her jaw, Jocelyn wriggled, attempting to force Harold to loosen his grip, but she refused to drop the cage. The knife pressed into her skin.

"Jocelyn, give him the damned bird," Blake ordered in a calm voice.

She heard the ominous undertone to his words. She hoped he didn't have a pistol. She didn't want Blake hanging for murder.

If she let Percy go, Harold would win. They would never be safe again.

Everything she'd hoped for the future would be transformed into bleak emptiness unless she fought back now. She would not let Harold destroy their happy nest—again.

"Jocelyn, give up the bird," Blake repeated, his voice steady.

"No," she declared, clinging to the cage. "I would rather you beat Harold senseless with the poker, please."

Harold stretched her chin higher, endangering her neck, but she still would not surrender. She prayed Blake did not expect her to, that he understood this fight was about more than a bird. It was about self-respect and fighting for what was right.

"I need that bird," Harold growled. "Release it before your little playmate tries anything stupid."

"Let him have the cage," Blake said calmly.

Oh, she'd let Harold have it, all right. She'd crack his skull with the cage, if she could. "Why?" she managed to mutter from her uncomfortable position, wondering if she could possibly let Harold have the cage and still rescue Percy.

"Oh, just a small matter of treason," her husband claimed with deceptive nonchalance.

Treason? Jocelyn tried to swallow. She heard Blake approaching. She had a strong suspicion that the calmer he sounded, the more dangerous he became. If Harold was a traitor . . .

She choked on bile. Her family could ruin Blake's good name forever. He would never take a position at Whitehall. He'd go to war and die, just as his mother feared.

She panicked, wondering if Blake was less likely to be blamed if she gave up the cage.

"A matter of survival," Harold corrected. "Your husband is a bit too clever for his own good if he's figured out the purpose of the birds, but he doesn't understand necessity." He forced her chin higher. "Play nice, and Antoinette's brother and his cronies will be happy, and the authorities need never know. Give me the bird, Jocelyn, or I'll blame everything on your new husband and see him hang."

She almost handed him the cage then. But she couldn't. She'd changed in these last months. She thought maybe Blake had given her the confidence to develop a backbone of sorts. She simply could not let the bully have his way.

"I don't believe thieves and liars, Harold," she declared proudly, "so nothing you can say will change my mind." Jocelyn knew she was pushing Harold to his limits, that she should not rely on a white knight coming to her rescue.

But this time, she had someone strong on her side, someone who believed in justice and honesty. This time, she was trusting Blake not to call her a flibbertiwidget but to see that she was right and act accordingly. Even if Harold was a traitor—*especially* if he was a traitor—he had to be stopped.

She knew when Blake reached her side, even if she couldn't see him from the awkward angle at which Harold held her. She could smell his shaving soap and the male scent. She had only one chance to distract Harold so Blake could reach him.

She shrieked at the top of her lungs and slammed her head backward into her brother's chin.

34

The blackest moment of Blake's life was hearing his brave Jocelyn scream and watching her crumple to the floor after the flash of Harold's knife.

The bastard may as well have stabbed him in the heart. Never could he survive Jocelyn's loss, even if she was a mule-headed nodcock for placing a bird's life above her own. She was *his* nodcock and he loved her beyond reason.

For England and honor, Blake knew his duty was to leap out the window and chase the traitor as he fled into the night. Percy's squawks made an easy trail to follow.

But he could not desert Jocelyn, as every other person in her life had done, not while the beautiful, laughing, defiant creature of moments earlier lay still in a puddle of silk upon the floor. What good were duty and honor if he lost her?

Shedding his hampering monk's robe, leaving him in shirtsleeves and trousers, Blake dropped to his knees.

Anguish washed over him as he dug in his waistcoat pocket for a clean handkerchief to stop the blood marring a loosened silver curl. The knife had slashed off the rope of diamonds, tearing the jewels from Jocelyn's slender throat. The cut left behind didn't look deep, but she was unconscious. *Had Carrington broken her neck?*

Blake's hands shook, and inside he screamed at the injustice as he very carefully examined the wound. Jocelyn did not deserve this. Finally, he saw her chest move. She was breathing, so must he. He applied the linen to staunch the bleeding and prayed as he'd never prayed before.

At his touch, her lashes fluttered open and frosty blue eyes glared up at him. "Stop him, Blake! Don't let the jackass escape!" she rasped.

She might as well have punched a fist to his chest and awakened his heart. Blood pumped through his veins again, air filled his lungs, and rage rushed to his head. Still, Jocelyn came first.

"He's stealing part of a French code machine. If I catch him and he's judged a traitor," Blake warned, "it will mean your family will be ostracized by all society."

"No." She shook her head, winced, and grabbed the linen he still held to her throat. "No, England and your future are more important. We can lose the house. I can live elsewhere. But I will not let the bully win. Stop him!"

Blake hoped she would someday forgive him for once believing she lacked depth of character. He wanted to cover her in kisses for giving him the freedom to do as he must. In relief, he pressed his lips to her forehead. She would not regret her sacrifice.

He left her to struggle to her feet and vaulted out the window to the side yard.

Outside, he had to determine Carrington's direction. Richard and half the party were running frantically about among the dark shrubbery, shouting and chasing a portly figure in a domino.

Bitty, the Pomeranian ball of fluff, had apparently escaped the kitchen. She ran yipping in happy circles around their guests, thinking this a new game designed just for her delectation.

Even as Blake watched, the domino-clad figure carrying a cage holding squawking Africa tripped over the mutt, splashed his way across the lily pond, and attempted to escape down the carriage drive. If Ogilvie wanted the duke's bird, the idiot was in the process of birdnapping the wrong parrot.

Harold would run in the opposite direction from the crowd, toward the front. He'd been clever to set Ogilvie as a diversion, but not clever enough. Percy's frightened cries gave him away.

Before Blake could race toward the darkened street, a pig squealed near the untrimmed yews at the front corner of the house. Harold's familiar curses followed, and with a grin of comprehension, Blake stuck his fingers between his teeth and whistled loudly.

The pig he had been training snorted, not at the intruder, but in anticipation of food. Nothing could come between a pig and his dinner, certainly not Harold. The villain's shouts reversed direction as he stumbled backward into the hedge, mowed down by a rampaging swine. Blake stalked toward the scoundrel. He kept a wary eye out for Harold's knife as he attempted to distinguish the wretch's shadow among the greenery.

A swathe of light suddenly illuminated the side yard.

Blake swung around to see Jocelyn on the windowsill, holding the fireplace poker in one hand and a lantern in the other. "Do you have pistols? Shall I find them?" she called.

Blake's sense of the ridiculous suddenly struck him, and he would have laughed at his once-docile wife's bloodthirsty suggestion, except he was still too enraged. Even his relief at knowing she was well wasn't sufficient to subdue his murderous urge to carve Harold into pig slop.

The lantern lit the shadowy shrubbery, where a fat figure slashed at a pair of irate hens while clinging to a birdcage. Percy's irate obscenities screeched louder.

At the lily pond end of the yard, a composed Lord Quentin held a lighted torch to illumine guests in togas and ball gowns chasing after a demented Richard. The boy was screaming and waving his spindly arms as he attempted to cut off the domino-wearing birdnapper, who was now in retreat from attack roosters.

Blake's attention was diverted by Harold fighting free of a flock of hens on his way toward the garden wall between this house and the next. Did he plan to climb a wall with cage in hand?

"The rabbit hutch," Jocelyn called. "He's heading for the rabbit hutch."

Before Blake could close in on his prey, a tall cloaked figure slipped from the deeper shadows. Harold passed the cage to the newcomer before scrambling for the roof of the hutch.

At last! The mastermind behind the nincompoops. "If you can jump down from there, Jocelyn, take the poker to your brother," Blake shouted. "This devil is *mine.*"

He merely had to follow the trail of Percy's squawks as the stranger leaped over the feral pigs with more athletic grace than clumsy Carrington had employed.

Relishing a more worthy opponent, Blake raced after him, taking a shortcut by using the head of a statue to vault over the yews. Damned good thing he knew this yard better than the stranger did because the leap jarred every sore muscle in his leg.

The bird thief attempted to elude him, but Blake had his powerful fury to fuel the race, and the brains to know there was only one way out of the fenced yard. He timed his next leap well and struck the thief broadside.

Percy's cage hit the ground and rolled under the hedge, but Blake was too busy pounding his fists into his opponent to rescue the obscenity-spewing parrot. In between the bird's curses, Blake detected a new shriek that sounded like *El Bear.*

El Bear. The parrot's French pronunciation of Albert. The name of Antoinette's brother—the big man now spewing French curses as he attempted to throttle Blake.

With one brutal swing of his fist, Blake slammed the thief's jaw squarely, and the fight was over. Damn. He wanted a good excuse to strangle the bastard who could steal his wife's reputation and happiness. But lacking his former frustration, Blake's propensity for violence had diminished. He couldn't kill the bastard in cold blood.

In disgust, he used *El Bear*'s own cloak to truss him up in knots that not even a magician could escape. Worried about Jocelyn's ability to restrain Viscount Pig, Blake grabbed Percy's cage and ran back toward the side of the house.

He was just in time to see his feral pigs snorting at Carrion's heels as the viscount climbed onto the roof of the rickety rabbit hutch so he might climb over the wall and escape. But the rotten wood of the hutch roof crumbled beneath Harold's excessive weight, and he lost his footing, falling back to the muddy ground. Jocelyn stood over him with her weapon raised.

"I have him cornered!" she shouted, swinging the poker at her brother's boots.

"I think I like living in the country," Blake announced, sauntering to his wife's side with a nonchalance he didn't feel. He set aside Percy's cage and forced himself to wait to see what she would do next.

He fought the urge to tell her to get the hell back inside before Harold tried some new trick. He had to allow her the opportunity to fight her own battles. Damnable to become victim of the same anxiety his parents had suffered all these years while they worried about his violent tendencies, but he couldn't deny Jocelyn this triumph.

Unable to climb the wall, seeing the crowd blocking his exit to the rear, Harold stupidly decided his chances were better through his sister. Clambering back to his feet, he rushed at her.

Jocelyn swung the poker at his knees. Harold howled.

As Harold stumbled forward, Blake balled up his already bruised knuckles and plowed them into the viscount's weak chin. A pig lurched, squealing, from beneath the collapsed hutch and ran directly into the back of Harold's knees. Between swine and fist, Viscount Pig toppled backward, hitting the wet ground again with a spray of mud.

Blake calmly stepped on Carrington's wrist, pinning him down.

"Hit him, just once more," Jocelyn cried, handing him the poker so she might drag her massive skirts from the ground. "Or can I kick him?" Not waiting for permission, she slammed her slippered toe into the bully's ribs. "That felt much too good. I believe violence is addictive." She kicked him again. "That's for terrifying Percy. I'd have to kill you for what you've done to everyone else." She lifted Percy's cage to coo soothingly at the screaming bird.

Blake bit back a grin, finding it hard to resist laughing at his wife's unusual display of fury. If she became comfortable with displaying what she really felt, he might come to regret it.

"Josie, Josie, I got him!" Richard cried from the backyard. "I got Africa and the bad man!"

"Ogilvie, one hopes," Blake said, hauling Jocelyn to his right side to press a kiss to her cheek while continuing to crush Harold's arm into the mud.

Harold grabbed at Blake's good leg with his free hand, trying to tumble him off, but nothing short of an earthquake would persuade him to let the bastard free after what he'd done to Jocelyn. With his left fist, Blake planted the poker square between Harold's ribs to prevent his rising. Holding Jocelyn at his side, he kissed the small wound on his wife's slender throat, inducing a purr of happiness. A pig began to sniff Harold's sleeve, causing him to curse and struggle.

"What the devil is going on here?" an authoritative voice boomed over the tumult of shouts and laughter and squawking parrot. "Is this a masquerade or a circus? I had to leave my footman tying up a Frenchie in the front yard. What is the meaning of this?" the new arrival demanded of Blake and Jocelyn, before roaring toward the melee in the backyard. "Ann, where the demmed hell are you?"

"Here, Papa. We have just caught a birdnapper." A poised figure in ivory and lace, Lady Ann separated from the crowd of guests.

The Duke of Fortham—Lady Ann's father—had

arrived. Blake cursed. There went any chance he had of keeping Harold's treason quiet and of protecting Jocelyn.

Needing to greet his noble guest properly, Blake stomped on Harold's shoulder until the scoundrel screamed and released his grip on Blake's leg.

Still cradling the cage in one arm, Jocelyn managed a graceful curtsy, attempting to hold her skirts above the mud and away from Harold as the duke stomped through the side yard. "Your Grace, it is a pleasure."

"Looks like you demmed well had your pleasure before I arrived. Montague, is that you?" Tall and built like a stout oak, the duke stepped into the light of a lantern and leaned his craggy visage forward to search their faces for recognition.

He gazed in contempt at the man whimpering under Blake's foot. "Carrion," he said with a sneer. "Upsetting the apple cart as usual? Are you responsible for the Frenchie out front?"

"Theft and possible treason, Your Grace," Blake murmured. "We will explain."

"No doubt. Is that my bird?" He squinted at Percy. "Don't look like him."

"He's Richard's bird, Your Grace," Jocelyn said sweetly.

Blake tried not to shake his head at his wife for arguing with a duke. It pained him not to protect her with every drop of his blood, but he had encouraged her to be honest instead of deceptive. No more flapping her lashes and hiding behind a fan. He couldn't stop her now. If they hung for her bravado, at least they would hang together.

In any case, he could not let Antoinette and her spies get away, so she and the viscount had to be denounced.

"I think you'd best rescue your nephew, Your Grace,"

Lord Quentin called from the back. "I do believe young Mr. Carrington is about to take Bernie apart for stealing his other bird."

Blake fought a grin at the duke's raised eyebrows. Now that Harold's fate was sealed, Blake's sense of the ridiculous was in great danger of taking over. He'd been in peril of becoming a bitter, cynical man until Jocelyn had showed him a lighter perspective on human behavior. He hoped more masquerades were in their future.

He turned to observe Nick in lace and Fitz in his knave's costume hauling a filthy Ogilvie off the ground while Richard clung to Africa's cage, raising his free fist and dancing around the thief.

"Bernard?" the duke said incredulously. "What the *devil* are you doing? Is that my bird?"

"It is, Your Grace," Bernard called sulkily. "They would not let me have him back, so I stole him for you."

"That's Africa," Jocelyn corrected. "The greengrocer's bird."

"I see." The duke eyed her with suspicion, then turned to Blake. "I think we'd better go inside and have some explanations. I hear you're a man of honor. Can I trust your word?"

"You can entrust the safety of all England to Blake," Jocelyn asserted proudly. "But we have to truss Harold up like the pig he is before we can offer explanations."

One look at the duke's startled expression, and Blake couldn't contain his laughter anymore. With his arm around his daunting wife, he howled his mirth.

Still dressed in billowing silk but without the diamonds she'd returned to Lady Bell—including the necklace they'd found in Harold's pocket—Jocelyn sent Richard off to bed while the men were hauling their prisoners inside for interrogation. Richard mercifully took Africa and Percy upstairs with him so they might calm down after their adventure.

With her brother out of the way, she joined Blake in saying farewell to their guests. She helped the servants find wraps and signal carriages, and prayed that the evening's events would not make her a laughingstock for all the kingdom. She'd been assured by many that the evening had been a delight, but that did not mean that by morning everyone wouldn't have concluded otherwise. The party had, after all, been a shocking hubble-bubble, with only a few knowing they'd caught an agent of Napoleon's government.

She'd refused to let Blake join his friends until she'd taken him to their chamber and wrapped his scraped knuckles. She promised she would not write his parents about the wound unless he continued breaking into inappropriate chuckles. Her husband still had the social graces of a turkey, but she could not prevent her giddy joy at hearing him laugh. He laughed so seldom, and happiness looked wonderful on him.

He kissed her so thoroughly, she almost forgot about Viscount Pig and his treachery, but a commotion rose in the front entry, jarring them from this stolen moment of bliss. From the shrill shrieking, Jocelyn thought one of the parrots must have escaped.

And then it dawned on her—Antoinette!

"Can we shoot her?" she whispered to Blake, who was already heading down the stairs ahead of her.

"Keep your fire poker handy," he suggested. "I can't throw her a facer as I did her brother."

"Out of my way, *chien*! You cannot keep me from my family." Below, Antoinette was wielding her berib-boned parasol to beat back the footman. Seeing the Earl of Danecroft step from the study to investigate her shouts, she flew in his direction. "Where is my Albert?"

she cried. "And where is that incompetent oaf who left me waiting in the cold all these hours?"

Blake finished the last few steps on the fly, grabbing the parasol in midswing and yanking it loose from Antoinette's grip.

Jocelyn sighed. It seemed the evening's entertainment was not quite over.

While Blake and Fitz held her sister-in-law's wrists, Jocelyn descended the stairs expecting Antoinette to foam at the mouth any moment.

"You!" her charming witch of a sister-in-law spat when she quit shouting long enough to see Jocelyn approach. "Why could you not invite us with all your other friends! There would not be such a scene if I had been here. Men are not to be trusted! They are all oafs. I could have had the birdies and been gone!" She twisted at the hands binding her. "Let me go, *bâtards*!"

Fitz nodded his head toward the study door. "The other two are ratting each other out as we speak. What do we do with this one?"

"We could just throw them all in the cellar with her brother and see who comes out alive," Blake suggested.

"We have guests," Jocelyn said, nodding toward the parlor, where she'd left Lady Danecroft and Lady Belden. "They might object to barbarity."

At Antoinette's continued shrieking of epithets, she turned and slapped her sister-in-law's face. The effect was immediate. Antoinette shut up and glared sullenly. "If you cannot behave with decorum," Jocelyn told her, "you may join Albert in the cellar."

With the shrieking silenced, Blake dragged his prisoner toward the study. The instant Antoinette saw Harold bound and trussed, she screeched again and berated him with a barrage of French and English that brought both ladies from the front parlor.

Jocelyn grimaced. She didn't understand the French, but enough of the English implicated all of them in parrot theft, if naught else.

"I will not tolerate such language in front of my wife. One of you must sacrifice your neckcloth," Blake demanded. "Tie her up and heave her in the cellar like the rat she is."

He used his own neckcloth to bind Antoinette's mouth, blessedly silencing the shrieks. Even Harold didn't complain as Atherton happily contributed his linen to tie the viscountess's hands. Jocelyn thought her brother just looked defeated, but Harold had stolen her necklace and ruined her party, and she had no sympathy for him.

Lord Quentin prodded their new prisoner out of the study, nonchalantly bowing to the staring ladies in the hall as he did so.

The men returned to interrogating their two aristocratic prisoners as if Jocelyn were not there. Apparently while she and Blake had been upstairs, both Ogilvie and Harold had squealed on each other, like the bullying cowards they were.

Ranting and shouting and throwing accusations now ensued—until Jocelyn grew tired of the senseless arguments. She left the study and summoned the maids hired for the evening to gather the remains of the buffet table and carry them to the front room.

When she returned to the study to announce that refreshments were being served, the lot obediently followed her out, keeping Ogilvie and Harold tied with wrists behind their backs.

Once she had the men sipping coffee and brandy and nibbling on sandwiches, she could breathe. Almost. She did not perfectly understand what treason Harold and Antoinette had perpetrated, but she was furious enough to lop off their heads.

"From what they've told us so far, Carrington's wife is a traitor, but we cannot prove that the viscount is more than an incompetent thief and bully," Blake told the duke. "He aided Albert in hiring a ruffian to break into the house and steal back Percy, so he is a danger to my family and cannot be trusted, but you know perfectly well that charging him with treason means his property and title will be forfeit and the reputations of innocent family members will be destroyed."

My family. Jocelyn wondered if he heard himself. The man who had wanted to be left alone was now claiming her and hers as his. She wouldn't argue with that. She had just discovered she liked being part of a pair, especially now that her educated husband had learned to listen to her.

"You would tar my nephew with the same brush!" the duke roared, as he had since he'd arrived. "I will not have it. He's an imbecile, not a traitor. Your wife's father warned me years ago that something was amiss with those birds. I couldn't nab both of them when Harold sold them, but I got the one and told Bernie to keep an eye on it. And that's what he's demmed well nearly killed himself doing."

"While attempting to kill me in the process," Blake asserted. "I was nearly maimed by a burr under my saddle acquired in your stable after an argument with your nephew."

An argument, *balderdash*, Jocelyn thought. It had been a duel. But she held her tongue and let Blake speak his piece while idly wondering why a mighty duke had bothered to accept her humble invitation. His arrival was a trifle too convenient.

"I almost broke my neck stumbling over an andiron after we had another confrontation, and an ale barrel nearly crushed me after a contretemps at the club. I cannot say Bernard is innocent," Blake continued. "He conspired with Carrington to steal birds that concealed the key to a French spy code. If my wife and her family are to be tarred by the taint of treason, then I demand equal treatment for your nephew."

Jocelyn tried to follow his logic. If Harold was a traitor, then she supposed the crown might reclaim his title and estate, not that he had much. But Richard, as his heir, would lose everything, and her sisters and all her relations would suffer abject humiliation.

Blake was trying to protect her family—by forcing the duke to condemn his nephew? Or by asking that he let Harold go? That did not sound right—unless he personally meant to tar and feather Harold and run him out of town on a rail. Then what would he do with Antoinette?

Lord Quentin had returned from placing her in the cellar and now stood in the doorway, hands behind his back, observing the shouting match. Lady Belden offered him a sandwich plate.

"Who the devil are you to tell me how I should conduct myself!" the duke raged, stalking up and down the small parlor.

"Blake is the man who both caught a French spy and broke their code." Jocelyn finally entered the fray on a note of exasperation with men who thundered and postured but could not communicate effectively.

"Blake can show the War Office how the code works," she continued. "He can give them the invention that Harold is claiming he was threatened into stealing, and teach the parrots to reveal more, if you like. Shouting at each other solves nothing."

"May I suggest, Your Grace—" Quentin started to say.

"It's your suggestion that brought me here, Hoyt!

Why the devil are you and the rest of these young scoundrels still about?" The duke scowled at Blake's friends. "Where did Lord Eldon and Westmoreland go? Weren't they just here? Let's hear from men with experience!"

"Your Grace." Jocelyn stood and stepped in front of the pacing tiger, handing him a glass of brandy with a practiced curtsy, hampered somewhat by her swinging panniers. "Our friends are here to vouch for Blake. He had naught to do with Harold and Bernie except catch them stealing my birds. Lord Westmoreland and Lord Eldon were friends of my father, and you may call on them as you like for their opinions, but Harold and his wife affect *me* and Mr. Ogilvie affects *you*, so it would be simpler to decide their fates quietly among ourselves. Albert is not English, so you may do as you wish with him."

Lady Belden and Lady Danecroft had refused to depart as long as the men were allowed to stay. They murmured approvingly and sipped their tea, forcing the men to choose their words carefully. Jocelyn imagined steam emerging from the duke's ears as he muffled his curses and was forced to think instead of shout.

She sent Lord Quentin a thoughtful glance. She appreciated his subtlety. The man never appeared to participate in events, but he was always behind them. He was the reason the duke had unexpectedly arrived on her doorstep.

In a distant corner, Harold protested, "I am no spy! Albert and his henchmen threatened to kill me if I didn't stop Montague from figuring out the bird code. Spying is for filthy tradesmen!" He shot Lord Quentin a look of scorn.

"You stole Lady Belden's necklace while trying to slit your sister's throat. You're a thief, worse than any pickpocket." Unlike their other guests, Quentin had worn boots beneath his domino, and the kick he gave Harold shut him up.

Looking dangerously competent in his role as guard, Mr. Atherton crossed his arms and leaned against the wall, standing over a sullen Mr. Ogilvie, who was too cowed by his noble uncle to speak or run.

Lord Danecroft flipped cards from one hand to the other with a player's skill while observing the scene.

"You can keep the parrot, Montague," the duke grumbled. "I'll find an estate in Scotland to stash Bernie where he can do no harm. But what the devil am I to do with Carrion there, if his wife is a traitor?"

"If I might?" Danecroft intruded quietly. At the duke's glare, he continued, not intimidated. "Montague has an encyclopedic mind. He has been trying to tell the War Office of Jefferson's code wheel for some time now, but they are in such disorder that they did not listen."

The earl waited a moment to see if the duke would deny the charge. When he didn't, he continued. "When the War Office ignored his warnings, Blake created a code wheel of his own and deciphered a French missive by using the key Harold's wife had taught the birds. Then he set a trap and caught the traitor. If Jocelyn's brother is charged with treason and brought to trial, Montague's affiliation with a traitor will ruin him for his efforts, and England will lose the use of his brilliant mind."

Jocelyn wanted to cheer for the earl's wisdom in grasping the crux of the problem. Really, people ought to celebrate intelligence more often. She would kiss the earl's cheek, but the petite countess would probably bash her with her Queen of Hearts scepter.

"And society will lose Jocelyn's refreshing company," Lady Belden added. "She has her father's astute political mind, Your Grace. You might well use her talents."

Since Jocelyn was sitting there in bedraggled silks

from a bygone era, her hair all a-tumble, and a sticking plaster on her throat, she did not think this a convincing argument, but she appreciated the support.

"Lady Bell's man of business has been investigating for me," Jocelyn said. "It seems Harold and his wife have run up gaming debts so steep they can never buy their way out," she explained, hoping to exonerate the Pig from treason, for Richard's sake.

"After you learn all from them that you can, they really need to be deported like common criminals, Your Grace," Quent suggested. "Would that not solve the problem better than a charge of treason that can only hurt the rest of the family, all of whom are innocent of treachery? I daresay you can interrogate Albert and charge him with spying without a public trial."

The duke rubbed his iron gray hair and nodded wearily. "The late Viscount Carrington was a friend. He warned me of his suspicions about Antoinette and her brother. I hate to see his heir—"

He shook his head in dismay, then straightened his broad shoulders and glared at everyone in the room. "I will hand the French spy over to the War Office for questioning and justice. Montague, I would speak with you in private. The rest of you—can I trust you to haul Carrington and his wife to a ship sailing for the penal colonies and heave them on it? I have it on good authority that Colonel Macquarie will be the next governor of New South Wales. I'll ask him to keep them under guard and well occupied. I'll take care of Bernie."

Jocelyn had never seen a room empty so fast, on such an air of triumph. Blake's friends were not only large and fiendishly attractive—they were also loyal and smart. Lord Quentin's shipping connections alone would answer the duke's orders. And Nick, the dandy, seemed to enjoy hauling Harold around like a trussed goose.

The penal colonies were said to be a terrible place, but she did not waste time pitying a bully. When a kitten leaped to her lap to comfort her, she buried her face in its fur.

The duke might think he was in control, but her world depended on the choices of one man. After this evening's events, she willingly surrendered her role as her family's protector and placed her future in her husband's competent hands.

35

In the wee hours before dawn, Blake entered the bed-chamber he shared with Jocelyn. After closing the door behind him, he sagged wearily against it. A candle still gleamed beside the bed, and his annoying, marvelous, terrifying wife sat ensconced against the pillows, petting a kitten and scratching a happy Bitty with her blanketed toe.

"I thought we agreed the pets belonged downstairs," he said, because saying that was easier than saying anything else that was in his head at the moment. Knowing she had waited up for him restored his draining energy. Understanding that she'd trusted him to decide her brother's—and her family's—future overwhelmed him and filled him with gratitude and bone-deep satisfaction, of a sort he'd never before experienced. He had a notion he would come to enjoy shouldering family responsibilities.

"They deserved a reward," she said. "And I needed company while I waited for you to decide what will happen to us."

She didn't speak with condemnation, just her usual acceptance that her fate rested in the hands of others. Blake needed no further incentive to cross the room and climb across the covers to sit beside her. His Jocelyn was a skilled and daring manipulator when it came to protecting those she loved. He would teach her that she could trust him as a partner in her endeavors.

He drew her into his arms until her head rested against his shoulder. He would not be so foolish as to underestimate her ever again. Had she not fought Harold and encouraged Blake to do as he must, the culprits would have absconded, and the evening would have ended very differently.

"I don't plan to die anytime soon, superstition or not," he declared firmly. "So your future is here, with me. Is that acceptable?"

She wiggled closer, and Blake was grateful the covers separated them. They needed to talk first. He prayed this was the end of the restraint between them, but he took nothing for granted.

"Very acceptable," she agreed. "May I say I love you, without fear of suffocating you?"

His dense genius might not readily recognize the value of others or how to respond to overtures such as this one. What he did know was that he wasn't idiot enough to deny his wife's worth any longer. He pressed a kiss to the thick cascade of hair she'd brushed out of its elaborate coiffeur and sought the words she needed to hear. "I nearly went insane tonight fearing I'd lost you. I think I understand better now why my family has fretted over me all these years. The thought of losing a loved one is crushing."

Startled blue eyes turned up to meet his gaze. "Loved one?"

"You," Blake admitted, holding her gaze and baring

his heart. "I love you. I think that's what it means when I fill with gladness every time I set my eyes on you, and panic like Richard if I think you're hurt. I don't want to imagine a world without you sitting across the table from me, even if you're mocking me or paying more attention to a damned dog."

She hastily scooped up her pets and returned them to the floor, then burrowed back against his side. "Love is a kind of madness, is it not? I love and adore you, but I will never be the clever, obedient sort of wife you wish."

Briefly, Blake closed his eyes and let her declaration sink in. *Love* had been a smothering emotion until Jocelyn entered his life. Now, he could see the freedom it offered.

"'Love is not love which alters when it alteration finds,'" he quoted, leaning over to kiss the upper curve of her lip. "Why would I be so dunderheaded as to wish to change anything about you?"

"Oh, unfair," she murmured against his mouth. "Does that mean I cannot try to change your manly stoicism and persuade you to tell me what you are refusing to say? I must accept your silence to prove my love?"

"If you are any more clever, you will outwit me." He chuckled and leaned back again. "I believe I have lost Quent his bays. You must teach me diplomacy so I might break the news without getting punched in the nose."

"I will punch Lord Quentin myself should he dare!" she said fiercely, before flinging her arms around Blake's neck, letting the covers drop away. "But he wagered you would have what you want by spring. Does his losing mean you are staying home?" she asked, trying to hide her trepidation.

"Ummm, not quite." Drowning in voluptuous breasts and diaphanous silk and an abundance of fair tresses, Blake lost his train of thought. He ran his hands up his wife's slender back and gave thanks that she had come to no harm. He needed to hold her for all the rest of his nights. He tugged the covers from between them and angled her so that she was kneeling astride his lap.

"Tell me that *all you want* is to stay home so we may play house," she whispered tauntingly, nibbling his ear and rubbing seductively against his trouser placket.

"I cannot say I'm staying home if I must spend my days in London," he warned, although he knew this would be no discouragement to his wife.

As expected, she covered his face with more kisses, and her wicked fingers began removing what remained of his attire. "We'll rent a flat," she declared happily. "Mother and Richard will be fine here alone. This can be our country estate."

"We think alike," he agreed, filling his hands with her breasts and hoping she unfastened his trousers soon. "In London, you may scream as you please when we make love."

She laughed and pressed kisses to his chest, working her way through his waistcoat, downward. "Naughty boy. And what else will we be doing in London?"

"I will be working for His Grace and the Foreign Office, in a gentlemanly, political sort of way that can offend no one."

She stopped what she was doing to sit up and stare at him. "What does that mean? How can you offend anyone by helping His Grace?"

"If he succeeds in arranging a crown appointment for me with the Foreign Office, as he's promised, that should be socially acceptable, but he's only doing that because he's paying me to act as his eyes and ears in Whitehall. You are the daughter of a viscount. I would not taint your reputation by reeking of trade."

Jocelyn punched his chest with her small fist. "You

could buy an iron foundry and a cotton mill and I would not care, if they made you happy. Does the duke offer a position worthy of your brilliance?"

"He does," Blake agreed, hiding a smirk as he rolled his defiant wife back to the mattress. "He is supporting Wellesley in the Portugal campaign and agrees that we need fresh ideas. I am to act as his assistant in his efforts while I am establishing myself at Whitehall."

"You are spying on Whitehall for the duke?" she translated mischievously.

"I'm keeping His Grace informed," he retorted. "It seems most of Parliament is unaware that the Post Office regularly reads diplomatic posts and has a Deciphering Branch, so I have already taught him something new. He believes I have more uses than cryptology, but for now he is insisting that I teach our continental ambassadors to secure their documentation with code. We shall see what the future brings."

"I do not understand, but if you are happy, I am happy." She arched her hips enticingly, expressing her happiness by rubbing seductively against him.

"Do you mean that? If I drag you into the city, away from your pets and family, will you be happy there?" Blake loved his wife, but that did not mean he fully understood her. He held his breath—and other parts—while waiting for her reply.

She laughed with delight, and he breathed again. And rubbed against her to ease his growing desire. With confidence that this night would finally end the way he wanted, he could be patient.

"You are giving me my dream," she said. "I adore the city and the parties and the theater. What I want most is a home I cannot lose, one where I can be myself. That can be anywhere." She ran her hands down his sides. "Anywhere you are, at least," she murmured, almost shyly.

With that reassurance, Blake rolled to one side and began unfastening his damned confining trousers. "Then tomorrow, we will ask Fitz if we might rent his town house. It is almost ready to be occupied."

"We can afford a whole house?" she asked, sounding slightly breathless as he stripped his shirt over his head.

He liked to think her excitement was for him as much as for the house, but he wouldn't count on it. "I believe my income will be more than yours. I think you may be able to buy a few new ribbons for your hair."

"And new linen for you," she taunted. "I cannot have a shabby husband if I sport new ribbons."

Blake tugged off his trousers, left the candle burning, and turned back to admire his wife's beauty as he drew her gown down over her rounded shoulders. He kissed the curve of each breast until he heard her breath hitch in that wonderful way he'd learned was a signal of her arousal.

"Changing me already," he warned, pressing his kisses further.

"Changing your linen is not changing you. You, I love as you are."

She freed her arms from her gown, wrapped them around his neck, and pulled his head down to her.

Jocelyn marveled at the long, hard masculine body pressing her into the feathered mattress. Her husband was a big man, one with very determined desires. Naked, he revealed the hugeness of those desires. She was no longer intimidated by his size, but she bit back her cry when Blake took her nipple in his mouth and ravished it. Her own desire scared her more than his.

She'd spent this last week learning the mysteries of his maleness, but there was yet one mystery to be solved. The place between her thighs ached and grew liquid with need. Was she ready for the babies that satisfying that need would inevitably bring?

Would Blake be there to share such a heavy burden?

"I love you," he declared, pushing up on his muscled arms to watch her, as if he knew what worried her. "I will want to smother and protect you against all harm. I know I cannot, but you must learn to be direct and tell me what you want, just as much as I must learn to listen."

His hips moved, and the hard heat of his maleness slid between her thighs, poised at her entrance.

I love you. She could never get enough of hearing such an extraordinary statement. He left her breathless, and she wanted nothing more than to give in to his demands. But he was right. Blake offered her the freedom to say what she wanted, and she could not throw away the opportunity. "I love you. I want you. I want your lovemaking. And maybe, someday, I want babies," she said. "But I need time . . . ," she admitted honestly, as she had not earlier.

"And time you shall have." To her shock and dismay, he rolled over and fumbled about in the wooden box he kept beside the bed.

Jocelyn wanted to drag him back, to tell him to keep on doing what he'd been doing, that she hadn't meant a word. That she *needed* him desperately right now. At the same time, she was fascinated as he produced a very odd packet with a ribbon drawstring.

She was even more fascinated with where he wore it. Her eyes grew wide, and excitement pulsed in her lower stomach. Could she have Blake without babies?

"You are a brilliant, brilliant man," she murmured in awe as he returned to her arms and began caressing her breasts into pouting, aching peaks again.

"I am glad you appreciate that," he said smugly, nudging her legs apart with his knees.

She laughed and kissed him everywhere she could reach and melted as his big hands cupped and caressed and drove her to those exhilarating heights he'd already taught her.

And when he entered her, at long last, she cried her delight and awe, wrapped her legs around his hips, and rocked to his driving thrusts until her whole world exploded in a vision of fireworks and stars. His shout of joy matched hers.

With Blake, she would willingly have babies. For the pure ecstasy of his hard arms around her and his heated body sprawled over her, she would give him anything he asked.

36

"I win," Lady Bell declared while examining the immense windows in the salon of Danecroft's newly renovated townhome. "I wagered Montague would not be buying colors on *my* money, and he will not."

Jocelyn had rather thought the money was *hers*, but she refrained from arguing with the marchioness, who had given her so much. She was much too enchanted with her newly wedded state and the possibility that she might own *two* homes. Well, she wouldn't own this one, but leasing was good enough.

Her security against disaster and upheaval was her husband, not a house. She'd finally found a useful man, one she could trust with her love, one who actually *listened*. Blake was her home. She could not begin to explain the wonder of such a discovery.

"But my wager was that Blake would have what he wants by spring," Quent argued. "Blake, do you have all that you want now?"

Blake was examining a nearly invisible seam in the

new wallpaper. At the question, he glanced at Jocelyn. "I wager I do," he agreed, laughing.

Just his look heated her blood until she blushed. What they had done these last nights . . . She sighed and tried not to think of that or she would have to find an excuse to run upstairs and inspect their new bedchambers.

"Blake is a man of action, not of violence," Jocelyn explained. "He did not wish to go to war so much as find an outlet for his energy and his intellect."

Quentin snorted but held his tongue.

"This wagering business is very complicated. We can't both win," Lady Bell argued, sweeping from the salon into the dining room. "These chairs are a disgrace. I believe I have some stored that will suit better, and you can have these sent off to be refurbished. You will need a great many chairs if you are to entertain Blake's colleagues at Whitehall."

"His Grace says Blake's code machine is a 'bloody brilliant device' for diplomatic correspondence," Jocelyn declared happily. "We will have many entertaining parties with people he would like us to meet."

Blake wrapped his arms around her waist to hush her and studied the room from over her shoulder. "I believe Fitz emptied his attics to furnish this place. We can send the chairs back to him, if you wish."

Jocelyn patted the back of an elaborately carved old mahogany chair. "The chairs do not matter as much as the people who sit in them do. I will have some nice pillows made."

She turned and looped her arm through Blake's to draw him into the room to admire the long dining table. "Lady Bell, I think you must bring Lord Quentin's sister out in the spring just so I might have the pleasure of introducing Lady Margaret to Blake's friends. And Lady

Sally is not yet attached, is she? Perhaps I should take up matchmaking."

Blake groaned. Lord Quentin looked interested. And Lady Bell raised her delicate eyebrows.

"If Quent will give up his bays to me, I will usher his sisters around, and we could call it even," the marchioness announced. "And I would be delighted to share the duties of helping the girls meet society. I do believe we can create a lively circle of eligible bachelors once we put our heads together."

"Nick has no intention of marrying," Blake said, warning them away from one of the bachelor possibilities. "He has no need of money or houses and is quite content the way he is."

"I wouldn't let the rake marry my sisters anyway," Quent said, "but I'll agree to the *loan* of my bays until my sisters are properly out. There is still the matter of the kiss you promised if I win." He watched impassively as Lady Belden flashed her fan and blatantly ignored his suggestive tone.

"I did not lose," she reminded him. "I owe you nothing."

Quentin smirked and continued with the earlier subject. "I cannot imagine how Jocelyn will manage come-out parties and political dinners and still have time for anything else. Your families will never see you."

"Chelsea is less than an hour's ride away. And we are going to Shropshire for Christmas," Jocelyn said. "Blake's family is thrilled that he's settling down. They have even invited my family to join them for the holiday. I think I might persuade Richard to leave his birds for a little while. I'm not so sure about my mother, but I suppose she can look after the pets if she chooses to stay home. She's researching Blake's genealogy now. I think she likes it best when she has her old home to herself."

"After enduring Harold in it for all those years, I can understand that," Quent said. "Was the duke satisfied with our handling of that situation?"

Jocelyn stood on her toes and pressed a kiss to Blake's cheek. Releasing her husband's arm, she followed Lord Quentin and patted the big man's coat sleeve reassuringly. "Harold and Antoinette could not go on as they were. You need not look so upset for your part in shipping them out. They cut themselves off from family, not the other way around. They had no friends. I'm not certain they even like each other. They either have to change or they will come to very bad ends. By writing the governor of the prison colonies, the duke has given them a second chance. My family is relieved by the choice."

"Richard shows more sense than the current viscount." Quentin pressed Jocelyn's hand on his coat sleeve and released her. "He has given me some ideas about raising fowl that I might put into production. I may have to hire him—discreetly, of course."

"Of course," Jocelyn agreed, biting back a smile. "I shouldn't think the heir to Carrington's title could go into trade. La, I'd be all atwitter."

Quent gave her a sharp look, but at Blake's and Lady Bell's laughter, realized she was hoaxing him. "You are a wretched minx and I wish Blake well of you. I don't believe Whitehall will know what hit them once you unleash your full skills. I suspect you will be as valuable to England as Blake is."

Blake took her in his arms and hugged her close. "Oddly enough, being part of a pair offers more freedom than living alone and doubles the opportunities for advancement. Two heads, working from different perspectives, really are better than one. Jocelyn is my secret weapon. Isn't it about time you found your own woman, Hoyt?"

Jocelyn snuggled against her husband's broad chest and laughed merrily at his conceit.

Tomorrow was another day, and for once in her life, she looked forward to planning it.

What happens when a rebellious younger son
is determined to reform his rakish ways?
Find out in

The Wicked Wyckerly

the first book in the Rebellious Sons series by
Patricia Rice.
Now available from Signet Eclipse.

Abigail Merriweather drove the sharp blade of her hoe into the weed that was daring to invade her rhubarb patch. The thick green leaves and red stalks of the rhubarb grew with a lushness that made a mockery of her arid existence since her half siblings had been taken away.

"The house is so quiet!" She cried her despair to the tailless squirrel perched on the fence.

The squirrel chattered his agreement, reaching with his little paw to grab the nutty reward she offered for his company. The tickle of his nails against her palm might be the only small hand that touched hers this day. She almost burst into tears.

"I cannot go on like this," she told her sympathetic friend. "I've written to the marquess asking for help and waited and waited, but he does not answer my pleas."

She didn't whine to the servants. That would be undignified. And her friends in the village thought she ought to be *relieved* to be rid of four rowdy young children. Certainly, she'd already sacrificed enough on their behalf. She had been twenty-three before she finally found a suitor in the local vicar, and twenty-four when he ran away rather than adopt the rambunctious half siblings whose responsibility she'd assumed upon her father's unexpected death. Her minuscule dowry hardly covered the expense of such a ready-made family. For a vicar hoping to advance his position, she had become a liability rather than an asset overnight.

She understood why Frederick had left, but she'd been crushed all the same. Losing both her papa and her fiancé in a single year had been devastating. But she loved the children and had given up marriage to keep them. Except now they were gone, too, shipped away by Mr. Greyson, her father's executor, to the safekeeping of a guardian *who could provide more effectual male guidance*. Tears welled at the still-fresh sting of the insult. A veritable stranger was more suitable because he wore trousers!

"They're all the family I have left," she told the squirrel, who would have switched his tail in approval had Miss Kitty not deprived him of it when he was just a nestling.

Brushing her short curls from her forehead, Abigail leaned on the hoe handle and surveyed the rhubarb bed with a sharp eye for nefarious dandelions and wild garlic. Soon, both rhubarb and strawberries would be plentiful, and Cook would prepare the tarts the twins so dearly loved.

But Cissy and Jeremy wouldn't be here to eat them.

"I need a man," she declared so decisively that the squirrel leaped from the fence and hid under the hedge. "I need to marry a rich solicitor," she amended. "A gentleman who loves children and would take my case to the highest courts. An upright, respectable man with enough money not to worry about the expense!"

Rather than cry more useless tears, she was stubbornly contemplating the solicitors of her acquaintance—which amounted to exactly none—when the mail coach rattled to a halt on the treelined road. The mail wasn't delivered personally to Abbey Lane, but Abigail couldn't prevent her heartbeat from skipping in hope. Perhaps a letter of response from a marquess required hand delivery. She wouldn't know. Her father's distant, titled cousin had never sent one.

Please, let him say he would help her fetch the children back. Jennie and Tommy were older than the twins, but they were still too young to be away from home. If she couldn't find a rich solicitor to marry, she needed a respectable, wealthy London gentleman, like the marquess, who would be willing to fight for her cause.

The coach lingered, and she hurried toward the gate, hoe still in hand. Perhaps their guardian had relented and sent the children home for a visit. The mail might stop out here for young children—

"Keep the demon bratling off my coach until you've tamed or caged her!" a cranky male voice bellowed.

"I hate you, you bloody damned cawker!" a child screamed.

Despite the appalling curse, Abigail hurried faster. She did not recognize the voice, but she knew hopeless desperation when she heard it. She would not let harm come to any child under her notice.

"Your generosity will not be forgotten," a wry, plummy baritone called over the thump of baggage hitting the ground.

Sophisticated aristocrats with rounded vowels and haughty accents were not a common commodity in these rural environs. Abigail's innate social insecurity kicked in, rendering her immobile while she tried to decide upon a course of action.

A small figure darted through the hedgerow, dragging a ragged doll and shouting, "Beetle-brained catch-farts can't catch me!"

"Penelope!" the gentleman shouted. "Penelope, come back here this instant."

Oh, that would turn the imp right around. With a sniff of disdain at such incompetence, Abigail intercepted the foulmouthed termagant's path. Crouching down to the child's level, she placed a hand on her arm. "If you run around behind the house," she murmured, "he won't find you, and Cook will give you shortbread."

Tearstained cheeks belied the fury in huge, long-lashed green eyes as the child gazed warily upon her. With her heart-shaped face framed by golden brown hair that was caught loosely in a long braid, she could have been a miniature princess, were it not for her threadbare and too-short gown. And the outrageous expletives that had polluted her rosy lips.

"Hurry along now. I will talk to the rather perturbed gentleman who is opening the gate."

The child glanced behind her and, setting her jaw in mulish determination, raced across the lawn toward the three-story brick cottage that Abigail called home.

"Penelope!" The fashionably garbed Corinthian caught sight of the child and strode briskly up the drive after her.

Abigail gaped at the intruder's manly physique, accentuated by an impeccably tailored, long-tailed cutaway, knit pantaloons, and Hessians polished to a fare-thee-well. She thought her heart actually stumbled in awe—until alarm startled her mind into ticking again.

She might be inclined to be generous and reserve

judgment for a man who made a child cry. Children cried for many reasons, not necessarily rational ones. She did not know a man alive who could deal successfully with tearful children, including her late, lamented father. But the gentleman's expensive frock coat and Hessians in the face of the child's pitiful attire raised distressing questions.

Abigail was even less inclined to be forgiving when he seemed prepared to race right past her as if she did not exist. She was painfully aware that she was small and unprepossessing, and she supposed her gardening bonnet and hoe added to her invisibility in the eyes of an arrogant aristocrat. But she wasn't of a mind to be treated like a garden gnome.

She stepped into the drive and wielded the hoe so it would knock the elegant stranger's knees if he didn't acknowledge her. He might be large and formidable, but no man would intimidate her into abandoning a hurt child. He halted with the quick reflexes of an athlete and gazed at her in startlement.

She scarcely had time to admire his disheveled whiskey-colored hair and impressive square chin before he ripped the hoe handle from her grip and flung it into the boxwoods. For a brief moment, she stared into long-lashed, troubled green eyes, and she suffered the insane urge to brush the hair from his forehead to reassure him. Except he was so formidably masculine from his whiskered jaw to his muscled calves, and smelled so deliciously of rich, male musk, that she trembled at the audacity of her impulse. Reverend Frederick had always smelled of lavender sachet.

"The little heathen first, introductions later." The Corinthian broke into a ground-eating gallop that would have done a Thoroughbred proud.

Discarding her disquiet, Abigail hastened up the

drive in the intruder's wake. Dignity and her corset prevented her from galloping. As did her short legs.

She arrived at the kitchen door to behold a scene of chaos.

Plump and perplexed, Cook stood with a tray of shortbread in her hand while the threadbare princess darted under the ancient trestle table, shoving a sweet in her mouth.

Miss Kitty yowled and leaped from her napping place on the sill, knocking over a geranium in her haste to achieve the top of the pie safe. The scullery maid cried out in surprise and dashed into the pantry, whether to hide or to secure a weapon was not easily discerned.

And the gentleman—

Abigail thought her eyes might be bulging as she regarded the captivating view of a gentleman's posterior upended under her kitchen table. She had never particularly noticed that part of a man's anatomy, but garbed in knit pantaloons, his was extraordinarily . . . muscled. And neither her insight nor his action was pertinent to the task at hand.

She sighed in exasperation and yanked the green coattail as the gentleman attempted to squeeze his broad shoulders between the table and Cook's favorite chair in an effort to retrieve the child. "Honestly, one would think you'd never seen a child have a tantrum before. Leave her be. She won't die of temper."

Unprepared for a rear attack, the intruder stumbled sideways, caught Cook's chair to steady himself, and knocked over a steaming teapot. He gracefully managed to catch the pottery before it crashed to the brick floor, but not before scalding his hand with the contents.

Abigail winced and waited for the flow of colorful, inappropriate invectives that the child had to have learned somewhere.

The gentleman's throttled silence was more evocative. Dragon green eyes glaring, he returned the pot to the table, clenched his burned wrist and ruined shirt cuff, and, ignoring Abigail's admonitions, again crouched down to check on the runaway.

If she had not already noted the family resemblance of matching forelocks that tumbled hair in their faces, Abigail would have known the two strangers were related by the identical mulish set of their mouths.

Bumping his head against a kitchen table while holding his scalded wrist, Fitz tried to recall why he'd thought learning to be an earl required turning over a new leaf. The moldy, crumbing old foliage he'd lived under all his life had been perfectly adequate for the lowly insect he was, although he must admit his impulsive actions in the past might occasionally give the flighty appearance of a butterfly. He snorted. In the past? If kidnapping his own daughter wasn't flighty, it was the most ill-conceived, most absurd, and possibly stupidest thing he'd ever done, as even the child seemed to recognize.

"I want my mommy." Beneath the table, Penelope stuck out her lower lip.

He peered in exasperation at the whining, scrawny six-year-old bit of fluff he'd accidentally begot in his brainless years, when he'd thought women would save his wicked soul.

The child had his thick brownish hair and green eyes, so he knew she was his, right down to the unruly swirl of hair falling across her forehead. The petulant lip and constant demands obviously belonged to her actress mother—may the woman be damned to perdition.

And yet, he was stupidly drawn to this imp of Satan who so resembled his neglected childhood self. He suffered an uncomfortable understanding of her rebelliousness. After all, she'd been ignored for years by a mother who had run off to marry a rich German and a father who thought good upbringing required only servants. He still preferred servants, but he obviously needed to find more competent ones.

"I will find you a better mother," he recklessly promised, if only to coax her from beneath the table.

"I want *my* mommy!" Big round eyes glared daggers at him.

"You have a daddy now. That ought to be enough until we have time to look around and pick a pretty new mommy for you." What in hell did she expect him to say? That her mother didn't want her? That was one truth that wouldn't pass his tongue, even though the damned woman hadn't seen her child since infancy.

"Mommy says you're a worthless toadsucker. I don't want you for a daddy," she declared.

Her real mother would never have lowered herself to such a common expression. Understanding dawned. "If you mean Mrs. Jones, she is a slack-brained lickspittle," he countered, "and she is *not* your mother. Do you think I'd pick dragon dung like that for your mother?"

He ignored the choking laughter—or outrage—of his audience in his effort to solve one problem at a time. The child's mother had chosen the nanny. He should have paid closer attention when he'd approved her choice, but at the time, Mrs. Jones had seemed affable and maternal, with all those qualities he imagined a good mother ought to have. Not that he had any experience with mothers or children, good or bad.

He couldn't remember even *being* a child. An undisciplined hellion, yes, but never an innocent. What the devil had he been thinking? That he wouldn't repeat the mistakes of his father? And his grandfather. They hadn't been called Wicked Wyckerlys for naught. Berkshire was littered with his family's bastards. Given the Dane-croft debt-ridden habit of marrying for money, producing legitimate spawn had been more of a challenge.

Still, he tried another tactic, plying the silver tongue for which he was known. "But I need a daughter very much, Penelope, and I would like you to live with me now."

No, he wouldn't, actually. He'd always assumed the child would be better off almost anywhere except with him. Therein lay the rub. There was nowhere else for her to go.

He suspected the banty hen breathing down his neck was prepared to dump the entire pot of steaming tea on him, if her tapping toe was any indication. If he'd learned nothing else in his wastrel life, he'd learned to be wary of vindictive women, which seemed to include all pinched, spinsterish females with time on their hands.

"If you will remove yourself from my table—" Right on schedule, the hen attacked, kicking at his boots in a futile attempt to dislodge him.

"I want my mommy," the child wailed in a higher pitch, rubbing her eyes with small, balled-up fists. "You *hate* me!"

"Of course I don't hate you," Fitz said, too appalled to pay attention to the hen. "Who told you that I hate you?" Gobsmacked by her accusation, he could only be blunt. "You're all the family I have. I *can't* hate you."

Sensing she'd shocked a genuine reaction from him, Penelope wailed louder. "You hate me, you hate me. I hate you, I hate you—"

"If you will give her time to calm down . . . ," the increasingly impatient voice intruded.

He didn't listen to the rest of her admonition. "Do the theatrics usually work with Mrs. Jones?" he asked the child, deciding on a nonchalant approach that generally shocked furious women into momentary silence.

At his unruffled response to her tantrum, Penelope fell quiet and stared, taken aback. Fitz crooked an eyebrow at her.

"While this is all very entertaining," the little hen behind him clucked, "you are preventing Cook from preparing dinner."

He winced at the reminder of the utter cake he was making of himself instead of impressing the household with his usual currency of sophistication and charm. Having been abandoned by the mail coach, they had nowhere else to go. Cheltenham and his prize stallion were still over a day's hard journey to the west.

The hen ducked down until Fitz was suddenly blinking into delectable blueberry-colored eyes rimmed with lush ginger lashes. A halo of strawberry curls framed dainty peach-and-cream cheeks. Whoa, why had she hidden such lusciousness beneath that ghastly bonnet? His gaze dropped to her ripe, cherry lips, and he nearly salivated as he inhaled the intoxicating scent of cinnamon and apples. He must be hungrier than he'd thought.

Ignoring him, she looked pointedly at Penelope and barked like a field sergeant instead of in the syrupy voice he'd anticipated. "Young lady, if you will refrain from caterwauling like an undisciplined hound, you may wash your hands and take a seat at the table."

Apparently expecting to be obeyed, the pint-sized Venus stood up, and her unfashionable but sensible ankle boots stalked away. Fitz stared back at his daughter. Over their heads, he could hear the exquisite little lady commanding her troops.

"Cook, I believe we will need your burn salve. And, sir"—she kicked his bootheel just in case he didn't realize he was the only man in the room—"if you will step outside for a moment, we will have a little talk while the salve is prepared."

"Just keep remembering, she eats sweets, not people," he whispered to Penelope before backing out to face his punishment.

PATRICIA RICE

THE WICKED WYCKERLY
The Rebellious Sons

**Nominated for a RITA Award by the
Romance Writers of America**

When he becomes seventh Earl of Danecroft, rakish
John Fitzhugh Wyckerly also inherits a crumbling
estate and massive debts. Determined to do right, he
reclaims his illegitimate daughter Penelope and heads
to London in search of a very rich wife.

Abigail Merriweather's farm has been quiet since she
lost custody of her four young half-siblings—until
a roguish gentleman named Fitz stops for a rest,
his rebellious daughter in tow. His etiquette is
questionable, his parenting deplorable—so why
does Abby delight in his flirtations? And when
she seeks a suitor to help her regain the children,
why does Fitz keep popping up?

**Available wherever books are sold or at
penguin.com**

S0198

PATRICIA RICE

Mystic Warrior

As Europe is torn by revolution, the fate of the Mystic Isle of
Aelynn also falls into question—its survival dependent on
recovering the elusive treasure known as the Chalice of
Plenty. Only the daughter of Aelynn's spiritual leader and a
renegade warrior can accomplish the dangerous mission.

Mystic Rider

Ian Olympus, skilled fighter and visionary, has left the isle of
Aelynn for the Outside World to retrieve a sacred chalice.
He finds it in the hands of Chantal Deveau, who plans to
buy her family out of prison.

But her outrage at his demand that she hand it over is
nothing compared to her powerful, sensual response to his
presence—and the startling conviction that their lives are
irrevocably entwined. And Ian will soon have to choose
between duty and desire.

Mystic Guardian

Off the coast of France lies the sun-kissed isle of Aelynn.
Guarded by Trystan l'Enforcer, its people use magical
abilities to protect a sacred chalice. An ambitious Trystan
intends to marry for convenience, but when a sultry beauty
washes up on his shore, she stirs in him a carnal hunger-and
his plans take a confounding turn. Now he must work with
her to recover Aelynn's most sacred object before chaotic
forces can lead to devastating destruction.

**Available wherever books are sold or
at penguin.com**

New York Times bestselling author

Jillian Hunter

A DUKE'S TEMPATION
The Bridal Pleasures Series

The Duke of Gravenhurst, the notorious author
of dark romances, is accused of corrupting the
morals of the public. But among his most
devoted fans is the well-born Lily Boscastle,
who seeks employment as the duke's personal
housekeeper. Only then does she discover
scandalous secrets about the man that she
never could have imagined.

**Available wherever books are sold or at
penguin.com**

S0205